"A WINNING COMBINATION OF HISTORY AND FICTION, FOCUSING ON THE FORMATION AND EARLY YEARS OF THE O.S.S., THE PRECURSOR OF THE C.I.A."

—*Publishers Weekly*

Richard Canidy—He never played by the book—but he was turning into one of Donovan's most trusted—and daring—agents

Eric Fulmar—The handsome, vulnerable son of a German industrialist and a beautiful Hollywood actress. Donovan had used him badly once—and this time the game is twice as dangerous

Ann Chambers—She was rich, headstrong and a determined newspaper woman—and madly in love with one of Donovan's top agents

Stanley Fine—A Hollywood lawyer turned flier—now on an impossible mission into the heart of Africa

James Whittaker—The hot-headed survivor of the Philippines. After he delivered a top-secret letter to Roosevelt from MacArthur, he became one of the elite—a Donovan man.

MEN AT WAR series by Alex Baldwin

#1: The Last Heroes
#2: The Secret Warriors

Published by POCKET BOOKS

MEN AT WAR

BOOK TWO

THE SECRET WARRIORS

ALEX BALDWIN

PUBLISHED BY POCKET BOOKS NEW YORK

Another *Original* publication of POCKET BOOKS

POCKET BOOKS, a division of Simon & Schuster, Inc.
1230 Avenue of the Americas, New York, N.Y. 10020

Copyright © 1985 by Alex Baldwin
Cover artwork copyright © 1985 Karen Chandler

MEN AT WAR was written on a Harris/Lanier Concept III Word Processor maintained by Gene Vajgrt

ISBN: 0-671-49779-0

First Pocket Books printing December, 1985

10 9 8 7 6 5 4 3 2 1

Printed in the U.S.A.

MEN AT WAR
THE SECRET WARRIORS

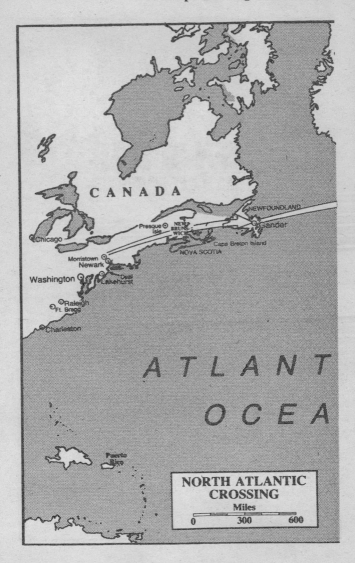

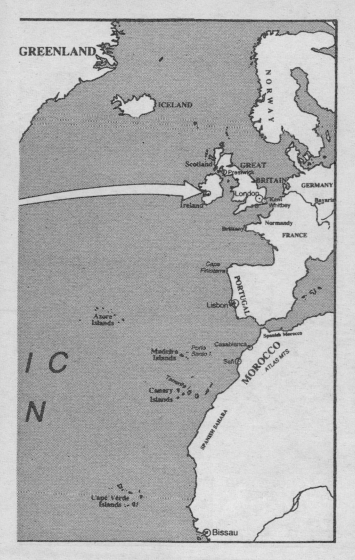

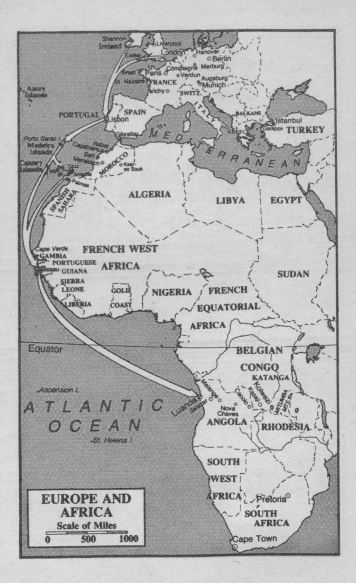

Shannon· Ireland °Liverpool
Easter °London Hanover
Brest° Compiègne Marburg °Berlin
Paris° Verdun
St Nazaire° FRANCE Augsburg °Munich
Vichy° SWITZ.

Azores Islands

PORTUGAL SPAIN
Lisbon BALKANS °Istanbul
Gibraltar GREECE Gallipoli TURKEY

Porto Santo I. M E D I T E R R A N E A N
Madeira Islands Casablanca° Rabat°
Safi°
Canary Islands Marrakech° MOROCCO °Ksar-
Sta Cruz es Souk
°Palmas

SPANISH SAHARA

ALGERIA LIBYA EGYPT

Cape Verde FRENCH WEST
GAMBIA
PORTUGUESE AFRICA
Bissau GUIANA
SIERRA SUDAN
LEONE GOLD NIGERIA FRENCH
LIBERIA COAST EQUATORIAL
AFRICA

Equator BELGIAN

CONGO
KATANGA
Ascension I. Malange° Kolwezi°
A T L A N T I C Luanda° Cicobo° Kisau°
Salazar°
O C E A N Nova MITUMBA MTS.
Chaves
·St. Helena I. ANGOLA RHODESIA

SOUTH
WEST
AFRICA °Pretoria
SOUTH
AFRICA

EUROPE AND
AFRICA
Scale of Miles °Cape Town
0   500   1000

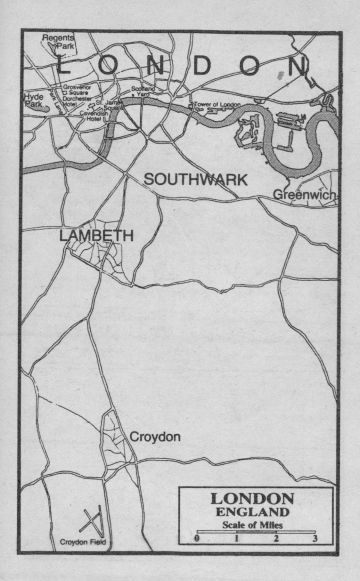

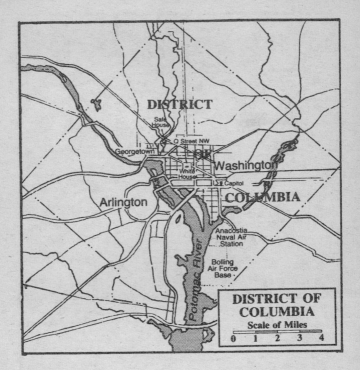

DISTRICT

Safe
House

Q Street NW

Georgetown

White
House

Washington

Capitol

COLUMBIA

Arlington

Anacostia
Naval Air
Station

Bolling
Air Force
Base

Potomac River

**DISTRICT OF
COLUMBIA**
Scale of Miles

0   1   2   3   4

One

1

THOUGH FOUR PASSENGERS were aboard the U.S. Navy PBY-5 from Pearl Harbor, Hawaii, most of the plane's interior was given to mailbags—regular mail from the fleet, official mail from various Army and Navy headquarters all over the Pacific, some from even as far away as Australia.

The Consolidated PBY-5 Catalina flying boat had not been designed as a transport but as a long-range reconnaissance aircraft. It had two 1200-hp Twin Wasp radial engines, mounted on its high wing. Two struts on each side reinforced the wing, the interior of which contained huge fuel tanks. What every Catalina pilot dreaded was landing shortly after takeoff, when the fuel tanks were full—and thus heavy. If the plane could not be greased in, all that weight was likely to tear the wings off.

There was little danger of that now. The fuel tanks were indicating close to empty. A head wind had been with them all the way across the Pacific from Hawaii. The pilot had even worried for a few rough moments that he would not have enough fuel to make it to Alameda. A few hundred miles from the coast, the navigator had wordlessly laid his calculation on the pilot's lap. His projection was that they would run out of fuel an hour and fifteen minutes short of Alameda.

At that point the pilot had two options: He could throw excess cargo out, or he could try fiddling with the engines. Since neither the official mailbags nor, obviously, the passengers could be thrown over the side, the only "excess" cargo that could be jettisoned was the fleet mailbags. The pilot was reluctant to throw away several thousand letters from home, so he elected to try the unusual.

He retarded the throttles, thinned the mixture more than he knew he was supposed to, and dropped from eight thousand feet to less than a thousand. The miles he gained by this maneuver would put them that many miles closer to the California coast, and thus increase their chances of rescue if he had to set down in the drink and wait for someone to come looking for them.

Since it was daylight and he was forced to fly dead reckoning, he had no reliable means of knowing whether or not what he was trying was working. He was flying on a course of 89° magnetic at an indicated airspeed of 140 knots. Simple arithmetic told him where he should be. But if he was, say, flying into a 30-knot head wind—which, very likely, he was—then he was making only 110 miles an hour over the water. And if the head wind was not coming directly at him, but from the side, he was liable to be far off his intended course.

He was genuinely thrilled, as well as enormously relieved, when the radio operator came forward, and, without asking permission, switched the frequency, and over his headset he could hear a marvelously unctuous, pure candy-ass voice announce that San Francisco could expect to experience evening temperatures of 68° Fahrenheit, with a slim possibility of early-evening fog.

"I make it about eighty-six degrees from here, Skipper," the radio operator said. Mounted on the wing, between the engines, was a loop radio antenna which could be rotated until it pointed toward the station transmitting the strongest signal.

"How far?" the pilot asked as he made the necessary small course correction to 86°.

"Don't know," the radio operator said. "I tried to raise Alameda, and couldn't. I'll try it again in a couple of minutes."

The radio operator went back to his desk. His voice came over the interphone in a moment.

"I'd suggest another degree north," he said. "To eighty-five degrees."

"OK. You try Alameda?"

"No reply," the radio operator said.

Which meant, of course, that they were still at least 150 miles at sea. The commercial broadcast station had a greater range than the shortwave transmitter at Alameda Naval Air Station.

But then, minutes later, Sparks's voice came over his cans again.

"Got 'em," he announced. "They can't read us, but we have them."

"Thank you, Sparks," the pilot said. "Keep us advised."

The pilot looked at the copilot to make sure he was awake, and then pushed himself out of his seat. He was now going to make the required airline pilot–type speech to the passengers.

Thank you for flying Transpacific Airways; we hope you have found our food and beverage service to your liking, and that you will give us the favor of your air travel business in the future, he thought wryly.

The four passengers were all captains. Three were from the Navy, four-stripers from BUSHIPS[1] in Wash-

---

[1] Navy Bureau of Ships.

ington, sent to Pearl to see what could be done to refloat a fleet after the carnage of the Japanese attack on Pearl Harbor four months before. Their party had originally been made up of three BUSHIPS captains and one BUSHIPS commander; but, over howls of outrage from the BUSHIPS captains, the BUSHIPS commander had been bumped from the flight by the fourth captain now aboard the PBY-5.

The PBY pilot found this one very interesting. He was an Army captain, which meant that he was two grades junior to the BUSHIPS commander he had bumped. He was also an aviator, and seeing an airman bump the Engineering Corps commander had not displeased the pilot.

And, although he was wearing wings on his ill-fitting, dirty, and mussed tropical worsted uniform, he was also wearing the crossed sabers of cavalry. The pilot had wondered about that. The crossed cavalry sabers had the numerals 26 affixed to them, identifying an officer of the 26th Cavalry. The 26th had not long ago been caught in the Philippines and apparently wiped out on the Bataan Peninsula. But this captain clearly hadn't come out of the Philippines, because no one had come out of the Philippines. The poor bastards had been deserted there.

No one, of course, except General Douglas Mac-Arthur, his wife and child, the child's nurse, and some brass hats, who had escaped from Corregidor on Navy PT boats. The pilot decided it was possible, though unlikely, that the Army captain was somehow connected with MacArthur. That seemed even more possible to the pilot when he considered the captain's travel priority. The end of the shouting session in Pearl Harbor over whether or not he was to go on the Catalina came after the admiral summoned to resolve the dispute read his orders and announced to the BUSHIPS senior brass hat, "Captain, it's not a question whether this officer is going with you or not, but whom you wish to send in the available space on the plane with him."

The pilot had planned to have a chat with the Army officer once they were airborne. But the first time he'd gone back into the fuselage, the man was sound asleep.

He had made himself a bed of mailbags in the tail of the aircraft, wrapped himself in three blankets, and was sleeping the sleep of the exhausted—and more, the sleep of the ill. His eyes were shrunken, and he was as skinny as a rail. He clearly needed rest, and the pilot didn't have the heart to wake him.

Though there was evidence he had eaten the box lunches provided, every other time the pilot had gone back he hadn't caught the Army officer awake. There was also proof that the captain was traveling armed. An enormous old-fashioned World War I Colt revolver lay on one of the mailbags beside him. No holster, which meant that the captain had been carrying the pistol under his blouse, stuck in his waistband.

Steadying himself by holding his hand flat against the fuselage skin above him, the pilot now made his way down the fuselage to the senior of the BUSHIPS captains and made his airline pilot's speech.

The other two Navy captains leaned forward in their seats to hear what he had to say. The Army captain was still asleep.

"Sir," he said, "we have just picked up Alameda. I thought you'd like to know."

"We're running late, aren't we?" the captain said.

"We've had a head wind all the way across," the pilot said.

"Is that so?" the captain said. "Thank you, Lieutenant."

Inasmuch as the captain's tone of voice clearly implied that the head wind was obviously the pilot's fault, a dereliction of duty which was inconveniencing him and seriously interfering with the war effort, the pilot did not as he had intended to do inform him that they would land in about an hour and fifteen minutes.

Instead, he walked aft and leaned over the Army pilot, frowning sympathetically at his sick pallor and sunken eyes. He touched and then shook his shoulder. The man did not stir.

Then he caught the Army pilot's breath. He chuckled, and felt around the mail bags until he found what he was looking for. It was a quart bottle of Scotch. And it was empty.

The pilot reburied the bottle and then, smiling, made his way forward to the cockpit.

"Charley," he said, "we may have a small problem at Alameda, unloading our passengers."

"How's that?"

"The Army guy? He's dead drunk. I found an empty quart of Scotch."

"No shit?"

"We didn't really have a fuel problem," the pilot said. "We could have got him to breathe into the tanks. We could make it to Kansas City on alcohol fumes."

"The brass know?"

"No. I don't think so."

"Let's keep it that way," the copilot said.

"Yeah," the pilot said. "I was thinking about that."

An hour and twenty minutes later, the Catalina touched down, none too smoothly, on San Francisco Bay.

"I'm glad we were a little light on fuel," the copilot said.

"Fuck you, Charley," the pilot said.

Two boats met the seaplane, a glossy motor launch for the passengers, the other a less ornate workboat to take the mail and tow the aircraft to its mooring.

The BUSHIPS brass, as they obviously thought was befitting their station in life, were sent ashore alone in the motor launch. The pilot told them that since the Army officer was ill, he would take care of him.

When the brass had motored away, he went back to the Army pilot.

He was awake, sitting up on the mailbags with blankets wrapped around his shoulders and wearing an aviator's leather jacket over his tunic. He was shivering.

Malaria, the pilot decided.

"Where are we?" the Army captain asked.

"Alameda Naval Air Station," the pilot said. "San Francisco."

"Well, I guess we have cheated death again," the Army captain said.

"As soon as we get these mailbags loaded in the boat, we'll take you ashore."

"Where's the brass?"

"They're gone," the pilot said.

"Good," the Army captain said. "I somehow got the feeling they didn't approve of me."

"Is there anything I can get you?" the pilot asked.

"You wouldn't happen to have a bottle around here anywhere, would you?"

"No, but I know where we can get you one once you're ashore," the pilot said. "Where are you headed in the States?"

"Washington," the Army captain said.

"I'll take you to base ops and arrange for another flight," the pilot said. "I gather you've got a priority?"

"Do I ever," the captain said.

"Can I ask you a question?"

"Why not?"

"How come the pilot's wings and the cavalry insignia?"

The captain looked coldly at him for a moment.

"Nosy bastard, aren't you?"

"Curious," the pilot said, with a smile. The army

officer was drunk. People got belligerent when they were drunk.

"The way they're running this war," the captain said, "is that when you run out of airplanes, they put you on a horse. And then when you have to eat the horse, they find something else for you to do."

"You were in the Philippines?"

The captain nodded.

"Bad?"

"Very bad, Lieutenant, very bad indeed," the Army captain said.

The pilot gave him his hand and pulled the captain to his feet.

"I'd like to keep the blankets for a while," he said. "OK?"

"Sure," the pilot said.

They loaded the Army captain into the workboat. Then he sat huddled under the blankets while the mailbags were loaded aboard and the plane was towed to its mooring.

After that the workboat delivered them to the amphibious ramp, where a pickup waited.

When they walked into base ops, the Army captain made an effort to straighten up, but he did not remove the blankets from his shoulders. Then he spotted a pay telephone.

"Can I mooch a nickel?" he asked.

"I think they would prefer you report in," the pilot said.

"Fuck 'em," the captain said matter-of-factly. "They can wait. I have a call to make."

"Then why don't you give me your orders?" the pilot asked as he handed the captain a nickel. "I'll get the bureaucracy working."

The captain went into his hip pocket for his orders. As he did so, the pilot saw that he had the old revolver in his waistband.

"Thanks," the captain said. "The call is important."
The pilot was handed only one sheet, instead of the stack of mimeograph copies he expected. He gave in to his curiosity as he approached the CONTINUING PASSENGERS counter, unfolded it, and read:

* * * SECRET * * *

SUPREME HEADQUARTERS ALLIED FORCES PACIFIC

BRISBANE, AUSTRALIA

Office of the Supreme Commander

28 March 1942

SUBJECT: Letter Orders
TO: Captain James M. B. Whittaker 0197644 AAC (Det CAV)
Office of the Supreme Commander
Supreme Headquarters, Allied Forces, Pacific

    1.   Verbal orders of the Supreme Commander re your relief from 105th Explosive Ordnance Disposal Detachment, Philippine Scouts, in the field, and assigning you to Supreme Headquarters are confirmed and made a matter of record.

    2.   You will proceed (Priority AAAA-1) via first available U.S. Government, Allied Powers, or civilian air, sea, rail, or motor transportation from Brisbane, Australia, to Washington, D.C., for the purpose of personally delivering to the Commander in Chief certain documents herewith placed in your custody.

    3.   Commanders of U.S. military installations are directed to provide to you whatever facilities and services are needed for the expeditious discharge of your mission.

    4.   After you have personally delivered the documents now in your custody to the Commander in Chief, you will report to Headquarters, U.S. Army, Washington, D.C., for further assignment.

BY ORDER OF GENERAL DOUGLAS MACARTHUR:

Charles A. Willoughby
Brig. General, USA

Official:
Sidney L. Huff
Lt. Colonel, GSC

* * * SECRET * * *

"What have we got? Who's the guy wrapped in the blankets?" the officer on duty behind the counter asked the pilot of the Catalina.

The pilot handed him the well-worn set of orders.

"Jesus Christ!" he said when he had read them.

2

Chicago, Illinois
April 4, 1942

The *City of Birmingham*, a Douglas DC-3 of Eastern Air Lines' Great Silver Fleet, could accommodate twenty-one passengers, two rows of seven seats against the right fuselage wall and a single row against the left.

When Mrs. Roberta Whatley, a brunette with 110 pounds arranged attractively about her five feet four inches, boarded the airplane, only an aisle seat halfway up the cabin was unoccupied. Although Mrs. Whatley was pleased to be on the airplane at all (she had a B-3 priority, which meant she had to wait for her boarding pass until all those with higher priorities had been boarded), she was displeased to see that the adjacent seat was occupied by a man.

She had hoped to find one of the single seats or, failing that, something next to another woman. Mrs. Whatley carried in her purse a just-issued bill of divorcement and was not at all interested in masculine companionship.

But there was nothing to be done. She would sit in

the one remaining seat and politely but firmly discourage any attempt by the young man to engage her in conversation.

She slipped into the seat, carefully avoiding looking at the man. That went well, she thought; he didn't even glance at her as she sat down. He had a folded newspaper in his lap and was working something like a crossword puzzle. It was some kind of code, she recalled, where you had to guess a famous quotation. With a little bit of luck, the puzzle would keep him busy for a long time.

The stewardess moved down the aisle making sure everyone had seat belts fastened. The young man ignored her, too. She had to touch his shoulder to get his attention.

With a look of annoyance on his face, he picked up his briefcase enough for her to see that his seat belt was fastened. Lowering it, he returned his attention to his puzzle.

He wasn't all that bad-looking, Roberta Whatley decided. Then she realized that he looked familiar somehow. It was just her luck to run into some brother naval officer of Tom's on the damned airplane. But then she concluded that that could not be the case. For one thing, now that the war was on, officers were required to wear their uniforms; and for another, the hair on this young man was much too long. Naval officers were careful about things like that.

Still, this young man was of military age and looked somehow military. Or at least athletic. She wondered why he wasn't in uniform.

The plane began to move. The young man's interest in the puzzle didn't wane until they had taxied to the beginning of the runway, where the pilots tested the engines, or whatever. The noise was bad and the airplane shook.

When the pilot did that, the young man beside

Roberta Whatley lifted his eyes from his puzzle, cocked his head, and listened carefully. Then he turned his attention back to the puzzle and kept it there, not even looking up when the plane started to move down the runway. It was only when they were up and making a sharp turn—a *bank*, Tom had called it—that he raised his head to the window and looked quickly out.

He hasn't looked at me yet, Roberta Whatley thought. She wondered if something like what had happened to her had happened to him, something that made him avoid the opposite sex.

When they were up in the air about as high as they were apparently going to fly, the stewardess came down and offered coffee, tea, or Coca-Cola to the passengers. When she got to them, the young man raised his head from his puzzle long enough to ask for Scotch and water.

"I'm sorry, sir," the stewardess said. "There is no cocktail service on this flight."

"Why not?"

"I don't make the rules, sir," the stewardess said.

"In that case, bring me two glasses of ice water, please," the young man said.

And in that moment, with his face turned to look up at the stewardess, Roberta Whatley recognized him. He looked at her too, but with neither interest nor recognition. He was a Navy officer, a naval aviator like Tom. The last time she had seen him was at Pensacola, and he had been wearing a high-collared white uniform with golden wings pinned to the breast.

She stole another glance at him to be sure. It was him, all right. His name was Richard Canidy, and he was a bachelor with a terrible reputation. If the stories could be believed, he had carried on with half the unmarried women at Pensacola—and some of the married ones. A dangerous man, a real wolf.

The stewardess appeared with a tray. He folded

down the little table on the back of the seat in front of him and put the glasses of ice water on it while Roberta did the same thing with her Coca-Cola.

After the stewardess had gone back down the aisle, Richard Canidy took a swallow of his water, then took a silver flask from his pocket and poured whiskey into the glass.

I know it's him! Tom had known Canidy's roommate, *Lieutenant (j.g.) Edwin H. Bitter, at Annapolis; and when they'd had Ed Bitter to supper, even they—men— had been upset at Canidy's romantic escapades.*

As if he sensed her looking at him, he looked at her. "Would you like a little taste?" he asked.

"No, thank you," Roberta said primly. "I think it's against the rules."

"It's the only way to fly," Canidy said.

And then he returned to his puzzle.

He looked at me. If I recognized him, he should have recognized me.

"You're Lieutenant Canidy," Roberta accused.

He looked at her.

"I'm used-to-be Lieutenant Canidy," he said. "Do I know you?"

He had very dark eyes. They seemed to look right inside her.

"I'm Tom Whatley's wife," Roberta blurted.

"Oh," he said. "And we've met?"

"At Pensacola," she said. "I didn't mean that."

"You didn't mean what?"

"I'm not Tom's wife," she said. "Not anymore, I mean. We were divorced. Just now. That's what I was doing in Chicago."

"Oh," he said. "In that case, are you sure you won't have a little nip? Either to celebrate or the reverse?"

He reached for the flask, and she didn't stop him.

Rule One had worked, Dick Canidy decided. *Rule One: The way to attract an attractive woman who is used to attention is to ignore her. When he had seen this one walking out to the airplane, and knew because it was the only vacant seat that she would be sitting beside him, he decided he would have a shot at her, if for no other reason than that it would make the Chicago–Cleveland–Washington flight pass more quickly. Now it looked as if he might strike gold. His experience was that divorced women had a hunger to prove to themselves that they were still desirable. It followed that that particular flame would burn especially bright a few days after a divorce.*

"Just now divorced, you said?" Canidy asked.

"I'd rather not talk about it," Roberta said.

Bingo! Canidy thought.

"You said 'used-to-be' Lieutenant?" Roberta asked.

"I'd rather not talk about it," Canidy said.

"Sorry," she said.

"I'm out of the Navy," Canidy said. "I got out about a year ago."

"I didn't know they were letting officers resign," she said.

"It was decided I would be of more value as an engineer than as an airplane driver," he said. "And I wasn't a very good aviator anyway—and a worse naval officer."

"You don't mind not being in the service?"

"They're shooting at naval aviators these days," he said. "Haven't you heard?"

I like that, Roberta Whatley decided. *Not only is it exactly opposite what Tom would say, but it's honest.*

"And you like what you're doing now?"

"It's all right," he said.

"What exactly are you doing?"

"Research in airfoil design for Boeing," he said.

"I don't know what that means," she said.

"An airfoil is a wing," he said. "As a wing approaches the speed of sound, strange things happen. We're trying to find out exactly what and why."

"You mean you're a test pilot?"

"The only thing I fly is a slipstick," Canidy said. "Behind a desk."

"Oh," she said.

"What happened between you and Tom?" Canidy asked. "If you don't mind my asking."

"I don't like to talk about it," she said.

"Excuse me," he said.

"He wasn't at Great Lakes three weeks before he started running around," she said.

"That's hard to believe," Canidy said.

"Why is it hard to believe?" Roberta asked.

"Look in the mirror," Canidy said.

She blushed.

By the time the *City of Birmingham* landed at Cleveland, Canidy's silver flask was almost empty. While they had a drink waiting for the plane to be refueled, he was able to refill it at the bar in the airport terminal.

Between Cleveland and Washington, she told him all about how Tom had been a rotten sonofabitch almost from the beginning. And he seemed to understand. He patted her hand comfortingly.

When they got to Washington, he confessed that he didn't know where he was going to stay, but that he would call her when he found a hotel room someplace. She replied that he didn't have any idea how hard it was to find a hotel room in Washington these days, and that what he should do was come with her to her apartment and use her phone to call around. Otherwise, he might wind up sleeping on a park bench.

While he was calling around to the hotels, she told him she certainly didn't want him to get the wrong idea, but she absolutely had to have a shower and get into something comfortable.

She was not surprised when he came into the bathroom and got into the shower with her. The only thing that surprised her was that she didn't even pretend to be furious. When she thought about it later, she decided it was all the Scotch she'd had on the airplane. Plus the fact that she had left Tom six months before, and she had the usual needs of a human being. Plus, in a flash of real honesty, she found it really exciting when she saw him with his thing already big.

3

The St. Regis Hotel
New York City, New York
April 4, 1942

When the ten gentlemen—the group known as the Disciples—gathered to brief and be briefed by Colonel William Donovan, they found him in pain in bed in his suite at the hotel. He had a glass dark with Scotch in his hand, and there was a Scotch bottle on his bedside table.

Though Colonel Donovan, a stocky, silver-haired, ruddy-faced Irishman, was not a professional soldier, neither was he a Kentucky colonel, nor the command-ing officer of a National Guard regiment. He had earned both his silver eagle *and* the Medal of Honor for valor on the battlefields of France in World War I. Between wars, he had become a very successful (and, it logically followed, very wealthy) attorney in New York City—and a power behind the scenes in Washington.

He was again in government employ, this time at an annual stipend of one dollar, as the Coordinator of Information, which meant he ran a relatively new government agency. Donovan reported directly to President Franklin Delano Roosevelt. Most people, to Donovan's joy, believed the COI was the United States government's answer to Joseph Goebbels's Propaganda Ministry.

COI did, in fact, have an "information" function (in

the propaganda sense) headed by the distinguished playwright Robert Sherwood. But it also had another "information" function, headed by Donovan himself, which had absolutely nothing to do with whipping the American people into the kind of patriotic frenzy that would impel them, for the sake of the "war effort," to abandon "pleasure driving" and donate their aluminum pans.

The kind of information that Donovan was charged with coordinating is more accurately described as intelligence. Each of the military services had intelligence-gathering operations, as did the State Department and the Federal Bureau of Investigation, and even the less warlike agencies of the federal government like Labor, Commerce, Treasury, and Interior, for example.

Despite sincerely-made claims of absolute objectivity, President Roosevelt realized that when, say, the Chief of Naval Intelligence made a report on a problem together with a proposal for a solution, that solution generally involved the use of the U.S. Navy. Similarly, the Army seldom recommended naval bombardment of a target. Heavy Army Air Corps bomber aircraft were obviously better suited for that.

It was the Coordinator of Information's duty (which is to say Colonel William J. Donovan's) to examine the intelligence gathered by all relevant agencies, and then to evaluate that intelligence against the global war effort. If asked, he would also recommend a course of action. This course of action might well be implemented by a different agency from the one providing the original intelligence.

To assist him in this task, Donovan intended to gather around him a dozen men, each of extraordinary intelligence and competence in his area of expertise. Like Donovan, they would offer to the government for one dollar per annum services that in the private sector would have cost thousands of dollars. Because there were supposed to be twelve of these men (he had managed to recruit only ten) and because they were answerable only to Donovan, it was natural that they came to be known as the Disciples. Donovan was Christ, answerable only to God—Franklin Delano Roosevelt.

Donovan's and his Disciples' mandate pleased virtually no one in the intelligence community. The Army and Navy were especially outraged that amateurs would oversee what their long-service professionals had developed.

Their disapproval, however, meant very little as long as Franklin D. Roosevelt (who had come to believe that Donovan's original suggestion was one of his own brilliant ideas) was pleased with the way things were going. He conferred at least twice a week with Donovan.

One of those meetings had occurred the day before, which was why the Disciples filing into Donovan's St. Regis Hotel suite found him in bed in his pajamas. On his way to Union Station in Washington, where he had gone to catch the 11:55 to New York, the White House car carrying Donovan had been struck broadside by a taxicab. Though his knee was severely—and painfully —hurt in the impact, he managed to catch the train.

In his compartment, the pain grew intense, and he had the conductor fetch a bucket of ice cubes from the dining car. He wrapped some in a towel and applied it to his knee. That helped, but when he began to experience pain in his chest as well, he knew he had a more serious problem than a bruised knee. After he got to New York and taxied to the St. Regis, he stopped in the lobby and asked the manager to send him a doctor.

The doctor listened to the symptoms, prodded the knee, and then announced he was going to call an ambulance and transport Donovan to St. Vincent's Hospital. What he had, the doctor told Colonel Donovan, was a blood clot caused by the injury to his knee. The clot had moved to his lung, which was why he had chest pains. The term for this condition was *embolism*, the doctor continued. If the clot completely blocked the flow of blood to his lungs, or if it moved to his heart or to the artery supplying the brain, he would drop dead. In a hospital, he would be given medicine intravenously which would thin the blood. If he were lucky, in a month or six weeks the clot would dissolve.

Reluctantly—and after pressure—the doctor told the colonel that the medicine which would be used to thin his blood was also available in a pill form. It was, Donovan was fascinated to learn, a pharmaceutical version of rat poison. The doctor also reluctantly admitted that giving him this medicine—and bed rest—was about all the treatment the hospital could offer.

"I can do that here," Donovan announced. "I can't go to the hospital now."

The doctor couldn't argue with that. So he had a pharmacy deliver the blood-thinning medicine, then watched as Donovan took a strong first dose.

"Take a couple of good stiff drinks too," the doctor said.

Donovan asked the natural question: "I thought you weren't supposed to mix drugs with alcohol?"

"This is the exception," the doctor replied. "Drink all you want. Alcohol thins the blood. Just stay in bed, and don't get excited."

Donovan was normally a teetotaler, but since whiskey was less repugnant than rat poison, he ordered up a bottle of Scotch.

After they had gathered in his room, Donovan told the Disciples how he had damaged his knee, but not about the blood clot.

The first item on the agenda, as always, was the super bomb. The Science Disciple, who was on leave from the Department of Physics of the University of California at Berkeley, reported that there was no question that the Germans were methodically, if not rapidly, engaged in nuclear research. As one proof of this, they had granted the same immunity ("for scientific contributions to the German State") to Jewish physicists and mathematicians involved in such research as they had to Jews involved in rocket propulsion. And further, a German delegation had not long ago returned from a visit to a plant in Denmark which had been engaged in research into a substance called heavy water. This substance, he explained—until it became apparent that no one else either understood or much cared about it—was water to whose molecular structure had been appended another hydrogen atom. The Germans were apparently trying to cause a chain—or explosive—effect by releasing the extra hydrogen atom so appended.

The Science Disciple then argued that it would be useful to "persuade" scientists engaged in German atomic research to come to this country—or, "persuasion" failing, to kidnap them. Though he was not convinced that these people would be able to make a contribution to the American nuclear effort, it was inarguable that if they were here, they could not contribute to the German effort.

The problem, Donovan said, was that if German nuclear people started disappearing, it would alert the Germans to American interest in the subject. Roosevelt himself had decided that the one American war plan that most had to be concealed from the Axis was the attempt to develop an atomic bomb.

"Even in the case of that obscure mining engineer we just brought out of North Africa," Donovan went on, "we thought about that long and hard before we went for him. In the end, because we need the uranitite ore from the Belgian Congo, we decided we had to have him. In other words, we'll have to go very carefully with this. As a general rule of thumb, anybody we got out would have to be very important. So come up with a list, and rate them twice. How important they are to the Germans and how important they are to our program."

The second item on the agenda was political: the question of Vice Admiral d'Escadre Jean-Philippe de Verbey, French Navy, retired. Not just for organizational but for personal reasons. This affair was the business of C. Holdsworth Martin, Jr., the Disciple who dealt with France and French colonies.

Like Donovan, Martin had served with the American Expeditionary Forces in the First World War. After the war, he had been appointed to the Armistice Commission. A civil engineer, he had met and married a French officer's widow, and had subsequently taken over the running of her late husband's construction firm. This he had turned from a middle-sized, reasonably successful business into a large, extremely profitable corporation. His wife's social position (she was a member of the deposed nobility) and his wealth had then combined to permit them to move in the highest social circles.

C. Holdsworth Martin, Jr., brought his wife and children to New York after the fall of France in 1940, purchased an apartment on Fifth Avenue overlooking Central Park, and promptly enraged the Franco-American community and large numbers of sympathetic Americans by proclaiming whenever the opportunity arose that French stupidity, cowardice, and corruption and not German military prowess had caused France to go down to such a quick and humiliating defeat. Even more outrageously, he made no secret of his belief that millions and millions of middle- and upper-class Frenchmen indeed preferred Hitler to Blum,[2] and had every intention of cooperating with Hitler's New Order for Europe.

---

[2]Blum, Leon. First Socialist Premier of France, 1936–1938.

One of the few people who agreed with any of this was Colonel William Donovan. And so far as Donovan was concerned, C. Holdsworth Martin, Jr., was the ideal man to be Disciple for France. He had spent more than twenty years there, knew the country and its leaders better than most Frenchmen, and, with very few exceptions, cordially detested most of them.

Over luncheon and golf, Donovan had learned from him that Martin detested most of the French as much for their chauvinism as for their inept army. His success with his wife's firm, because it was an "American" and not a "French" success, earned him more jealousy than respect among his French peers. His wife's late husband's family, for instance, referred to him as *le gigolo américain."*

On January 11, 1942, C. Holdsworth Martin, Jr., entered the service of the United States government, at the usual remuneration of one dollar per annum, as a consultant to the Office of the Coordinator of Information. Three days later, C. Holdsworth Martin III, a 1940 graduate of the École Polytechnique in Paris, by enlisting in the U.S. Army as a private soldier, entered the service of the United States government at a remuneration of twenty-one dollars per month.

Although he acted, and sounded, like a French boulevardier, C. Holdsworth Martin, Jr., was almost belligerently an American.

Now C. Holdsworth Martin, Jr., was engaged in a description of what he referred to as *"l'affaire du vieux amiral vicieux."* The old, vicious admiral, Vice Admiral d'Escadre Jean-Philippe de Verbey.

When the war broke out, *Admiral* de Verbey was recalled from retirement. He was assigned to the French naval staff in Casablanca, Morocco, and had there suffered a heart attack, which nearly killed him. By the time he'd spent nine months in the hospital, France had fallen and an upstart, six-foot-six brigadier general of tanks, Charles de Gaulle, who had gotten out of France at the last minute and had appointed himself chief of the French government in exile and commander in chief of its armed forces.

The majority of French officers still on French soil considered themselves honor-bound to accept the defeat of France and the authority of Marshal Pétain, the aged "Hero of Verdun" who now headed the French government in Vichy. Admiral de Verbey did not. He considered it his duty as a French officer to continue to fight. He managed to pass word to de Gaulle in London that he approved of de Gaulle's actions. He announced further that as soon as he could arrange transportation (in other words, escape house arrest in Casablanca) it was his intention to come to London and assume command of French military and naval forces in exile.

So far as the admiral was concerned, it was as simple as that. Once he reached London, he would be the senior officer outside Vichy control. He had been an admiral when de Gaulle was a major. If de Gaulle wanted to pretend that he was head of some sort of government in exile, fine. But the commander of Free French military forces would be the senior officer who had not caved in to the Boche, in other words, Vice Admiral d'Escadre Jean-Philippe de Verbey.

Brigadier General de Gaulle was not pleased with the admiral's offer, which he rightly saw as a threat to his own power. De Verbey's very presence in London, much more his assumption of command of Free French military forces, would remind people that de Gaulle was not anywhere near the ranking Free French officer and that his self-appointment as head of the French government in exile was of very doubtful legality. He couldn't have that.

Admiral de Verbey shortly received orders, signed by a major general—in the name of Charles de Gaulle, "Head of State"—ordering him to remain in Casablanca, "pending any need for your services to France in the future."

Early in 1942, de Verbey, furious, took the great risk of offering his services to Robert Murphy, who was American consul general in Rabat. The Americans, he told Murphy, could use him in any capacity. Murphy related the information to Washington, where eventually it reached C. Holdsworth Martin, Jr. Martin knew de Verbey, and suggested to Donovan that the old man be brought to the United States. It might be useful to have a lever available if de Gaulle—who already showed signs of being very difficult—became impossible.

Donovan was aware that since Roosevelt looked fondly upon de Gaulle he was safe in his self-appointed role of head of the French government in exile. Further, even if they were to have a de Gaulle replacement waiting in the wings, he felt they could find someone better than a long-retired admiral with a serious heart condition. He had not then rejected Martin's recommendation, however. But he believed that he would ultimately decide that getting the admiral out of Morocco would be more trouble than it would be worth.

But later there came the necessity of bringing out of Morocco the French mining engineer who knew about the stock of uranitite in the Belgian Congo. That operation had a very high priority and it was top secret. Which meant they would need really good cover for it.

Donovan's deputy, Captain Peter Douglass, USN, had suggested, and Donovan had agreed, that should something go wrong with the snatch-the-mining-engineer operation, the Germans would begin to suspect an American interest in atomic fission. If, however, the operation had the escape of the admiral as its cover and the operation blew up, there was at least a good chance the Germans would not suspect what was really up.

Thus C. Holdsworth Martin, Jr., had been told that Donovan had decided to bring the admiral to the United States. He had not been told about the mining engineer. The operation had been a success. The admiral and the engineer had arrived at the Brooklyn Navy Yard aboard a submarine which had picked them up fifteen miles at sea off the Moroccan coast.

The admiral and the engineer were then taken to a seaside mansion in Deal, New Jersey, where they could be kept on ice until a decision was made what to do with them. Afterward, Martin told his wife that the admiral was safe in America, and where he was being kept. Madame Martin, who had known the admiral all her life, then drove the fifty miles to Deal, loaded the admiral in her Packard, and took him to the Martin duplex on Fifth Avenue.

When the formidable Madame Martin arrived, the naval officer charged with the security of the mansion incorrectly decided there was nothing he could do to keep the admiral in Deal. And besides, Madame Martin was the wife of a Disciple. So he had helpfully loaded the admiral's one suitcase into the Martin Packard, and then saluted crisply as it drove off. As a result of this failure of judgment, he would spend the balance of World War II as a supply officer in the South Pacific, but the damage was done. The admiral was in New York City, prepared to tell anyone who would listen that Brigadier General Charles de Gaulle not only was a megalomaniac but had no legal authority whatever for declaring himself the head of the French government.

"This will never do," Donovan told Martin. "Maybe we'll need to let the admiral have his say. But for the time being he has to be kept on ice at Summer Place. If you have to take him back to the mansion by force," Donovan went on, "then do that. But we absolutely have to keep him away from the press. I have had a word with the *New York Times,* and they are not going to run the interview they did with him. But it's only a question of time until the story gets out. God help us if Colonel McCormick gets wind of what we've done."

"Who's Colonel McCormick?" Martin asked, confused.

"He publishes the *Chicago Tribune*," Donovan said. "He volunteered for active duty on December 8. Since Franklin hates his guts—the feeling is mutual—Roosevelt turned him down, ostensibly because of his age. As a consequence, the colonel would be very sympathetic to another old warrior denied active service by that socialist in the White House."

"I can get de Verbey back to Deal, Bill," Martin said. "But how are you going to keep him there?"

"For the time being . . . I really don't want to lock him up unless I have to . . . I think we should keep stalling him," Donovan said. "Maybe pay him some Navy attention. That will infuriate de Gaulle when he finds out about it—and he will. But I still think we can peacefully stop the admiral from calling him a megalomaniac on the front page of the *Chicago Tribune*."

"What do you mean by 'Navy attention'?" Martin asked.

"Send some Navy brass to ask his opinion about invading North Africa," Donovan said. "That might appeal to his ego, keeping his role in the invasion a secret."

"And he might even be helpful," Martin said, just slightly sarcastic. "He *was* the naval commander in Casablanca."

"Well, you make him feel important, and I'll arrange with Captain Douglass to send some Navy brass down to confer with him."

"What about some of the French naval officers in Washington? Can we get him some kind of a small staff? Otherwise, he'll know we're just humoring him."

Donovan thought that over. The moment Free French naval officers were assigned to de Verbey, de Gaulle would hear about it—and be furious. Perhaps that might not be a bad idea. It was Machiavellian. Or perhaps Rooseveltian.

"I'll speak to Douglass," Donovan said. "I'm sure we can find several otherwise unoccupied French naval officers to serve the admiral."

"I'll have him at Summer Place by noon tomorrow," Martin promised.

The third item on the agenda was financial. Five million dollars in gold coins had been made available to finance secret operations in Africa, France, and Spain. More would be made available when needed. Five million was enough to get started.

Project Arcadia had two basic objectives: to keep Spain from joining the German-Italian-Japanese Axis, and to keep the native populations of French North Africa (Morocco, Algeria, and Tunisia) from throwing in their lot with the Germans. Five million was a lot of money, but worth it. Ten times that much was available if necessary from the President's secret war appropriation. It was much cheaper to spend fifty million to keep Spain neutral than to spend two weeks at war with her.

Donovan and his Disciples knew that it had been decided to invade French North Africa as quickly as possible. That would be called Operation Torch. Donovan now told the Disciples something he had learned from the President only the day before: The Army and Navy were shooting for August or September, but he and Roosevelt privately believed the operation could not be begun until October or November.

In addition to the logistical nightmare of sending an invasion force from the United States directly to Africa, there were geopolitical problems. If Spain joined the Axis, the Germans could legally move troops into Spanish Morocco, from where you could almost spit on Gibraltar. The Vichy government was almost certainly going to resist TORCH with whatever they had. And they had troops and warships, including the battleship *Jean Bart*, in Casablanca. This problem would be compounded if the natives decided to support the Franco-Germans against an American invasion. Some of their troops were not only good but in French service; and even the least modernized of their forces could function effectively as guerrillas. On the other hand, the French Army had never been able to pacify the ones who disdained French service.

Donovan ordered the five million to be spent with the missions of Project Arcadia alone in mind. As little as possible would be spent for "general war objectives." It was further not to be regarded as supplemental funds by intelligence operators on the scene.

Gold then was worth $32.00 an ounce, $512.00 a pound. Five million dollars' worth of gold weighed almost ten thousand pounds, nearly five tons. A man named Atherton Richards, a banker on the fringes of the Disciples, would pick up the gold at the Federal Reserve Bank in Manhattan, transport it by Brink's armored cars to the Navy base in Brooklyn, and load it on a U.S. Navy destroyer, which would then make a high-speed run across the Atlantic to Gibraltar.

Donovan's visitors had plans and suggestions, and sought instructions, and the session continued for two more hours before it died down.

"Is that all?" Donovan finally asked. He was tired and wanted some sleep. The rat poison and the Scotch were getting to him.

"I have one thing, William," the Near Eastern Disciple said. "Has there been any decision about whether, or how, we're going to deal with Thami el Glaoui?"

"No," Donovan said, adding dryly, "there are many schools of thought on Thami."

The Disciple, previously professor of Near Eastern Studies at Princeton, believed that Thami el Glaoui, pasha of Marrakech, was not only a very interesting character but that he had every likelihood of becoming king of Morocco.

Who?" the German Industry Disciple asked, chuckling. "That sounds like an Armenian restaurant."

He was given a withering look by the Near Eastern Disciple.

"Thami el Glaoui," the Disciple began, patiently, pedantically, *"bridges,* one might say . . . he's sixty-some, maybe seventy . . . the Thousand and One Nights and what it pleases us to consider modern civilization. He reigns over his tribesmen like a sheikh in the desert, as absolute monarch, exercising the power of life and death. But he also owns wineries, farms, a bus company, and phosphate mines. God only knows how much he made by taking a percentage for smuggling diamonds and currency out of Morocco and France."

"Can he do us any good?" the Italian Disciple interrupted impatiently. "And if so, how?"

The Near Eastern Disciple was not used to being interrupted, and produced another withering look.

"We could not have gotten the mining engineer Grunier out of Morocco without his permission," he said. "That cost us over a hundred thousand dollars. If I may continue?"

"Please," Donovan said, spreading oil on troubled waters.

"If Thami el Glaoui were to come to believe that we were in favor of his becoming king, or at least that we would not support the present monarch—who would, I should add, like to behead him—it could be quite valuable to us, I think."

"Sorry, Charley," the Italian Disciple said contritely. "No offense."

The apology was ignored.

"The one, as it were, who has led Thami el Glaoui into the twentieth century is another interesting chap," the Disciple went on, as if picking up a lecture. "He is the old pasha of Ksar es Souk. For years and years and years he was the éminence grise behind Thami's maneuverings. He was assassinated on December 6 last, probably by the king. Probably with the tacit approval of the Germans. Possibly by mistake—they could have easily been after his son instead. The son was involved in high-stakes smuggling.''

"I don't get the point of all this, Charley," C. Holdsworth Martin, Jr., said.

"On the death of the pasha, the eldest son became pasha. The pasha is dead. Long live the pasha. The new pasha of Ksar es Souk is Sidi el Ferruch, the Disciple went on. "Twenty-five years old. Educated in Switzerland and Germany. A product of *this* century.''

"What about him?" East Europe asked impatiently. "Can *he* do us any good?"

It was time for Donovan to interrupt.

"He already has," Donovan said. "He smuggled . . . with el Glaoui's permission . . . Grunier out of Morocco. Charley feels that he could be very useful when we invade North Africa. So do I. But there is, to reiterate, more than one school of thought on the question.''

"You're thinking about causing a native rebellion, then?" The previously skeptical Italian Disciple was now fascinated.

"The Army's weighing the pros and cons," Donovan said, not wanting to get into a lengthy discussion of that now. "It's something for the back burner. A rebellion could quickly get out of hand, but simply ensuring that Thami el Glaoui's Berbers stay out of the fight seems worth whatever effort it would take. I'll let you know what's decided.''

The Near East Disciple was used to concluding lectures when he wished to conclude them, and not before. He was also, Donovan decided, not immune to the romance of his first venture into international intrigue.

"With an eye to using el Ferruch in the future, and for other reasons," the Disciple said, "we decided not to bring Eric Fulmar out when we brought Grunier out.''

East Europe took the bait. "Who is Eric Fulmar?" It was the first he had heard about this operation.

"Still another interesting character," the Near East Disciple said. "His father is the Fulmar of Fulmar Elektrische Gesellschaft, and his mother is Monica Carlisle, the actress."

Now that Charley had the other Disciples' rapt attention, Donovan knew that silencing him was going to be damned near impossible.

"I didn't know she was even married. Or was that old," C. Holdsworth Martin, Jr., said.

"Very likely to make sure that her dark secret . . . a son *that* old . . . did not become public knowledge," the Near East Disciple went on, "she sent him to school in Switzerland. Where Sidi el Ferruch was in school."

"This is off the wall, Charley," Martin said. "But *where* in Switzerland? What school?"

"Bull's-eye, Holdsworth," the Near East Disciple said. "La Rosey. Where your boy was."

C. Holdsworth Martin snorted. "I'll be damned," he said.

"And then el Ferruch and Fulmar went to Germany, to Marburg, for college. Where they apparently took honors in Smuggling One-oh-one. The pair of them have made a fortune smuggling gold, jewels, currency, and fine art out of France—not to mention the hundred thousand we paid them to get Grunier out. Fulmar now has over a hundred thousand in the Park and Fifty-seventh Street branch of the First National City Bank. And I wouldn't be at all surprised if there was more money in Switzerland."

"This Fulmar chap supposed to come out with Grunier?" Italy asked, and when the Near East Disciple nodded, asked: "Then why didn't we bring him out?"

"That was part of the deal," the Disciple said, relishing his role as spymaster. He had a surprising talent to be a sonofabitch, Donovan thought, so long as it was in a good cause. "He *thought* we were going to bring him out. The Germans were breathing down his neck. They knew about the smuggling, and the son of a Nazi should be in uniform, preferably with the Waffen-SS in Russia. Since he knew that it was a bit below the salt to have made himself rich by helping the French move their assets out from under the benevolent control of the Thousand-Year Reich, he really wanted to get himself out of Morocco. It made him very *cooperative.*"

"If we said we would bring him out, then why didn't we?" Italy continued, his sense of fair play offended.

"It wasn't nice, Henry," Donovan said. "But it was considered necessary. It gave Sidi el Ferruch a choice. He could turn Fulmar in, and cover himself with the Germans. Or he could continue to protect him, and leave the door open to us. And of course, when we're talking about el Ferruch, we're talking about Thami el Glaoui. For the moment, at least, he's decided to leave the door open. Fulmar is in the palace at Ksar es Souk."

"And what does this Fulmar think of us for leaving him behind when we promised to get him out of Morocco?"

"I don't suppose he thinks very kindly of us," Donovan said. "We'll have to deal with that when we come to it. *If* we come to it. As I said, the decision whether or not to try to use Thami el Glaoui's Berbers has not yet been made."

"If I were Fulmar," the Italy Disciple said, "I would tell you to . . . go straight to the devil."

Donovan suppressed a smile. "We'll have to burn that bridge when we get to it," he said. "I don't think waving a flag at him will be very effective, but he likes money."

"Good God!" the outraged Disciple said in disgust.

"Anything else?" Donovan asked, looking at them one at a time.

There were only verbal reports, nothing that required discussion. When these were concluded, Donovan's visitors shook his hand and left.

He drained the Scotch in his glass, had another, and then turned the light off. But his mind would not let him go to sleep. He poured more Scotch and drank that. He wondered if he would die. He didn't want to die now. Not, he thought, until the tide had turned. Not while he was having so much fun. He went to sleep vowing to obey the doctor's command to stay in bed until the embolism dissolved.

He had been asleep an hour when one of the telephones on his bedside table rang. He had three telephones there: a house phone, a scrambler telephone, and his personal, unlisted telephone. The last was ringing. It was probably Ruth, he thought as he reached for it. He wondered what his wife wanted at this time of night.

Instead, it turned out to be Barbara Whittaker. Barbara owned Summer Place, the mansion in Deal, and had made it available without cost or question when Donovan told her he needed it. Barbara Whittaker was a very old friend of both Ruth and Bill. She was also the widow of his lifelong friend Chesty Whittaker, and, he remembered, the aunt of Jimmy Whittaker, who was in the Philippines in the Air Corps. Turning over Summer Place and the house on Q Street to Donovan was the only way she could imagine of helping Jimmy.

"I'm sorry if I woke you, Bill, but I had to say thank you."

"For what?" Donovan asked, confused.

"Jimmy just called. He's in San Francisco."

Donovan concealed his surprise. The best hope he had had for Chesty Whittaker's nephew was that he would somehow survive both the debacle in the Philippine Islands and the certain confinement in a Japanese POW camp.

"He's in San Francisco?" he asked, still confused.

"All right, Bill," Barbara Whittaker said. "I understand. But thank you and God bless you."

"He got out of the Philippines?" he asked.

"OK, I'll tell you," she said, gently sarcastic, humoring him. "So in case anyone asks you, you'll know. He got out of the Philippines with Douglas MacArthur, and Douglas sent him from Australia with a letter to Franklin Roosevelt. They're flying him to Washington tonight with it."

"I had nothing to do with this, Barbara," Donovan said. "But of course I'm delighted to hear it."

"God bless you, Bill," Barbara said emotionally. "You're really a friend."

"I hope I am," he said.

Then the phone went dead.

She really thinks I went to Franklin Roosevelt and got him to give Jimmy special treatment.

And then he had another thought, a professional thought. Douglas MacArthur, whom Bill Donovan had known since they had both been young colonels with the AEF in France in 1917, was very likely up to something devious. God only knew what that letter contained. Whatever it said, it could not be allowed to fall into the wrong hands. Donovan realized that the wrong hands were not only those of Colonel McCormick of the *Chicago Tribune* but those of George Marshall as well. Marshall and MacArthur despised one another.

What Roosevelt did with the letter was his business, but it had to reach him, not get "mistakenly" released to the press, or "misplaced" in the Pentagon. Or "lost."

Donovan picked up the scrambler telephone and called the White House. The President was not available, he was told, but would be in half an hour. He left a message for the President: Jimmy Whittaker was in San Francisco, en route to Washington, bearing a personal letter to Franklin Roosevelt from Douglas MacArthur.

After he hung up, he realized that wasn't enough. Interception of the letter was possible now that he had announced its existence.

He picked up the scrambler phone again and called the COI duty officer in the National Institute of Health building. He told him to find Captain Peter Douglass and have him call immediately.

Captain Douglass, whom Donovan had recruited from naval intelligence to serve as his deputy, was on the phone in three minutes.

Donovan told him what he had just learned.

"I want you to find out how Whittaker is traveling to Washington," Donovan said.

"If he flew from Hawaii," Douglass said, "he went to NAS Alameda. I'll call there and get the details."

"I want to ensure that he delivers that letter to the President," Donovan said. "Which means I want you to have the airplane met when it lands in Washington. I would prefer that you're not personally involved, but if need be, meet him yourself. Is there anybody available?"

"Canidy is in Washington," Douglass replied. "He came back today from visiting his father in Cedar Rapids. He and Whittaker are close. I think I can lay my hands on him. And Chief Ellis is at the house on Q Street, of course."

"Where's Canidy, if he's not at the house?" Donovan asked.

"He called up and said he was staying with a friend," Douglass said dryly. "He left her number with Ellis."

"Aside from his catting around," Donovan asked, chuckling, "is he giving us any trouble?"

Canidy was a naval aviator who had been recruited by General Claire Chennault for his Flying Tigers in China. Canidy had been the first ace of the American

Volunteer Group. He had then been recruited again, this time by the COI, to bring Grunier and the old admiral out of North Africa. After he and Eric Fulmar had been left floating in the Atlantic off Safi by the submarine they'd both expected to escape on, Canidy decided he no longer wished to offer his services to COI.

Shortly after his safe return to the States, Canidy had informed Captain Douglass that now that he'd had the opportunity to play Jimmy Cagney as a spy, he'd decided that flying fighters off an airplane carrier didn't seem nearly as dangerous or unpleasant as what he'd gone through in Morocco, and that he would be grateful if Captain Douglass would arrange for his recommissioning in the Navy.

There were several reasons why Donovan could not permit this. At the top of the list was Canidy's involvement with the "movement" of Grunier from Morocco to the United States. Canidy knew nothing about why Grunier was important, of course, but he knew about Grunier, and that meant he was privy to a nuclear secret, and that in itself was enough to deny him return to the Navy.

And that wasn't the only secret he knew. He had been in contact with Sidi Hassan el Ferruch, pasha of Ksar es Souk. Donovan believed that Roosevelt in the end would decide in favor of the notion of using el Ferruch's Berbers in the invasion of North Africa. But even if he didn't, the necessity for absolute secrecy about American plans for North Africa was such that Canidy's knowledge of them—presuming he was not a cheerful, willing, obedient, loyal Boy Scout's honor COI volunteer—made him a security risk.

So would his very knowledge of the inner workings at the top of COI. For these reasons—if he became "difficult"—Donovan would have to have him sit out the war at a remote base in Alaska or Greenland. It might even be necessary for Donovan to order his "hospitalization for psychiatric evaluation." In the opinion of Roosevelt's attorney general, the legal right of habeas corpus did not apply to mental patients. If Canidy were "hospitalized," it would be for the duration.

Captain Douglass could not threaten Canidy with any of this when he asked to return to the Navy. What he did say to him was that he should sit and think a moment about why it might be impossible for him to pin his golden naval aviator's wings back on. Canidy, who was by no means stupid, saw what the writing on the wall was, and agreed (though not eagerly) to stay on.

"No," Douglass said to Donovan. "He's hardly what you could call a happy volunteer, but he seems to have reconsidered his situation."

"If he were a happy volunteer," Donovan said, *"that* would worry me." Donovan was pleased, and relieved. He liked Canidy personally, and it would have been unpleasant to order his "hospitalization." And he agreed with Eldon Baker, the longtime professional intelligence officer in charge of the Moroccan operation, that Canidy was one of those rarities who have the strange combination of intelligence, imagination, courage, and ruthlessness that an agent needs. It would have been a pity had it been necessary to lock those talents up for the duration.

Captain Douglass chuckled.

"OK," Donovan said. "Then he's the man. Have Chief Ellis get him out of the lady's bed, tell him what he has to know, and then let him handle it. Didn't you tell me you'd gotten him a marshal's badge?"

"It's in the safe."

"Well, give it to him," Donovan said. "Send Ellis along with him."

Chief Boatswain's Mate Ellis was an old China sailor from the Yangtze River Patrol. Ellis was Douglass's jack-of-all-trades in Washington.

"Yes, sir."

"And maybe you better go with them too. Sit in the car or something, where nobody can see you. Just make sure that letter is not intercepted."

"If I have any trouble, I'll call you back," Douglass said. "Otherwise, I will call you when Whittaker is safe in the house on Q Street."

"Fine."

"How are you, Colonel?" Douglass asked.

"I'm sitting up in bed drinking rat poison and Scotch whiskey," Donovan said. "Thank you for asking, Peter."

"Good night, sir."

Somewhat bitterly, Donovan thought he was spending much too much time in political warfare with the ranking member of the American military establishment. But it couldn't be helped. His allegiance belonged to Roosevelt, and no one else.

Two

1

THE TWIN-ENGINE B-25 Mitchell medium bomber taxied up to the Alameda transient parking ramp and killed its engines. Mounted just below the pilot's side window on the fuselage was the single silver star insignia of a brigadier general on a red plate the size of an automobile license plate.

A door opened in the bottom of the fuselage and then a short ladder appeared. A lieutenant, wearing aviator's wings and the insignia of an aide-de-camp, descended the ladder and started toward base ops just as a Navy captain and an Army captain walked out of the base ops building.

The lieutenant and the Navy captain exchanged salutes. The Army captain, hands jammed into his pockets, nodded at the lieutenant.

"Hold it down there a minute," a voice called from the pilot's window of the B-25. A moment later, the pilot, who wore the stars of a brigadier general on the epaulets of his horsehide zippered jacket, came out of the airplane and walked toward the others.

39

Another salute was exchanged.

"Good evening, Captain," the general said, offering his hand. "I'm General Jacobs. What's this all about?"

"Captain Farber, sir," the Navy officer said. "I'm the air operations officer. This is your passenger."

"My name is Whittaker," the Army officer volunteered conversationally.

Brigadier General Jacobs did not like the appearance of the captain. He was wearing a horsehide aviator's jacket over his tropical worsted uniform; that was not only against uniform regulations, it was unsightly, for the leather jacket did not cover the blouse. Moreover, he was annoyed at being ordered to divert to Alameda to pick up a priority passenger who turned out to be nothing but a lowly captain.

"Your appearance, Captain," he said, "is disgraceful."

"I've been traveling, General," Whittaker told him.

"And you have been drinking," the brigadier general snapped. "I can smell it!"

"Yes, sir, I have been drinking," Whittaker confessed cheerfully.

"I have been informed that he is on a high-priority mission," Brigadier General Jacobs said to the Navy captain. "My first reaction is to order him back to his unit."

Whittaker chuckled.

"You're amused?" the general flared.

"That might be a little hard to do," Whittaker said.

"General," the Navy captain said, "this officer just came out of the Philippines."

"Oh?" The general's tone softened, but just barely. He looked at Whittaker. "I'm sure," he said, "that you have seen difficult service. But that's really no excuse for looking slovenly. Or drinking on duty. Let me see your orders, Captain."

"Sir," the Navy captain said, "Captain Whittaker's orders are classified secret."

"You've seen them?"

"Yes, sir," the Navy captain said. "Captain Whittaker has the highest possible priority to facilitate his movement to Washington."

That explained, then, General Jacobs thought, why he had been ordered to Alameda Naval Air Station. Brigadier generals bound for Washington on their own important business are not routinely ordered to divert for passenger pickups.

Curiosity got the better of him. He looked at Whittaker.

"How did you get out of the Philippines?"

"In a PT boat," Whittaker said.

The story of MacArthur's escape (the general thought of it as "personal retreat") from the Philippines was well known. It was logical to conclude that this young officer had been with him.

"Well, get aboard, Captain," he said. "We're flying straight through."

"Thank you, Captain," Whittaker said to the Navy captain.

General Jacobs waited until Whittaker and his aide had disappeared into the fuselage. Then he looked at the Navy captain.

"You can't tell me what this is all about?"

"I've had two telephone calls already from Washington," the Navy captain said, "asking for his schedule. All I know is that he's headed right for the White House."

"Very interesting," General Jacobs said. He gave his hand to the Navy captain, and then walked to the airplane. As he started up the ladder, the port engine starter began to grind.

2

It was a long and cold flight from San Francisco to Salt Lake City. The aircraft's weapons had been removed, but the pieces of Plexiglas intended to cover the weapons ports had not been replaced, and cold wind whistled through the fuselage from the moment they began the takeoff roll.

When they were at altitude, General Jacobs went back into the fuselage and expressed regret that it was uncomfortable for Whittaker, but that he could unfortunately do nothing about it.

In Salt Lake City, while they took on fuel, Whittaker stole a case of paper towels from the men's room in base operations. As soon as they were airborne again, he stuffed the towels in the openings in the nose. It wasn't a perfect solution, but it helped.

When they refueled again at the Air Corps field at Omaha, Nebraska, it was a toss-up, Whittaker reflected, whether the general was more annoyed with him for the appearance of the airplane, or with the people at Omaha for not having the parts to fill the gaps in the windows.

The paper towels were removed and replaced with strips of blanket, taped in place. General Jacobs's ire had preceded them to the Air Corps base at Columbus, Ohio, and when they landed there to refuel again, a captain and two sergeants were waiting with the missing pieces of Plexiglas.

From Columbus to Washington, it was not quite as cold in the fuselage, but Whittaker's blood was still thin from the tropics, and he spent the flight huddled under a thick layer of blankets.

When the B-25 landed at Bolling Field, a Follow Me pickup led it far away from the lights of Base Operations and the hangars to a distant spot on the parking ramp. When Whittaker climbed down the ladder and, ducking his head, walked away from the airplane, he found a number of people waiting for the B-25. There were two cars, an olive-drab Chevrolet staff car, driven by a buck sergeant, which Whittaker presumed was for him, and a black Buick Roadmaster sedan, driven by a Navy chief boatswain's mate.

A tall, erect General Staff Corps colonel approached him first and asked if he was Captain Whittaker. When Whittaker nodded, he announced that he was from the Office of the Chief of Staff and that he had been sent to take possession of the letter Whittaker was carrying.

"Excuse me, Colonel," another voice (oddly familiar, Whittaker thought) broke in, "but I have been sent to welcome Captain Whittaker home, and to take charge of him and the letter."

"I'll be a sonofabitch," Whittaker said, really surprised. "Canidy!"

Richard Canidy had been James M. B. Whittaker's best friend since they had been adolescents at St. Mark's School. Until this moment, Whittaker had believed that Canidy was in China as a Flying Tiger. Which meant that Canidy, if he wasn't dead, was in the deep shit there at least as much as he himself had been in the Philippines.

"May I ask who you are?" the colonel asked.

"I'm a deputy United States marshal, Colonel," Canidy said. He took a small wallet from his pocket and extended it, open, for the colonel's examination.

"What the hell is all that?" Whittaker asked.

"Just shut up and get in the Buick, Jimmy," Canidy said. "I'll explain later."

"I can't imagine how the Department of Justice has become involved in this," the colonel said. "But I'll tell you this, Mr. . . . what did you say your name was?"

"Canidy," Canidy furnished.

"I'll tell you this, Mr. Canidy," the colonel went on. "Perhaps you didn't understand me. I am from the Office of the Chief of Staff, and I have every intention of assuming responsibility for this officer and any material he may have in his possession."

"Colonel," Canidy said, "the Justice Department has just assumed responsibility for this officer. If you have any questions, may I suggest you refer them to the attorney general?"

"This officer's not important," the colonel said. "You can have him, if you like. But I must have the letter he has in his possession."

"Colonel," Whittaker said matter-of-factly, "General MacArthur told me to deliver the letter in person."

"And I'm telling you, Captain, that I am here to take it from you. That's an order."

The muscular, stocky Navy chief petty officer who was driving the Buick walked up.

"Chief, would you put Captain Whittaker in the car, please?" Canidy said.

"Yes, sir," Ellis said. "If you'll come with me, please?"

"Now, just a minute!" the colonel fumed. "I *will* have that letter!"

"I'm sorry about the mix-up, Colonel," Canidy said. "But I have my orders. I'm sure you'll understand."

He walked quickly after Whittaker and Captain Ellis.

The colonel made one last attempt. "I order you, Captain," he called after them, "to give me that letter."

"Sorry," Whittaker said, over his shoulder. The confrontation and the colonel's frustration seemed to amuse him. "I don't know who you are, Colonel, but Marshal Wyatt Earp and I are old friends. I think I'd better go with him."

He opened the rear door of the Buick and got in. There was a man sitting against the far door, wearing a blue overcoat.

"Welcome home, Captain Whittaker," he said. "My name is Douglass."

"What about your luggage, Captain?" Chief Ellis asked.

"Luggage?" Whittaker parroted incredulously. *"Luggage?"*

Chief Ellis grinned, closed the door, and quickly got behind the wheel. Canidy trotted in front of the Buick and slipped beside Ellis.

"Get out of here, Chief," he said, "before that colonel has a chance to think of something to do."

After they were moving, Whittaker asked, "What the hell was that U.S. marshal business all about? What are you doing here, anyway? The last I heard, you were a Flying Tiger in China."

"That was fun for a while," Canidy said. "But then they started shooting at me, so I came home."

"And became a U.S. marshal?" Whittaker asked. "Clever, Richard! An essential occupation that keeps you out of uniform."

"We're from the Office of the Coordinator of Information," Douglass said.

"What the hell is that?"

"Colonel Donovan runs it, Jimmy," Canidy said.

"And we work for Colonel Donovan," Douglass said, "and he wants to make sure you deliver that letter to the President."

"Where are we going?" Whittaker asked.

"To your house," Douglass said. "We're using it now, as sort of a hotel. We'll see that you get a good night's sleep—you must be exhausted—and in the morning, we'll see about you delivering your letter."

"I was wondering about that," Whittaker said. "How I would do that. I can hardly walk up to the White House gate and announce I've got a letter for Uncle Franklin."

"We'll take care of it in the morning," Douglass said.

"Who the hell are you guys?" Whittaker asked again.

"What do you mean, Dick, you're working for Bill Donovan? What's he got to do with this?"

"Can you hold your curiosity overnight, Captain?" Douglass asked. "We'll explain it all in the morning."

"Jimmy," Canidy said. "For tonight: Colonel Donovan tells us what to do, and he told us to meet you. Asking questions around here is like farting in church."

Whittaker and Chief Ellis laughed.

"Are you hungry, Captain?" Douglass asked.

"Starved," Whittaker said.

"We asked the cook to stay up," Chief Ellis said, "in case you would be."

"You're in the house, Dick?" Whittaker asked. "Living there, I mean?"

"Your house is now sort of a fraternity house for strange people," Canidy said. "Like you and me."

"I'll be damned," Whittaker said.

"And you'll be surprised, no doubt, to hear that our house mother is Cynthia Chenowith," Canidy said.

"No kidding?" Whittaker said. Cynthia Chenowith was a young woman he had known—and loved—since they were both children.

"There's something you ought to know about her, Jim," Canidy said.

"I really think that should wait until morning," Douglass said quickly.

"I don't," Canidy said. "I think he should know before he sees her, and she's likely going to be there when we get there."

"What should I know?" Whittaker said.

There was a moment's hesitation. Whittaker realized Canidy was waiting for permission to continue.

"OK," Douglass said. "Tell him. Maybe you're right."

"They did get word to you about Chesty?" Canidy asked.

"Yeah," Whittaker said. "I know about that."

"He was with Cynthia when he died," Canidy said. "At the house."

It took Whittaker a moment to digest that.

"Jesus Christ!" he said softly. "Does my aunt know?"

"He was at a ball game in New York, with Colonel Donovan, when they got the word about Pearl Harbor," Canidy said. "Then he came to Washington with Donovan. Donovan went to the White House. Chesty went to the house on Q Street. To Cynthia's apartment. He suffered a stroke. Just dropped dead."

"In the saddle?" Whittaker asked lightly.

Canidy, embarrassed, did not reply.

"Jesus," Whittaker said. "That's only supposed to happen in a dirty joke."

"Cynthia called Donovan at the White House. He couldn't leave, so he sent Captain Douglass and the chief. They took care of things, so there was no scandal. I don't think your aunt knows."

"How did they 'take care of things'?" Whittaker asked.

"We fixed it so the body was found in his shower," Ellis said.

"You carried his body from her apartment to his room?" Whittaker asked.

"Yes, sir," Ellis said.

"Thank you," Whittaker said. And then, a moment later, he asked, "How tight a secret is this?"

"It's known only to the people in this car, plus, of course, Colonel Donovan and Miss Chenowith," Captain Douglass said.

"How did you find out?" Whittaker asked Canidy.

"I was afraid you'd ask that," Canidy said.

"How did you?"

"I've had several run-ins with Cynthia," Canidy said. "It came out during one of them."

"What kind of run-ins?" Whittaker asked.

"Does it matter?" Canidy asked.

"You put the make on her?" Whittaker asked. "You sonofabitch!"

"No," Canidy said. "I didn't put the make on her."

"Then what?" Whittaker asked angrily.

"Your beloved, Jimmy, almost got me killed," Canidy said.

"How?"

"Stop right there, Canidy!" Douglass said.

"I want to know what the hell he's talking about!" Whittaker said.

"I'm sorry, that's out of the question."

"I was somewhere," Canidy said. "Doing something. And the end of the game was when they sent a submarine to pick us up."

"What the hell are you talking about?"

"When we reached the submarine, the skipper said he was sorry as hell, but he had orders to keep us from coming aboard. 'By force of arms if necessary' is the way he put it."

"Who are 'we' and 'us'?" Whittaker asked.

"*No*, Canidy!" Douglass said. "Don't even start into that."

"At the time, I thought somebody else was responsible for that order," Canidy said. "I was going to feed him his balls the next time I saw him. So Captain Douglass decided he had better tell me who had really made the decision. It wasn't who I thought it was, it was Cynthia."

"Cynthia? She's involved in whatever it is you're doing?"

"Donovan was so impressed with the way she handled herself . . . when Chesty died, I mean . . . that he gave her a job," Canidy said.

"Doing what?" Whittaker asked.

"No, Canidy," Captain Douglass said again. "Be very careful."

"I was so goddamned mad, Jimmy, that I told Captain Douglass that Cynthia wasn't the sweet maiden he apparently thought she was."

"That was a pretty shitty thing to do, Dick," Whittaker said.

"Under the circumstances, Captain, Canidy's reaction was understandable," Douglass said.

"What circumstances?" Whittaker asked. "Is she now fucking somebody else? Donovan, maybe?"

"That's not what I meant," Douglass said.

"Is she, or isn't she?"

"For what it's worth, I don't think so," Canidy said. "Certainly not Donovan, and I don't think anybody else. She's too busy playing master spy."

"That's enough of that, Canidy!" Douglass snapped. In a moment, he went on: "Under the circumstances, I thought it necessary to fill Canidy in on the circumstances surrounding your uncle's death."

"Jesus Christ!" Whittaker said. And then he laughed.

"Well," he said. "At least Chesty went out happy. All's well that ends well, they say."

Canidy looked at him curiously. That was not the reaction he had expected.

"Tell me this, before the joyous reunion," he said. "Does Cynthia know that I know she was fucking my uncle?"

"No," Canidy said. "And she doesn't know that I know, either."

"Then let's keep it that way," Whittaker said. "OK?"

"So far as I'm concerned," Douglass said, "there is no reason to bring up this subject ever again."

3

When the Buick reached the house on Q Street, the driveway gate was open and Ellis drove right in, stopping the car on the cobblestone drive in front of the garages.

"Who's the guy on the gate?" Whittaker asked. "He looks like a cop."

"There's a security arrangement here," Douglass said.

"I feel like I'm in a Humphrey Bogart movie," Whittaker said.

"I'm going to have Ellis take me home," Douglass announced. "I think it would be a good idea to put the letter Captain Whittaker has in the safe."

"I'll put it in the safe, Captain," Ellis said, "if it can wait until I get back."

"No, you won't," Whittaker said. "I've kept it this far, I'll keep it the rest of the way."

Douglass thought that over.

"Whatever you wish, Captain," he said. "I'll be back here around eight in the morning. We can arrange for you to deliver it then."

"OK," Whittaker said.

Douglass got out of the car. He leaned in again and gave Whittaker his hand, but didn't say anything more to him.

Ellis tapped the Buick's horn ring. The plainclothes security man started to open the gate again as Canidy and Whittaker walked toward the kitchen.

There was a skinny black woman sitting at the kitchen table. She looked somewhat disapprovingly at them, Whittaker in particular.

"Is Miss Chenowith here?" Whittaker asked.

"No, but she should be soon," the black woman said.

And then, indicating Whittaker with a nod of her head: "He's staying?"

Candidy nodded.

"She know?"

Candidy shook his head no.

"She told me that if anybody came in she didn't know about, they was to be put in the second-left bedroom," the black woman said. "She said she'd be back by now. I don't know why she's not."

"Who's in the master bedroom?" Whittaker asked.

The black woman looked at him curiously. "They save that for important people."

"Can you fix the captain something to eat?" Candidy asked, amused.

"I suppose so. If he's hungry."

"Steak and eggs?" Whittaker asked. "And french fried potatoes?"

"This time of night?"

"Make him whatever he wants," Candidy ordered flatly.

The black woman shrugged.

"Is there anything else we can get for you, Captain?" Candidy asked, as if Whittaker were a total stranger.

"I need clean clothes. I need a razor, and a comb and brush. And underwear and socks. I have to see a dentist, and I think I caught the crabs," Whittaker said. "Where would you like to start?"

Candidy laughed. "You're a real basket case, aren't you, Jimmy?" he asked.

"And you, on the other hand, are not only well fed but here, and not wearing a uniform. I'm going to have to find out how you did that, you clever sonofabitch."

"Cowardice. It works every time," Candidy said.

"Bullshit. I'm the biggest coward you ever met, and you won't believe what those sonsofbitches had me doing."

"You look like hell, and you smell like a barroom floor, but I'm glad to see you anyway."

"Fuck you, Dick," Whittaker said fondly.

"We can give him pajamas and a robe," the black woman said practically, "and a comb and a razor and a toothbrush and that sort of thing . . ."

"Pajamas and a robe? Christ, I'd forgotten there were such things," Whittaker said.

". . . but I don't know what to do about the crabs," the black woman went on matter-of-factly. "Unless you go to that all-night drug store on Massachusetts Avenue."

"I'll send the chief when he comes back," Canidy said.

"I didn't mention that I also don't have any money," Whittaker said.

"Don't worry about that," Canidy said. "I'll trust you. You have an honest face."

Ellis returned as the black woman was frying a steak. Canidy told him what Whittaker needed, and handed him money. "Get him whatever else you think he needs," he added.

"Right," Ellis said. "It won't take me long. You going to be all right?"

"We'll be fine," Canidy said.

"I only look this way, Chief," Whittaker said. "I'm not really crazy."

"You really want eggs with this steak?" the skinny black woman asked.

Whittaker nodded. "Four, sunny-side up. And toast."

She shrugged and went to the refrigerator.

"And coffee," he said. "And milk."

While he ate at the kitchen table, Canidy took a cup of coffee and sat down with him. The black woman went out of the kitchen and returned with pajamas and a robe.

"I couldn't find slippers," she said.

"Thank you," he said.

She saw that all the food which she had heaped on his plate was gone. "If that's all you want to eat, I'll show you your room," she said.

Whittaker was unsteady on his feet. It was entirely possible he couldn't make it upstairs by himself.

"I'll show him," Canidy said quickly, and went with him. He was glad he had. Whittaker had to haul himself upstairs on the banister railing.

In the upstairs foyer, Whittaker stopped at the door to the master bedroom.

"As I recall," he said, "the shower in here has two heads. I'll use this."

"The way it works around here," Canidy said, "is that rooms are assigned by Miss Chenowith. Miss Chenowith goes into a snit when someone dares disobey her. Miss Chenowith, I think you should know, is very impressed with her role in the hierarchy around here."

"Fuck Miss Chenowith," Whittaker said, laughing, "which seems to be a splendid idea, come to think of it."

"You going to be all right in there?" Canidy asked seriously. Whittaker looked terrible. His eyes were bloodshot and burning, he was thirty or forty pounds underweight, and he looked as if he were teetering over the edge of exhaustion.

"I look that bad, huh?"

"Yeah. You want me to wait?"

"If you hear a loud crash, come after me," Whittaker said. "But I'd rather do it myself, thank you."

"I'm really glad to see you, you bastard," Canidy said. "And now that you're here, I don't want you cracking open your skull falling down in the shower."

"I'm planning on fucking myself to death," Whittaker said. "Don't worry."

"Come on down when you're clean," Canidy said. "If you feel up to it. I've got a bottle of Scotch we can work on."

"Yeah, sure," Whittaker said.

Canidy, shamed, realized that drinking was the last thing the poor, beat-up sonofabitch wanted to do. He wanted to fall into bed, but his ego required that he accept the offer to booze.

We'll have one drink, Canidy decided, *and then I will announce I'm beat, and head for bed.*

He went back down the stairs and into the kitchen.

Cynthia Chenowith came into the kitchen fifteen minutes later. She was a tall, lithe, fair-skinned woman in her late twenties, but she looked younger than that. Canidy noticed, as he always did when he saw her, that she had perfect breasts. Not too big, but big enough. She was expensively dressed, and the purse hanging from her shoulder was alligator.

She gave Canidy an impersonal nod by way of greeting. It was all he expected. He didn't like Cynthia Chenowith and she didn't like him.

She went to a wall telephone hanging by the door to the dining room and dialed a number from memory.

"This is Miss Chenowith," she announced. "I'm at the house and will be until further notice."

She was checking in with the duty officer. *She loves it,* he thought. *It makes her feel important.*

What would be nice, Canidy thought, *would be for her to go upstairs and fuck that poor, beat-up, exhausted sonofabitch who thinks he's in love with her. But that won't happen.*

She sensed his eyes on her.

"Something, Canidy?" she asked.

"No," he said. "Nothing at all."

"He brought a man in," the black woman volunteered. "Him and Ellis."

"Who, Canidy?" Cynthia demanded. "I asked if there was anything."

Fuck you, you cold-blooded bitch.

He said, "Donovan sent Douglass, Ellis, and me out to Bolling Field to pick him up and bring him here."

"What are you doing here anyway?" she asked.

"I'm not sure you have the need to know, Miss Chenowith," Canidy said, openly mocking her. "Suffice it to say that I, too, am on duty."

"You're here in connection with our problem with the admiral," she flared.

He smiled, very broadly, very artificially, at her. He didn't know what the hell was she talking about, except that "the admiral" was more than likely Vice Admiral d'Escadre Jean-Philippe de Verbey, French Navy, whom he had loaded aboard a submarine off Safi and sent to the States, but he was damned if he would let her know he didn't know.

"No comment," he said. "I'm sure you understand."

White-faced, she tried to stare him down and failed.

With a little bit of luck, he thought, *she'll take a swing at me with her purse.*

She did not. She turned to the black woman. "Is the man upstairs a French naval officer?"

The black woman shook her head and told her that the new guest was an Air Corps captain; that he had arrived looking as if he hadn't had a meal in a week and without luggage; that he had crabs; and that she had put him in the second room on the left, as ordered.

Cynthia, Canidy saw, with pleasure, was annoyed. She turned to him. "Crabs?" she asked incredulously. "Body vermin?"

"Crabs," Canidy confirmed happily. "I sent Ellis for crab medicine."

"I'll have to have the room fumigated!" she said.

"They also serve who fumigate," Canidy said.

Ellis, as if on cue, came through the kitchen door carrying a large kraft paper bag.

"He's in the master bedroom, Ellis," Canidy said. "Take it up to him."

"The *master* bedroom?" Cynthia demanded. She turned furiously on the black woman. "I told you to put anybody who came in unexpectedly in the second room, left."

"She told me," Canidy said. "But I decided, what the hell, it wasn't being used."

He thought for a moment that she was about to lose her temper. But then, as if she understood that was exactly what he wanted her to do, she gained control of herself and smiled at him just as warmly and patently artificially as he was smiling at her.

"Well, we'll just have to move him where he's supposed to be," Cynthia said, "won't we?" She reached for Ellis's package. "Give me that, please. What's in it?"

"Personal-comfort items," Canidy said, winking at Ellis. "And crab killer."

She took the bag and stormed upstairs to the master bedroom, which was actually a suite. She had, as she always had when she went to its door, a mental picture of Ellis carrying Chesley Haywood Whittaker, naked, wrapped in a sheet, dead, into that bedroom.

And now Canidy had taken it upon himself to put some vermin-infested character in Chesty's room, to leave his filth in the shower where they had put Chesty.

There was no answer to her knock on the master bedroom's door, so she walked in. As she did, the sound of the shower died.

"Hello, in there," she said. "I'm Miss Chenowith. I'd like a word with you."

"I was hoping it was the guy with the stuff for my crabs," he said.

"I have it," she said. "Open the door a crack."

It opened wide enough for a hand to pass. Steam billowed out. She offered the bag to a scarred hand with battered fingernails. She had a quick, steam-fogged glance at a face with gaunt and sunken and very bright eyes. Uncomfortable, she immediately averted her eyes.

Whoever he was, she thought, he looked like the sort of person who would pick up body vermin.

The door opened and he came out in a robe and pajamas.

She didn't want to face him, so she pretended to fuss with the clock on the bedside table.

"There seems to be some misunderstanding," she said. "This room is reserved for VIPs."

"Not while I'm here it's not," he said.

"I don't know who you think you are!" she flared, and turned to face him, to glare at him.

"I think I'm Jim Whittaker," he said, in the moment recognition dawned, "and I own this house. How the hell are *you*, Cynthia?"

"That sonofabitch!" Cynthia fumed.

"What sonofabitch is that?" Whittaker asked. "And when did you start using dirty words?"

"Canidy!" she snapped. "He didn't tell me it was you!"

"Maybe he thought a surprise would be nice," Whittaker said.

Barely audibly, shocked both to see him and at his appearance, she said, "I don't know what to say."

"How about 'I'm glad you got out of the Philippines'?" he suggested. "Or better yet, how about 'Hi, Jim, let's screw!'"

"Oh, Jimmy, for God's sake! Please!" Cynthia Chenowith said, and with tears in her eyes turned and fled.

She heard him laughing happily behind her. She had amused him. She remembered that when she used to amuse Chesty, he laughed almost exactly like that.

She went into the kitchen. Canidy, obviously very pleased with himself, was sitting at the table with Chief Ellis. There was a bottle of Scotch between them.

"That was a rotten thing to do, Canidy, you son-ofabitch!"

"What rotten thing was that, Cynthia?" he asked innocently.

"You *bastard!*" she screamed, and then she fled.

She would die, she thought, before she gave the sonofabitch the satisfaction of seeing her cry.

4

Chicago, Illinois
April 5, 1942

The arrival of the radiogram turned out to be a disappointment for the doorman of the tall apartment building on Lakeshore Drive. It was his usual practice to relieve Western Union messengers of their yellow envelopes, hand them a dime, then turn the envelope over to the elevator operator. The elevator operator would then deliver it. With rare exceptions, every tenant in the building was worth a quarter, and some of them, like the Bitters, were worth more. The Bitters kept a supply of dollar bills in a vase just inside the door of their penthouse apartment to be dispensed whenever a service was done for them.

But this delivery boy was difficult. For one thing, he wasn't a boy, but a young man. For another, he adamantly refused to turn his RCA envelope over to the doorman unless the doorman got the addressee on the house phone and asked to send the messenger himself up with the message.

Somewhat reluctantly, the doorman passed him to the elevator, and the RCA messenger rode up to the penthouse atop the twenty-seven-story building. At the door, he then made the butler sign for the envelope. Only then did he hand it over. The butler, annoyed, reached into his pocket and handed him a quarter rather than one of the dollar bills in the vase.

Then the butler delivered the cablegram to Mr. Chandler H. Bitter, the fifty-five-year-old, silver-haired president of the Chandler H. Bitter Company, Commodities Brokers. Chandler Bitter was drinking a second cup of coffee with his wife on the small patio outside the second-story master bedroom.

She presumed it was business. Seeing him frown, however, she asked him what it was.

"I think it would be better if you read it yourself," he said gently, and passed it to her.

MACKAY RADIO I330GREENWICH 2APR42
CHUNKING CHINA VIA RCA HONOLULU
MR MRS CHANDLER BITTER
2745 LAKESHORE DRIVE
CHICAGO ILL USA
DEEPLY REGRET INFORM YOU YOUR SON FLIGHT LEADER
EDWIN H BITTER WOUNDED IN ACTION AGAINST JAPANESE
AIRCRAFT VICINITY CHIENGMAI THAILAND MARCH THIRTY
STOP COMPLETE RECOVERY INJURY RIGHT KNEE EXPECTED
STOP AIR EVACUATED US ARMY HOSPITAL CALCUTTA INDIA
STOP LETTER FROM CHINESE AMBASSADOR TO US FOLLOWS
STOP CLAIRE CHENNAULT BRIG GENERAL COMMANDING
AMERICAN VOLUNTEER GROUP END

"Oh my!" she said, in frightened wonderment, and turned her face up at him.

She had said the same words, he remembered with sudden brilliant clarity, and looked at him in exactly the same way, in just about the same place, when her waters broke, just before he took her to Women's Hospital to deliver Eddie.

"Helen," Chandler H. Bitter, Jr., said very tenderly, "I want you to listen to me carefully."

Her eyes locked on his, she waited for him to go on.

"He's alive," Chandler Bitter said. "And he has

been taken to an American Army hospital, where he will receive the best of care. The important thing is that he is alive."

There was a barely perceptible nod of her head.

"And this may very well be a good thing," he said.

Her face now registered pain and surprise and shock —and an unspoken question: How could he say such a thing?

"I don't mean to be brutal, Helen," Chandler H. Bitter, Jr., went on, "but he has been injured in the knee. That's bad, because knee injuries are difficult to repair and take a long time to heal."

"Chan . . ." she said.

"Which means, Marjorie, that he won't be able to fly for a while, perhaps never again. Which means that they'll probably send him home for recuperation. He may well be out of it, Helen."

"Oh," she said thoughtfully.

"The military have a thing, Helen," he said. "They call it the million-dollar wound. It means a wound like his."

She stood up and went to him, and he put his arms around her.

He saw the butler watching them.

"Eddie has been hit, Morton," he said. "In the knee. I think it means he will be coming home. Read the cable, if you like."

Morton went to the glass-topped table and picked up the radiogram and read it.

"Thank God he's alive!" he said emotionally.

"Would you please see if you can get Mr. Chambers on the telephone for me, Morton?" Chandler H. Bitter said.

"Yes, sir," Morton said.

"Brandon," Chandler H. Bitter said, into his wife's hair, "has people over there, correspondents. I think he may be able to find out something more for us."

There was a letter and a small package, sent registered special delivery, from the Chinese embassy the very next day, but it had nothing to do with Edwin's being wounded, and Mr. Bitter had to explain to his nearly hysterical wife that the Chinese were not insane, but that the embassy had already mailed this letter before they heard about what had happened in China.

THE EMBASSY OF CHINA
Washington, District of Columbia
March 22, 1942

Mr. and Mrs. Chandler H. Bitter
2745 Lakeshore Drive
Chicago, Illinois

My dear Mr. and Mrs. Bitter:

It is with pleasure, pride, and gratitude that I am able to inform you that your son, Wingman Edwin Howell Bitter, of the American Volunteer Group, was on March 1, 1942, invested with the Order of the Cloud Banner of the Republic of China, at the direction of Generalissimo Chiang Kai-shek, and simultaneously promoted to the rank of flight leader.

Flight Leader Bitter was cited for his valor in the air, specifically the downing of five Japanese aircraft in aerial combat during the period from December 23, 1941, through March 1, 1942. I have learned that he has since then sent two more enemy aircraft down in flames.

You must certainly take pride that your son is one of that group of brave and farsighted young men who sensed the danger not only to China, but to America and to freedom throughout the world, in the ruthless and predatory course of Japanese militarism. Not waiting to be called, this group went forward to meet the enemy, prepared to sacrifice themselves, if need be, in order that the democracies might gain precious time, that freedom might live, and that countless other lives might be saved.

The record already made by the American Volunteer Group in aerial combat against the Japanese is one of which every American may be proud.

You may have heard that the American Volunteer Group has adopted as its emblem a Flying Tiger. The figure chosen was designed by Walt Disney Studios and shows a winged tiger leaping out of a Victory V. It is worn as a lapel insignia by your son and his comrades, and also appears in color on the fuselages of their planes. I have the honor to send, herewith, a gold replica of this insignia, as well as a gold miniature of the Order of the Cloud Banner.

As Foreign Minister of the Republic of China, I want to express to you on behalf of my countrymen and Generalissimo Chiang Kai-shek personally the sense of honor that is ours that your son has allied himself with the Chinese people in the cause of freedom. Like Lafayette in America, these gallant young men will ever be gratefully enshrined in the memory of the Chinese people.

Very truly yours,
T. V. Soong
Minister for Foreign Affairs

5

The St. Regis Hotel
New York City, New York
April 7, 1942

Colonel William J. Donovan, in white silk pajamas, was propped up against the headboard of the double bed when Captain Peter Douglass and Richard Canidy were shown into his room.

"Good morning," Donovan said, offering his hand. Douglass took it first, and then Canidy.

"Nice to see you again, Canidy," Donovan said. "Has Captain Douglass told you what's wrong with me?"

"Yes, sir," Canidy said.

"And the medicine? Rat poison?"

"Yes, sir," Canidy said, and grinned.

"It's enough to drive a man to drink," Donovan joked. "And it has." He gestured at a bottle of Pinch

Bottle Haig & Haig on his bedside table. "I used to be, almost, a teetotaler."

Donovan waited for the chuckle he expected, and then went on.

"I consider this affair of MacArthur's letter to the President important," he said. "Which is why I asked you to come up here and tell me exactly what happened."

"Yes, sir," they said, almost in unison.

"So let's start at the beginning," Donovan said. "You first, I guess, Peter, but I want you to feel free to interrupt, Dick, whenever you think it's necessary."

"Well, after I spoke with you, Colonel," Douglass said, "I called Alameda Naval Air Station. An old shipmate is in command, and he knew about Whittaker's return. He was traveling on orders signed by MacArthur's G-2, General Willoughby, which directed him to personally deliver to the President 'certain secret documents' placed in his possession. The last leg of his journey to the United States was, as I suspected, from Pearl Harbor to Alameda on that Catalina courier plane service the Navy operates."

Douglass hesitated. "You said 'exactly what happened,' Colonel. Captain Whittaker was dead drunk on arrival."

Donovan smiled. "He do anything wrong?"

"His priority bumped a naval officer," Douglass said. "The senior officer of those who didn't get bumped felt it his duty to report Whittaker. The first thing Whittaker did on arrival was make a telephone call. I don't know to whom."

"He told me he called Mrs. Whittaker," Canidy furnished.

"Just the one telephone call?" Donovan asked.

"Yes, sir, I think so."

"His orders," Douglass went on, "were brought to

the attention of the air station commander, my friend, who called around and found the next available space, military space, was on a B-25 being flown to Washington by a Brigadier General Jacobs. He arranged to have Jacobs diverted to Alameda. Shortly after Jacobs picked Whittaker up, I called out there."

"And what does Jacobs know, other than Whittaker had a high priority?" Donovan asked.

"Just that, sir," Douglass said. "Nothing about the letter. I then arranged to keep tabs on the flight as it came across the country. When it was due at Bolling, Canidy, Ellis, and I were there to meet it. I stayed in the car, and Canidy went to the plane to meet him. Dick?"

"There was a colonel there, who said he was from the Office of the Chief of Staff," Canidy said. "He knew about the letter."

"The word was probably sent from Hawaii," Donovan thought aloud. "Or perhaps even from Australia."

"Well, this colonel knew about it, sir," Canidy said. "And he told Whittaker he had come for him and the letter. I then showed him my marshal's badge, and said that I had been sent for him."

"Any trouble?"

"The colonel was pretty upset, sir, but that marshal's badge worked. I told him if he had any questions, he should direct them to the attorney general. Anyway, Jimmy came with us because he knew me. In the car, we told him—I thought we should, and I think Captain Douglass reluctantly agreed—about Miss Chenowith and his uncle."

"I thought he knew about that," Donovan said.

"I mean the business about where Mr. Whittaker died," Canidy said.

"Oh," Donovan said. "Was Cynthia at the house when you arrived?"

"She got there shortly after we did," Canidy said.

"So Whittaker took a bath and went to bed. In the master bedroom, which annoyed Miss Chenowith somewhat. . . ."

"Canidy, please keep your differences with her out of this," Donovan said, more reasonably than sharply.

"Yes, sir," Canidy said.

"What shape was he in?" Donovan asked.

"Sick and exhausted," Canidy said. "I'm sure he has malaria, and Christ knows what else is wrong with him."

"Vermin," Douglass said. "He was vermin-infested."

Donovan shook his head. "MacArthur must have had him on the first plane out of Australia."

"Yes, sir," Canidy said. "He told me he left Brisbane two hours after he got there."

"At eight the next morning, Colonel," Douglass said, "I went to the house on Q Street and checked on him. Then I called Steve Early. I thought the President's Press Secretary ought to be able to reach the President immediately. I told him that Whittaker had just flown in from Australia with a letter from General MacArthur, and that he was under orders to deliver it personally to the President. I had the feeling, sir, that Steve was surprised to hear about it."

"And he carried the word to the President?"

"Thirty minutes later, the White House switchboard called. The President wished to speak with Whittaker. The Roosevelt and the Whittaker families have been friendly for decades, you'll recall. If Whittaker was asleep, the White House said, we need not wake him, but he was to call as soon as he woke up."

"Was he awake?"

"No, sir," Douglass said. "And I decided to let him sleep."

Donovan nodded approval.

"At half past two," Douglass said, "I called you, and you told me you thought he had to return the President's call. Canidy and I woke him up. He was sick. Shivering, and nauseous. He insisted we give him something to drink. We did. That might have been the wrong thing to do."

"Much?"

"A good stiff pull at the neck of a Scotch bottle," Canidy said. "He said it would 'keep the worms happy.'"

"And then I placed the call to the White House," Douglass said. "The President came on the line in a minute."

"Do we know what was said?" Donovan asked.

"I had a stenographer on the line," Douglass said. "I have the transcript. But there wasn't much. The President welcomed him home, expressed his condolences about Mr. Whittaker, and said that he wanted him to come for supper. Whittaker told him that he had MacArthur's letter, and the President said he knew he did, and he could bring it with him."

"You told Early, and Early must have told him," Donovan said.

"Yes, sir," Douglass said. "And then Whittaker said, if it would be all right, he wanted to bring a friend with him."

"Canidy," Donovan said.

"Yes," Douglass said. "And the President said fine, and that he and Mrs. Roosevelt both looked forward to seeing him."

"Whittaker then said he wanted to catch up on his sleep," Canidy said. "And asked us to wake him when it was time."

"And you did?"

"We sent up a tray, in case he woke and was hungry. And we did what we could to make him look presentable," Canidy said. "A rush dry-cleaning job on his uniform. At five-thirty, I went up and woke him again, and shaved him."

"You shaved him?"

"He wanted more to drink," Canidy said, "and I didn't think he should have it. When I told him so, he held up his hands, which were shaking, and asked me how the hell he was supposed to shave, so I told him I'd shave him, and I did."

"At six-fifteen I sent them to the White House, in the Buick," Douglass said.

"Had he been given anything else to drink?"

"I gave him a drink in the car," Canidy said.

"I told you not to," Douglass said.

"I thought it was necessary," Canidy said, unrepentant. "He was shaking, and he said he hurt. I think he had cramps. The drink seemed to help. In view of what was waiting for him at the White House, I think it was the right thing to do."

"The press, you mean?"

"Yes, sir," Canidy said. "There was a Marine officer waiting for us. He took us into the Oval Office. The press was already there. Whittaker didn't know they would be, of course, and he didn't like it. I was glad he'd had something to drink."

"Where was the letter all this time?"

"He had it."

"There was no chance for you to see it?" Donovan asked.

"It was sealed, sir," Canidy said.

"We didn't have time to risk opening and resealing it, Colonel," Douglass said. "I made that decision."

"I'd love to know what the hell it says," Donovan said.

"Whatever it says, General Marshall didn't like it," Canidy said. "As soon as Whittaker gave it to the President, he gave it to General Marshall, and Marshall didn't like what it said."

"We're getting ahead of what happened," Donovan said. "Take it in sequence."

"There were half a dozen photographers, and eight, ten, reporters, and crews from Fox Movietone newsreel and The March of Time," Canidy said. "The President was already propped up. Standing, I mean, leaning against a back support. It was very carefully rehearsed, apparently. Early got Jimmy in position, and then they turned on the floodlights, or whatever they're called, and started to operate the cameras. The President started out and said he wanted them to meet an authentic hero who had just escaped from the Philippines with MacArthur and flown to Washington with a message from the general. He said—with his grin—that it was normal for an officer to salute the Commander in Chief, but in this case he was going to give him a hug, because he was the son of one of his best friends, and he had known him since he was in diapers.

"Then Early pushed Jimmy into camera range, and the President hugged him and introduced him by name. Then he gave him the Silver Star for his heroic escape and told the press that Jimmy had already won medals for valor in the air and on the ground."

"Very touching," Donovan said. There was a hint of sarcasm in his voice. "Roosevelt is marvelous at that sort of thing."

"The press wanted to ask Whittaker all kinds of questions," Canidy went on, "but the President wouldn't let them on the grounds that Whittaker was exhausted, and that after he and Mrs. Roosevelt had a family supper with him, he was going to let him go to bed. Somebody turned off the bright lights, and the press was ushered out."

"You weren't involved at all in the press conference?"

"I almost had to fight my way into the room," Canidy said.

"But none of the press made any connection between you and Whittaker?"

"If anything, they thought I was Secret Service," Canidy said.

"Good," Donovan said. "Then what?"

"The orderly put the President in his wheelchair," Canidy said, "and we went upstairs."

"General Marshall was in the living quarters?" Donovan asked. "Not in the Oval Office?"

"He was waiting for us in the living quarters," Canidy said. "He and Mrs. Roosevelt."

"And there was liquor?"

"Yes, sir. But I don't think . . . I don't know how to say this. Whittaker was weak, and the alcohol got to him more than it normally would. So he was probably drunk, but I don't think that's the reason he did what he did."

"Get into that," Donovan said.

"Mrs. Roosevelt kissed him, then asked him if he'd been in touch with his mother and Mrs. Whittaker. He told her he'd talked with them, and one of the stewards passed hors d'oeuvres. . . ."

"You were introduced how?"

"As an old friend, who worked for you, sir," Canidy said.

"OK," Donovan said. "Go on."

"Then we went in to dinner," Canidy said.

"The only other guest was General Marshall?" Donovan asked.

"Yes, sir," Canidy said. "He introduced himself and welcomed Jimmy home. He sat on one side of the table. Jimmy and I were on the other, and the Roosevelts at the ends. A steward poured wine, and the President said he had a toast to make, but he thought it should wait until after grace."

"He said grace?" Donovan asked.

"A brief grace," Canidy said. "Standard Episcopal, with a couple of added lines, one about Jimmy making it home, and another asking for a speedy victory. When he was finished, he toasted Jimmy's return, and then Jimmy gave him MacArthur's letter. He read it, and then gave it to General Marshall, who, as I said before, didn't like what it had to say."

"Did Mrs. Roosevelt read it?"

"No, sir," Canidy said. "When the President got it back from General Marshall, he put it in his pocket."

"What next?"

"We made small talk—prep school, Harvard, that sort of thing—and the food was served. That's when Jimmy went off."

"What, exactly, did he do?"

"Jimmy asked the steward for an extra glass and an extra plate," Canidy said. "I thought it was a little odd, but nothing to worry about. It was also odd that he hadn't eaten any of his soup. And then, when the steward tried to take the bowl away, he wouldn't let him remove it. I thought that was odd, too, but I didn't think it was alarming. I was more worried that he was going to get sloppy drunk, and that didn't seem to be happening.

"Then the meal, roast beef, was served. That's when I realized he was up to something. He sliced a small piece off his baked potato, and put that on the plate he'd asked for. Then he did the same thing with the slice of beef. And a piece of butter, and a roll. Then he carefully spooned a small portion of the clam chowder into the glass he had asked for.

"I asked him what the hell he was doing, and he smiled at me and winked. Then he stood up and walked around the table to George Marshall. He leaned over and pushed Marshall's plate to the center of the table. Then he laid the plate he'd made up in front of Marshall and poured the clam chowder over everything.

"And then he made his speech: 'That, General, is a three-eighths share of our ration. The troops in the Philippines have been on a three-eighths ration for months. Except the men on Bataan and Corregidor have no beef. What they're eating, if they have meat at all, is caribou and what's left of the mules and horses of the Twenty-sixth Cavalry. And there is no butter, no bread, and no clam chowder.'"

"Jesus Christ!" Donovan said.

"I told him to sit down," Canidy said. "He looked at me. He was excited, flushed in the face. He just grinned at me. And then he looked at the President, came to attention, and saluted. Very crisply."

"You couldn't have stopped him?" Donovan asked.

"This all happened very quickly," Canidy said. "I didn't know what he was up to."

"Did he say anything to the President?" Donovan asked.

"He said he was sure the Commander in Chief and the Chief of Staff would like to know what a three-eighths ration was, and that he hoped they would enjoy it, but that he begged to be excused, because he seemed to have lost his appetite."

"What did Marshall do?"

"Nothing," Canidy said. "Mrs. Roosevelt looked like she was about to cry. The President looked at me and said that he thought it would be a good idea if I took Captain Whittaker home, he was obviously exhausted."

"By the time they got back," Captain Douglass said, "General Marshall had called. He told me that Whittaker was on the way back to the house, and that since he obviously required medical attention, an ambulance had been dispatched. Marshall went on to say he had been ordered by the President to make sure that Whittaker was given this attention as soon as possible. It wasn't until I saw Canidy that I learned what Whittaker had done."

"The ambulance was there no more than two minutes after we got to the house," Canidy said. "An Army ambulance, from Fort Myer."

"There was a Medical Corps colonel with it," Douglass said. "I didn't know what to do but turn him over to them."

"I tried to go along with them," Canidy said. "But they wouldn't let me, and Whittaker said there was no reason to go. So he got in the ambulance, and they took him away."

"And then, sir, I called here," Douglass said.

"Well," Donovan said, after a moment's thought, "first things first. You certainly can't be blamed for his behavior, Canidy. And we accomplished what we set out to do. The President has MacArthur's letter. If he chose to share it with General Marshall, that's his business. And, from what you've told me, Jim Whittaker does need medical help. I'll see if I can find out what they've done with him. If I can, Canidy, I'll let you know."

"I don't think he's crazy, Colonel," Canidy said. "I don't think he deserves to be locked up in St. Elizabeths."[1]

"I said I'll try to find out what they've done with him. If I find out he's in St. Elizabeths, I'll do what I can about that then."

"Yes, sir," Canidy said.

"Would you mind waiting outside for a few minutes, Canidy?" Donovan said. "I've got a few things for Captain Douglass."

"I'd hoped to have a minute of your time, Colonel," Canidy said.

"About this?"

"About me, sir."

"What about you?"

"I'd like to know what you have in mind for me,"

---

[1]The Federal Government's psychiatric hospital in the District of Columbia.

Canidy asked. "Captain Douglass has been unable or unwilling to talk about that."

"I was told," Donovan said, "that you were no longer so determined to leave the comforts of Washington for the glory of aerial combat in the wild blue yonder."

"Captain Douglass has managed to make it perfectly clear that my enlistment in your Navy was for the duration. I think I understand why I can't go back to the other Navy, but I would like to know what I'm going to be doing in yours."

"For the time being, Canidy, you're going to baby-sit Admiral de Verbey," Donovan said. "He's at Summer Place."

"Cynthia said something about trouble with him," Canidy said, making it a question.

"We have to keep the admiral at Summer Place and away from the press," Donovan said. "Preferably amicably, but by force if necessary. Captain Douglass is arranging to have some Free French officers assigned to him as a staff, and there will be consultations between the admiral and various staff officers from the Navy. So far as the admiral is concerned, you will be his liaison officer. He knows you, of course, and we hope he will swallow that line. You'll wear the uniform of an Air Corps major. The Navy is providing a security force, and they will be told they will take their orders from you."

"How long will that go on?" Canidy asked.

"Until it has been decided by me that it is no longer necessary," Donovan said.

Canidy shrugged but said nothing.

He takes orders, Donovan thought. *That's good.*

"For the long term, Canidy," Donovan went on, "I'm sure we'll find things for you to do, taking into consideration both your flying background and your demonstrated ability to do other things. Just what, and when, hasn't been decided. The ever-resourceful Chief Ellis has scrounged an airplane for us, and we want you to pick that up and take it with you to New Jersey."

"What kind of an airplane?"

"A Beech D18," Donovan said. "Is that right, Peter?"

"Yes, sir."

"I'm a fighter pilot," Canidy asked, more of a question than a challenge.

"And an aeronautical engineer," Douglass said, "who knows how to fly a D18S. Isn't that correct?"

"I got a couple of hours in the one the AVG had," Canidy said.

"Well, you'll have plenty of time in New Jersey to become proficient," Douglass said. "And we'll try to arrange it so that you can get checked out in other aircraft as well. When you can spare the time from taking care of the admiral, of course."

Canidy nodded his acceptance of this.

"Any other questions, Canidy?" Donovan asked.

"No, sir."

"I think there's a coffeepot in the sitting room," Donovan said, politely dismissing him.

"Thank you," Canidy said again, and left the bedroom, closing the door behind him.

Three

1

A BLIMP WAS about to take off as Canidy approached the field in the twin Beech D18S. The tower ordered him to circle east of the field in order to get out of the way. Canidy was pleased. He hadn't seen that many blimps, and he'd never before seen one take off. It apparently required a great deal of skill on the part of the pilot and the large ground crew. He could see them now, six and eight men to a line, pulling the blimp's nose into the wind while simultaneously keeping the machine from being blown crossways.

As large as blimps were (there were three others on the ground), they were in turn dwarfed by their hangar. This monster had been built, he remembered, when he was a kid, at a time when important people seriously believed that dirigibles were going to be the warships of the future. A series of disastrous crashes, including that of the German *Hindenburg* right here at Lakehurst, had killed that idea.

The blimp he was watching finally sailed gently into

the air and headed due east, out to sea. It was going on a war patrol to look for German submarines.

"Lakewood clears Navy Six-one-one for landing on runway two-seven," his earphones announced, waking him up. "The winds are five, gusting to fifteen, from the west. The barometer is three-zero-zero-zero."

He banked the Beech back toward the field. It was brand-new, a VIP transport, neither the navigation trainer nor the bare-to-the-ribs small transport he had expected. It had been intended for a senior admiral who had been given a command at sea before he could take delivery. As was his way, Ellis had heard about this and "somehow" had arranged for it to be diverted to COI. A useful man, Ellis.

"Six-one-one on final," he said into the microphone as he lowered the wheels and put down the flaps.

He had a little trouble putting it on the ground, and he was farther down the runway than he wanted to be when he heard the wheels chirp. He'd like to put blame, he thought, on the flight characteristics of the aircraft, but the truth was that the fault was his. Despite his newly issued Army Air Corps flight records claim that he was rated as pilot in command of C-45, C-46, and C-47 aircraft (the three standard Air Corps transports), he had never even been in the cockpit of a C-46 or a C-47, and when he had taken this Beech D18S off the field at the Beech factory in Wichita, it was the first time he had flown what the Air Corps called the C-45 solo.

"Lakehurst, Six-one-one," he reported to the tower. "I'm on the ground at ten past the hour."

"Six-one-one, take the taxiway to your left, and taxi to the east door of the dirigible hangar."

The hangar looked even bigger on the ground than from the air—simply incredibly vast. As he approached, with the building looming over him, a Navy officer walked from the hangar, stood in his path, and made "come to me" ground handler signals. Canidy thought it was odd that an officer should be parking aircraft, but his signals were even stranger. The officer with the commander's shoulder boards was giving him a left-turn signal, into the hangar itself.

Canidy made the turn, but stopped. One does not taxi airplanes inside hangars. Prop blast does interesting things inside confined spaces such as hangars—like turn other airplanes over on their backs.

But inside the hangar was a proper plane handler, a white hat with wands in his hands. And he too was giving "come to me" signals.

Canidy released the brakes, opened the throttles a crack, and obeyed. There was, he thought, an exception to every rule, and this hangar was obviously the exception to the one about not operating engines in a hangar.

There were six other aircraft inside. A Catalina with its engines running taxied toward the far door. It looked at least a mile away.

The ground handler, walking quickly backward, led him a hundred yards into the hangar and then signaled for him to turn left, turn around, and shut it down.

When Canidy climbed out of the D18, the officer who had met him outside the hangar was standing there, waiting for him.

Canidy saluted, and the commander returned it, then offered his hand.

"Major Canidy?" the commander asked. When Canidy nodded, he introduced himself as Commander Reynolds, the air station commander.

"I like your hangar," Canidy said.

Reynolds laughed. "It's supposed to be the largest covered area without roof supports in the world," he said.

"I can believe that."

"The sun gets hot here," Reynolds said. "When we have the room, we like to park airplanes inside, keep them from baking."

He is a nice guy, Canidy decided, but that isn't the only reason he's being so charming. He is a professional, keeping the apple polished. NAS Lakehurst had orders coming directly from the Office of the Chief of Naval Operations to provide whatever guard force was deemed necessary for Summer Place, and to place that guard force under the absolute authority of a United States deputy marshal who would make his identity known to them.

And that morning the "deputy U.S. marshal," who was in fact one of the FBI agents on loan to COI, had told the commander, NAS Lakehurst, that he was being relieved by an Air Corps major named Canidy, who would be arriving in a Navy airplane.

"Mr. Delaney said that he'd like to turn over to you at Summer Place," Commander Reynolds said. "And I thought, if you had no objection, I'd tag along. I don't know what your requirements are going to be, and it might save time if I was there from the beginning."

"I'm glad you can spare the time," Canidy said.

"I understand the importance of your mission," Reynolds said.

Translated, Canidy thought, *that means you don't want me to make any waves.*

Commander Reynolds drove Canidy to Summer Place in his Navy gray staff car. The last time he had been in a Navy car with a white-hat driver had been at Pensacola, Canidy thought. The admiral had dispatched his car and driver to fetch Lieutenant (j.g.) Canidy from the beer hall to the admiral's quarters, where he had been introduced to a leathery-faced old Army fighter pilot named Claire Chennault. Chennault promptly announced that he was asking for volunteer pilots to fly Curtiss P-40B Tomahawks for the Chinese, and that Canidy had been selected.

"It's a beautiful place," Commander Reynolds volunteered. "A turn-of-the-century mansion right on the ocean."

"I know," Canidy said. "I've been here before."

Reynolds obviously thought he meant in connection with whatever was going on there now. But what Canidy meant, what Canidy was thinking, was how often Jimmy Whittaker's aunt and uncle had entertained him—and Eric Fulmar—here when the three friends had been in St. Mark's School together.

Mounted every hundred feet or so on the fence that surrounded the estate there were signs announcing that this was a U.S. Government Reservation, where trespassing was forbidden, and that trespassers would be prosecuted.

And far enough inside the gate not to be seen from the road, a guard shack had been set up. A white hat in puttees carrying a Springfield rifle stepped onto the road and barred their passage until Commander Reynolds identified Canidy.

The "deputy U.S. marshal" and a young lieutenant (j.g.) who was in charge of the guard detail were waiting for them at the house. Canidy recognized the ex–FBI agent from the house on Q Street. If the ex–FBI agent was surprised to see Canidy in a major's uniform, it didn't show.

"Just as the weather turns nice here," the ex–FBI man joked, "I have to go back."

"Virtue is its own reward," Canidy announced unctuously.

The details of the guard arrangement were explained to Canidy: there were, in addition to the man who met Canidy, four more "deputy U.S. marshals" at the house working eight-hour shifts in rotation. They supervised the Navy guards, who worked four to a shift around the clock guarding the road and making irregular patrols of the fence and along the beach.

A telephone switchboard had also been installed. This was operated by the "deputy marshals." There were direct lines to Lakehurst, to the Coast Guard station three miles down the beach, and to the police department in Asbury Park.

Ten minutes after the turnover had begun, it was over. On his way back to Lakehurst, Commander Reynolds gave the ex–FBI agent a ride to the train station in Asbury Park.

Canidy then formally presented himself to the admiral, who was a tiny little man who looked both very fragile and very intense. Canidy had liked him from the moment he met him in Morocco.

"Monsieur l'Amiral," Canidy said, saluting. *"Je suis encore une fois à votre service."* He had rehearsed the French.

"It is my pleasure to see you again, Major," the admiral said in excellent English, returning the salute. "I have often wondered what had happened to you after you were left behind by the submarine that carried me to this country."

"I have been told," Canidy said dryly, "that there were compelling reasons to leave us behind."

"Well," the admiral said, touching Canidy's arm, "what is important is that you finally got out, and are here. I think you'll like it. We are guests of a Mrs. Whittaker," the admiral said. "She is a gracious lady, and an even more gracious hostess."

"I know Mrs. Whittaker, *mon Amiral,*" Canidy said. "Before the war, I was often a guest in this house."

"And is that why you have been sent here?"

"I am honored to have been named your liaison officer," Canidy said.

"Odd," the admiral said dryly, "I somehow got the idea that you were my new jailer."

Canidy, flustered, couldn't think of a reply.

"Well, I don't suppose it matters, one way or the other. As there were good reasons for you to be left behind off Safi, I am sure there are good reasons for my house arrest here," the admiral said, without apparent bitterness. "Come, I will introduce you to my staff."

The staff consisted of a French Navy captain, an old man who had served aboard the battleship *Jean Bart* when the admiral had been her captain; a much younger lieutenant commander (Douglass had warned Canidy to be very careful dealing with this one; he was suspected of having strong ties to de Gaulle); and a middle-aged petty officer who looked pathetically absurd in his bell-bottomed trousers, seaman's blouse with flap, and hat with red pom pom. He performed the dual functions of orderly and clerk.

Half an hour later, Barbara Whittaker returned from shopping in Asbury Park. When Canidy caught sight of the old, sedate Rolls-Royce moving majestically up the drive, he excused himself and went down to meet her.

The Rolls had an A ration sticker stuck on the windshield. The A ration was for nonessential personal vehicles, and provided three gallons of gasoline a week. That would be enough, he thought, to get the Rolls to Asbury Park, but not back. Barbara Whittaker's ration was obviously being augmented, probably from Navy stocks.

She was out of the car and helping the chauffeur unload grocery bags from the trunk before she saw him. Then she smiled and strode up to him, a tall, silver-haired woman of great dignity.

"Would you be terribly embarrassed if I put my arms around you and kissed you, Dick?" she asked. "I'm so very glad to see you!"

"I'd be unhappy if you didn't," Canidy said.

She hugged him tightly. He was surprised at the depth of his own emotion at seeing her again.

"Help Tom and me with the groceries," she said. "And then we'll sit on the porch and have some of Chesty's Scotch and bring each other up to date."

She'll want to know about Jimmy, Canidy thought. *And obviously, I am expected to tell her as little as possible. Well, fuck that, she's no German spy. I'll tell her as much as I can.*

She meant it about drinking Chesty's Scotch. The bottle she produced was older than Canidy. And she asked him about himself and what he was going to be doing while he was at Summer Place, but fortunately she steered away from asking about Jimmy.

This was not an indication of lack of interest in him. It was rather because she was a great lady whose sense of duty forbade asking questions.

"I met Jimmy when he flew into Washington," Canidy said.

"I don't think you're supposed to talk about him, are you, Dick?" she said.

"He has apparently been running around in the jungles of Bataan," Canidy went on. "I'm sure he has malaria, and he told me he had a tapeworm named Clarence," Canidy said.

"Oh my!" she said. "Chesty had one years ago and had a terrible time passing it."

"He was thirty pounds underweight," Canidy went on, "and he's going to have to have some serious dental work."

"What of his attitude?" she asked.

She means, Canidy thought, *'is he out of his mind?'*

"The President had him to dinner, after that business with the newsreel cameras," Canidy said, and went on to tell her what Jim Whittaker had done to demonstrate what a three-eighths ration was.

"Even under the circumstances, that was extremely rude to Franklin and Eleanor," Barbara Whittaker said.

"Well, please don't apologize for him," Canidy said. "If you do, they'll know who told you about this."

She waved her hand to show him she understood, then asked, "Is that why he's been hospitalized? Why I can't see him?"

"I think he's hospitalized because he needs hospitalization," Canidy said, hoping she would believe it.

"It said in the newspapers that he carried a letter

from Douglas MacArthur to the President," she said. "And General Marshall was there for dinner. Do you know how much Marshall and Douglas MacArthur loathe each other?"

"I've heard," Canidy admitted.

"Does that have anything to do with Jimmy's hospitalization?"

"I don't know," Canidy said, after a moment. "I just don't know."

She thought that over.

"Chesty and Franklin Roosevelt were not the best of friends," she said. "But I am unable to believe that Franklin would . . ."

"Colonel Donovan said he was going to find out what he could," Canidy said. "I think the thing to do is wait for him to do that."

She leaned over and patted first his knee and then his cheek.

"Thank you," she said. "I'm sure you shouldn't have told me any of this, but I'm glad you did."

"Just make sure Colonel Donovan doesn't find out," Canidy said.

"He won't," she said.

She stood up.

"When I heard you were coming," she said, "I had Commander Nadine moved out of your old room. He didn't like it much, but I told him you were an old friend of the family. Now I'm sorry I said that."

"Excuse me?" Canidy asked, confused.

"I should have said you were family, period," she said. She looked down and met his eyes. "We generally have a cocktail at half past six, and then dinner around seven. If you can't make it until then, you know where to find the refrigerator."

"Thank you."

"Welcome home, Dick," she said, and then she walked off the porch.

2

2745 Lakeshore Drive
Chicago, Illinois
April 21, 1942

Despite Brandon Chambers's assurance to Chandler H. Bitter that he would immediately have one of his war correspondents in India send a report on Ed Bitter's condition within a matter of days, the first amplification of what had happened came to Chandler in the morning mail two weeks after the radiogram from General Chennault.

The envelope was cheap brownish paper, and the letter itself appeared to have been typed on mimeograph paper on a battered portable.

> HQ, 1st Pursuit Sqdn, AVG
> APO 607 S/F Cal.
>
> 25 Mar 42

Dear Mr. Bitter:

By the time you read this you will have heard that Ed has been hurt. I thought you would like to know what happened.

We mounted a two-flight (10 a/c) low-level strafing assault on the Japanese air base at Chiengmai, Thailand. Our squadron commander led one flight, I had the other, and Ed was in line to take the place of either of us if anything should happen.

We went in on oxygen at 20,000 feet, and went down near the field for a strafing run. Some of the ships had 50-pound HE bombs in their flare chutes. There was a lot more antiaircraft on the way down, and many more heavy machine guns on the deck when we got there, than intelligence had led us to expect.

The skipper took a hit and was shot down his first pass, and Ed took a hit just below his right knee on his third pass. I think it was a glancing shot or a rickoshay (sp?), because the wound, while unpleasant, isn't nearly the mess it would have been had he taken a direct hit from a .50, which is what the Japs use, we having obligingly showed them how to build them.

Ed managed to get his aircraft up to altitude again, but on the way home he went on the radio and said that he was feeling bad, and faint, and wanted to set down (rather than risk losing consciousness while still in the air).

Luck was with him. There was a riverbed in the middle of nowhere that looked like it was hard enough to take a landing, and he set it down without trouble. Once he was there, and we knew it was safe to land, we were able to land another plane, load him into that, and with the pilot sitting on Ed's lap and ducking his head to get it out of the prop blast, he was able to make off and get Ed back to the base.

That was the worst part. Once he was on the ground, they gave him something for the pain, did what they could here for his knee, and arranged for him to be flown to India, where there is a brand-new General Hospital (US Army) in Calcutta.

Probably the best indicator of his condition is that he told me just before he left for Calcutta that he will be back in six weeks. I don't think so. I think they will probably ship him home just as soon as they can arrange for it. He is not in danger, so the worst that will happen is that he may have a stiff knee.

I have to cut this off now, because I'm now the squadron commander and I'm finding that means a lot of work.

Ed and I had become good friends, and what I've been thinking is that if something like this had to happen, this wasn't so bad. We're really going to miss him around here, but he's going to come out of it all right.

Sincerely,
Peter Douglass, Jr.

Chandler Bitter showed Helen the letter, then suggested she call Brandon and read the letter to him. After that he left for work.

When he returned that evening, she mentioned to him that she had also called Ann Chambers and read the letter to her. Ann was Brandon's daughter and their niece, and she was working on Brandon's newspaper in

Memphis. Margaret had also called Mark and Sue-Ann Chambers in Mobile. The rest of the afternoon she'd spent having Peter Douglass's letter photographed so that she could send copies to other friends who would be interested.

There was a second letter from the Chinese embassy the next day. Eight flowery paragraphs proclaimed that a second gold miniature Flying Tiger was being sent with the personal gratitude of the Chinese people and Generalissimo Chiang Kai-shek.

Mrs. Bitter had that letter photographed, too, so that it could be sent to sundry and assorted relatives and friends. When things calmed down a bit, she was going to have the letters framed. She was also going to have the second gold Flying Tiger mounted and take it to The Plantation in Alabama (which was the family vacation residence). She would hang it all in the library there with the other family war memorabilia. Some of this went back to the War Between the States.

Helen's behavior astonished Chandler. He had been married to her a long time, and thought he knew her. What seemed to be the strange truth was that the traditional roles were reversed. He was nearly sick with fear and relief for their child, and she was reveling in his heroism.

3

Memphis, Tennessee
May 28, 1942

A reporter-photographer team from *Time-Life* visited the U.S. Army General Hospital in Calcutta in early May looking for "upbeat" stories. The United States of America had been taking a hell of a whipping in the opening months of the war, and with the exception of

Lieutenant Colonel Jimmy Doolittle's B-25 raid on Tokyo the month before, there was a surfeit of depressing stories of courage in the face of defeat.

It didn't take them long to find out there were several Flying Tigers in the hospital. One of these had a story that would go over well in New York.

The first story about him appeared in *Time* of May 28, 1942. There was a one-column photograph of Edwin Howell Bitter in a hospital bathrobe, sitting in a wheelchair with his right leg in a cast sticking straight out in front of him. The cutline under the photograph read: *"Civilian" Ed Bitter*.

The story itself seemed sure to satisfy the editor's demand for something upbeat:

There are five American "civilian" patients in the new U.S. Army General Hospital in Calcutta. Their bills are paid by the Chinese government. They are employees of the American Volunteer Group who were "injured on the job." The job 24-year-old ex-Navy pilot Edwin H. Bitter, of Chicago, was injured doing was strafing the huge Jap air base at Chiegnmai, Thailand, in a worn-out Curtiss P-40B Warhawk, an aircraft the Chinese were able to get for their American volunteer pilots to fly only because the British turned them down as obsolescent for service against the Germans in Europe.

Bitter downed nine Japanese aircraft in his "obsolete" P-40 before he himself was downed by ground fire in Thailand. He was rescued from certain imprisonment and possible execution as a "bandit" when another "civilian" Flying Tiger pilot managed to land his Warhawk on the dry riverbed where Bitter had crashed. He squeezed the wounded flier into his cockpit and took off again. Names of AVG pilots still fighting the Japanese are not released.

Annapolis graduate ('38) Bitter sees no future for himself in the U.S. Navy, which, he says, "has no use for people with stiff knees." When he is able, he will return to his "civilian job" as a Flying Tiger.

Life magazine, ten days later (it took time to get all the photographs necessary for a photo-essay to the

United States), had a longer story about the AVG men in Calcutta, but by then *Time* had been published.

It was not known whether the order had come from President Roosevelt himself, or from Secretary of the Navy Frank Knox, who had been wounded as a sergeant charging up San Juan Hill with Teddy Roosevelt in the Spanish-American War, but the word came down from way up high:

"Get that fellow Bitter back in the U.S. Navy as soon as he can be sworn in, even if you have to do it with him on a stretcher."

Not long afterward a letter addressed to Miss Sarah Child which bore the return address, LtComdr E. H. Bitter, USN, Det of Patients, USA Gen Hospital, APO 652, San Francisco, Calif. appeared in Sarah's and Ann's box in the Peabody Hotel in Memphis. Before Sarah saw it, Ann Chambers took the letter and kept it in her purse until she found time to steam open the envelope over a teakettle and read it. Ann had opened all of Sarah Child's mail since the visit to Memphis of Sarah's mother.

When Sarah's mother had asked her husband to take her to Memphis to see her daughter, Joseph Child had desperately wanted to believe that time and the maternal instincts of his wife had overcome her first reaction to the news that their unmarried nineteen-year-old daughter was pregnant. Her first reaction—rage and fear—put Sarah's mother in the Institute of Living, a private psychiatric hospital in Hartford, Connecticut, for six weeks. But Joseph Child had taken his wife out of the IOL against medical advice when she asked to go to Memphis.

Sarah shared a suite in the Peabody Hotel in Memphis with her best friend from Bryn Mawr, Ann Chambers. There was no question in Joseph Child's mind that Ann, the daughter of Brandon Chambers, the newspaper publisher, was in Memphis as much to give Sarah refuge from her mother in New York as she was to work for her father's newspaper.

But with the world in flames, with the European continent in the hands of the Germans, with most of their European relatives either missing or in hiding from the Nazis, with the United States fighting what looked to be a losing battle for its very existence, Joseph Child reasoned that his wife would see that their daughter's pregnancy was a joyful thing and an affirmation of life.

In Memphis, at his first sight of Sarah, Joseph Child's eyes filled with tears. Not tears of sadness, he realized, but rather because she looked like a living madonna. Her skin glowed, her somewhat solemn eyes glistened.

"Bitch!" his wife had screamed at their daughter in the suite in the Peabody. "Godless whore! Why don't you and your bastard die!"

Joseph Child had to physically restrain his wife until the hotel could find a doctor who would come to the suite and sedate her.

The instant her mother and father were gone, Sarah went into an emotional nosedive. Two days later, she still had not recovered when, on the day the radiogram from General Chennault arrived in Chicago, she was delivered of a healthy, seven-pound-five-ounce boy in Memphis's Doctors Hospital.

Ann Chambers decided that this was not the moment to tell Sarah that Eddie had been injured, had almost been killed. Postnatal depression had come sooner than it usually did, and with a greater severity than the doctor had expected. In the delivery room he had thought admiringly that Sarah was a tough little cookie.

Sarah was in the hospital ten days, and then—still depressed—returned to the suite in the Peabody. There was a nurse all day, but she was alone when the nurse left at five until Ann came home from the *Advocate*. Which meant that Ann often had to rush home when she would have preferred to work.

In their suite, Ann steamed open the letter over a teakettle on a hot plate, read the letter, carefully resealed the envelope, and then went to Sarah's door. She flung the door open and, waving the letter, went inside.

"Poppa is finally heard from!" she cried.

Sarah turned the envelope in her hands and saw the return address.

"Oh, my God!" she said. "He's in the hospital!"

Then she tore it open and read it.

Calcutta, India
7 April 1942

Dear Sarah:

I have continued to receive your fine and regular letters, and regret that I have been such a terrible correspondent. I was involved in a small accident, slightly injuring my leg, and am spending, as you might have noticed from the return address, some time in the hospital. I hasten to say that I am really quite well, and there is no cause for concern. And being in the hospital finally gives me a chance to answer your many letters.

My big news (which you may also have noticed from the return address) is that I am back in the Navy. An officer from the staff of the Commander, Naval Element, U.S. Forces in India came to see me yesterday. He got right to the point. Now that I wasn't going to be of much use to the AVG, had I given any thought to "coming home"?

I told him that I was obliged to fulfill my contract with the AVG, which has until July 4 to run, but he told me that the AVG was willing to let me out of it. My leg will be in a cast for another month or six weeks, and probably a little stiff after that, and by the time I'd be ready to fly again, my contract would just about be over.

I thought it was really quite decent of the Navy to take me back as a temporary cripple, but they went even beyond that. We were promised (I guess I can now tell you) that we would be taken back into the Navy with no loss of seniority, and that if we were promoted while in the AVG, we would receive a promotion in the

Navy. It seems that the Navy has a policy by which lieutenants (junior grade) with six months in the war zone are considered eligible for promotion, so they took that into consideration, and then also made good their word to promote me since I had been promoted in the AVG.

What that means is that I'm back in the Navy with a grade (temporary, of course) two grades higher than I was the last time I saw you. I find it hard, frankly, to think of myself as Lieutenant Commander Bitter (all the lieutenant commanders I knew were old men), but it must be so, for that's what it says on the sign on my bed.

The other good news is that I will be returned to the United States. A hospital ship is en route here, and as soon as they have enough people to fill it up (and there probably will be more than enough by the time it gets here) I'll be returned to the United States. There is a good chance that I'll be gone before any letter you might write could get here, so you can save stamps.

I have no idea where I'll be stationed in the States, but perhaps I'll be able to come to Memphis to see you. I would like very much to buy you the most elaborate dinner the Peabody dining room has to offer.

Please say hello to Ann, and if you'd like to risk the paper and a stamp, write your

Fond Pen Pal
Ed

"He's been hurt," Sarah said to Ann. "Not seriously. He had some kind of an accident."

"He's lying through his teeth," Ann said.

Sarah looked at her in surprise. Ann walked back out of the bedroom and returned with the manila envelope in which she had all the rest of the story, copies of the radiogram and the letters from the Chinese embassy and from Peter Douglass, Jr., and the clippings from *Time* and *Life*.

"He looks terrible," Sarah said when she saw the photographs. "He looks starved."

"He's alive," Ann said. "And he's coming home."

"Why didn't you show me this stuff before?" Sarah demanded.

Ann shrugged her shoulders.

"I was suffering from perfectly normal postnatal depression," Sarah said furiously. "I wasn't crazy!"

Ann smiled at her.

Sarah thought of something else. "Have you heard from Dick Canidy?"

"Not from or about," Ann said.

"Well, they're probably keeping him busy," Sarah said, "and he just hasn't had time to write."

"Sure," Ann said. "Either that, or there is a Chinese girl, or girls, or an American nurse, or an English nurse, or all of the above."

"You don't know that," Sarah said.

"I know Richard Canidy, damn him," Ann said.

4

Warm Springs, Georgia
June 8, 1942

The President of the United States and Colonel William J. Donovan took their lunch, fried chicken and a potato salad, on the flagstone patio outside Roosevelt's cottage. The two were shielded from the view of other patients and visitors at the poliomyelitis care center by a green latticework fence.

Roosevelt had a guest, who vanished immediately on the arrival of Donovan by car from Atlanta. Donovan wondered why he was surprised and shocked. Roosevelt was a man, even if his legs were crippled. Eleanor, he well knew, could be a pain in the ass. Barbara Whittaker was far more charming, and certainly better looking, and Chesty Whittaker had died in the bed of a woman young enough to be his daughter. Why should he expect Roosevelt to be a saint?

And, he told himself, in any event it was none of his business. He had come to Georgia to discuss the war, and what COI was doing to help win it. Whether Franklin Roosevelt was getting a little on the side had nothing to do with that.

The most important thing on Roosevelt's mind at lunch was neither the beating the nation was taking in the Pacific nor even the first American counterstroke, Operation Torch, the invasion of North Africa, scheduled for the fall. What he wanted to discuss was the super bomb.

Donovan had previously learned that while the experiments at the reactor at the University of Chicago were by no means near completion (they had yet to try for a chain reaction), Dr. Conant of Harvard had reported that the scientists were more and more confident that things were going to work. After these reports Roosevelt had been so confident (or, Donovan thought, so desperate) that he had authorized a virtual blank check on his secret war appropriations funds to go ahead with the effort. As of June 1, under an Army Engineer officer, Brigadier General Leslie R. Groves, the Manhattan Project came into being, with the mission of developing a bomb whose explosive force would come from atomic fission. Manhattan was chosen for the project name in the hope that the enormous expenditures about to be made would be connected with Manhattan Island, rather than the facilities being built at Oak Ridge, Tennessee, and in the deserts of the Southwest.

The Office of the Coordinator of Information had so far been involved in this program in the operation that located and brought to the United States Grunier, the French mining engineer who had worked before the war for Union Minière in the Belgian Congo. One of the very few known sources of uranitite ore, from which it was theoretically possible to extract uranium 235, was in Katanga Province of the Belgian Congo.

From Grunier it had been learned that there were in fact many tons of uranitite in Katanga Province lying around as by-products of other Union Minière mining and smelting operations. Some of it had simply been removed and pushed aside as slag during copper and tin mining operations. A few people questioned how much to trust Grunier, for he had been brought involuntarily to the United States from Morocco where he was working in phosphate mining. His family was in France, and he was understandably concerned for their welfare. This concern was promptly used as leverage by COI.

He was thus prevailed upon to draw maps. Donovan then sent an agent to the Belgian Congo from South Africa who had returned with fifty pounds of uranitite ore in twenty bags. The source of each bag was labeled according to which pile of spillings it came from. Twelve of his packages turned out to be useless. They were not what Grunier thought (or at least so he told the COI interrogators) were supplies of uranitite. Seven more samples had not contained enough uranitite to make refining possible. One of the three good samples had contained an adequate parts-per-million ratio, and the last two, on spectographic and chemical analysis, proved to be very desirable.

The next question was: Were the samples truly representative of the pile they were taken from, or were they a fluke?

This problem was magnified greatly because of the enormous quantities of uranitite ore required to produce even minute quantities of pure uranium 235. There was, so far as anyone knew, less than 0.000001 pound of the stuff in all the world.

Some scientists believed that as little as an ounce of pure U-235 would be enough to make up the critical mass of an atomic fission bomb. But others, just as knowledgeable, said the minimum figure would have to be at least a hundred pounds.

Thus, to determine how many thousands of tons were going to be necessary to produce as much as fifty pounds of uranium, it was necessary to have refinable quantities. In laboratory terms, that meant a minimum of five tons. For now. And of course much more later, if things went the way everyone hoped they would.

As of December 12, 1941, the German government had informed the Belgian government that under the terms of the armistice agreement between them, the export of copper and other strategic minerals and ores from Belgian colonies to the United States of America was no longer permitted. And all other exports would henceforth be reviewed to make sure they would not accrue to the enemy's benefit.

Worrying about how to smuggle several hundred tons of ore out of the middle of darkest Africa would, however, have to wait. The job now was to determine if the Katanga ore was what was needed, and the way to do that was to get five tons of it to the United States.

And the way to do that, Donovan decided, was to fly into Katanga and get it.

"You're working on flying the stuff out, then. Is that right, Bill?" Roosevelt said.

"Yes, sir," Donovan said.

"How are you going to do it?"

Donovan was a little annoyed with Roosevelt's interest in details. It was, in a way, flattering, but it took time. He was often saying to his subordinates that of all the shortages that interfered with the war effort, the greatest was time. There simply wasn't enough time to do what had to be done. The few minutes it would take to tell the President how he planned to get the uranitite ore from the Belgian Congo would have to come from the total time Roosevelt was able to give him. He would have much preferred to spend this talking about other things.

But Franklin Delano Roosevelt was the Commander in Chief, he reminded himself, and could not therefore be told to stop wasting time with unimportant questions.

"You remember the young man who came to dinner with Jim Whittaker?" he asked.

"Canidy . . . something like that?"

"Richard Canidy," Donovan said. "Ex–Flying Tiger, and more important now, an MIT-trained aeronautical engineer."

"I'm a little confused. Isn't he the chap you sent to North Africa after the mining engineer and Admiral Whatsisname?"

"That, too," Donovan said, impressed but not really surprised that Roosevelt had called that detail from his memory. "At the moment, he's at Chesty's house on the Jersey shore, trying to keep the admiral happy and away from newspaper reporters. But he's also working on this."

"How is he working on this?"

"He has been provided with the details . . . weight and distance, I mean, not what has to be hauled or where the stuff is. And he has been told to recommend a way—in absolute secrecy—to move that much weight that far. He's been getting a lot of help from Pan American Airways."

"Why not the Air Corps?"

Donovan was very much aware that he had just walked out on thin ice. Pan American Airways beyond question had greater experience in long-distance trans-oceanic flight than anyone else—including the Army Air Corps. But their greatest expert in this area was Colonel Charles A. Lindbergh, "Lucky Lindy," the first man to fly the Atlantic solo, the great American hero who had not long before enraged Roosevelt and a large number of other important people by announcing that in his professional judgment the German Luftwaffe looked invincible. Lindbergh had then rubbed salt in the wound by involving himself deeply in the America First movement, throwing his enormous prestige behind the notion that America should stay out of Europe's wars.

Immediately after Pearl Harbor, Lindbergh, who was a colonel in the Air Corps Reserve, had volunteered for active duty. Roosevelt, predictably, had no intention of letting that happen. Franklin Roosevelt would allow Lindbergh to serve in uniform over his dead body.

Donovan and Lindbergh, however, were friends. And Lindbergh had proved eager to help when Donovan asked for flight-planning advice. When Donovan had told Roosevelt Canidy was getting a lot of help from Pan American, he meant help from Charles A. Lindbergh personally.

"Because Pan American knows more about this sort of thing than the Air Corps," Donovan said.

Roosevelt grunted, but accepted that. If he had asked if Lindbergh were involved, Donovan would not have lied to him. But he hadn't asked, which was just as well as far as Donovan was concerned.

"And you think it can be done?" Roosevelt asked.

"Canidy tells me it can," Donovan said.

"You seem to place a good deal of trust in him, Bill," the President said. "He seems possessed of a number of interesting secrets."

"There are two schools of thought about multiple secrets, Mr. President," Donovan said. "If people are limited to one secret at a time, you wind up with a lot of people who have to be watched. On the other hand, if one man has a number of secrets, we only have to worry about security for him. And, right now at least, I don't intend to send Canidy himself to the Congo. He's just setting the operation up. In the end, I think it will turn out that we'll use an Air Corps crew."

Roosevelt thought that over a moment.

"They would like that, I think," he said, grinning. "They have the responsibility, you know, of dealing with airplanes."

"Yes, I know," Donovan said, just as sarcastically, "and as I understand things, I'm supposed to be dealing with intelligence. You will doubtless be surprised to learn that sometimes, despite our best efforts, that puts me and the Air Corps in conflict."

"Is that just a general philosophical observation, Bill? Or do you have something specific in mind?"

"German fighter aircraft propelled by jet engines," Donovan said, after a pause.

The President smiled very broadly, his cigarette holder cocked high between his teeth. He was enjoying the exchange.

"*You* will doubtless be surprised, Bill," he said, "when I tell you that when I mentioned those aircraft to George Marshall, he told me that the Air Corps was not very concerned about them. In fact, they had—with great tact, of course—asked if such aircraft weren't really a tactical concern of theirs, rather than a strategic concern of yours."

"Then they're wrong about that, too, Franklin," Donovan said flatly.

"Are they indeed?"

"Will you listen to me?"

"Of course," Roosevelt said. "How can I refuse?"

"As it has been explained to me, the Air Corps tactic for Europe is massive bombing from high altitude of German military targets by heavy bombers, B-17s and B-24s. The Air Corps believes that the massed heavy armament of a large flight of carefully arranged bombers can throw up a relatively impenetrable wall of fire against German fighters."

"And you don't think they can?"

"Not against German fighters, armed with cannon,

that are flying three times as fast as the bombers," Donovan said.

"The Air Corps disagrees with that, of course," Roosevelt said. "And they also believe that the Germans are a long way from having fighters powered with jet engines off their drawing boards."

"The first flight of a jet-powered German aircraft took place on August 27, 1939," Donovan said, "at an airfield near Berlin."

Roosevelt looked at him sharply.

"The Luftwaffe will flight-test within a month or so one of the twelve Messerschmitt ME-262 fighter planes currently being built in underground, bombproof facilities in Augsburg. The ME-262 is powered by a centrifugal Junkers oh-oh-four engine, designed by a man named von Ohain, which is supposed to be a great improvement over the radial jet engine they've used up to now."

It was a moment before Roosevelt spoke.

"I was about to insult you, Bill, by asking if you were sure of your information," he said. "I won't do that, of course. But do you realize what a spot you're putting me in with the Air Corps?"

"If the Germans get these fighters operational, Franklin, we will not be able to accept the losses they will inflict on our bomber force—either in a tactical sense or a public-relations sense. That, I respectfully submit, is indeed a strategic consideration."

"And how do you suggest we stop them?" Roosevelt asked.

"That would be the Air Corps' business," Donovan said. "Once they recognize the problem, I'm sure they'll know how to handle it. My people tell me that manufacturing jet engines is considerably more difficult than building piston engines. Not only are they more complex, but they require special metals and special metallurgy. If we can take out the smelters, the special steel mills, or the machining facilities, perhaps we can slow down their development. I doubt if we can stop it, but I think we should be able to slow it."

"Damn!" Roosevelt said.

"I don't think you can ignore the problem. It will not go away, Mr. President," Donovan said.

Roosevelt turned and glared at him, his eyes cold, his eyebrows angrily raised. "What exactly is it, Colonel Donovan," he asked icily, "that you wish me to do?"

"Mr. President, I respectfully suggest that you tell the Air Corps you have given COI intelligence responsibility vis-à-vis German jet aircraft, and then direct them to turn over to me what intelligence they have in their files."

Roosevelt snorted. "That's all you want, their files?"

"I want the authority to look into German jet planes," Donovan said. "And I don't want to be in competition with them while I'm at it."

"They're not the enemy, Bill," Roosevelt said, his temper now in check.

"Their intelligence, Franklin, is being evaluated by Air Corps officers who simply cannot ignore their knowledge that *every* one of their superiors, *every* one of them, is dedicated to the theory that heavy-bombardment aircraft can defend themselves. None of them wants to hear about any challenge to that devout belief."

They were back to first names. The crisis had passed.

"Very well," Roosevelt said. "George Marshall's going to call at five this afternoon. I'll tell him then."

"Thank you," Donovan said.

"Anything else?"

There was a just-detectable hesitation before Donovan said, "No, sir."

Roosevelt picked up on it. "Yes, there is," he said. "Let's have it."

Donovan shrugged. "I'd like to know what's happened to Jim Whittaker," he said.

"Would you, now?" the President said coldly.

"Chesty and I were friends for as long as I can remember," Donovan said. "As you, and he, and a certain lady are old friends."

Roosevelt's head snapped toward him. There was fire in his eyes again.

Oh, God! He thinks I'm talking about Whatsername, his lady friend! I simply forgot about her.

"And what lady would that be, Bill?" Roosevelt asked.

"Barbara Whittaker," Donovan said quickly.

"Oh yes," Roosevelt said. "How is Barbara?"

Now he thinks that the famous glower has made me back down!

"She's probably more than a little upset," Donovan said. "She hasn't heard a word from Jimmy since he called her from San Francisco."

"If you think I should," Roosevelt said, "I will call Barbara and assure her that we're doing everything possible for Jimmy."

"I've already told her that. What she wants to know is where he is, so that she can go see him."

"That's going to be impossible, I'm afraid."

"Because of his condition?"

Roosevelt nodded.

"What exactly *is* his condition?" Donovan asked.

"Somehow, Bill, I think you know," the President said.

"I know he's being held virtually a prisoner at George Marshall's personal order in the hospital at Fort Knox, Kentucky. And I would like to know why."

"Where did you get the notion he's a prisoner?"

"When Barbara told me she couldn't get any information out of the hospital there, I told her that it was probably just the military system at work, and that I would call down and have Jimmy telephone her. But I couldn't get through to him. They denied all knowledge of him. So I called Georgie Patton, since he's in command there and an old friend of mine, and at first he wouldn't tell me anything either. I pushed him hard, and he finally told me he had specific orders from 'very close to heaven' and that he simply couldn't tell me anything more."

"The orders came from me," Roosevelt said. "Not George Marshall."

Donovan's surprise registered on his face.

"Jimmy Whittaker is being given every comfort and the best of medical attention. He was a very sick young man on the edge of physical collapse. He was forty-five pounds underweight. His teeth were about to fall out of his mouth, and he had, I have been informed, three kinds of intestinal parasites."

"Why can't he talk to Barbara—or me, for that matter—on the telephone?"

"You know what happened in the apartment, Bill," the President said.

"Canidy told me," Donovan said. "I think Douglas MacArthur might have done the same thing. It doesn't mean that he's crazy."

"I'm the President," Roosevelt said.

"And you were playing the role of Uncle Franklin," Donovan said. "In Jimmy's condition, I can see where the two roles might be blurred in his mind."

"That's Eleanor's argument," Roosevelt said. "George Marshall argues—after taking into consideration that Jimmy probably knows what MacArthur wrote—that keeping him at Knox is the prudent thing to do."

"What did MacArthur write?" Donovan said.

"You don't know?" Roosevelt said. "I'm a little surprised."

"I only intercept enemy mail, Mr. President," Donovan said.

"Touché, Bill," Roosevelt said. "General Marshall thought you might be—what shall I say?—more efficient."

"And according to Canidy, Jim Whittaker said he had no idea what the letter said."

"Then far be it from me to violate Douglas MacArthur's confidence," the President said. "Suffice it to say that when I showed Douglas's letter to George, he wanted MacArthur to be given the chance to resign. And if he didn't, George wanted me to court-martial him."

"It was that bad?" Donovan asked.

"One of the kinder things Douglas said was that he has had no reason to reconsider his opinion that George Marshall is only marginally fit to command a regiment, and that giving him the authority I have seen fit to give him borders on an impeachable offense. Oh, how the *Chicago Tribune* would love to have that letter."

"And because George Marshall thinks Jimmy Whittaker may know the contents of that letter, you intend to hold him incommunicado indefinitely?" Donovan asked.

"You obviously don't think that's necessary?"

"For one thing, it presumes—and *this* presumes he knows what the letter said, and I don't think he does—that the moment he has the chance, he would rush to Colonel McCormick with it. But really, Franklin, I don't think he'd do that to you—not as an officer, and certainly not as a friend."

"Marshall believes that MacArthur, in his usual Machiavellian way, hopes Jimmy would do just that."

"Bologna!" Donovan said.

"Eleanor's word, exactly," the President said. "All right, Bill, tell me what you would do."

"Assign him to me," Donovan said.

"And what would you do with him?"

"He's entitled to a thirty-day home leave," Donovan said. "I'd give it to him—at Summer Place in Deal. Canidy's going to be there, and he's privy to much of this anyway. I can tell him enough more to make sure that Jimmy doesn't do anything to embarrass George Marshall."

"George would argue that Jimmy requires psychiatric care," Roosevelt said.

"George is saying Jimmy's crazy?" Donovan snapped. "I don't think he's mad. I think he was under a terrible strain. And besides, I don't think he's the only officer who would like to do to George Marshall what he did."

"You don't think his actually *doing* it raises the question of his mental health?" Roosevelt asked.

"He's as sane as you or I," Donovan said. "Christ, Franklin, you've got Putzi von Hanfstaengl,[1] a certified Nazi, in the Hotel Washington, and you have him for dinner here . . . how can you keep that boy under what amounts to arrest?"

"Putzi is an *ex*-Nazi," the President said coldly. "And you know, Bill, how valuable he's been to us."

Though he let his displeasure show, Donovan didn't back down.

"I would say that Jim Whittaker has done his fair share of being valuable to us," Donovan said. "At the very least, if he has to be—what shall I say?—restrained, then we can do that as well at Summer Place as Fort Knox."

"You may have a point," the President said.

"There's one more thing," Donovan said. "Jim

---

[1]Ernst "Putzi" von Hanfstaengel, a classmate and close friend of Franklin Delano Roosevelt at Harvard, was one of the early aristocratic supporters of Hitler and the Nazi party. Later, disillusion came. This became known to Heinrich Himmler, who ordered von Hanfstaengel murdered. Von Hanfstaengel learned of the plot and managed to escape with his family through Spain. Roosevelt established him in an apartment in the Hotel Washington, where von Hanfstaengel spent the war offering his knowledge of the Nazi inner circle to Roosevelt and the several intelligence services.

Whittaker's name has come up in connection with the North African invasion, in connection with a man named Eric Fulmar."

"Who's he?"

"Another valuable-to-our-cause-German, Franklin," Donovan said. When Roosevelt glared at him, Donovan went on: "We used him to help us get the mining engineer out of Morocco. He's close to the pasha of Ksar es Souk, who, Holdsworth Martin suggests, might just be able to arrange for a rebellion when we invade."

"What's his connection with Jimmy?"

"He, Jimmy, and Canidy were in boarding school together. St. Mark's," Donovan said. "We used Canidy to get to him in the Grunier operation, but that burned Canidy out for Fulmar after we decided to leave Fulmar in Morocco although we'd promised to take him out. If we go ahead with the idea of stirring up the Berbers, we'll need another contact. Among the names that the researchers came up with, absolutely independently, was James M. B. Whittaker."

Roosevelt didn't reply for a moment. Finally he asked, "Again, Bill, exactly what is it you want me to do?"

"Turn Jimmy over to me," Donovan said. "I'll guarantee his silence."

"I'll discuss it with George," Roosevelt said.

"We both know what he'll say," Donovan protested.

"As I've told you, George doesn't always get what George wants," the President said. "But under the circumstances, I think I should ask him what he thinks."

Donovan just looked at him.

"And under the circumstances, I think you should relay my gratitude to Barbara for her hospitality to the admiral. You may tell her that I said I have every hope that she will soon be able to see Jimmy."

Four

1

San Francisco, California
June 15, 1942

LIEUTENANT COMMANDER EDWIN H. Bitter returned to
the United States aboard the Swedish passenger liner
Kungsholm. The *Kungsholm* was then engaged in
returning diplomatic and civilian personnel of the various belligerent powers to their homelands. Its last
voyage in this capacity had been to Japan, carrying
among others a hundred Japanese of American citizen-
ship who preferred Japan to detention in the camps
established for them in Arizona and elsewhere.

The Swedish ambassador to the Empire of Japan
then received Japanese permission to charter the vessel
to the United States for service as a hospital ship. On
instructions from Berlin, the German ambassador sup-
ported the Swedish request. The German Foreign
Ministry believed that Germany might require similar
services at some time in the future. The German
request overcame reluctance from some quarters in the
Japanese Foreign Ministry.

The *Kungsholm*, its white hull with the huge red
cross painted on it floodlit, steamed under the Golden

106

Gate Bridge and docked at the Treasure Island Naval Base in San Francisco Bay. Most of the Navy and Marine Corps personnel aboard were transferred immediately to a hospital train for transportation to the Navy hospital in San Diego. But since Lieutenant Commander Bitter was ambulatory (he required a cane) he was driven to the Alameda Naval Air Station in a Navy station wagon.

After a complete physical examination he was given an interim classification of convalescent and a partial pay, then ordered to report to the Great Lakes Naval Station. He was then to be allowed a fourteen-day convalescent leave to his home of record. Reservations had been secured for a roomette aboard a train to Chicago the next day.

Bitter arrived in the United States wearing Army-issue khakis with an Army major's golden oak leaf on each collar point. There had been no Navy-size (smaller) rank insignia available in Calcutta.

As soon as he could, he went to the officers' sales store and outfitted himself with uniforms off the rack. These would do for the time being. When he left for the Orient a year before, he had sent most of his Navy uniforms from Pensacola Naval Air Station, where he had been stationed with Dick Canidy, to his parents' home in Chicago.

He bought two sets of khaki tunics, trousers, and shirts; two sets of khaki shoulder boards (two white, two blue); and the appropriate metal insignia of rank. He purchased a set of naval aviator's wings to replace the set he had taken to China. That one was now either misplaced or stolen.

The clerk had never heard of the Order of the Cloud Banner, so he could not buy a ribbon to represent that. And he was further disappointed when he realized that since he'd gotten his wound while he was in Chinese service, it did not qualify him for the Purple Heart medal. The clerk told him, however, that anybody with ninety days' service in the Pacific was entitled to a Pacific Theater ribbon, but Bitter decided he wasn't entitled to that either, since he did not have ninety days' *U.S. Navy* service in the Far East. He also did not choose to wear the single ribbon everyone in the service was entitled to, the American Defense Service Medal. Finally, he pinned his American Volunteer Group wings above the right breast pocket and his Navy wings above the left, where regulations prescribed they should be worn.

When he examined himself in the mirror, he was pleased with what he saw. It was good to be back in a Navy uniform, and he thought that the AVG wings would more than make up to anyone who knew what they were (and he didn't care about anyone who didn't) for the lack of campaign ribbons on his left breast.

In the men's room of the officers' club that night, he ran into a nonflying rear admiral who did not know what the AVG wings were and was drunk enough to inquire.

"Commander," the admiral asked, "what the *hell* is that pinned to your jacket?"

"They're AVG wings, sir," Ed replied, properly modest.

"What say?"

"AVG wings, sir," Ed repeated, and when there was no glint of understanding in the admiral's eyes, he explained: "The American Volunteer Group, sir. In China."

"Chinaman's wings?"

"Americans flying for China, sir."

"I would suggest, Commander," the admiral said nastily, "that you remove those immediately from the uniform of the U.S. Navy. *Chinaman's* wings! Good Christ! On a naval officer!"

The admiral stormed out of the head.

Fuck the old———FART! Bitter thought angrily.

Dumb chair-warming shore sailor didn't even know what the AVG is! I earned those wings, and I'll goddamned well wear them!

In ninety seconds he was calmed down enough to realize that he was reacting like Dick Canidy (who questioned every order he was ever given) and not like a lieutenant commander, Regular Navy, Annapolis graduate. He wondered again what had become of Canidy. He had thought often of writing to him after Canidy had been sent home in disgrace, but had never done so. He really hadn't known what to say. It was uncomfortable to say anything at all to a man who had shown the white feather in combat, even though he himself now understood with insight born of his own combat experiences how close anyone could come to that.

But as he stepped to the men's room mirror to comply with the admiral's order, he realized that his feelings really had nothing to do with Canidy. He had earned the wings as a Flying Tiger, and so far as he was concerned, AVG wings lent distinction to the Navy uniform rather than shaming it. He didn't take the wings off, then, and he was wearing them the next morning when he went by the transportation office and picked up his tickets for the trip to Chicago.

The first couple of days were a euphoric emotional bath.

On the third day, there was a telephone call for him. One of the maids came out on the patio. She was carrying a telephone on a long extension cord and wordlessly she handed it to him.

"Hello," he said.

"Commander Bitter, please," a crisp military voice demanded.

"This is Commander Bitter," Ed said. He was still not used to his new rank, and rather liked the way that phrase sounded.

"Hold one, Commander, please, for Admiral Hawley," the crisp voice said.

Faintly he heard, "I have Commander Bitter for you, Admiral," and then another voice came on the line, deeper, older.

"Commander Bitter?"

"Yes, sir."

"Admiral Hawley, Commander," the admiral said. "I'm Chief, Aviation Allocation, BUAIR."[1]

"Yes, sir?"

"First, let me welcome you home, both to the States and the Navy."

"Thank you very much, sir."

Who the hell is he? I know the name from someplace. What does he want with me?

"Commander, I need an aide-de-camp, preferably someone like yourself, Annapolis, who has been in harm's way, and one who is not at the moment on flight status. What he'll be doing, rather than passing hors d'oeuvres, is helping me distribute our assets where they will do the most good. Unless you have objections to the assignment, BUPERS[2] says I can have you. Interested?"

"Yes, sir."

"Now, I don't want you rushing down here to Washington, son. You take your leave. From what I hear, you damned well have earned it. The reason I called now is so that we can get the paperwork moving."

"I'm on a fourteen-day leave, sir."

"Well, you take the full fourteen days, and however much longer you feel you need. I don't want you returning to duty before you feel up to it."

"Fourteen days will be enough, sir."

---

[1] U.S. Navy Bureau of Aeronautics.
[2] U.S. Navy Bureau of Personnel.

"Welcome aboard, Commander," Admiral Hawley said, and hung up.

Ed Bitter was pleased at this development. It would be some time before he could get back on flight status, if ever. Thus, he had been afraid that when he reported for duty, he would find himself officer in charge of enlisted recreation, or in some other "essential" occupation which could be handled by a grounded aviator. This was different. Not only would he be on the staff of a BUAIR flag officer, but that flag officer wanted him because he was Annapolis, and had been in harm's way, not just because he was an available body. Duty as an aide-de-camp was considered an essential part to the advancement of an officer's career, and he was now getting that chance. He was no longer the shallow junior officer who had gone to China. He was an ace, nearly a double ace, and he was quite sure that Admiral Hawley would not object to his wearing his AVG wings. Admiral Hawley obviously knew what they represented.

By the end of the week, however, the euphoria palled, and his mother and the procession of friends she marched to hover over her son the wounded hero had made him more than a little uncomfortable. By the weekend, he knew he had to get away.

"I'm sorry, Mother," he said when she told him she'd planned a cocktail party in his honor on Sunday, "I should have said something sooner. But I won't be here over the weekend."

"But the invitations have already gone out . . ."

"I'm going to Memphis tomorrow," he said firmly. "For a couple of days. Navy business. I called the airfield. They have planes running to the Memphis NAS and I can catch a ride on one."

"Whatever do you want to go to Memphis for?" his mother asked.

The reason he wanted to go to Memphis was to see if the little girl who had been so passionate in bed at the

Chambers' vacation home in Alabama would give him the same kind of welcome she had given him before he went away, but he could hardly say that to his mother.

"Navy business," he said again. "The Navy has a large air station at Memphis. I thought you knew."

"No," she said unhappily. "And I don't see why the Navy's making you go all the way to Memphis," his mother said. "With your knee in the shape it is."

Having me as a naval hero, he thought, *works both ways.*

"Mother," Bitter said. "I'm a naval officer. The country is at war."

She swallowed that whole. "Yes, of course," she said. "Your duty comes first. I was only thinking of your well-being."

At Glenview Naval Air Station, he was given space aboard a Navy R4D[3] bound for the Memphis NAS.

At Memphis, when he asked in Base Operations where he could find a cab, the aerodrome officer took a quick look at the cane and the AVG wings and announced: "We have cars for people like you, Commander. Welcome home, sir!"

It probably is unfitting and childish of me, Ed Bitter thought, *but under circumstances like these, there is much to be said for being a hero returned from the wars.*

He had the driver take him to the Peabody Hotel rather than to the newspaper. He didn't really want to see Ann Chambers. He wanted to see Sarah Child and get her off somewhere before Ann could guess his intentions and throw up obstacles. With a little bit of luck, Sarah Child would be alone at the Peabody.

He drew a blank with the hotel operator when he asked for Miss Child, but when he asked for Miss Chambers, she said, "Oh, you meant Mrs. *Schild.* I'll ring."

---

[3]U.S. Navy designation for the Douglas DC-3 (USAAC C-47).

Who the hell was Mrs. Schild?

"Hello?"

"Hello, yourself, pen pal," he said. There was silence on the line for a long moment. "Sarah? That is you, isn't it?"

"Where are you, Ed?" Sarah asked, calmly, distantly.

"In the lobby."

The announcement, he thought, *has not sent the lady into paroxysms of ecstasy.*

"Give me fifteen minutes, Ed," Sarah said. "Make it twenty."

"And then what?"

"And then come up."

"Caught you in the shower, did I?"

"Twenty minutes," she replied, and hung up.

He went into the bar and had a Scotch, and then another. There were a number of possibilities. She could have been in the shower, or had her face covered with mud, or the other things that females did to achieve beauty. Or she could have some guy up there. If she had a guy up there, a likely prospect considering her hot pants, she would either have to get rid of him or explain me to him.

It was a dumb idea coming here in the first place, he thought. He should have left things as they were. Pen pals. He waited precisely twenty minutes from the time he had spoken with her on the house phone and then walked across the lobby to the elevators.

He had just given the floor to the operator when he heard a familiar female voice shout, "Hold that car!"

It was Ann. That's why Sarah had needed twenty minutes. To summon Ann. She was afraid that he would open the door, carry her to the bedroom, tear off her clothes, and rape her.

"If *you* say 'Hello, Ann,'" Ann said, "*I* will say, 'Hi, there, Cousin Edwin. How's tricks?'"

"She called you, right?" Ed Bitter snapped.

"Right."

"What the hell for?"

"I don't really know," Ann said. "Did Dick Canidy get home yet?"

An hour after Ann Chambers first set eyes on Dick Canidy, she decided she was going to marry him. That was a year before, when both Ed and Dick were flying instructors at the Navy base in Pensacola, Florida. Ed brought Dick, his roommate, to The Plantation, the antebellum mansion sitting on several hundred thousand acres of pine her father, Ed's uncle, hoped one day to turn into newsprint.

Dick Canidy looked like the answer to a maiden's prayer in his white Navy uniform with the gold wings of a naval aviator pinned to his manly breast, and she would have cheerfully given him her pearl of great price right there on the carpet in the library of The Plantation had he asked for it. Or shown a slight interest in it. He hadn't; he regarded her as a college girl, beneath his consideration, and a relative of Eddie to boot.

But that hadn't changed her dream of catching Dick Canidy. All it made her do was realize that the way to capture *this* man was *not* to stare soulfully at him and wiggle her tail. She would have been perfectly willing to do that, too, but that wasn't going to work. The way to catch this man was, she *knew*, to become his pal, his friend, a buddy in skirts. The birds and the bees business would come later. She barely managed to start this—talking flying with him (Ann had her commercial single-engine license, and 520 hours in her father's Stagger-wing Beechcraft), asking intelligent questions, putting him at ease—when Dick and Ed set off for China to save the world for democracy.

That reduced her campaign to letter writing. Funny letters, the envelopes containing more clippings she thought would interest him than text. But she did just happen to mention that she had quit college and was working for the *Advocate* and hoped to get overseas as a correspondent. He had responded as a pal. Without even mentioning what he was doing in the war, he wrote about China and about the problems of navigation where there were no navigation aids and about how difficult it had been to reassemble crated airplanes with a Chinese work force.

And then the letters had stopped. She had no idea why, but there was a chance that Ed Bitter knew something she didn't.

"Why do you ask about him?" Ed Bitter replied as the elevator doors closed. And then he remembered that Ann had a schoolgirl crush on Dick Canidy.

"Yes or no," she said. "Simple question, simple answer."

"He's been home for some time," he said.

The way he said that alarmed her. It was evident in her voice. "He's been hurt?"

"No," he said. "He has not been hurt."

"Then what?"

"He was sent home months ago," Ed said.

"Why?"

"Is that important?"

"It wouldn't be if you weren't reluctant to tell me."

"If you have to know," Ed said, "he was relieved."

"What does that mean?" Ann asked.

"He was . . . discharged . . . from the AVG," Bitter said. "Under not quite honorable circumstances."

"What, exactly, were those 'not quite honorable circumstances'?" Ann demanded.

"It was alleged that he refused to engage the enemy."

She looked at him intently, convincing herself that he was telling her the truth.

"He must have had his reasons," she said loyally. "Where is he?"

"I have no idea," Ed said. "Under the circumstances, I don't think he wants to see me. Or, for that matter, you."

"I would like to hear his side," Ann said.

"I really don't know where he is, Ann," Ed Bitter said. "My advice is to leave it that way."

The elevator was by then at the eighth floor. The operator opened the door and they stepped into a corridor. He followed Ann down the corridor. She stopped before a door, took a key from her pocket and unlocked it, and stepped inside.

She waved for him to follow her inside. There was a sitting room, with doors opening off either side.

"Sarah!" Ann called.

A door opened. And Sarah stood framed in it—with an infant in her arms. She looked at Ed Bitter and then away. Ann went to her and took the child.

What the hell is all this?

"Don't tell me that's yours," he said to Ann.

"OK. I won't tell you it's mine," Ann said agreeably. "It's not mine. It's yours."

She walked to him and abruptly handed him the infant.

"He's mine," Sarah said. "You're the father, but you don't have to think of him as yours unless you want to."

"I don't believe this," Ed Bitter said.

"Scout's honor, Cousin Edwin," Ann said. "Cross my heart and hope to die."

"I'm glad you're home safe, Ed," Sarah said.

"Goddamn it, don't get off the subject!" he said. "Why wasn't I told?"

"Theoretically," Ann said, "because you were off saving the world for democracy, and she didn't want to trouble you. Actually, because she was afraid of what you would do when you found out."

"Ann!" Sarah said.

"Jesus Christ!" Bitter said.

"So now that you know, Ed," Ann pursued, "what are you going to do about him?"

"Ann!" Sarah said again.

Ed Bitter looked down at the child in his arms. He felt no emotion whatever. This boy was unquestionably his child, if for no other reason than that a practical joke of this magnitude was beyond even Ann. If it was his child, he certainly would have to recognize it, legitimatize it, marry the mother, give it and her his name.

He looked at Sarah. She was staring out a window.

He looked down at the child again. He had no sense of recognition, he thought, no animal sensing that this was the fruit of his loins. It was simply a baby, indistinguishable from dozens he had held as reluctantly as he held this one.

"If I seem somewhat stunned by all this," he said, "I am. I came here with the intention of rushing Sarah into becoming engaged before my leave was up."

"You took your sweet time getting to Memphis, Romeo," Ann said.

"And now," he said, ignoring the remark, "it would seem that it is not a question of whether she'll marry me, but how soon."

"You don't have to marry me," Sarah said, not meaning it.

"I love you, Sarah," he said, surprised at how easy the words, the lie, came to his lips. "And we owe it to Whatsisname here, don't you think?"

Ann laughed. "Give me Whatsisname," she said. "And I'll take him for a walk."

"No," Bitter said. "You take a walk, Ann. But leave him here. I want to get to know him."

Ann looked at the two of them and left, saying nothing.

Sarah finally turned to him.

He looked gaunt, she thought, but even more handsome than the first time she had seen him. She was reacting to him now as she had reacted to him then. Except now she understood what that reaction was. He was more than the most handsome man she had ever seen, he was the sexiest. Perhaps that was really what handsome meant.

She wanted very much to rush to him, to put her arms around him, to feel his body against hers. But that, she sensed, was not what she should do right now. There had been shock in his eyes when he looked at her, maybe even fear. Certainly not lust.

"How's your friend Canidy?" Sarah asked. "Ann hasn't heard from him in a long time, months."

"To hell with Canidy," he snapped. "Let's talk about this." He raised the baby in his arms.

"He's very healthy," Sarah said. "And most of the time very happy."

"He looks like you," Bitter said.

"Too early to tell," she said. "You like him?"

"I like him," he said, and looked at her and smiled happily.

"I'm glad," she said. She smiled back. It was the first time she had smiled since he had arrived.

"Me, too," he said. "Glad, I mean. Happy. Stunned, but happy and glad."

"It wasn't what you expected, was it?"

"I came with evil designs on your body," he said.

Sarah met his eyes.

He means that, Sarah realized. *He came hoping for a quick piece of ass, and was instead presented with his child. But that is not important. I am not offended, or hurt. He didn't know, and he came. That is enough.*

"He's sound asleep at half past five," she said. "And he sleeps like a log until it's time to feed him again."

He was strangely excited. He recognized it as sexual excitement. *What the hell,* he thought, *what's wrong with that?*

"We'll have to get rid of Ann," he said.

"If she can't hear the baby cry, she couldn't hear us," Sarah said.

She saw the surprise on his face, and added: "I've

been thinking about you that way, too. Does that shock you?"

"I don't think anything will ever shock me again," Bitter said.

2

Newark, New Jersey
June 25, 1942

Dick Canidy had come up to Newark from Summer Place in Deal in a business suit, something he had been doing for the past several days; and he was right now in the fuselage of a Curtiss C-46 Commando at Newark Airport. Two men were with him there, an airframe mechanic from Pan American Airways and Colonel Charles Augustus Lindbergh, U.S. Army Air Corps Reserve, Inactive. Lindbergh and the airframe mechanic were trying to come up with a simple, reliable means of augmenting the C-46's fuel-carrying capacity with auxiliary tanks that could be jettisoned in the air.

Canidy no longer felt awed in the very presence of Lindbergh, for Lindbergh had made it almost immediately plain that since Canidy was another flier, he was thus an equal. He had then proved in any number of small ways that he meant that. Canidy had shared a dozen cold and soggy hot-dog lunches with the tall, shy hero. Twice, wearing Pan American coveralls, Lindbergh had walked the half mile to the terminal to buy them himself. He had not been recognized. He looked like just one more airplane mechanic trying to fix a broken bird.

That was not to say that Canidy had grown entirely comfortable around Lindbergh. He hadn't been sure what to call him, for one thing. He certainly couldn't call him Slim—considering Roosevelt's recent actions

—and he wasn't sure how Lindbergh would like to be called Colonel.

Finally, he asked him.

"How about Slim?" Lindbergh said.

"I don't think I could do that," Canidy said.

"Well, then, Major, call me Colonel if that's more comfortable for you."

"Colonel," Canidy blurted, "I'm not a major. I'm not really in the Air Corps. I'm just wearing the uniform."

Lindbergh hadn't liked that.

"It was Colonel Donovan's idea," Canidy said.

"I see," Lindbergh said.

After that, Canidy had not worn the major's uniform. And two days later, when he walked into the Pan American hangar at Newark Airport, he knew from the look on Lindbergh's face that he had offended him.

"Mr. Canidy, as someone who will probably never again wear a uniform, who has never heard a gun fired in anger, I feel a little foolish being called Colonel by the first ace in the American Volunteer Group. Why didn't you tell me about that?"

Canidy shrugged uncomfortably.

"Well, from now on it's Slim and Dick," Lindbergh said. "All right?"

"Yes, sir," Canidy said.

He still could not bring himself to call Lindbergh Slim.

Connecting one casually dropped fact with another, he learned that Lindbergh had personally laid out, then flown himself, most of Pan American's long-distance flight routes in South America and across the Atlantic and Pacific oceans, and that he had an awesome amount of experience with all of the Sikorsky amphibians and seaplanes Pan Am used.

But Lindbergh had already concluded that large commercial seaplane transports had outlived their usefulness.

"I think," he said, "that we've already reached the point of diminishing return in seaplane design. Since the engines must not take in water on takeoff or landing, they have to be placed very high. But because the engines have to be that far above the water, we can't use aerodynamically efficient wings and engine locations. And if we make these planes any larger, we will have to make their hulls correspondingly stronger, and the weight penalty there is too high. There's no question in my mind that the next step in transoceanic flight is going to be an aerodynamically efficient airframe, designed for flight at very high altitude. Howard Hughes showed me some preliminary drawings of a really beautiful airplane that will carry seventy people at thirty thousand feet at nearly four hundred miles an hour for three thousand miles. The *big* leap forward will come when they come up with a reliable jet engine. With jets, transport aircraft will actually approach the speed of sound."

Canidy, who had only heard the most vague references to jet engines, said so, and was astonished to learn from Lindbergh that both the English and the Germans had test-flown jet-powered aircraft.

Lindbergh had already rejected Donovan's notion that a seaplane, one of Pan American's Sikorskys, be borrowed for the long-distance cargo flight he wanted. And Lindbergh also had quickly deduced where that flight was headed.

"Bill Donovan won't tell me where this flight is going," Lindbergh said, "and if you know, I suppose you can't tell me either. But unless you tell me it's a waste of my time, I'm going to work on the idea that it's probably some place on the west coast of Africa."

"I really don't know," Canidy had told him.

Lindbergh shrugged. "And since there is some question about where my sympathies lie in this war, I don't suppose I'll be asked to fly this mission. That means, I suppose, that you will."

"I don't know that, either," Canidy said.

"Huh!" Lindbergh snorted, and then went on: "Well, we'll proceed on the notion that you'll be flying it."

"I really don't know, Colonel," Canidy pursued. "I've never flown anything but fighters—and a Beech D18S."

"They're sending kids with a hundred twenty hours' total time to Europe as B-17 aircraft commanders," Lindbergh said. "How many hours did you say you have, Ace?"

Canidy didn't reply. Lindbergh chuckled, and then went on: "Far down the west coast of Africa. Perhaps as far as South Africa. The way to do that is with a Curtiss."

"Why?" Canidy asked simply.

"Because it can fly faster and higher than a Sikorsky, and when we solve the problem of auxiliary fuel tanks, maybe a thousand miles farther."

Lindbergh had then arranged for a Pan American Stratoliner, the civilian version of the Commando, to be flown to Newark. The story was let out that it had been requisitioned by the Air Corps. While one crew of workmen stripped the seats, the carpets, and the sound-deadening material from the cabin, another crew removed the glistening white paint and Pan American insignia from the outside skin. Then the hangar was isolated and placed under guard by Air Corps military policemen. Canidy came to understand that isolating aircraft and cargo was a routine procedure these days.

Whenever a crew from Pan American was doing something that did not require his expertise, Lindbergh talked to Canidy at length about long-distance, high-altitude flight. In the course of these discussions, Lindbergh and Canidy prepared more than a dozen flight plans, all based on the idea that the departure point would be either the Azores or one of the American air bases in England. Though they didn't know where they were going, or even where they would leave from, Lindbergh seemed determined to have a flight plan prepared for every possibility.

Lindbergh also spent long hours showing Canidy around the Curtiss's cockpit, familiarizing him with the controls and the peculiarities of the aircraft, while delivering conversational lectures on how to milk the most mileage from its twin two-thousand-horsepower Pratt and Whitney Twin Wasp engines. He gave no consideration to the fact that Canidy had never flown the Curtiss. Lindbergh seemed to believe that little problem could be solved in an hour or two in the left seat, going around the pattern shooting touch-and-go landings.

Although Canidy was by no means modest about his flying ability—he was, after all, a pretty good fighter pilot—flying the Curtiss when the time came made him a little nervous.

And (there being no question in his mind that Lindbergh had correctly deduced where the plane was headed) what he had come to think of as the African flight wasn't all Canidy had to deal with.

His primary duty was still the baby-sitting of Admiral de Verbey at Summer Place. He and the admiral had quickly dropped the polite fiction that Canidy was his liaison officer. The admiral knew that he was being politely held prisoner. To pretend otherwise would have been insulting. And there were always other problems for Canidy, small but time-consuming ones with the guard. They developed colds. One of them fell over a piece of driftwood on the beach, dislocated his shoulder, and nearly died of exposure before he was found. And then disputes between the guards over the duty roster had to be resolved.

And the admiral placed yet another demand on Canidy. In what Canidy came to think of as his Great Summer Place Mistake, on his second or third night in Deal—caught up in the excitement of the game—he had played some first-class bridge, wiping out the admiral and Mrs. Whittaker and awing the ex–FBI agent who had been drafted for a fourth.

The admiral thereafter saw in Canidy a bridge player worthy of his own considerable talent. From then on, whenever Canidy sat down near a flat surface, the admiral started drawing up chairs and shuffling cards. Canidy soon realized that he should have dropped the cards on the floor the first night.

And then there was the question of what to do with the great battleship *Jean Bart,* currently at anchor in Casablanca harbor. The admiral planned to steal the *Jean Bart.*

The first time Canidy learned this, he was torn between amusement and concern for the admiral's mental health. Telling himself that humoring the feisty little old man was the price he was going to have to pay to keep the admiral happy, he had reluctantly presented himself at Admiral de Verbey's war plans room (a glassed-in porch on the second floor) to be "briefed."

Charts of Casablanca harbor, the mouth of the Mediterranean, and the eastern Atlantic had been thumbtacked to the walls. The halves of a Ping-Pong table, resting on folding chairs, now held large sketches —drawn from memory—of the battleship itself. Deadly serious, the admiral had used the charts and drawings to show Canidy how the vessel could be seized by a small force and by judicious use of watertight doors, and how the vessel could afterward be refueled under way at sea.

By the time the admiral finished outlining his plan to steal the sixth- or seventh-largest naval vessel in the world from under the noses of the German forces in Casablanca, Canidy was no longer convinced that the old man was living in cuckoo land. *Improbable* was not quite the same thing as *insane.*

First of all, the admiral had made it clear that his chief and only reason for stealing the *Jean Bart* was as a symbol. Removing the ship from the shaming control of the Germans would not just humiliate them; more important, it would profoundly challenge the belief now held by most Frenchmen that since nothing could be done against the Boche, the logical thing to do was accommodate them.

And Admiral de Verbey's plan to seize the battleship met the first test of any good naval tactic, simplicity.

In compliance with the terms of the Franco-German armistice, the battleship still remained in French hands with her full crew and enough ammunition for both her main turrets and her extensive complement of antiaircraft cannon and machine guns. In the event of an attack by any enemy (read English or American) against the sovereign soil of neutral France, the *Jean Bart* was expected by the Germans to respond with all its firepower.

For several reasons, the Germans were not particularly worried that her crew would turn the *Jean Bart*'s weaponry on them or suddenly decide to let loose the lines and go to sea. For one, the honor of the French Navy was at stake. France had signed an armistice with Germany. Marshal Pétain, as Chief of the French State, had through official channels ordered her captain to remain in port.

More practically, the *Jean Bart*'s fuel tanks were virtually dry. She was regularly refueled, but with only enough oil to run one of her four engines for twelve hours. That was not nearly enough fuel for a dash for the open sea. It was, however, sufficient to provide electrical services and power for her turrets and separate cannon and their ammunition hoists. Each of her four engines was run in turn, which kept all four in good running order.

There were thus only two major problems to be

overcome in the "liberation" of the *Jean Bart*. The first was the question of the willingness of her captain to fly in the face of his honor and violate his orders.

The presence of Vice Admiral de Verbey on the scene would handle that problem. He was not only the former captain of the *Jean Bart* but was also now the senior admiral not under the German thumb. If he ordered her to sea, his orders would be obeyed.

The second problem, fuel, was by no means as hopeless as it might first appear. Though the main tanks were officially empty, there was still residual fuel in each of them, tons of it left there because it was beyond the reach of fuel pumps. But by setting up portable pumps, the "empty" tanks could rather easily be pumped dry of their "residual" fuel, and that fuel transferred to the "active" tank. The admiral's calculations had determined that there would be enough fuel in the "active" tank to run all *Jean Bart*'s four engines at full power for almost two hours.

That would see her out of the harbor and into the Mediterranean. There she would be met by an American tanker and an escort, preferably of destroyers and a cruiser. If the escort could provide defense against the aircraft the Germans would send after her, sufficient fuel could be transferred in an hour to give the *Jean Bart* the means to sail into the Atlantic out of range of German aircraft. Then refueling could be accomplished more or less at leisure.

What the admiral still required, and what Canidy decided to get for him, were a few technical facts: How much fuel per minute could be pumped from a tanker into the *Jean Bart*'s tanks? Using how many lines? What was the pressure of the lines? At what speed could the tanker steam while her fuel lines were attached to the *Jean Bart*? In what sea conditions?

"I wasn't aware that delusion was contagious," Captain Douglass said when Canidy called him in Washington.

"What would it hurt to give the old man the information he wants?"

"Well, for one thing, I'm sure that's classified."

"Who are you afraid he'll tell?" Canidy asked.

"I'll work up some figures, then," Douglass said.

"Get him the right ones," Canidy said. "He's no fool."

"You ever think of making an investment in a bridge, Canidy?" Douglass said. "I'm sure the admiral has one he'd be willing to sell you cheap."

But two days later, probably because Douglass had decided it would keep the admiral happy and away from the press, a messenger delivered an enormous stack of technical manuals containing details of U.S. Navy tanker refueling techniques and capabilities.

3

Deal, New Jersey
June 25, 1942

Dick Canidy, dressed in a business suit and carrying a briefcase, stepped off the New Jersey Central train at Asbury Park. The Rolls-Royce was waiting for him.

After making another killing on Wall Street, home comes Richard Canidy, well-known international financier, to be met by the faithful family retainer in the Rolls.

When the Rolls delivered Canidy in his stockbroker's uniform to Summer Place, the admiral, Barbara Whittaker, and the admiral's chief of staff were drinking wine at an umbrella-shaded cast-iron table on the lawn. The lawn was green and lovely and it stretched down to the beach. Without being asked, the admiral's middle-aged orderly brought Canidy some of Chesty Whittaker's older-than-Canidy Scotch.

With a breeze coming off the ocean, it was so

pleasant at the table that Barbara Whittaker ordered that their dinner be served there. And they lingered over coffee and brandy until it was dark and fireflies came out.

The admiral finally announced he was going to take a stroll along the beach, and Canidy was flattered when the old man asked if perhaps he would care to join him.

They caught up with one of the Navy sentries, who was patrolling the beach with a Springfield rifle on his shoulder and an allegedly ferocious German shepherd on a leash.

The shepherd obligingly chased pieces of driftwood for the admiral, proudly delivering them with his tail wagging. Finally, the sentry resumed his rounds, and Canidy, without thinking, idly asked a question he immediately regretted. He asked the admiral about his family.

"My wife lives as I do, on charity," the admiral said calmly. "When I was court-martialed—"

"Court-martialed?"

"In absentia, almost immediately after I left Morocco," the admiral said matter-of-factly, "I was convicted of treason. The court stripped me of my rank and decorations. That of course stopped my pay, and my property was forfeit."

"Jesus Christ!" Canidy exploded.

The admiral shrugged. "My son was dismissed from the Navy shortly after my court-martial. As my son, he was obviously not trustworthy. He has been arrested by the Germans. I don't know where he is."

"I'm sorry."

"I have old friends in New York," the admiral said, "Madame Martin and her husband, who have been kind enough to provide a little pocket money for me, enough that I can share a little with my staff."

"You don't get money from the Free French?"

"I have a letter from *Brigadier* de Gaulle," the

admiral said, his tone making it quite clear what he thought of de Gaulle, "in which he states that he, representing the Free French, does not of course regard my court-martial as valid, and that so far as the Free French are concerned, I am in honorable retirement. He went on to express his profound regret that because of other, more pressing claims upon the limited funds made available to him, he will unhappily be forced to delay the payment of my pension until after the war."

"That sonofabitch!" Canidy said.

"You are referring, *mon Major,*" the admiral said dryly, "to the head of my government. But under the circumstances, I do not believe I will offer you the choice of a duel or an apology."

They walked along the beach in silence for a couple of minutes, nodded to the sailor when he came walking back down the beach with the German shepherd, then turned and headed back to Summer Place.

When they got back to the house, Barbara Whittaker was waiting for them. Captain Douglass had called, she said. Canidy was to fly the Beech to Anacostia Naval Air Station in Washington first thing in the morning. Someone would meet him at the airport.

4

Memphis, Tennessee
June 26, 1942

Two signs forbidding personal long-distance telephone calls were tacked to the employee bulletin board of the *Memphis Advocate.* One was a poster published by the Office of the Coordinator of Information. It showed an Air Corps officer sitting at a desk with a telephone to his ear. He was wearing a look of pained frustration in response to a balloon coming from the telephone: "Sorry, Captain, all the lines are busy." In black letters was the legend **Telephones are tools of war! If you *have* to call, make it quick!**

The second was smaller and more succinct. It was hand-lettered.

A record of long-distance calls is now being kept. Charging personal long-distance telephone calls to the *Advocate* is grounds for dismissal.

Ann Chambers ignored both. For one thing, she doubted that one two-minute telephone call from Memphis, Tennessee, to Cedar Rapids, Iowa, was really going to lose more battles than were already being lost. For another, the *Memphis Advocate* was one of nine newspaper properties owned by Chambers Publishing Corporation. The president of Chambers Publishing was Brandon Chambers, and Brandon Chambers was Ann's father.

She had begun thinking about making the telephone call to Iowa in the elevator in the Peabody Hotel the day her cousin Ed Bitter had told her that Dick Canidy had been sent home in disgrace from China for "refusing to engage the enemy."

Ed obviously believed that was true. And it certainly would explain why her pen-pal letters to Canidy had gone unanswered. It was possible that he was a coward, though she didn't feel it was likely.

In fact, the truth was that even if Dick did run away from the Japs she didn't care. The truth was that she loved him more than she'd ever believed she could love any man. And what she wanted more than anything in the world right now was to get his head on her shoulder. Or her breast.

"This is Reverend Canidy," the voice on the telephone said curiously.

"Reverend Canidy, this is Ann Chambers," she said. "I'm Ed Bitter's cousin, and, more to the point, a friend of Dick's."

"Oh, how nice!" he said, puzzled.

"The reason I'm calling is that I'm going . . . I live in Memphis . . . east, and I seem to have lost Dick's address."

"He's home from China," the Reverend Canidy said, "as I guess you know . . ."

"Yes," Ann said.

"And he's found work with the National Institute of Health, as a pilot."

The National Institute of Health?

"I'd heard," Ann lied.

"Could you give me his address in Washington? And his phone number? I'd really like to say hello when I'm there."

"Just a moment," he said. "I've got it somewhere."

Later, when she called the number Canidy's father gave her, a woman answered and denied any knowledge of anyone named Canidy. When Ann called the National Institute of Health, they had never heard of him either. When she called the Washington information operator, she said she had no listing for the address Reverend Canidy had given her on Q Street, NW.

Ann walked into the teletype room and sat down before the Chambers News Service teletypewriter. She typed rapidly, a service message to the Chambers News Service Washington Bureau. She asked for ALLINFO, FACT AND SPEC the Washington bureau could develop SOONEST on what was going on at the address Reverend Canidy had given her on Q Street, Northwest. She signed it CHAMBERS ADVOCATE. If they thought her father had sent the service message, so much the better. Her name was Chambers, too, and if they were inspired to drop something unimportant and get on this right away, fine.

As she'd hoped, the response was quick, but it was not quite the one she expected. Two hours after she sent the service message, she had a telephone call.

"Exactly what is your interest in that address on Q Street?" her father began without other preliminary.

"Hello, Daddy," she said. "I'm fine, how are you?"

"What are you into?" he said. "What have you heard?"

"How did you get involved in this?" she asked.

"That address, so far as we're concerned, doesn't exist," Brandon Chambers said. "Do you take my point?"

"No, I don't," she said.

"It's a government installation," he said. "We don't know it's there. We don't write about it."

"Oh," she said.

"When you signed my name to that service message, they checked with me."

"I didn't sign your name to it," she said. "My name for the time being is Chambers, too."

She heard him sigh in exasperation, but he chose not to argue about that.

"I have to know, honey," he said, "what you're working on."

"I was looking for Dick Canidy," she said. "I got that address from his father."

There was a long pause.

"Eddie returned from China with an unpleasant report on Mr. Canidy," Brandon Chambers finally said.

"That he was a coward," Ann said. "Eddie told me."

"And Canidy's father gave you the Q Street address?"

"And two telephone numbers," Ann said. "I called both of them, and they said they had never heard of Canidy."

"What's behind your deep interest in Canidy?"

"I swore Mother to secrecy," Ann said, "but I

thought she'd tell you anyway. I'm going to marry him."

"For Christ's sake!" he said. "This is not a joking matter, Ann."

"Who's joking?"

"Now, listen to me," he said. "Drop your inquiry right now. Right here. If you don't, you can do us a great deal of harm. I've come to an agreement with certain people . . ."

"It's a military secret, right?" she challenged. "And I'm a Nazi agent."

"It is a military secret, Ann," her father said.

"Odd, wouldn't you say, that a coward is involved with military secrets?" she said.

"Just drop it, Ann, OK?" he said. "I want your word."

"Or what?"

"Or you're fired. This moment."

He's absolutely serious.

"It's that important?"

"It is."

"All right, then," she said.

"And I don't want you talking to anybody . . . even Eddie or your girlfriend . . ."

"Mrs. Edwin Bitter, you mean?" Ann said.

"Goddamn it, I'm serious."

"I know," she said. "OK, Daddy, you've made your point."

"I really hope so, Ann," he said.

Thirty minutes later, Ann walked into the office of the *Advocate*'s managing editor and told him her father wanted her to come to Washington for a couple of days, and she was thinking of going Saturday night after they'd gotten the Sunday edition to bed. She hated to ask, but if she could have a business travel priority certificate for an airplane ticket, that would get her back to work that much quicker.

"Yeah, sure, Ann," he said. "We can work that out."

Being in love does strange things to you. So far this morning, I have lied to an Episcopal priest, my father, and my boss. And I'm not ashamed of myself.

Then she called Sarah Child Bitter at the Willard Hotel in Washington and announced that she would be in Washington on Saturday and needed a place to stay.

Sarah and Ed Bitter were living in Sarah's father's suite in the Willard. Ed was probably going to be more than a little annoyed when she showed up. Ed and Sarah had gotten married only a few days earlier. Having Ann around would be like having your sister on your honeymoon. To hell with him, Ann thought. He owed her for taking care of Sarah.

Five

1

Lakehurst Naval Air Station
Lakehurst, New Jersey
June 27, 1942

WHILE CANIDY WAS doing the preflight, Commander Reynolds's Plymouth staff car came down the hangar and stopped beside the Beechcraft.

"I didn't know where you were going, Major," he said. "But I thought you could use a thermos of coffee and a couple of sandwiches."

"Washington," Canidy told him. "Thank you."

Commander Reynolds was impressed. There was something about Washington that impressed professional naval officers, Canidy thought, as if the place were the residence of God.

"I'm glad you're here," Canidy went on. "I didn't know about starting the engines inside the hangar."

"We drag aircraft to the center lane," Reynolds said, "and make sure that both hangar doors are open. Then you might as well be outside. You've already been refueled."

"I noticed," Canidy said. "Thank you."

"Sailor," Reynolds said somewhat pompously to his

driver, "would you round up some men to move the major's aircraft?"

"Aye, aye, sir," the white hat said. Canidy winked at him, and he smiled back, as if to say that it was all right, Reynolds was a little salty, but a good guy.

Canidy climbed into the Beech, released the brakes, and strapped the thermos and the bag of sandwiches in the copilot's seat. He wasn't going to need the sandwiches between Lakehurst and Washington, but it had been a nice thing for Reynolds to do.

He started to leave the cockpit when the airplane lurched. A half-dozen white hats had started to push it to the center of the hangar. He went aft and closed the door, then returned to the cockpit and strapped himself in. He saw another pair of white hats roll up an enormous fire extinguisher on what looked like wagon wheels.

The plane stopped moving.

Canidy looked at the window. "Clear!" he called.

"Clear!" one of the white hats called back. Canidy set the mixture, primed the port engine, and hit the engine start switch. The starter whined and then the port engine bucked, backfired, and finally caught. He started the other and looked out the window.

Commander Reynolds was standing there with his fist balled, thumb up.

Canidy smiled and gave him the gesture back, whereupon Commander Reynolds saluted. Canidy smiled again, returned the salute, and advanced the throttles.

Once he was clear of the hangar, he got on the radio and asked for taxi and takeoff instructions.

"Navy Six-one-one," the tower replied, "you are cleared to taxi to the threshold of runway nine. Hold on the threshold. We have an aircraft on final."

The aircraft on final was a Curtiss C-46. Canidy thought he was coming in way too high, and he was right.

"Six-one-one," the tower promptly announced, "hold your position. The forty-six is going around."

"Six-one-one, roger," Canidy said.

He followed the C-46 with his eyes as it rose again and made a low turn over the pine barrens. It glistened in the sunlight. A new one, Canidy thought. The next time the C-46 came around at an altitude Canidy saw was much too low. He was right again. Even over the racket of his idling engines, he heard the roar of the C-46's engines as the pilot gave them enough throttle to make the end of the runway.

When the C-46 flashed by Canidy, he wondered what it was doing here. There were no markings on either wings, fuselage, or tail. The only time aircraft did not have at least identification numbers on them was when their paint has been stripped off, as the paint had been stripped from the Pan American Curtiss at Newark Airport. Was this the Pan American Curtiss? If so, what was it doing here?

The Beech, caught in the C-46's air disturbance, rocked. Canidy was reminded how big the C-46 really was and how powerful its engines.

"Six-one-one, you are clear for takeoff as soon as the forty-six clears the runway."

"Roger," Canidy replied as the forty-six moved past him. When it turned off the runway, its prop blast again rocked the Beech. Canidy waited until it stopped shaking, then spoke one final time into the microphone.

"Six-one-one rolling."

A few minutes after ten, over eastern Maryland, Canidy raised the Anacostia tower and requested landing permission.

When he went into Base Operations to arrange for the refueling of the airplane, a Navy captain, curious about an Army pilot flying a Navy airplane, looked at the paperwork, grew even more curious when he read it. He had heard about this strange Beech D18S. Officially, he had been informed that by authority of the Chief of Naval Operations "the naval liaison officer to the Coordinator of Information" would from time to time be basing a D18 aircraft at Anacostia. The aircraft was not to be considered part of the Anacostia fleet, and no one was to use the aircraft without the specific permission of Captain Peter Douglass, USN, the naval officer assigned to COI.

"You at this place, too, Major?" the Navy captain, whose name was Chester Wezevitz, asked. "The information coordinator, or whatever it is?"

"Yes, sir."

"What the hell is it?" the captain asked. "I guess what I'm really asking is what the hell is a Navy *captain* doing at the 'Coordinator of Information'?"

The temptation was too great for Canidy (who had even been encouraged during one briefing or another to offer "disinformation" when questioned), and he gave in to it.

"You know those comic books, Captain? Warning the white hats about the lasting effects of VD?" he asked. "Urging them to use pro kits?"

"I wondered where the hell they came from," the Navy captain said.

By appearing at that moment, Chief Ellis made things even better.

"Good morning, Major," he said, saluting crisply. "I have the major's car."

"Jesus Christ," the Navy captain said. "A *chief*, driving a staff car."

When they were outside, Canidy asked: "What's going on, Ellis?"

"We're going to the office," he said. "Mr. Baker's there with the captain."

"What does that sonofabitch want with me?"

"I dunno," Chief Ellis said, "but don't do nothing dumb, Mr. Canidy."

"I'd like to feed him his balls," Canidy said.

"That's what I mean by dumb," Ellis said.

"You know what's going on, don't you, you bastard?" Canidy said. "And you won't tell me."

"I'm surprised at you." The old sailor laughed. "Didn't anybody tell you loose lips sink ships?"

"Screw you, Ellis," Canidy chuckled as he got in the front seat of the Buick beside him.

When they got to the National Institute of Health building, Eldon C. Baker, a pudgy, bland-appearing man, was sitting on a red leather couch in Captain Douglass's office bent over what Canidy in a moment realized were the flight plans Lindbergh had made up.

That seemed to prove that the Curtiss he had seen landing at Lakehurst was indeed the Pan American aircraft.

"How are you, Canidy?" Baker said, leaning forward and offering his hand.

Canidy ignored the offered hand. The last time he had seen Eldon C. Baker had been in the palace of the pasha of Ksar es Souk in the foothills of the Atlas Mountains in Morocco. Baker had known then that Canidy was not going to be loaded aboard the sub then at sea off Safi. He had not told Canidy.

Baker shrugged. "I'm sorry you still feel that way," he said.

"Do you know what you're looking at?" Canidy asked.

"I have a general idea," Baker said. "I'm sure you can explain anything I can't figure out myself."

Captain Douglass, carrying an armful of military service records, walked into the office.

"Good morning, Dick," he said. "Nice flight? How's the admiral?"

"A little restive, but under control. Did you know that de Gaulle sent him a letter saying he couldn't afford to pay him?"

"No, I didn't," Douglass said.

"I would have guessed you were reading his mail," Canidy said.

"His mail is being read," Douglass corrected him. "But his pay status has not until now been brought to my attention. I'll see what I can do. Obviously, you think it's important, or you wouldn't have brought it up."

"Do I detect an ever-so-subtle reprimand?"

"Not at all," Douglass said, and smiled. "As a matter of fact, I was about to tell you that a number of people have been saying nice things about you. After that I was going to tell you I think you're doing a fine job keeping the admiral happy."

"Is that what this is all about?" Canidy asked.

"You're not interested in the nice things people have been saying about you?"

"Go ahead," Canidy said.

"Our friend at Pan American told the colonel that you are an unusually bright, unusually capable young man."

Canidy was embarrassed.

"Perfectly capable of supervising the Curtiss flight by yourself, from here on in," Douglass finished.

"I saw that you had the plane moved to Lakehurst," Canidy said. "But before we go any further, there is one little detail that seems to have been overlooked: I've never flown a C-46."

"No problem," Baker said. "You won't be flying it anyway."

"Who will?" Canidy asked.

"I'm not finished with the nice reports," Douglass said. "I had occasion last night to discuss you with an Air Corps officer. To hear him tell it, you combine the character traits of a Boy Scout with the flying skill of Baron von Richthofen."

It took Canidy a moment to guess what was up. Then he broke into a broad smile. "Oh," he said, "have you by any chance been talking to your son and namesake? Is Doug back?"

"He's been back about a month. He was home. He stopped off here, on his way to Alabama. He's been made a major, and they gave him a fighter group, P-38s."

"I'm glad to hear that," Canidy said.

"I took what he said about you with a large grain of salt, of course," Douglass said. "But I thought I would pass it on."

Canidy laughed. "Who is going to fly the African mission?" he asked.

"*African* mission?" Baker asked incredulously.

"That depends in large part on you," Captain Douglass said, ignoring Baker and acknowledging that Canidy's suspicions were correct.

"I don't understand," he said.

Douglass handed him one of the service records. "This is the man we would like to make the flight," he said. "Do you think he could handle it?"

Canidy took the records, and found the Air Corps captain's flight records. The officer had entered the service with several hundred hours of single-engine civilian time, taken a quickie course in a basic trainer, and then gone right into B-17s. He had picked up not quite two hundred hours as a B-17 pilot in command, and was currently commanding a bomber squadron.

The first thing he thought was that the captain was not especially qualified for either a quick transition course to the C-46 or to fly across the Atlantic to Africa. And then he glanced at the pilot's name.

Captain Stanley S. Fine. There were, he thought, probably fifteen Stanley S. Fines in the Washington telephone directory, and three times that many in the directories of Los Angeles, New York, and Chicago, but he knew this was his Stanley S. Fine.

Canidy had first met Fine in Cedar Rapids, when he

and Fulmar were kids. Fine was a lawyer who worked for his uncle who owned most of Continental Motion Picture Studios. His responsibilities included keeping the secret that "America's Sweetheart" Monica Carlisle had not only been married but had a thirteen-year-old son. When he and Eric, horsing around with matches fired from spring-loaded pistols, had managed to set an automobile on fire, Fine had rushed to Cedar Rapids to buy the guy a new Studebaker, free them from the clutches of a fat lady of the Juvenile Authority, and, most important, keep the whole escapade out of the newspapers.

The last time he had seen Fine had been here in Washington just before he and Eddie Bitter had gone off to the Flying Tigers. They had had dinner with Chesty Whittaker and Cynthia Chenowith. Fine had some business with Donovan's law firm. It would be an extraordinary coincidence if this were *not* the same Stanley S. Fine.

"I think I know this guy," Canidy said.

"The colonel thought you might remember Captain Fine," Douglass said.

"The question you were asked, Canidy," Baker said, "is whether you think he can handle the mission."

"According to this, he's a qualified multiengine pilot with long-distance navigation experience," Canidy said. "But certainly there ought to be better-qualified people around for something like the African flight."

"But he could handle it?" Douglass pursued.

"Yeah, I think he could."

"We'll arrange for an experienced crew to go with him," Douglass said. "That's presuming you can talk him into volunteering."

Canidy looked at Douglass thoughtfully for a moment.

"You don't mean talking him into volunteering for

just this flight," he said. "What you want him to do is enlist in Donovan's Dilettantes."[1]

Douglass laughed. "You heard about that, did you?"

"We get newspapers in Deal," Canidy said.

"The colonel was rather amused by that piece," Douglass said. "And told me it would probably do us more good than harm."

"You didn't answer my question, Captain," Canidy said.

"You're right, we want Captain Fine permanently."

"Why?" Canidy asked.

"You ask entirely too many questions, Canidy," Baker said.

"He's another good friend of Eric Fulmar," Captain Douglass said.

"You gave me that too easily," Canidy said. "Which means that isn't the reason you want him."

"You're getting very perceptive, Dick," Douglass said. "But we're not playing twenty questions. If you don't like that answer, I'm sorry, but it's all you get for now."

"Why have I been picked to recruit him? I hardly know him."

"When I said that's all you get for now, Dick," Douglass said, "I meant it."

---

[1] Newspaper columnist Drew Pearson, who loathed Franklin Roosevelt and seldom passed over an opportunity to attack him, had pieced together one or two facts with a good deal of vague hearsay and written a column in which he accused Roosevelt, through Colonel William J. Donovan, of keeping his rich, famous, and social dilettante friends out of combat service by recruiting them for his propaganda organization. Pearson had even heard about the house on Q Street, calling it a "luxurious mansion requisitioned to serve as a barracks for Rooseveltian favorites," but had mislocated it in Virginia.

2

Chanute Field, Illinois
June 28, 1942

An eight-ship flight of B-17Es appeared in the air in the north. Canidy watched from a pickup truck. The truck was painted in a checkerboard pattern, and a large checkerboard flag was flying from its bed. The tail-end B-17E dropped its nose and made a steep descent for a straight-in approach to the runway.

"That'll be Captain Fine, sir," the assistant base adjutant, who was driving the pickup, said to Canidy. "He likes to sit on the taxiway so that he can offer 'constructive criticism' of their landings."

Canidy smiled. The translation of that was "eat ass."

The assistant base adjutant, a captain, was very impressed with Major Richard Canidy. This was his first encounter with an officer assigned to General Headquarters, Army Air Corps, who was traveling on orders stamped SECRET. That he was flying a Navy airplane added a delightful touch of mystery.

"This is Major Canidy, Captain," the base commander had told him. "I want you to take him where he wants to go and do whatever you can to assist him. But don't ask him any questions."

The remaining seven B-17Es circled the field in formation. As they passed over, the roar of their engines was awesome. They were simply enormous— and seemed invincible. Canidy let himself dwell for a moment on the incredible logistics problem involved in just getting them into the air. How many gallons of avgas had it taken to fill their tanks? How many mechanics were required to service that many engines?

144

For that matter, how many parachute riggers had to be trained just to pack all those parachutes?

One by one, at ninety-second intervals, the B-17Es detached themselves from the formation and began to land. By the time the first wheels touched down on the wide concrete runway, Fine's plane had stopped a third of the way down the parallel taxiway, shut down its inboard engines, and turned its nose toward the runway.

The captain drove the pickup over next to it, and Canidy saw in the pilot's seat a thin-faced, ascetic man with horn-rimmed glasses. He wasn't at all like the man Canidy remembered. Captain Stanley S. Fine was wearing a leather-brimmed cap with a headset clamped over it. He looked down at the pickup truck, and then turned his attention to the first plane landing.

A minute later, a sergeant in sheepskin high-altitude clothing came to the pickup. He saw Canidy's gold leaf and saluted.

"Captain Fine wants to know if you're waiting for him."

"Yes, I am, Sergeant," Canidy said.

When the message was relayed to him, Fine looked down at the pickup truck again, without recognition. His eyebrows rose in curiosity, and he smiled. Then he looked away and didn't look back at Canidy until the last of the B-17Es had landed. Finally he held up his index finger as an "I'll be with you in a minute" signal and disappeared from view.

He appeared on the ground shortly afterward walking around the tail section of the aircraft, with his cap held on his head with his hand against the prop blast. He was wearing a tropical worsted shirt and trousers and a horsehide leather A-2 jacket.

He saluted Canidy. "Is there something I can do for you, Major?"

"We've met, Captain Fine," Canidy said.

Fine's eyebrows rose in question.

"The first time was when Eric Fulmar and I tried to burn down Cedar Rapids. The last time was in Washington the spring before the war. We had dinner with Colonel Wild Bill Donovan and Cynthia Chenowith."

"Dick Canidy," Captain Fine said, extending his hand. "I don't know why I didn't recognize you. I guess I expected you to be halfway around the world."

"I'm much better looking than I used to be," Canidy said.

Fine laughed. "I saw in the papers, of course, that Jim Whittaker got out of the Philippines. I wondered what happened to you."

"I got out of China," Canidy said.

"But you were in the Navy," Fine questioned, indicating Canidy's Air Corps uniform.

"And you were a lawyer," Canidy said as they shook hands. "Things change. The war, I hear, has something to do with that."

Fine laughed again, then said, "Well, I'm glad you did, and I'm glad to see you. But I suspect this is not a coincidence."

"Can your copilot handle parking that aircraft?" Canidy asked.

"Interesting question," Fine said dryly. "I suppose he has to learn sometime, doesn't he?"

He turned to the airplane and made gestures telling the copilot to take the airplane to its parking place.

"Curiosity is about to overwhelm me," Fine said to Canidy.

The conversation was interrupted by a roar from the B-17's outboard port engine. The copilot, Canidy thought, was running the engine much too fast to taxi.

The copilot retarded his throttle to a more reasonable level, and the B-17E began to move.

Fine and Canidy exchanged the smug smiles of veteran pilots over the foibles of new ones. Then Fine said, "He's got a hundred thirty hours' total time. He'll learn."

"Can we talk in your BOQ? Do you have a roommate?"

"We can talk there," Fine said.

When they reached Fine's room, which was in a frame barracks so new it smelled of freshly sawn lumber, Canidy told Fine to close the door, then reached into his tunic and took from it a small American flag on an eight-inch pole. He waved it at Fine.

"In case you miss the symbolism," he said, "I'm waving the flag at you."

"I don't think I'm going to like this," Fine said, laughing. "You always carry a flag around?"

"No," Canidy said. "I stole this one from your group commander's desk while he left me to check out my orders."

Fine smiled. "They apparently checked out," he said. "What do they say?"

Canidy handed him the orders.

"They don't say much, do they?" Fine said when he had read them. "Except that whatever you're doing has the approval of the Air Corps. And that it's secret. I used to be in the motion-picture business, you remember, and this has all the earmarks of a Grade B adventure thriller. A mysterious officer appears, carrying secret orders. Are you now going to ask me to volunteer for a secret, dangerous mission, from which there is virtually no chance of returning alive?"

"I'd say the chances are sixty–forty," Canidy said, "that you'll get back all right."

Fine looked at him long enough to see that he was serious. "Jesus Christ!" he said.

"There is a mission, a long-distance flight, that we would like you to undertake," Canidy said.

"We?" Fine asked. "Who's 'we'?"

"I can't tell you that yet," Canidy said.

"Hey, come on!"

Canidy shrugged and smiled.

"Well, let's see, Dick," Fine said. "This wouldn't have anything to do with Colonel Donovan, would it?"

"Colonel who?" Canidy asked innocently.

"And you are also forbidden to tell me where I would be going, or for how long, or why. Right?"

"How long will it take you to pack?" Canidy asked.

"That would depend on where I would be going, and how long I would be gone. Will I need my fur coat or short sleeves?"

"If I were you, I wouldn't leave anything behind."

"I'm usually not much of a drinker," Fine said. "And taking a drink right now probably isn't very bright, but I'm going to have one anyway. Scotch all right with you?"

"I'm driving, thank you just the same," Canidy said.

Fine took a bottle of Scotch from a shelf in his closet and poured two inches of it into a water glass.

"And if I tell you, 'Thanks, but no thanks'?" he asked.

"They wouldn't have sent me after you," Canidy said, "if they didn't need you."

Saying that seemed to embarrass him, Fine saw, although Canidy tried to cover it by waving the little American flag again.

I don't know why I am surprised about this, Fine thought. *I should have known that sooner or later the service would require me to do what it wants me to do, as opposed to indulging me in the acting out of my personal fantasies.*

On December 9, 1941, Stanley S. Fine, vice president, legal, Continental Motion Picture Studios, Inc., who had been in New York on business when the Japanese attacked Pearl Harbor, took the train to Washington to see Greg Armstrong, a friend from law school who had given up corporate law to serve his country in uniform.

When he found Greg, who was working in one of the temporary buildings (from World War I) near the Smithsonian Institution, he quickly saw that his friend thought Stanley Fine had gone off the deep end. Even though Greg professed to understand why Fine wanted to come into the service, and even why Fine wanted to fly, it was clear that Greg thought that flying was the last thing Stanley should be doing. But still, he went through the motions.

"There's two ways you can handle the flying thing, Stanley," he said. "You can apply to one of the aviation cadet selection boards. If you've got a pilot's license . . . what did you say you have?"

"I've got a commercial pilot's certificate with five hundred ten hours, and an instrument ticket, single-engine land."

"OK. What I'm saying is that you can certainly get into the aviation cadet program. Which means after you got your wings, you would be either a flight officer or a second lieutenant. Or, Stanley, you can go in the service as a lawyer. With your years of practice, you can start out as a captain."

"I don't want to be a lawyer."

"Hear me out. You're a *captain*. I can have that paperwork for you in two weeks. You get a commission, and they tell you to hold yourself ready for active service. While you're waiting to be called, you apply for flight duty. Send them a certified copy of your licenses, and so on. They'll probably jump at you. But you do have a senator in your pocket who can do you a favor, don't you?"

"Do I have to do that?"

"You don't even have to go in the Army, Stan. You're a married man with three kids. And movies are going to be declared an essential war industry. I heard that last week. If you want to play Errol Flynn in *Dawn Patrol,* though, you're going to need a senator."

On February 7, 1942, they gave a going-away party at Continental Studios. It was held on soundstage eleven, and Max Lieberman had it catered by Chasen's, so the people in the Continental commissary could attend. There was one big head table on a four-foot platform built especially for the occasion. It sat sixty-eight people, and it was draped with bunting. Behind it hung an enormous American flag. Everybody else sat at ten-seat round tables.

With the exception of Max and Sophie Lieberman, the guests at the head table were Continental employees about to enter the armed forces.

The honorees were introduced alphabetically, and Max Lieberman made it through best boys and truck drivers and clerks and scenery painters and even two actors until he got to Stanley Fine, who was his nephew—Sophie's sister's Sadie's boy—and who was the nearest thing he had to a son. That was when he got something in his throat, and then in his eye, and so Stanley took over for him at the mike and introduced the others while Uncle Max sat blowing his nose and wiping away tears.

The founder and chairman of the board of Continental Studios got control of himself by the time Stanley had finished the introductions. He reclaimed the mike and announced that in case anybody was wondering, everybody had his job waiting for him, so they should get the lead out of their ass and win the war. Meanwhile, Continental had movies to make.

Captain Stanley S. Fine, Judge Advocate General's Corps, had entered upon active duty for the duration plus six months on 1 May 1942.

His initial duty station was the U.S. Army Air Corps Officers' Reception Station, Boca Raton, Florida. The Adjutant General of the United States Army was led to understand that assigning Fine to the Army Air Corps would please the junior senator from California, and he so ordered.

When Captain Fine reached Boca Raton, he learned that the U.S. Army Air Corps Officers' Reception Station had only three weeks before been the Boca Raton Hotel and Club, an exclusive, very expensive resort. The Air Corps had taken it over for the duration, rolled up the carpets, put the furniture in storage, closed the bar, installed GI furniture and a GI mess, and turned the place into a basic training camp for newly commissioned officers.

Fine's fellow student officers had also been lawyers, or doctors, dentists, engineers, wholesale grocers, paper merchants, trucking company executives, construction engineers, or other civilians whose occupations had a military application and who had been directly commissioned into the services.

He had been at Boca Raton six weeks when his senator's influence was again felt.

Captain Fine was engaged in a class exercise in the administration of military justice. He was playing the role of prosecutor in a mock court-martial when a runner summoned him from the classroom (which had been the card room of the Boca Raton Hotel) to the station commander's office.

"I don't understand this, Captain," the station commander said, "but we are in receipt of orders assigning you to the Three-forty-fourth Heavy Bombardment Group at Chanute Field. It says for transition training to B-17 aircraft. You're not a pilot, are you?"

"I have a civilian license, sir."

"I never heard of anything like this before," the colonel said. "But orders are orders, Captain."

When he reported to the 344th Bombardment Group at Chanute, he was sure there was no way he would be permitted to become a pilot.

"The only time you have is in Piper Cubs and a Beechcraft?" the colonel asked.

"I'm afraid so, sir," Fine said.

"I hope you can fly, Fine," he said. "And not just because you know some important politicians and the general told me to give you every consideration."

"I wanted to fly very badly," Fine said. "I thought I needed some help. That now seems rather childish."

"If you can fly," the colonel said, "I'd like to make you a squadron commander. I've got a lot of very healthy, very impetuous young men who need a stabilizing influence. In my day, it took ten years to make captain. Now we're making them in a year, and then making them B-17 aircraft commanders with a hundred ten hours' total time. It's working better than I thought it would, but I would still like as many officers like you as I can get. I really *need* officers with five hundred hours and some instrument experience. Who can *really* navigate."

"I was about to say that I might well be more use as a lawyer," Fine said.

"That's not my decision to make," the colonel had told him. "I have one other officer, Major Thomasson, who was an aircraft commander before last week. I'm going to introduce you to him, explain the situation, and see what he thinks."

"Yes, sir," Fine said.

"On the basis of your extensive civilian aeronautical experience, Captain Fine," the colonel said dryly, "Headquarters, Army Air Corps, has seen fit to designate you as a military aviator. You are now a pilot, Captain Fine. Congratulations."

He tossed Fine a pair of aviator's wings still pinned to a piece of cardboard.

"If you can't handle the seventeen," the colonel said, "and I really hope you can, there are other places where you can be put to good use."

The next day, Fine began what he was sure would be at least a two-week course in the B-17 aircraft. Major Thomasson turned out to be a bright-eyed twenty-three-year-old West Pointer who told Fine that he had graduated from the last prewar, yearlong pilot training course.

Thomasson almost casually went through the B-17E dash-one with him for most of the day, and then took him to the flight line for what Fine expected would be a hands-on explanation of the aircraft.

"I've never seen one up close before," Fine confessed.

"It's a pretty good bird, Captain," Thomasson said. "It's the E model. I picked this one up in Seattle last week."

Fine had been introduced to the crew. There was a navigator and a bombardier, both officers, and an engineer, a radioman, and tail and turret gunners. There was no copilot.

"I don't think you'll have any trouble with it, Captain," Thomasson said to him, and then raised his voice. "You guys get aboard."

It took a moment for that to sink in. They were obviously about to take the B-17 aloft—without a copilot. The incredible truth seemed to be that on his first time up in a B-17E, he would fly as copilot.

"I think I should tell you," Fine said as he sat down in the copilot's seat and looked around the cockpit, "that I have a total of zero hours' twin-engine time."

"That's exactly as many as I had when I first came down here," Major Thomasson said. "They sent me to seventeens right out of primary."

"Jesus!" Fine said.

"The way you fly this thing," Thomasson said, "is that the copilot reads the checklist out loud." He handed Fine a sheet of cardboard three inches wide and six inches long. "And the pilot does what it says. Got it?"

"We'll find out," Fine said. He read the first item on the list: "Master power buss on."

"Master power buss on," Thomasson parroted.

"Uncage gyros."

"Gyros uncaged."

Fine looked at the artificial horizon on the instrument panel before him. There were two sets of instruments, one for the pilot and one for the copilot. He reached out and uncaged his gyro. The ball inside began to move.

"Verify crew in position, crew hatches closed," Fine read. He didn't understand that and looked at Thomasson.

"You have to get on the intercom to do that," Thomasson explained, and showed him how to switch it on.

"Crew report," Thomasson's voice came over the intercom. One by one, the crew reported their presence.

"Navigator, yo!"

"Bombardier here, forward hatch closed and locked."

"Radio here, sir."

"Tail here, sir."

"Belly, yo!"

"Engineer, rear door closed and locked."

"Fire extinguisher in place," Fine read. "Ground crew clear."

Thomasson looked out his window and reported: "Clear!"

"Number one engine, full rich," Fine read.

"One full rich."

"Prime number one engine."

"One primed."

"Start number one engine," Fine read.

"Starting number one," Thomasson replied.

There came the whine of the starter, and then the cough of the engine as it tried to start, and the aircraft began to tremble. The engine caught, smoothed out.

Fine looked across the cockpit to the left wing. He could see the propeller turning.

"Number one running smoothly," Thomasson said.

"Lean and idle number one," Fine read. "Number three engine, full rich."

"Number one lean and idle," Thomasson replied. "Number three full rich."

"Start number three," Fine read.

"Starting number three."

The propeller on the engine at Fine's right began to turn slowly as the starter ground, and then the engine caught.

"What you do," Thomasson said dryly, "is taxi to the threshold with just two engines."

"I see," Fine said.

"Then when you get there, Captain, before you take off, I suggest you start the other two."

Fine looked at him in disbelief.

"Go ahead," Thomasson said, smiling. "There always has to be a first time."

Fine had picked up the microphone.

"Chanute, Air Corps Four-oh-one in front of the terminal for taxi and takeoff."

"Well, at least you know that much," Thomasson's metallic voice came over the intercom. "I've had guys in the right seat who got on the horn and called 'Yoo-hoo, Tower! Anybody there?'"

The tower came back: "Air Corps Four-oh-one, taxi left on taxiway six to the threshold of the active. The active is three-two. You are number one to take off. There is no traffic in the immediate area. The altimeter is two-niner-niner-niner, the time one-five past the hour, and the winds are five, gusting to fifteen, from the north."

"Where the hell are the brakes on this thing?" Fine asked.

The pilot showed him how to release the brakes.

Fine put his hand on the throttles and ever so gently nudged them forward. The pitch of the engines changed, and the B-17E had started to move.

A week later, he was certified as B-17 qualified, and a week after that as pilot in command. Two weeks after that, he scrawled his signature to a document of the 319th Bomber Squadron: "The undersigned herewith assumes command, Stanley S. Fine, Captain, Air Corps, Commanding."

He then set about to make the 319th Bomber Squadron the best squadron in the group, in the wing, in the Army Air Corps. He was as happy as he could ever remember.

I should have known it couldn't last, he thought, looking balefully at Dick Canidy.

"Cue the rolling drums and the trumpets," he said. "Our hero is about to volunteer."

"Then let me be the first to welcome you, Captain," Canidy said, "to Donovan's Dilettantes."

"I thought so," Fine said. "What would happen if I changed my mind again?"

"Then there would be questions about your mental stability," Canidy said. "Psychiatric evaluation would be ordered. It would take a long time. For the duration, at least."

"Can they do that?" Fine the lawyer asked, surprised.

"They can, and they do, Captain Fine," Canidy said.

3

When Canidy and Fine landed at Anacostia, Chief Ellis was there with the Buick to meet them.

"Give Captain Fine a hand with his gear, please, Chief," Canidy said, "I've got to see about getting this thing fueled, and I want to check the weather."

When they had Fine's Val-Paks and his footlocker in the Buick, Chief Ellis led Captain Fine into base ops, where they found Canidy in the weather room getting a three-day forecast from a Navy meteorologist.

As the weatherman was concluding, Chester Wezevitz—the Navy captain who believed the COI's job was suppressing VD—came into the room.

"VD must be a hell of a problem in the fleet," he said. "I had a look at your airplane, Major. Carpets, upholstered leather seats, and everything."

"You noticed, I'm sure," Canidy said, "that the seats fold down into couches. We think of it, Captain, as our airborne prophylactics-testing laboratory."

"Shit," Wezevitz said, grinning.

"It is considered so important to the overall war effort," Canidy said, "that I have been given a copilot to share the strain of my burden. May I present Captain Fine?"

As Fine, baffled, was shaking hands with Wezevitz, Lieutenant Commander Edwin H. Bitter, with the golden rope of an admiral's aide hanging down his arm, walked into the weather room.

He and Canidy looked at each other for a moment without speaking.

"Well," Canidy broke the silence, "look at the dog robber."

Bitter offered his hand.

"It's good to see you again, Dick," he said a little stiffly. "In the Air Corps, are you?"

"That's right," Canidy said. "Captain Fine, Commander Bitter. Do you remember him? He was at that dinner in Washington."

"Of course," Fine said. "He went off to the Flying Tigers with you."

The eyebrows of the Navy captain rose in surprise.

"The Air Corps, eh?" Bitter asked.

"The Air Corps," Canidy said.

The awkwardness and tension between Bitter and Canidy was evident to Ellis, Fine, and Wezevitz.

"The admiral's flight is all laid on, Commander," Wezevitz said. "I presume that's why you're here?"

"Yes, sir," Bitter said. "The admiral asked me to check on it."

"All laid on," Wezevitz repeated awkwardly.

"Are you stationed here?" Bitter asked.

"No. But I come in here from time to time," Canidy said. "I'm assigned to the Office of the Coordinator of Information."

Canidy saw no comprehension on Bitter's face.

"How's the knee?" Canidy asked, to change the subject.

"I have a cane," Bitter said. "I left it in the staff car. It keeps me from flying. I'm assigned to BUAIR."

"You're a lieutenant commander, so congratulations are in order," Canidy said, adding mischievously, "How do you like being a dog robber?"

Bitter was not amused.

"Obviously, I can't fly," he said. "I can't even get limited duty at sea."

"And that bothers you?" Canidy said. "Be grateful, Edwin."

Bitter didn't like that either, but he didn't respond to it. Instead, he asked, "Have you got a minute?"

Canidy nodded. Bitter took his arm and led him out of the weather room into the corridor.

"Do you remember Sarah Child?" he asked.

"Sure," Canidy said. "Your pen pal. The little Jewish girl with the sexy eyes and the marvelous boobs."

"We're married," Bitter said levelly.

"Ooops!" Canidy said.

"And we have a child," Bitter went on. "A little boy. His name is Joseph after Sarah's father, and he was born last March. We were secretly married before we went over there."

Canidy's eyebrows went up, and then he understood.

"I remember," he said. "I was your best man. How could you have forgotten?"

"She's really a fine woman, Dick," Bitter said.

"I know she is," Canidy said.

"Thank you, Dick," Bitter said.

Canidy was embarrassed. He was being thanked, he understood, for his unspoken promise not to tell anyone, should the occasion arise, that Lieutenant Commander and Mrs. Bitter were not married when Bitter went off to the Flying Tigers.

Quickly Canidy said, "So tell me all about your little nest. You got a picture of the kid?"

Bitter took several from his wallet and handed them over.

"Unfortunately, he looks just like his old man," Canidy said. "I'm happy for you, Eddie."

"Come see us, Dick," Bitter said.

"That would be difficult, Eddie," Canidy said.

"We're in the Willard Hotel," Bitter said in a rush. "We absolutely couldn't find a place to live, so Sarah's father turned his apartment in the Willard over to us."

"You get along all right with Sarah's father, huh?"

"Our mothers are the ones who give us trouble," Bitter said.

"Oh?"

"Sarah's is—well, crazy. She's in and out of mental hospitals. And mine—disapproves."

"She's probably sore you didn't tell her you were secretly married," Canidy said. "She'll get over it."

"I really would like to talk to you, Dick," Bitter said.

He means about my cowardice in China. He wants an explanation. That's touching. But I can't. That would violate the Donovan's Dilettantes' code of honor.

"Tell me, Eddie, did your kid inherit your undersized wang?"

Bitter shook his head in resignation, but then, surprising himself, he said, "He can lie on his back and piss on the ceiling."

"Here's to a kid who can piss on the ceiling," Canidy said, lifting his hand high, then, "Eddie, I have to go."

They shook hands again, and Canidy went to the weather-room door to motion to Fine and Ellis to come with him.

When they were gone, Wezevitz asked, "Old pal of yours?"

"We were at Pensacola as IPs before the war," Bitter said.

"And now he's in the Air Corps?"

"He left the service in 1941," Bitter said.

"Now he's an Air Corps major flying a VIP transport for the VD comic-book people," Wezevitz said. "Seems like a hell of waste of a naval aviator."

Bitter, not quite sure he had heard correctly, asked, "Sir?"

"What the Coordinator of Information does, Commander," Wezevitz said, "is publish those *Use a Pro Kit* comic books they issue to the white hats. Why they need an airplane to do it is beyond me."

Bitter looked at him curiously, but didn't say anything. He thought it was highly unlikely that the Navy would assign a C-45 to airlift VD comic books. It was even more unlikely that the Air Corps would commission as a field-grade officer someone with Canidy's record. At the same time he remembered a cryptic remark from Doug Douglass once when Canidy's name had come up, that people should not jump to conclusions before they had all the facts. Doug wouldn't say anything else, but he obviously knew something else.

When I get back to the office, Ed Bitter decided, *I will get to the bottom of this. While there's a hell of a lot wrong with being an admiral's dog robber, it has certain benefits. When you call somebody up and identify yourself as the aide to a vice admiral, you get answers a lieutenant commander wouldn't be given.*

Two hours later, when he walked into the office, the admiral's Wave said the admiral wanted to see him immediately.

"Close the door, Commander," Vice Admiral Enoch Hawley said. When Bitter had done that, he went on: "I've just had a strange telephone call about you, Commander. You will consider the following an order: From this moment on, you will make no attempt to contact Major Richard Canidy, U.S. Army Air Corps. Nor will you discuss him with anyone, nor make inquiries regarding him or the Office of the Coordinator of Information. Is that clear?"

"Yes, sir," Bitter said.

"Whatever this is about, Ed," the admiral said, "it doesn't seem to bother you. You're smiling."

"In a way, sir, it's very good news."

4

The House on Q Street, NW
Washington, D.C.
June 29, 1942

"Is this the 'requisitioned mansion' Drew Pearson wrote about?" Stanley Fine asked as Ellis drove through the gate of the house on Q Street.

"The one he wrote about is in Virginia," Ellis said.

"This is Jim Whittaker's house, isn't it?" Fine asked as they got out of the car. "What did you say happened to him?"

Canidy shrugged and threw up his hand, but Fine had seen the look in his eyes.

"Something else you know and can't tell?" Fine said.

"People get pissed around here if you ask questions, Stanley," Canidy said. "After a while you'll get used to it."

Cynthia Chenowith came into the library as Canidy was helping himself to a drink.

"It's nice to see you again, Captain Fine."

"And it's nice to see you, Miss Chenowith," Fine said.

"Miss Chenowith is our housekeeper," Canidy said. "You need extra towels, that sort of thing, you just let her know."

She glowered at him but didn't respond.

"You'll be staying here for a couple of days, Captain Fine," she said. "We've put you on the third floor, first door on the right at the head of the stairs."

"Thank you," Fine said. "May I ask a question? I don't know who else to ask."

"That would depend on the question, Stan," Canidy said.

"What is it?" Cynthia asked.

"What do I tell my wife?"

"I would suggest," Cynthia said, "that you drop her a note telling her that you are on temporary duty in Washington, and that as soon as you have an address you'll be in touch again."

"I generally telephone her every few days," Fine said. "She'll expect a call from me today or tomorrow."

"I don't think that calling her right now would be a very good idea," Cynthia said. "But if you'd like to write her a note, I'll see that it's posted right away."

Fine was sitting at a Louis XIV escritoire writing his wife when Colonel Donovan walked into the library. Donovan was wearing a mussed seersucker jacket. It was already hot and muggy in Washington.

"Good to see you, Fine," he said, mopping his forehead with a handkerchief and then offering his hand. "Welcome aboard."

"Thank you," Fine said.

"What's Dick told you about all this?"

"That I shouldn't ask questions," Fine said.

"We don't have many rules around here, but that's an important one. You don't ask questions, and you don't volunteer information. Dick, however, seems to have volunteered the information that I'm connected with all this."

"Only after he swore true faith and allegiance to the Dilettantes, sir," Canidy said.

Donovan chuckled. "Did you see Pearson's column, Stanley?"

"Yes, sir," Fine said.

"There are—aren't there always?—some administrative things to be taken care of," Donovan said. "That'll take a day or two. Then Dick's going to take you to a house we run in New Jersey. What we want you for involves a rather interesting long-distance cargo flight."

"Yes, sir," Fine said.

"Tomorrow Dick is going to take to Fort Knox a man

you'll be working with. His name is Eldon Baker, and you'll meet him at dinner tonight. By the time they get back, you should be ready to go to Jersey with Dick."

"Why is Baker going to Knox?" Canidy asked.

"He'll explain that to you when he's ready," Donovan said. "Oh hell, there's such a thing as carrying secrecy too far. You're going to talk to Jimmy Whittaker."

"Really?" Canidy asked, but Colonel Donovan chose not to say anything more.

Over dinner, however, the African flight was discussed.

"You'll function as flight engineer, as well as the mission commander," Baker told Fine. "And before you go, there will be time to—what is it they say?—'transition' you in the airplane."

Now that it was official that he was not going, Canidy did not feel relief. Instead, he felt left out.

Don't be a goddamn fool, he told himself.

"Incidentally, Canidy," Baker said, "we have decided that you, too, should transition into the C-46."

"My feelings weren't hurt about being left out," Canidy said.

"Your feelings have nothing to do with it," Baker said. "What is important is that something might happen to Captain Fine, in which case you would go on the flight."

"You've considered, I'm sure, the possibility that either one of us might bend the bird learning how to fly it?" Canidy asked dryly.

"That was considered," Baker answered matter-of-factly. "According to your records, both you and Captain Fine are rather good pilots. The chances are that there will be no damage to the aircraft. But in case something does happen, we have acquired another aircraft on standby, in case it is needed."

The next morning Canidy flew the D18S southwest across Virginia, with the Appalachian Mountains on his right wingtip, to Roanoke. There he turned more westerly, crossed the Appalachians, then the Alleghenies and the lower tip of West Virginia, and then set down at a small airport in Wheelwright, Kentucky, for coffee and a piss break.

"Where are we?" Baker asked as Canidy walked through the cabin.

"Eastern Kentucky, a place called Wheelwright," Canidy said.

Baker followed him out of the airplane and went into the terminal, a small frame building with a sign on it advertising flying lessons for five dollars. Canidy watched as the tanks were topped off, checked the oil, signed a U.S. government purchase order for the gas, and then went to the foul-smelling men's room.

Baker was waiting for him outside the small building.

"Let's stretch our legs," he said, gesturing down the single dirt and pebble runway.

They had walked half its length when Baker touched his sleeve. "This is far enough."

No one, Canidy thought, could possibly overhear what Baker was about to tell him.

"We're going to Fort Knox to see your friend Whittaker," he said.

"Donovan told me," Canidy said.

"And there's somebody else there you know," Baker said.

"Are you going to tell me who, or just tease me with your superior knowledge?"

"Eric Fulmar," Baker said, enjoying Canidy's surprise.

"If you wanted to surprise me, you've surprised me," Canidy said. "How'd you get him out of Morocco? More important, why? And what is he doing at Knox?"

"Getting him out was simplicity itself," Baker said. "Even though he didn't want to come. We had a little talk with Sidi el Ferruch, and Fulmar, tied up like a Christmas turkey, was delivered to Gibraltar. There he was loaded on a destroyer, taken to Charleston, and then to Fort Knox."

"What for?"

"We have need for friend Fulmar again," Baker said.

"Why?" Canidy asked. "How?"

"Putting him together with Whittaker at Knox was my idea," Baker said, ignoring Canidy's questions. "He feels about you—about *both* of us—much as you feel about me. Since we need his cooperation, I thought it might be a good idea to let him know, via Whittaker, that we can make things very unpleasant for him if he doesn't cooperate."

"You are indeed a true sonofabitch," Canidy said, more in resignation than anger. "You like pushing people around, don't you?"

Baker didn't reply.

"What kind of cooperation?" Canidy asked.

"In connection with the North African invasion," Baker said.

Canidy thought that over for a moment.

"Bullshit," he said. "First of all, you gave me that too quick, and second, we don't need Fulmar. You've already compromised Sidi el Ferruch. He has no choice but to do what you want him to do."

Baker smiled patronizingly at Canidy. "Very good, Canidy," he said. "Let us say, then, we *tell* everybody who has the need to know that we want Fulmar for Operation Torch."

"What do we really want him for?"

"*You* don't have the need to know, just yet," Baker said.

"Fuck you," Canidy said.

"You really should learn to control your mouth," Baker flared. "One day it's going to get you in trouble."

There was a pause while Baker waited for an apology. He went on after none came: "It is important, Canidy. You'll have to take my word for it."

"If you say so, Eldon," Canidy said sarcastically. He was trying to get under Baker's skin, and succeeded.

"You don't really think we recruited Fine just to fly that airplane, do you?"

"I wondered about that," Canidy said.

"Fine has some interesting contacts in Europe," Baker said. "And we have reason to believe his uncle has made substantial contributions to the Zionist movement."

"I don't understand that," Canidy said.

"The Zionists have a very skillful intelligence service," Baker said, as if patiently dealing with a backward child.

"I didn't know that," Canidy confessed.

"Much of what we know about German jet-engine development we got from the British, who got it from the Zionists," Baker said. "And you're shortly going to be joined at Summer Place by Second Lieutenant C. Holdsworth Martin III."

"The Disciple, Junior?" Canidy asked, surprised. "Wait till Drew Pearson hears about that."

Baker ignored him again. "He was at La Rosey in Switzerland with Fulmar," Baker said.

"What the hell is so important about Fulmar?" Canidy asked.

"Important enough that I may order responsibility for Captain Whittaker transferred from Fort Knox to you, at Summer Place—*if* he can bring Fulmar with him."

"How can I get Whittaker to talk Fulmar into anything if neither of us has the slightest idea what you want Fulmar to do?"

"We tell Whittaker that it's something connected with the invasion of North Africa. That's credible. But we simply cannot even suggest what we really want from Fulmar at this point."

"I'll be a sonofabitch if I understand any of this," Canidy said.

"Good. You're not supposed to."

"What makes you think Fulmar will believe anything you have to say?" Canidy asked. "I suppose it's occurred to you that you destroyed your credibility with Fulmar when you left him and me floating around in the Atlantic off Safi," Canidy said.

"That's where you come in," Baker said. "Why do you think you were left behind? You ever wonder about that?"

"I was too mad to wonder about it," Canidy said.

"Police detectives have an interrogation technique," Baker said, "where one is a heartless sonofabitch, and another is kind, gentle, and understanding."

"And I'm to be the good guy, right?"

"Now you're getting the picture," Baker said. "You're not a sonofabitch like Baker; you were left behind, too."

"The truth is that you are a genuine, heartless sonofabitch, and like being one," Canidy said.

"I'm sorry you feel that way," Baker said.

"OK," Canidy said. "I get the picture. Is this class about over now?"

"I was about to suggest it was," Baker said, and waved his hand back down the pebble runway to where the D18 sat waiting for them.

Six

1

SARAH CHILD BITTER was kneeling on the floor of what at one time had been the suite Child and Company, Merchant Bankers, maintained in Washington. The suite was now what she thought of as her first married home. What she was trying to do was force mashed carrots into Joe, a losing battle that was thankfully interrupted when the telephone rang. Long distance was calling for Commander Bitter.

"I'm sorry, operator, he's not here," Sarah said.

"If that's Mrs. Bitter, operator," the voice said, "I'll talk to her."

"This is Mrs. Bitter," Sarah said.

"Go ahead, sir," the operator said.

"This is Doug Douglass, Mrs. Bitter," a pleasant voice said. "I'm an old friend of Ed's."

"I know," she said.

Doug Douglass was more than an old friend. He was the man who had saved Ed's life when Ed had been wounded. Doug Douglass had landed his own P-40 on a dry riverbed, manhandled Ed from the cockpit of his plane into his own cockpit, and then somehow managed to take off again.

"When I called his folks to ask if they knew where he was, they gave me your number."

"You don't know how glad I am to hear you're back," Sarah said.

"So am I," he said. "I never thought I would be delighted to be stationed in Selma, Alabama, but—"

"Is that where you are?" Sarah asked. "Alabama?"

"They gave me a fighter group down here, Mrs. Bitter," he said.

I will thank him, she thought, *for my husband's life, for Joe's daddy, but this isn't the time.*

"Oh, please call me Sarah," she said.

"I hear there's a baby, too, I didn't know about."

"Yes, there is," Sarah said.

"I'd like to see Ed," Douglass said. "And if he's going to be available, this weekend. I'm coming up to Washington."

"He'll be available," Sarah said. "And you'll stay here with us."

There was a perpetual shortage of hotel rooms in Washington for civilians. And so many officers were visiting the city, Ed had told her, that rooms in transient bachelor officers' quarters had become nothing but wall-to-wall cots.

Sarah was at first delighted to have room to offer Doug Douglass, until she remembered that her old friend Charity Hoche was coming on Friday afternoon and Ann Chambers on Saturday, which meant there would be no spare room. Well, they would just have to make do, have the hotel send up cots or something. Both Ann and Douglass had large claims on her. And Charity was a dear. Fortunately, it turned out there wasn't going to be a problem after all.

"Well, that's very kind, Sarah, but I already have a place to stay," Doug said.

"A nice place?" she challenged.

"Very nice." He chuckled. "I'll be staying with my father."

"Well, there's a bed here if you need one," Sarah said. "Are you going to be here on business?"

"I am solemnly informed that the entire war effort will collapse unless I immediately acquire some cross-country time," he said. "So I decided to cross the country to our nation's capital instead of Hogwash, Wisconsin."

He has a nice voice, Sarah thought. And seems like a nice fellow.

"Well, if the fate of the nation depends on it," Sarah said. "How long can you stay?"

"Overnight, anyway," he said. "If you can find a baby-sitter, I'd like to take you out to dinner."

"No, you won't," Sarah said. "We'll have a party. I even know some girls."

"You don't have to do that," he said.

"I want to," Sarah said. "When and where are you arriving?"

"I'll leave here say six, six-thirty," he said. "I should touch down at Bolling no later than half past ten."

"You can't make it from Alabama that quickly, can you?" she said.

"You can in a P-38," he said.

"I really look forward to this," Sarah said.

"Me, too, Sarah," he said, then: "Gotta go! See you Saturday."

She broke the connection with her finger. What I really would like to do, she thought, is call Ed and tell him. But he doesn't like me to call him there. She meditated a moment, then lifted her finger off the switch. When the operator came on the line, Sarah gave her Ann's number at the *Memphis Advocate*.

"Ed's friend Douglass is going to be here Saturday, too," she announced. "If he's going to see Ed, maybe he'll see Dick Canidy, too."

"At least I should be able to corner him and see if he

has a number or an address," Ann said. Then: "Just for the hell of it, why don't you try the National Institute of Health again for me? Save me the price of a call. If he comes on the line, hang up."

Sarah giggled. "OK," she said. "I will."

Ann gave her the number, said, "See you Saturday," and hung up.

Just as before with Ann, the operator at the National Institute of Health informed Sarah that no one named Canidy worked there.

"I'm sure there's some mistake," Sarah said. "I was told to call him at the National Institute of Health building."

There was silence on the line, and Sarah had just about decided the operator had hung up on her, when there was the sound of a phone being rung.

A woman answered and said, "Hello?"

The one word was enough for Sarah to judge that she was young, sophisticated, and intelligent.

"Major Richard Canidy, please," Sarah said.

There was a hesitation.

"May I ask who's calling?"

"My name is Sarah Bitter," Sarah said. There was another pause. Sarah suspected she was about to be put off again, so she quickly added: "My husband is Commander Edwin Bitter. He and Major Canidy were in the American Volunteer Group."

There was another pause, not as long.

"May I ask where you got this number?" the young woman asked.

"From another Flying Tiger," Sarah said. "Major Doug Douglass."

"I see," the young woman said, her inflection explaining a good deal. "Well, I'm sorry, miss, there is no one here by that name."

"I see," Sarah said. "Thank you very much, anyway."

The young woman hung up without another word.

2

Godman Army Air Field
Fort Knox, Kentucky
June 29, 1942

The parking ramps of Godman held a large number of what looked like brand-new Lockheed P-38 aircraft. At least two squadrons, Canidy judged. He wondered why so many were in the middle of Kentucky, and decided that they were here to protect the United States gold reserves.

That made perfect sense: two squadrons of brand-new airplanes here to protect something that not only was safe but far beyond the range of any enemy bomber.

"They expect us," Baker announced. "I have a number to call."

"Go call it," Canidy said and went to find somebody to top off the D18's tanks.

A few moments later, Baker returned to the airplane and announced a car was coming for them; it would be a couple of minutes.

Canidy looked at the other man carefully. After considerable thought he had made up his mind to do something he now concluded was not unduly colored by his dislike for Eldon C. Baker.

"Let's stretch our legs," he said, mimicking Baker's manner at Wheelwright. When he had him out of earshot of the ground crew servicing the Beech, he said, "I've been thinking that I'm not going to feed Whittaker your line of bullshit about some kind of unspecified dangerous mission. I'm not going to lie to him."

"Your sense of humor, or loyalty, or whatever it is, is

misplaced," Baker said. "Though commendable," he added.

"Well, I'm not going to do it, so do whatever you have to do with that in mind," Canidy said.

"Are we going to have to call Captain Douglass on the phone to get this straightened out?"

"Call anybody you want," Canidy said.

"There's a scrambler phone at post headquarters," Baker said. "I'll use that."

Canidy shrugged.

"What are you thinking, Canidy?" Baker asked, en route to post headquarters in an Army olive-drab staff car. "That he would learn the truth anyhow and be upset?"

"I don't think you understand trust," Canidy said. "I don't think the elaborate bullshit is necessary with this guy. And it damned well could be counterproductive. When you finish tattling on me to Douglass, that's the argument I'm going to make."

As he got out of the car before the brick post headquarters building, Baker turned to Canidy.

"We'll tell him as little of the truth as necessary, agreed?"

"But the truth," Canidy said.

Baker nodded.

Either he realizes the profound wisdom of my position, or else he's afraid to go to Douglass with it. Which means that I may have more influence with Douglass than I think I do—or he wants me to know I have.

Canidy had hoped to meet the post commander, a general named Patton whom he knew to be quite a character. General Patton had not only traveled around the prewar Army with his own string of polo ponies, but he designed a uniform for armored troops that made them look like characters in the "Buck Rogers in the 21st Century" comic strip. Unfortunately, it turned out that Patton was in Washington.

Though Patton's deputy, a brigadier general, was

expecting them, he had no idea why they were coming. And when Baker showed him the identification of a deputy U.S. marshal, he was visibly uneasy—and even more nervous when Baker produced an order of the United States Court of Appeals directing him to give Baker access to Captain James M. B. Whittaker and Eric Fulmar. Baker was to be further allowed—if he so chose—to take one or both of the aforesaid patients into his personal custody.

"I'll have to check this, you understand, sir," the brigadier general said.

A telephone call to the Chief of Staff confirmed that he was to comply with the court order. The brigadier general then called in the post provost marshal, who drove Canidy and Baker to the station hospital in a Chevrolet sedan with a chrome siren on the fender.

The station hospital was a sprawling complex of single-story frame buildings. It was brand-new—still smelling of freshly sawn lumber and paint—and it was built on gently undulating land a half mile from the brick buildings of the main post. After the hospital commander, a tall, heavy, white-mustachioed full colonel, was shown the court order, he told them that Whittaker and Fulmar were in private rooms in a private ward, and that he would personally escort them there.

"Whittaker first," Canidy said.

The private ward was in a fenced-in portion of the neuropsychiatric division of the hospital. Sections of hurricane fence enclosed a small porch. Others were nailed over the windows. A military policeman was in the corridor, and another sat outside the fence on a folding chair under a small tree.

"What's his physical condition, Colonel?" Baker asked.

"Physically," the hospital commander said, "and so far as I am concerned mentally, there is nothing wrong with Captain Whittaker. He was a mess when they brought him here, but once we got rid of his parasites and got some food into him, he came right around."

"I'm glad to hear that," Baker said.

"I've been told to ask you no questions, and as a soldier I'll obey my orders. But I don't mind telling you that I don't like a hospital ward being used as a prison," the hospital commander said. "I don't think it's either ethical or legal."

"Wouldn't you say, Colonel," Baker said coldly, "that the attorney general would be the best judge of that?"

The colonel did not back down.

"The Supreme Court, perhaps," he said. "I'm not sure about the attorney general."

Canidy chuckled, and Baker glared at him.

The MP unlocked the door to a room, then held it open for Canidy, Baker, and the hospital commander.

"Captain Whittaker," the doctor said. "These gentlemen have been sent from Washington to see you."

"I'll be goddamned," Whittaker said. He was in a red hospital bathrobe, pajamas, and slippers. He had been reading *Life* magazine.

"Thank you, Doctor," Baker said, "I'll take it from here."

The hospital commander left, closing the door after him, and almost immediately Canidy heard the lock being snapped shut.

Whittaker looked suspiciously at Canidy but got out of his chair and offered his hand.

"Hello, Jimmy," Canidy said. "How the hell are you?"

"This is the nut ward," Whittaker said. "Or the prison ward. Or the prison nut ward. How the hell do you think I am?"

"I hear you got rid of Clarence," Canidy said.

"Yeah," Whittaker said. "And he was a persistent bastard. It took about ten pounds of quinine to kill him. I was as yellow as a daisy for a while."

"It must run in the family," Canidy said. "Your aunt Barbara told me that Chesty had one in—somewhere in the Far East."

"I've heard that story," Whittaker said, and then he looked coldly at Eldon C. Baker. "Who're you?" he asked.

"His name is Baker," Canidy said. "Watch out for him. He's a sonofabitch. But be nice to him. He has the power to get you out of here."

"Uncle Franklin is no longer pissed?" Whittaker asked. "I am to be sprung from durance vile?"

"That's up to you," Canidy said. "Some people think you're a bomb about to go off. Others think you may be useful to them. Once you hear why, you may want to stay in the loony bin."

Whittaker looked at Baker curiously.

"Has Dick told you about Morocco, Captain Whittaker?" Baker asked.

"No," Whittaker said simply.

"You know, Baker," Canidy said. "Loose lips lose ships."

"You are aware that he and I work for the Office of the Coordinator of Information?"

"Yes," Whittaker said.

"Would you mind telling me what you know about the COI?"

Whittaker shrugged. "It's a hush-hush outfit run by Bill Donovan," he said. "It's probably involved in very strange things, like espionage. Who knows what else?"

"Dick tell you that?" Baker asked.

"If he had, I wouldn't tell you and get him in trouble," Whittaker said. "I got some of it from that captain, Douglass, and some of it from the President. The rest I put together myself, like Sherlock Holmes."

Baker smiled. "Very good," he said.

"You get two gold stars to take home to Mommy," Canidy said.

Whittaker chuckled. Baker gave Canidy a dirty look.

"Why don't we stop the bullshit?" Canidy said.

"Why don't you?" Whittaker said.

"You first," Canidy said. "Do you know what was in that letter from MacArthur to the President?"

"No," Whittaker said. "I know it made General Marshall mad."

"That's one of the reasons you're down here," Canidy said. "They're worried you'll give the press the contents of the letter."

"I have no idea what it said," Whittaker said.

"And you'd take a polygraph, a lie-detector, test about that?" Baker asked.

Bull's-eye! Canidy thought. *I knew damned well they hadn't locked him in a loony bin for pissing off the general.*

"It was that embarrassing, was it?" Whittaker asked. "Yeah, I'll take a lie-detector test. Why not? Anything that'll get me out of here."

"The next question," Canidy said, "is, would you be willing to stick your neck out, mission unspecified?"

"No," Whittaker said, after a split second's hesitation. "I don't think I would."

"Your move, Baker," Canidy said. "He just proved he's sane."

"You've had a chance to talk to Eric Fulmar?" Baker asked.

"Of course, I have," Whittaker said.

"Did he tell you what happened in Morocco?" Baker asked.

"Why do I feel that no matter how I answer that, it will cost me?" Whittaker asked.

"Answer that one, Jimmy," Canidy said. "It's important."

Whittaker looked at Canidy, as if making up his mind whether or not to trust him.

"Yeah," he said finally. "He told me all about Morocco."

"Including him and me getting the shaft off the coast?" Canidy asked.

"Yeah, that, and how he finally got out. Tied up in the bilge of an Arab dhow, or whatever they call those little boats. . . . He didn't like that much either."

"I didn't think he would," Canidy said.

"A betrayal, followed by a kidnapping," Whittaker said. "You guys play dirty."

"Baker plays dirty," Canidy said. "I got left behind too. I'm one of the good guys, Jimmy."

"You're doing fine, Canidy," Baker said angrily. "Keep it up."

"Why not?" Canidy said. "This way you can tell Douglass and Donovan that I was the one who told him all the secrets and you had nothing to do with it."

"So tell me a secret," Whittaker said. "Things have been a little dull around here."

"Eric Fulmar is close to an important man in Morocco," Canidy said. "We want to use that again. We used him once."

"So he told me," Whittaker said. "And now you know that he's going to tell you to go fuck yourselves."

"If he does, then both of you stay here," Baker said.

"You just can't do that," Whittaker flared.

"We can, Jimmy," Canidy said. "And we will."

Whittaker looked at him.

"I notice you said 'we,' Dick," he said.

"Yeah, I said 'we,'" Canidy said. "I'm part of this."

"Otherwise you get locked up, too?"

"Partly that," Canidy said. "And partly because I think that what we're doing is so important that the usual rules don't apply."

"What's got me pissed off," Whittaker said, "is that just as soon as I got home, they started treating me like the enemy."

"You got in a cross fire between Marshall and MacArthur," Canidy said. "You were an innocent bystander who got in the line of fire. Nobody thinks you're the enemy."

"That's why there's a fence over the window and an MP outside, right?"

"We've come with the authority to take you out of here, Captain Whittaker," Baker said.

"What's the price?"

"You heard it," Canidy said. "You volunteer for the classic dangerous, secret mission, like Errol Flynn."

"I couldn't just go back to flying fighters?" Whittaker asked.

"Not any more than I can," Canidy said.

"OK," Whittaker said, after a moment's thought. "What the hell." He saluted Canidy, crisply but mockingly. "I await my orders, sir, and stand prepared to give my all for our noble cause. Whatever the hell that might be."

"This really isn't a joking matter, Whittaker," Baker said.

"I didn't think it was," Whittaker said coldly.

"You are now a member, more or less in good standing," Canidy said, "of Donovan's Dilettantes."

"What the hell is that?"

"I'll tell you later," Canidy said.

"And what's the 'more or less in good standing' mean?"

"Now we have to get Fulmar to cooperate," Canidy said.

"My getting out of here really depends on that?" Whittaker asked.

"I'm afraid so," Baker said.

"No," Canidy said firmly. "No, it doesn't, Jimmy. Baker, I'll go to Donovan himself about that. Jimmy's coming with us no matter what happens with Eric Fulmar."

Baker didn't reply.

"Well, Mr. Baker?" Whittaker asked after a moment.

"I can see no point in keeping you here any longer, Captain Whittaker," Baker said finally.

"OK," Whittaker said. "You guys are going to have a problem with Fulmar. He's really pissed. He's tried to escape four times."

"I didn't hear about that," Baker said. "Are you sure?"

"Yeah, I'm sure. The only reason he hasn't escaped is that everytime he was about to go, I squealed on him."

"He know about that?" Canidy asked.

Whittaker shook his head no. "It wasn't time to try something like that," Whittaker said. "It was getting close, but it wasn't time yet. I sort of thought there was a reason my childhood chum just 'coincidentally' wound up in the adjacent cell."

"You are very perceptive, Captain," Baker said approvingly.

"Lucky for you I am," Whittaker said. "*I* could have gotten out of here."

"How could you have done that?" Baker said scoffingly.

"Would you like to watch me take that forty-five away from that kid?" Whittaker said, nodding at the MP sitting on a folding chair in the fenced-in yard. "I'm surprised at you, Mr. Baker. I thought that surely Major Canidy had regaled you with tales of my exploits on Bataan."

"I'm well aware that you were decorated for valor, Captain Whittaker," Baker said condescendingly.

"I didn't get any medals for what I did," Whittaker said. "You could call my medals political medals. It pleased the people who gave them to me. It had nothing to do with what I did."

"What exactly did you do?" Baker asked.

"I blew a lot of things up," Whittaker said. "Sometimes after the Japs had captured them. I'm awfully good at explosions."

"Really?"

"That meant we had to take out sentries," Whittaker said conversationally.

"Indeed?" Baker said impatiently.

The next thing Baker knew, he was on the floor. Whittaker's knee against his back held him immobile. Whittaker's left hand was on his chin, twisting his neck so that it was exposed. Whittaker drew the index finger of his right hand across Baker's Adam's apple.

"I don't think," Whittaker said, still conversationally, "that I would have to cut that kid's throat to get his gun. All I would have to do is say 'Boo!'"

"Let him up, Jimmy," Canidy said, laughing. "I think you've made your point."

Baker rose awkwardly to his feet and straightened his clothing. Then he surprised Canidy.

"You're very good," Baker said. "I don't think I've ever seen anyone that fast."

That surprised Whittaker, too, and seemed to embarrass him.

"You figured out how to handle Fulmar?" Whittaker asked. "Or are you open to suggestion?"

"Let's hear it," Canidy said quickly.

"If you go in there and give him the business about volunteering, he's going to tell you to go fuck yourselves."

"What do you suggest?"

"Take him someplace now, without conditions. Maybe the house on Q Street, or better Summer Place. Dangle the carrot in front of his nose. Sugar catches more flies than vinegar. Right now you've got him trapped in a corner. Even Pekingese dogs will fight when you get them in a corner."

"Christ, I don't know," Baker said uncomfortably. But Canidy saw that he had not out of hand rejected Whittaker's reasoning.

"And you stay the hell out of sight," Whittaker said.

"He really hates you. Let Canidy go in there and tell him he's been sent to get us out of here."

"Would he believe that?" Baker asked.

"Why not? The last time he saw Canidy was after they'd both been left behind in Morocco. And he would probably take his cue from me."

"And what if he tries to escape?"

"Canidy and I can handle him until we get where we're going," Whittaker said.

"I'll have to have permission," Baker said.

"No," Canidy said. "If you ask for permission, Douglass is going to say no. You get on the telephone after we're airborne and call Washington, and tell them we're on the way. Whittaker's right, and you know he is. Your coming here was stupid."

Baker thought that over for a moment, then walked to the door and knocked. When the MP opened it, he asked him to fetch the provost marshal. When the provost marshal came, he told him that he was serving the court order which directed that Whittaker and Fulmar be placed in his custody.

"I won't be going with them," Baker said. "Can you provide transportation for me to post headquarters?"

He turned and spoke to Canidy.

"Unless you hear to the contrary while you're en route," he said, "go to Lakehurst. I'll have someone meet your plane."

And then he was gone.

3

The D18S was an hour out of Godman Field at Fort Knox when, very faintly, Canidy heard Cincinnati calling him.

"This is Navy Six-one-one. Go ahead, Cincinnati."

"Navy Six-one-one," Cincinnati replied so faintly that they had to repeat it four times before Canidy could understand, "this is a Navy Department priority in-flight advisory. You are directed to divert to Pope Field, North Carolina. Acknowledge."

Canidy acknowledged the message. But it took him several minutes to find the place, which was on the Fort Bragg reservation, just about as far on another heading as Washington. He turned the plane in the general direction of North Carolina, gave the controls over to Jim Whittaker, with an admonition to keep it as straight and level as his limited ability would permit, and went back in the cabin to plot the course.

Eric Fulmar, in hospital pajamas, robe, and slippers (another very bright idea of Whittaker's had been to tell Fulmar that his clothing had been misplaced; people in bathrobes are less prone to try something foolish), was sitting in the leather upholstered chair intended for the admiral whose plane the Beech was to have been.

There was something about Fulmar, Canidy thought, that made the purple U.S. Army hospital robe look like a silk dressing gown.

"Change of plans," Canidy announced. "We're going to North Carolina."

"Why?" Fulmar asked, concern in his voice.

"I really don't know, Eric," Canidy said. "But I wouldn't worry about it."

Fulmar raised himself out of the leather chair and, fascinated, watched over Canidy's shoulder as Canidy went through the business of plotting their new course.

"As closely as I can figure it," Canidy said when he had finished, "we will either make Pope Field with an hour-thirty's fuel aboard, or we will run out of fuel and crash-land somewhere along around here in the foothills of the Great Smoky Mountains."

Fulmar laughed dutifully. "You really know what you're doing, don't you?" he asked. "Whittaker know how to do this, too?"

"Yes, he does."

When Canidy went back to the cockpit and handed Whittaker the marked chart, he saw that Fulmar had followed.

"Is it all right if I stand here?" he asked.

"Sure," Canidy said quickly.

"Just don't touch anything," Whittaker snapped. That surprised Canidy, until he realized that Fulmar was being reminded he was a nonflier, an outsider, that there was an Order he was possibly, probably, not worthy of joining.

Whittaker, Canidy realized, seemed to have a Baker-like talent for manipulating other people.

Between that point and Pope Field, Navy Six-one-one received three more of the priority in-flight advisories ordering diversion to Pope. Whatever was going on at Pope, Canidy thought, someone considered it important enough to make one hell of an effort to make sure they went there.

As they approached Pope Field, Canidy took the controls and made the landing, wondering whether he had done so because Whittaker had never landed a C-45 before, or whether it was because he wanted to establish his superior position in the pecking order.

A Follow Me jeep met them at the threshold of the runway and led them to the transient parking ramp in front of base operations. When Canidy opened the door, a captain and a second lieutenant of the 508th Parachute Infantry Regiment of the 82nd Airborne Division were standing there. They were wearing gabardine jumpsuits, glistening jump boots, and steel helmets covered with netting. Over their jumpsuit tunics they wore an arrangement of straps and web belting from which hung canteens and pouches for first-aid kits, spare magazines for their .45 Colt pistols, compasses, and leather holsters for the pistols. The second lieutenant had a Thompson submachine gun dangling from his shoulder, and at his feet was a stuffed canvas Val-Pak.

"Major Canidy, sir?" the paratroop captain asked, saluting crisply and holding it until Canidy made a vague gesture in the general direction of the leather brim of his uniform cap.

"I'm Canidy," Canidy said.

"I have a classified message for you, sir," the captain said, "if you'll be good enough to show me your AGO[1] card."

Canidy found the card and passed it to him, and the captain said, "Thank you, sir," and handed him an envelope. Canidy tore it open and read it.

SECRET
PRIORITY
WAR DEPT WASH DC
COMMGEN FT BRAGG NC
DELIVER FOLLOWING MESSAGE MAJ R CANIDY USAAC EN
ROUTE POPE FIELD ABOARD USN R5D AIRCRAFT TAIL NO
SIX ONE ONE QUOTE PROCEED ANACOSTIA SIGNED

---

[1] The Adjutant General's Office issued plastic officers' identity cards.

CHENOWITH END QUOTE ADVISE DELIVERY MOST
EXPEDITIOUS MEANS FOSTER BRIG GEN

Canidy chuckled. That explained all the in-flight advisories. Cynthia Chenowith was wallowing in her role as spymaster.

"I am under instructions to deliver this officer into your custody, Major," the captain said.

"Who are you?" Canidy asked the young second lieutenant.

"Martin, sir, Second Lieutenant Holdsworth C., III."

The Disciple's son.

"Would you please sign for Lieutenant Martin, sir?" the captain said, and extended a clipboard and a pen. Canidy scrawled his name and handed it back.

"Would you be good enough to fill in the date-time block?" the captain said, giving it back to him. Canidy did so.

"Thank you, sir," the captain said crisply. "Now, sir, is there anything else you require before your departure?"

"I've got to put gas in the bird, and I would like to take a leak," Canidy said.

"Refueling has been arranged, sir," the captain said. "The truck should be here directly. There is a latrine in base operations, sir. Lieutenant Martin has visited the latrine. If you would like, sir, he can secure your aircraft while you are gone, sir."

Whittaker jumped out of the airplane. He was hatless, his necktie was pulled down, and his tunic was open. The paratroop captain looked at him with a mixture of shock and outrage. Whittaker promptly made it worse.

"And who are these two ferocious warriors?" he asked.

"Shut up, Jimmy," Canidy said. "I'm going to take a

leak. If you want to come with me, button your tunic, pull up your tie, and put your hat on."

"Yes, sir, Major, sir," Whittaker said. "I'm sorry to have embarrassed you, sir."

"Lieutenant," Canidy said to Martin, "under no circumstances is our passenger to leave the aircraft."

"Yes, sir," Lieutenant Martin said. Then, having taken a look at Fulmar, who was staring out the door, he went on in some embarrassment, "Sir, I feel I should tell the major I know this . . ." He searched for a proper word and finally came up with "individual."

"Fine," Canidy said. "Then you will have a chance for a little chat while Captain Whittaker and I are taking our leak."

"Yes, sir," Lieutenant Martin said militarily.

The captain was gone when they returned to the plane, and the fueling crew had topped off the tanks. Canidy made the preflight, and then motioned for Second Lieutenant Holdsworth Martin III to get aboard.

"Sir, may I inquire as to my destination?"

He had an accent. But not much, considering that Martin had been born in France, had a French mother, and had come to the United States for the first time just over two years before.

"I'm not sure if I have the authority to divulge that highly classified information," Canidy said. "But, once we get in the air, if you've got a class A uniform in your Val-Pak, you'd better change into it and hide that tommy gun someplace, or you're going to scare hell out of a bunch of bureaucrats."

"I was told to prepare myself for immediate overseas shipment, sir," Martin said.

"I don't know anything about that, Lieutenant," Canidy said. "But where you're probably going to spend the night is on the New Jersey seashore."

Second Lieutenant C. Holdsworth Martin III looked more disappointed than surprised.

4

"Anacostia clears Navy Six-one-one to land on runway three-one," the tower said. "The winds are negligible, the altimeter is three-niner-niner-eight."

"Understand three-one," Canidy replied.

"You've got it," Jim Whittaker said, taking his hands off the wheel.

"You don't think you can land it?" Canidy asked.

"What the hell, why not?" Whittaker replied, putting his hands back on the wheel and banking to the left to line himself up with the runway.

"Six-one-one on final," Canidy said to the microphone. "Wheels going down," he said, pressing the intercom switch. "Flaps going to twenty percent. It gets dirty quick, Jim. Don't chop too much power."

"Got you."

"Wheels down and locked. Flaps at twenty percent. Jesus Christ, I said *don't* chop the throttles!"

"Whoops!" Whittaker said, advancing the throttles to increase his glide path.

"Now it's too much," Canidy said.

"Work them yourself, goddamn it!" Whittaker snapped.

"You're flying it; go around if you have to," Canidy replied.

"Oh shit," Whittaker said, cut the throttles again, and flared out, too high, over the runway. They landed hard, bounced into the air, landed again, bounced again, and finally touched down, again hard; but this time they stayed on the ground.

"The next thing you do is lower the tail," Canidy said dryly as Whittaker made a violent move to keep on the runway.

"Fuck you," Whittaker said as he eased back on the stick to raise the nose and lower the tail.

"Anacostia, Six-one-one on the ground at five past midnight. . . . And at five and a half past midnight, and *finally* at six past midnight."

"Fuck you, wiseass," Whittaker said as he began to brake.

There was laughter in the tower operator's voice when he came back on the air. "If you're sure you're finally down, Six-one-one, take taxiway three left to the transient parking area. Your ground transportation is waiting for you."

"We have apparently cheated death once again, Anacostia. I came on the airways from Raleigh. Will you close me out with Washington control, please?" Canidy said.

"Will do, Six-one-one," the tower operator said, still laughing.

"And will you arrange to have me fueled, please?"

"A fuel truck will meet you, Six-one-one."

"What happens here?" Whittaker asked.

The translation of that is, Canidy thought, *am I going to get to see Cynthia Chenowith?*

"We'll have to wait and see, Jimmy," Canidy said.

As they taxied past base operations Canidy saw Chief Ellis standing inside the glass door.

"That landing was a little rough, wasn't it, Dick?" Fulmar asked when Canidy walked through the cabin to open the door.

Canidy looked at him. He was mopping at his bathrobe with a paper towel. He had apparently been drinking a cup of coffee when Whittaker had made the landing.

"I didn't think it was all that bad, Eric," Canidy said.

"So far as I know, that was Whittaker's first landing in a twin-engine airplane."

He saw that Second Lieutenant Holdsworth C. Martin III's eyes grew very wide.

Canidy went the rest of way down the aisle, opened the door, and jumped onto the ground.

Ellis was there. And so was the gas truck and a crew of white hats. Ellis saluted, which he would not have done if no one had been there.

"Captain Douglass's compliments, Major," he said. "And would the major come to the base ops building?"

Canidy looked at his watch. It was twelve minutes past midnight.

"I have passengers aboard, Chief," he said as formally as Ellis. "What about them?"

"They're to remain aboard the aircraft, sir," Ellis said. "I'm to see to that."

"Be careful, Ellis," Canidy said softly. "One of them has a Thompson submachine gun and high hopes that he can shoot it at somebody."

"Oh, Christ!" Ellis said, chuckling. "What are a pair of old sailors like us doing in this fucked-up outfit?"

When Canidy walked into base ops, he was directed to an office on the second floor. Captain Douglass and Stanley Fine were inside, sipping on coffee in heavy china mugs.

"Everything go all right?"

"Young Martin has a submachine gun," Canidy said, "that scares me a little."

"When you get to Deal, take it away from him," Douglass said.

"Was all that priority in-flight advisory business necessary?" Canidy asked. "And the secret message ordering me here? Didn't Miss Spymaster of 1942 get a little excited?"

"So far as you're concerned, she does nothing right, does she?" Captain Douglass said coldly. "But just to keep the record straight, she did what she did because I told her to. And I was really doing you a favor, or so I thought. If we hadn't managed to divert you, you would have found yourself flying back here for Captain Fine from Deal tonight, and flying to North Carolina to get young Martin tomorrow."

"Why?" Canidy asked. "There's no more trains or planes? Or we don't get a priority?"

"Christ, you don't give up, do you? The colonel said you were to pick Martin up at Bragg. He didn't tell me why. If you like, the next time you see him, you ask him. And I ordered you here. Can you get all that straight?"

Canidy touched his forehead in sort of a salute.

"How's Whittaker?" Douglass asked.

"He landed the plane just now," Canidy said. "He's all right."

"Baker is very impressed with him," Douglass said.

Canidy laughed.

"Why is that amusing?"

"Did Baker tell you Whittaker demonstrated how easily he could have cut his throat?"

"Yes, as a matter of fact, he did," Douglass said, which surprised Canidy. "He thinks we should put Whittaker in charge of training in that sort of thing at the school."

"What school?"

"We're starting a school for agents, new people in COI," Douglass said. "When we can find the time, we're going to run you through it."

"I'm not sure I'd like that," Canidy said.

"No one asked you," Douglass said. "Baker also told me Whittaker has some good ideas about how to deal with Fulmar."

"Yes, he does."

"Well, for the time being, keep a close eye on them, but let Whittaker try his method."

"I'd planned to," Canidy said.

"Good," Douglass said tightly. "Now to the business at hand. From this point, you and I will be talking about the African flight. It is classified top secret."

"Yes, sir."

"Captain Fine has been briefed on certain aspects of the mission and provided with certain documents. You will note that he has also been provided with a pistol and that there is provision to handcuff the briefcase containing the documents to his wrist."

Canidy looked at Fine, then at the briefcase he held in his hand. It was handcuffed to his wrist.

"The documents placed in Fine's possession are to be in one of five places," Douglass said. "In his possession; in your possession; in Commander Reynolds's safe at Lakehurst; in Eldon Baker's possession; or in mine."

"Yes, sir."

"The lock has a sequence counter," Douglass said. "It counts every time the case is opened. You will keep a record of those numbers. If you should ever open the briefcase and the number does not tally, you are immediately to notify Cynthia, Baker, or me. In that order."

Canidy nodded.

"And any documents removed from the briefcase are to be returned to it before the case is shut again. The documents are not to be separated. Understood?"

"Yes, sir."

"The details of this operation are known in full only to Baker, myself, and Chief Ellis. And, when we have finished filling each other in, to you two. Understood?"

"Yes, sir."

"I have explained to Captain Fine your other responsibilities at Summer Place," Douglass said. "And that you will have your hands full for the next few days getting everybody settled. So what I suggest you do,

Dick, is put all this material in Reynolds's safe tonight, when you get there, and forget it until after the Fourth."

"When we get there this *morning,* you mean," Canidy said, and then, puzzled, asked, "The Fourth?"

"The Fourth of July," Douglass said. "You remember, Independence Day? Parades? Fireworks? Patriotic speeches?"

"Jesus, are we going to celebrate it in the middle of a war?"

"Even more enthusiastically than before the war," Douglass said. "Now it's considered important for morale."

"I know," Canidy said, straight-faced. "I'll see if I can't come up with the makings, lobsters, beer, corn on the cob, that sort of thing, and then we'll have a clambake on the beach."

"That's an idea, certainly," Douglass said. "Why not?"

"If that's all, Captain? And presuming you're ready, Stanley?"

"Anytime," Fine said. His eyes were smiling. He had caught Canidy's sarcasm, even though it had sailed right over Captain Douglass's head.

"Have a good flight," Captain Douglass said. "Tell Chief Ellis I'll be in the car."

Seven

1

The Willard Hotel
Washington, D.C.
July 2, 1942

CHARITY HOCHE, SARAH's friend from Bryn Mawr, had arrived at half past five the day before. She was a tall, sharp-featured blonde. And she was so very Main Line that Sarah and Ann Chambers had joked behind her back that there was no way to tell whether Katharine Hepburn had lurked in the shrubbery at Bryn Mawr to study Charity before she made *The Philadelphia Story*, or whether Charity had gone to the movie over and over so that she could faithfully copy the actress's mannerisms and nasal speech.

Despite the heat, Charity had swept into the suite with an ankle-length mink coat over her shoulders. Under this she wore the college-girl uniform of sweater and pleated plaid skirt. She had large breasts, which Sarah and Ann called behind her back the Hoche Dairy and which the sweater did little to conceal.

"Daahling!" she cried. "I can't *wait* to see it."

"You can't wait to see what?" Sarah asked, although she knew perfectly well that Charity meant the baby.

"Your *child*, Little Mother! What else?"

Charity searched through the suite until she found the crib, and then picked up Joe with a skill that surprised Sarah.

"He's adorable!" Charity said.

"Thank you," Sarah said.

"I would never have dreamed you had it in you," Charity said. "But then, no one did, did they? Still waters, daahling, that sort of thing."

I should be offended and angry, Sarah thought, *but of course I'm not. Charity is Charity.*

"If this precious little bundle is the wages of sin, daahling, you're just going to have to find a sailor for me."

Sarah laughed, although she knew she shouldn't. "The sailors seem to be spoken for," she said. "Would you settle for an Air Corps fighter pilot?"

"Have you one?" Charity asked, bright with interest.

"I've got one coming in the morning," Sarah said. "He's the man who saved Eddie's life."

"A bona fide hero? Marvelous! I wanted to see you, of course, and the bundle of joy here, but I wasn't really looking forward to a whole weekend of watching you change his diapers. Which, incidentally, is necessary now."

She handed the baby to Sarah, and then gestured at the furniture in the room. It had been furnished with the reputation of Child and Company, Merchant Bankers in mind. Most of the Louis XIV furniture was genuine, and so were the Matisse and the Gainsborough and the other paintings hung on the brocade walls.

"It looks like a museum," Charity pronounced. "The only thing that's missing are velvet ropes and signs saying Please Do Not Touch."

"It belongs to the bank," Sarah said. "My father turned it over to us. You just can't find anywhere to live in Washington."

"Being rich is nice, isn't it?" Charity said. "What about the admiral? How did he react to finding out that supporting you isn't going to be the usual problem?"

"Ed is a lieutenant commander," Sarah said. "He can support us."

"Not like this," Charity said flatly.

She followed Sarah into the bedroom and sniffed loudly as Sarah changed Joe's diaper.

"My God, do they all smell that bad, or have you been feeding that innocent child something you shouldn't have?"

"You get used to it," Sarah said, and then: "Ed's father is a commodities broker in Chicago. His mother is Ann's father's sister."

"In other words, the Chambers Publishing Company," Charity said.

"Uh-huh," Sarah said.

"So you won't have to take in washing, will you? What did you get from them for a wedding present?"

"They pretended they believed that Ed and I were married secretly before he went off to the Flying Tigers."

"That got them off cheap, didn't it?" Charity said.

"They wanted to give us a car," Sarah said, "but my father had already given us one."

"Hold out for a newspaper," Charity said. "That would be a nice little nest egg in case the admiral misbehaves when the novelty wears off."

"Before he gets here, Charity," Sarah said sharply. "I want to ask you not to make fun of his being in the Navy. He's an Annapolis graduate, a career officer, and he might not understand you."

Somewhat to Sarah's surprise, Charity and Ed got along very well. They quickly came up with a half-dozen mutual acquaintances. Then, again surprising Sarah, Charity firmly insisted that Ed take Sarah to dinner while she baby-sat Joe.

Ed even laughed heartily when Charity said that she had to "get in practice, if I'm to believe half of what Sarah says about your friend Douglass."

In the morning, after Ed had gone off to work, they dressed Joe, took Sarah's 1941 Cadillac Fleetwood from the Willard garage, and drove to the airport.

"I think I should have told Ann to take a cab," Sarah said. "This is nearly out of gas, and I don't have any more ration coupons."

"Then buy some on the black market," Charity said.

"Oh, I couldn't do that," Sarah said. "My God, Charity, my husband is a naval officer."

"What's that got to do with being out of gas?"

"If you can't figure that out, I certainly couldn't explain it to you," Sarah said coldly.

At the airport, Charity Hoche went into the terminal to meet Ann while Sarah and the baby waited in the car. When Charity reappeared with Ann, there was a Marine officer Ann had picked up on the plane to carry her bags.

"I promised the lieutenant we'd drive him into town," Ann said.

They drove back across the Potomac into Washington and dropped Ann's bag carrier at the Temporary Navy Department buildings across from the Smithsonian.

"Now what?" Ann asked.

"We go to Bolling Field to meet Doug Douglass," Sarah said. "Praying that we don't run out of gas."

"Out of ration coupons?" Ann asked.

"And, my God, don't suggest buying black-market gas," Charity said. "Sarah will turn you in as a Nazi agent."

"Well, if it gets to push and shove," Ann said, "she'll just have to swallow her patriotism. I've got coupons for twenty gallons."

"Where'd you get them?"

"Journalism is an essential occupation," Ann said. "I stole them from my city editor."

"You two may think you're clever," Sarah said. "But I don't."

"Amazing, isn't it," Ann said, "what marriage does to a girl? One moment she's making whoopee with sailors in the backseat, and the next she's delivering lectures on patriotic duty."

I was about to say something I would have later regretted, Sarah thought. *But these are my best friends in the world, Ann especially.*

"Sailor," Sarah said. "Singular. One sailor."

But I will not put black-market gas in this car, if we have to walk back to the hotel.

Getting into Bolling Field wasn't as easy as they'd expected. The captain they went to had orders that only journalists on his list (they'd hoped Ann's press card would see them waved through) were to be admitted. But Ann finally charmed the captain into passing her in as a guest and not as a journalist.

There was a chain-link fence beside the base operations building, and Sarah pulled the Cadillac's nose against it. Then, because she had a naval dependent's ID card, Sarah went into base operations to ask what they knew about the arrival of an Air Corps plane from Selma, Alabama.

Very politely they told her they could not give out that information to her, dependent or not.

"What do we want to know?" Charity asked. After Sarah told her, she went into base operations. Five minutes later she came back and told them that an Air Corps P-38, probably theirs, had called in extending his ETA by forty-five minutes, but he should be on the ground in ten or fifteen minutes.

"How did you do that?" Sarah asked.

"She kept brushing lint off her boobs," Ann said. "Right?"

"That, too," Charity said. "But I think what got to him was the way I kept licking my lips."

"You two are disgusting!" Sarah said.

Five minutes later, there was unusual activity on the field. Two red fire engines, what looked like a water truck, an ambulance, and several pickup trucks, all with flashing red lights, raced across the field and stationed themselves on either side of the main runway.

"I don't like the look of that," Ann said seriously.

"What kind of an airplane are we looking for?" Charity asked.

"A P-38," Ann said. "It has twin engines and a dual tail structure."

"Like that?" Charity asked, pointing.

"Like that," Ann said.

A P-38, its polished aluminum skin glistening in the bright sunlight, straightened up from a steep bank and lined up with the runway.

"One of its things isn't working," Charity said.

"Engines, idiot," Ann snapped. "He's coming in on one engine."

The fire trucks and crash equipment proved to be unnecessary. The P-38 touched down in a perfect three-point landing (*a greaser,* Ann thought), then turned off the runway. It disappeared for a minute or two. But then, trailed by one fire truck and several of the other vehicles, it reappeared on the taxiway right in front of them. A ground handler showed the pilot where to park.

The canopy was back and they could see the pilot clearly as he taxied into position. He was bareheaded and wearing sunglasses. Ten red and white Japanese Meatballs and the legend *Major Doug Douglass* were painted on the nose of the fuselage.

"Now, there's a sight," Charity Hoche said softly, "that would make the Virgin Mary, much less any red-blooded American female patriot, say this one, jump on her back and spread her knees."

"Charity!" Sarah said.

Ann Chambers grinned. "I think that's yours, Charity," she said. "Say thank you to Sarah."

"Thank you, Sarah," Charity said.

"I don't know you two," Sarah said, trying hard to suppress a smile.

"I'm glad he didn't hear her," Ann said. "But she's right, Sarah. Nature takes care of that, making the warriors powerfully attractive before they go off to get killed. She wants them to impregnate the maidens while they still can."

Sarah looked at her. "Are you trying to say that's what you think happened to me?"

"If the shoe fits, Cinderella." Ann laughed, and then, when she saw that Douglass had shut the P-38 down and climbed down to the ground, she reached over and tapped the Cadillac's horn: *Shave and a haircut, two bits.*

It caught Douglass's attention, and after a moment's confusion he smiled, waved, and, ignoring the people who were now fussing over the engine that had failed, walked over to the fence. Ann stepped out of the car, then Charity, and finally Sarah, carrying Joe.

"You're Sarah," Doug Douglass said. "I've seen your picture."

He now had a battered cap on the back of his head and was wearing a battered horsehide jacket on the front of which was painted the Flying Tiger insignia. On its back was a Chinese flag and an extensive legend in Chinese calligraphy.

"What happened out there?" Sarah asked.

"I blew a jug in my right fan," he said. "That's why I was late."

"What does that mean?" Charity asked breathlessly.

"He lost a cylinder in the engine," Ann explained.

"And I know who you are, then," Douglass said to Ann. "You're the one with the stagger-wing Beech. Canidy told me about you."

"Guilty," Ann said.

I must be in love, she thought. *All it took to get my heart thumping was to hear that sonofabitch has been talking about me.*

"And I'm Charity," Charity said, brushing lint off her sweater front and looking right into his eyes.

"God, I hope so!" Douglass said. "Well, ladies, your welcome makes me feel like a conquering hero."

"That was the intention," Sarah said.

Douglass took a close look at the baby. "I hate to tell you this," he said, "but he looks like his father."

"He's handsome, you mean," Sarah said.

Douglass laughed. "It'll take me a couple of minutes to do the paperwork about the blown jug," he said. "I'll make it as quick as I can."

It took him, in fact, closer to an hour.

"Sorry it took so long," he said when he finally appeared. "But there was a silver lining. The maintenance officer, his chin on his knees, just told me there's no way he can swap engines for me before the Fourth of July. Which means I can be here longer than I thought I could."

"Great," Sarah said. "Would you mind driving? I think we could make it off the base easier if you did."

"Sure," he said, and slipped behind the wheel. "Where's Eddie?"

"He had to work," Sarah said, "but he should be home by one o'clock."

"Where's your friend Canidy?" Ann asked.

"God only knows," Douglass said. "He works for my father. Whatever they're doing, they're not supposed to talk about it, and they don't. When we find somewhere where there's a phone, I'll see if I can run him down."

Wonderful! Ann thought.

They were well into the District before Douglass happened to glance at the fuel gauge. "Does the fuel gauge work?" he asked.

Ann giggled.

"If it does, we're running on the fumes," Douglass said.

"Sarah's out of ration coupons," Ann said.

"Well, we'll just have to get some on the black market," Douglass said.

"How does that fit in with your patriotism?" Ann asked innocently.

"What's running out of gas got to do with the patriotism?" Douglass asked.

Ann and Charity were now both giggling.

And then Douglass suddenly pulled the car to a curb.

"Don't tell me we're out of gas?" Ann asked.

"Not yet," Douglass said. "Just almost. There's a cop. I'm going to ask him."

"Ask him what?"

"Where I can get some gas," Douglass said. He got out of the car and walked toward a policeman.

In a minute, Douglass was back behind the wheel.

"There's a Shell station," he said. "Second right, and then two blocks up on the left. He said he wasn't sure if they had coupons too, but he thought they did."

Fifteen minutes later, the fuel gauge of the Cadillac indicated past full, and there was a sheet of ration coupons in the glove compartment.

Sarah wasn't pleased, but she didn't say anything.

When they got to the Willard, Ed was already there, and Admiral Hawley was with him.

"I didn't want to intrude on this reunion," the admiral said. "But I did want to meet you and shake your hand, Major Douglass. That was an incredible bit of flying you did when you picked Ed up."

With genuine modesty, Douglass downplayed what he had done, but there was no question in anyone's mind, least of all Sarah's, that Doug Douglass was a storybook hero.

There were drinks. Then, without asking, Sarah

called room service and ordered shrimp salads—it was too hot to eat anything else—and the women watched while Douglass and Ed, using hand movements, explained the fine points of attacking a Japanese bomber formation in diving sweeps.

It was nearly two-thirty before the admiral left. Ann decided it was time then to again bring up Dick Canidy—before Douglass and Ed Bitter had more to drink.

Douglass settled himself comfortably on one of a pair of couches facing a low table that was in front of the fireplace. After Charity had brought him another drink and Ann the telephone, he consulted a small pocket notebook for the number and dialed it.

Ann moved close so that she could hear both ends of the conversation.

"Liberty 6-4133," a male voice said.

"Captain Peter Douglass, please," Douglass said.

"May I ask who's calling?"

"This is Major Peter Douglass, Jr.," Doug said.

"Oh, sure, just a moment, Major, I'll ring."

"Captain Douglass's office," a female voice said.

"This is Major Douglass. May I speak with my father, please?"

"Oh, I'm sorry, Major, he's in conference. I could interrupt, but it would be better if you could call back in an hour."

Damn! Ann thought. *In an hour he's either going to be drunk, or else in a closet somewhere with Charity, or both.*

"Miss Chenowith in there with him?"

"No, she's not."

"Could you switch me to her?"

There were some clicking noises, and then another female voice came on the line.

"Twenty-eight," she said.

"Cynthia, this is Doug Douglass."

"Well, we've been expecting you, Major. How

was the flight? I guess you need a ride. Where are you?"

"The flight was fine, thank you," he said. "But what I need is Dick Canidy's phone number. My dad's holding yet another conference and won't be free for an hour."

"He's not here," Cynthia Chenowith said.

"Where is he?"

There was a perceptible hesitation before she replied.

"Actually, he's in New Jersey."

"Will you give me the number, please?"

There was a longer hesitation before she finally gave him the number. "When the switchboard answers, Major," she continued, "you ask if this is the Foster residence. Got that? Foster. Otherwise, they won't put you through."

"Foster residence," Douglass parroted. "Got it. Tell my father I'll catch up with him later."

"I will," she said.

Douglass broke the connection with his finger, and then gave the operator the number Cynthia had given him.

"Asbury 4-9301," a male voice answered.

"Is this the Foster residence?"

"Yes, it is," the male voice replied.

"Can I get Dick Canidy on this?"

"I'll ring the major for you," the man said.

Canidy came on the line, answering with his name.

"Early Bird Leader, this is Early Bird One," Douglass said.

Canidy laughed happily. "Early Bird" had been their plane-to-plane call sign in China.

"You bastard, where are you?"

"I am sitting here with *Commander* Bitter, no less, three good-looking ladies, gallons of booze, and a baby. The important question is, where the hell are you?"

"I'm sitting here up to my ass in fuel-consumption charts," Canidy said.

Ann became aware that her heart was beating; and when she put her fingers to her cheek, she confirmed that her face was flushed.

"Where's there?"

There was a hesitation before Canidy answered.

"On the seashore, near Lakehurst NAS," he said.

"Well, drop whatever you're doing, get on a train, and come here before Bitter drinks all the booze."

"Christ, I wish I could, Doug," Canidy said. "But it's out of the question."

"Why is it out of the question?"

"I've got the duty."

"Over the whole goddamned Fourth of July weekend?"

"Over the whole goddamned Fourth of July weekend," Canidy confirmed. "I'm really sorry, Doug. I just can't."

"Ah shit!" Douglass said, disappointed but understanding. "It would have been fun. Well, at least say hello to *the commander* and the girls."

He handed the telephone to Bitter.

"What was that 'Early Bird' business?" Charity asked.

"That was our call sign in China," Douglass said.

"What's this story I heard about Canidy being sent home for cowardice?" Ann asked.

"Bullshit is what it was," Douglass said. "They used that story to explain why he suddenly took off to work for my father. Christ, the first time out, he attacked by himself nine Jap bombers and shot down five of them. He was the first ace in the AVG."

Ann looked at Ed Bitter in triumph. Then she took the telephone from him.

"Hello, Dick, how are you? This is Ann Chambers. Remember me?"

"What's a nice girl like you doing with those two?" Canidy replied.

"It's all right," she said. "We have Sarah as a chaperone."

Sarah took that as her cue to take the telephone. Ann gave it up willingly.

Now that I finally got to talk to him, I couldn't think of a damned thing to say.

But by the time everybody including Charity had talked to Canidy and the phone was back in its usual place, she did have something to say.

"I think I know where he is," she said.

Douglass looked at her curiously.

"I was there once with my father," Ann said. "'On the seashore, near Lakehurst.' He and Chesley Haywood Whittaker were friends. And Chesty Whittaker had a big place on the shore at Deal. Summer Place."

"I think you're right," Douglass said. "Donovan and my father have taken over the Whittaker place here in D.C. That makes sense. But so what?"

"So, no matter what he's doing, I don't think he'll be doing it on the Fourth. If you two wanted to see him, I mean."

"Damn right I want to see him," Ed Bitter said, a little thickly. The alcohol was getting to him. "Jesus, I owe him an apology."

"Yes, I think you do," Ann said, reinforcing that argument.

"The seashore sounds splendid to me," Charity offered. "Anyplace but this steam bath."

"But how would we get there?" Bitter asked reasonably. "I don't want to take the baby on a train. And it would take forever. And we don't *know* he's where you think he is."

"We can drive," Douglass said.

"You need gas to drive," Bitter said.

"The tank in your car is full," Douglass said. "And

there's a hundred gallons' worth of coupons in the glove compartment.''

Ed Bitter, surprising his wife, accepted the black-market gasoline and ration coupons without comment. But, as if he sensed that they really shouldn't be going through with their plan, he offered a last objection.

"Who's going to drive?" he asked, focusing his eyes with an effort on Douglass. "I'm a little tiddly myself, and you're obviously in no condition to drive.''

"I'll drive," Ann said.

2

Summer Place
Deal, New Jersey
2230 Hours 3 July 1942

Even with a priority, there had been no airline seat available from Louisville for Eldon Baker. And he had elected not to use his priority to evict from their berths officers traveling by train from Fort Knox northward. He had consequently caught what sleep he could sitting up in a passenger car to Washington, and it had been nearly six in the evening of July 3 when he finally reached Summer Place.

He was not especially pleased with what he found. First, Canidy had allowed Second Lieutenant C. Holdsworth Martin III to call his parents. Mrs. Chesley Haywood Whittaker had then taken it upon herself to invite Mr. and Mrs. C. Holdsworth Martin, Jr., to come out of the brutal heat of Manhattan and spend the Fourth of July with their son at Summer Place.

"*I* said they could come," an unrepentant Canidy told Baker after the damage was done. "Martin *père* came to the horn and asked me if it would be all right.''

"You should have politely told him no," Baker said.

"I was not about to do that. From where I sit, one of Donovan's Disciples ranks the hell out of a lowly Dilettante like myself. And I also thought it would please the admiral."

"And you didn't think you should keep them away from Fulmar?" Baker demanded. At this moment, Eric Fulmar, wearing trunks and a beach robe, was sitting with the Martins and the admiral beneath one of the umbrellaed tables on the lawn.

"Again, Eldon, when Martin *père* asked to speak to him, I didn't think it was my place to tell him no."

The damage has been done, Baker decided. *First thing in the morning, I will report what's happened to Captain Douglass. In the meantime, I will do what I came here to do.*

"Captain Douglass thought it would be a good idea if I sat in on the first session between you and Fine. In case the two of you don't have everything you should have."

"He told me to put the briefcase in Reynolds's safe at Lakehurst and start on it fresh after the Fourth."

"Then, inasmuch as Commander Reynolds doesn't know me, I think that you and I had better ride out there to get it," Baker said.

"What about waiting until after the Fourth?"

"I plan to leave here at five tomorrow afternoon," Baker said. "So it's either tonight or tomorrow morning."

"Tonight, then," Canidy said. "Tomorrow we're going to have a clambake on the beach. I wouldn't want anything to interfere with that."

"Let's go, then," Baker said.

"You realize we'll have to make the trip twice? Once to get it, and once to put it back?"

"Unless you elect to sleep with it handcuffed to your wrist," Baker said.

When they returned from Lakehurst, Canidy politely asked Admiral de Verbey if he might use his war room.

He then collected Fine, who had been sitting on the porch with Mrs. Whittaker, and led him up to it.

"In the somewhat changed circumstances," Baker said, "I think the best thing to do is run briefly through the whole mission. If either of you have questions, interrupt me. It may not be necessary to remind both of you, but I will: the classification of this operation is top secret cabinet level. And the cabinet's access is on a need-to-know basis. For your general information, the President has decided that Vice President Wallace does not have the need to know."

"We're impressed, Eldon," Canidy said. "Can we move on now?"

Baker opened the briefcase, made note of the lock-open sequence count, and took out a large-scale map. He spread the map out on the table so that it was right-side up in front of Canidy.

"If you will look, you can see, halfway down the leg of Africa near the Portuguese Angola, Rhodesia, and Belgian Congo borders, a town called Kolwezi," Baker said. "It's in the Mitumba mountain chain in Katanga Province."

Canidy found it and pointed. Lindbergh's guess had been off by no more than two or three hundred miles.

Baker next handed him a sheaf of photographs: brand-new ten-inch-square aerial photographs, some eight-by-ten-inch prints, which were also new, and some other photographs that appeared to have been blown up from old snapshots.

These showed a small town of frame buildings with several huge excavations around it. The excavations were so large that roads had been carved into its sides. There were also smelters and mountains of smelter and mine tailings. There was an airfield, which looked unpaved, except perhaps with mine or smelter tailings which were often used for that purpose. The "tower" was about ten feet off the ground, and none of the airplanes on the parking ramp was multiengined.

"What we have to do, in *absolute* secrecy," Baker said as Canidy worked his way through the pictures, "is remove from Kolwezi ten thousand pounds of a very special cargo and bring it here."

"What kind of cargo?" Canidy asked.

"An ore," Baker said. "Please do not ask any further questions about the ore. All you have to know is that it is a dry, nonexplosive substance. Some of it has the characteristics of ordinary dirt, and some of it is what they call spillings, which means with rocks in it. The rest of it is in the form of smelter residue. It will all be packed in canvas bags, each weighing approximately ninety pounds."

Canidy nodded. "That's a lot of weight," he said. "But it's within the weight/range limitations of several of the flight plans Colonel Lindbergh laid out."

"What did you say, Dick?" Stanley Fine asked, shocked.

"I don't think you should talk about that," Baker said.

"Oh, for Christ's sake!" Canidy flared. "Stan, the transport expert who laid most of this on was Colonel Charles Lindbergh. But don't say anything. The President thinks he's a Nazi sympathizer."

Fine shook his head in disbelief.

"The departure point will be Newark Airport," Baker resumed. "You will fly the bomber stream to Ireland, via Gander Field, Newfoundland, and from Ireland to Portugal and then down the west coast of Africa, stopping here, and here, and here. To Kolwezi. There will be a crew of three. We have recruited a pilot and copilot from the Air Transport Command. They were both formerly Pan American pilots who have flown to South Africa before. Not, it is germane to note, in land aircraft. They flew Sikorsky seaplanes.

"They will transition both of you into the C-46, so that if it becomes necessary you can fly the aircraft. Coming out of Kolwezi, there will be a passenger."

"Who?" Canidy asked.

"Grunier," Baker said.

"Grunier?" Canidy asked. "Oh, Christ! Again?"

"We hope to have his family in England within two weeks," Baker said, again ignoring him. "That was his price for his cooperation in this, and we met it."

"He's in the Belgian Congo?" Canidy asked.

"He will be," Baker replied. "That's one of the things holding us up. We have to put him in and then make sure he's in place before we send the airplane."

"What's he going to be doing there?" Canidy asked.

"He's going to make sure that the bags contain what we're paying for," Baker said. "We're going to send a substantial sum of money into the Belgian Congo with him to pay for all this. An even more substantial amount will be paid after you pick it up."

"How much is 'substantial'?" Canidy asked.

Baker thought it over before he replied.

"The deposit was a hundred thousand dollars' worth of Swiss francs, gold coins. The payment due on delivery is four hundred thousand."

"And why do we trust Grunier? Not only with a hundred thousand dollars, but after what we've already done to him?"

"Because we told him that it would be even easier to send his family back to France than it was to sneak them out," Baker said matter-of-factly. "And because he has been told that if he does what we want him to, his family will be brought here and he will be given a job in Colorado."

"And he believes you?"

"Well, for one thing, it's true," Baker said. "And for another, people believe what they want to believe."

"What the hell is this stuff?"

"I told you, you're not to ask that sort of question," Baker said. "Now, about the aircraft. If I'm wrong about anything, Canidy, please interrupt."

He was looking through the papers on the table when

there was a knock at the door. Baker looked at it impatiently.

"Yeah?" Canidy called.

"I think you had better come downstairs, Mr. Canidy," a voice said. Canidy recognized it as the security duty officer's.

"Won't it wait?" Canidy replied. "We're almost through in here."

"I think you had better come right down, Mr. Canidy," the ex–FBI agent said doggedly.

"Duty apparently calls, Eldon," Canidy said. "What would you suggest I do?"

"Let's wind this up," Fine said. "If all we're going to do is talk about the airplane, I'd really prefer to look at it myself."

Baker thought that over a moment and then nodded. He started folding the map.

"Be down in a minute," Canidy called to the security man.

When Baker had the documents back inside the briefcase, he locked it and handed it to Fine.

"You'd better use the handcuff, Captain," he said.

"Christ, yes, Stanley. For all we know, Joseph Goebbels *and* Hermann Göring are downstairs upsetting the guards," Canidy said.

I hope it's something as simple as that. From the security guy's tone of voice, I am more than a little afraid he's going to tell me the admiral has had a heart attack.

They went quickly down the wide stairway to the foyer. There, surrounded by both COI security guards and rifle-armed sailors, were Lieutenant Commander Edwin Bitter, USN; Major Peter Douglass, Jr., USAAC; and three women, one of them with a baby in her arms.

"I'm really embarrassed about this, Major Canidy," the crew-cut young lieutenant (j.g.) in charge of the Navy guard detail said. "My sentry at the gate passed them into the compound. Because one of them was a naval officer, he said, and because they said they were here with your permission."

"Oh, Christ!" Canidy said in exasperation, and then he laughed.

He had taken a close look at Douglass. Not only was his face smeared with lipstick, but somehow the buttons on his fly did not match the holes.

"You two need keepers," he said to Douglass and Bitter.

"Who are these people?" Baker snapped.

"The one with the lipstick on his face is Peter Douglass, Jr.," Canidy said. "Doug, say hello to Eldon Baker. He works for your father."

"What are they doing here?" Baker demanded icily.

"I guess they came for the clambake," Canidy said. He turned to the young Navy officer of the guard. "I can't say there's no harm done," he said. "But they're not dangerous. You can let the white hats go."

"None of these people are to leave the grounds without my specific permission," Baker said.

"Until I'm relieved, Eldon—and you don't have the authority to do that—I'm in charge. Which means you issue orders through me," Canidy said. Then he looked at the others. "But he's right. I'm sorry; now that you're here, you'll have to stay here until they decide what to do with you."

"Sounds fine to me, Dick," Douglas said. "You said something about a clambake?"

"Baker, why don't you get on the phone and tell Captain Douglass about our guests," Canidy said, laughing. "I know you're dying to do that."

Baker walked quickly into the library.

Canidy looked at the others.

Sarah Child Bitter seemed close to tears, and her husband, Canidy thought, looked as if he had just farted in church.

"The first thing we have to do is get everybody bedded down," he said. "All right, lady prisoners, follow me. There's a butler around here someplace, and we'll get him to bed you down. The male prisoners will find the bar to the right."

3

Summer Place
Deal, New Jersey
1005 Hours 4 July 1942

As his Packard rolled past the sailor guarding the private road to the Whittaker estate, Colonel William J. Donovan wanted to believe the affair at Summer Place was something like *The Marx Brothers at the Seashore*—because he thought it was so real, so immediate, and the security implications were so monumental that his mind couldn't take it all in.

It was proving impossible on a bright Fourth of July, in your own car with your wife sitting beside you, riding up to a house and friends you knew well, to see a bona fide threat not only to the coming amphibious landing on the North Coast of Africa but to the Army Air Corps' plans for the bombardment of Germany, and even to the development of the weapon that might, very likely, decide the outcome of the war.

When they approached the house, they told the chauffeur (who was not really their chauffeur) to go around to the front. The chauffeur, in fact, was a former FBI agent who had a .38 in a shoulder holster. There was a Thompson .45 ACP machine pistol on the floorboard. Donovan himself carried a .38 Colt Banker's Special on his belt. He had not taken off his seersucker jacket, because he knew the sight of a pistol disturbed Ruth.

As the car rolled to a stop before the broad stairway, he saw three groups of people. Sitting at umbrellaed tables on the lawn were an extraordinarily handsome collection of young people. He recognized Canidy, Jimmy Whittaker, and young Douglass. The other men, a Navy lieutenant commander and two handsome, muscular young men wearing swim trunks and bathrobes, were obviously Bitter, young Martin, and the very interesting Eric Fulmar. Three young women were with them. One of them held a baby on her lap. On each of the tables were pitchers of iced tea, and a galvanized tub was sitting on the grass full of ice and beer.

It was significant to Donovan that Canidy was on the lawn with the intruders, and not with one of the two groups that had formed on the porch.

The group on the right was made up of Vice Admiral d'Escadre de Verbey; his staff; their hostess, Mrs. Barbara Whittaker; and Mr. and Mrs. C. Holdsworth Martin, Jr. Two silver wine buckets held a half-dozen towel-wrapped bottles.

On the left—with an iced-tea pitcher—sat "the forces of shamed righteousness": Captain Peter Douglass, Sr., USN; a Navy commander and a young lieutenant (obviously these two were officers from the Lakehurst guard detail); Mr. Eldon C. Baker; Miss Cynthia Chenowith; and Captain Stanley S. Fine, USAAC. Donovan thought it was especially interesting that Fine sat with Douglass, Baker, and the others.

Pete Douglass had the night before accepted full responsibility for what had happened and had offered his resignation. Donovan had no intention of accepting it, but when he glanced at Douglass's crestfallen face he realized that Douglass had imagined the worst possible scenario for the situation. To judge by *his* face, Baker simply looked angry. Cynthia Chenowith seemed embarrassed and ashamed. The two Navy officers had

faces Donovan recognized from his own military service: The big brass hat has just arrived, and there is no
telling what will happen next. Fine, as always, was a
lawyer, privy to the mess before the bar but not
personally involved in it.

Donovan suppressed a smile when the young lieutenant, carried away as the big brass hat started up the
stairs, came to attention and saluted. That triggered an
automatic reflex from the other officers on the porch.
They all saluted, even the admiral.

"Good morning," Donovan said as he reached the
top. He offered his hand to Douglass and Baker,
introduced himself to the other naval officers, smiled at
Cynthia, and then took Ruth's arm and crossed the
porch to where Barbara Whittaker and her group
waited.

The women embraced while Martin introduced Donovan to the admiral and his staff.

"We have a little problem, Barbara," Donovan said,
"that has to be talked out. Is there someplace we can
go?"

"Captain Douglass suggested that we clean up the
breakfast room for you, Bill," Barbara said.

"Fine," Donovan said. "Holdsworth, if you don't
mind, I'd like you to sit with us. I'm going to need your
advice."

*With a little bit of luck, if it becomes necessary to put
your son on ice, you will hear enough to agree that it is
necessary.*

"I am not a disinterested observer, Bill," Martin
said.

"None of us is," Donovan said. "Will you excuse us,
please?"

He walked toward the front door of the house.

"Pete," he said, "you want to come along, please?"

"Yes, sir," Captain Douglass said, and followed
them into the breakfast room.

A glass-topped table had been equipped with legal pads and a glass full of sharpened pencils. The security people had connected two telephones. One had a scrambler line.

"I will begin, Pete," Donovan said, "by saying your resignation is declined, that while I will be very interested in your worst possible scenario, I don't think the war has been lost."

"I think," Martin said, "that much ado is being made about nothing."

"I must respectfully disagree with Mr. Martin, Colonel," Captain Douglass said, and then he outlined his theory that every operation now under way, planned, or discussed was compromised by the current security breach. Donovan was impressed with Douglass's presentation, and he suspected that Douglass had worked on his speech from the moment Baker had called him the night before.

"All right, Pete," Donovan said when he had finished. "That's just what I wanted. Will you send in Baker, so that we get all the bad news at once?"

Baker was in fact angry; more than angry, outraged. He was a professional intelligence officer, and furious that a number of well-laid plans were apparently going down the toilet not only because of the inexcusable carelessness of a bunch of amateurs, but because— more seriously—certain individuals who could have been expected to know better had acted sloppily.

He didn't mention Captain Douglass's name, Donovan thought, *but he left no doubt who he means.* And then he had another thought: *No, that's not all that he means. The "certain individuals," plural, includes me.*

Baker had apparently spent as much time as Douglass preparing his opening statement. He likewise had specific recommendations.

Canidy should be relieved of his responsibilities and put on ice at least until after the African flight and

Operation Torch. After that his case would be reviewed and a decision made about what to do next with him.

Whittaker and Fulmar should also be put on ice, at least until after Operation Torch. Their cases would be reviewed then. Fulmar, considering the projected use of him, would require special attention.

Although it had to be presumed that they knew more than they had a right to know, Commander Bitter, Major Douglass, and Lieutenant Martin could probably be made aware of all the relevant security implications and so could be returned to their units and trusted to keep their mouths shut. Bitter's wife could also doubtless be trusted.

The wild cards were Ann Chambers and Charity Hoche. Hoche, Baker said, had the brains of a gnat as well as an automatic mouth. There was no doubt that no matter how carefully everything was explained to her, she would promptly talk to whoever would listen about the fascinating people she had met at Deal.

"And Ann Chambers is a journalist," Baker concluded. "She smells a story, and she's skilled at pulling facts from people. There is no question that at this very moment she is skillfully milking facts to fill in what didn't come out last night when Canidy and company were in their cups."

The Misses Chambers and Hoche consequently should be put under close supervision, regardless of the consequences, until after the African flight and Operation Torch, Baker said flatly.

That's a wish list he's offering me, Donovan concluded. *Everything he would like to have but knows he can't get. Still, he has gone on record that if something goes wrong, the onus will not fall on him.*

But he was right about one thing. Ann Chambers is a loose cannon rolling around on the deck of a ship in a storm.

"As for Captain Fine," Baker concluded, "he is the

silver lining. We can turn the African flight over to him. Presuming he returns safely from that, he can be put to work on the other projects."

"If we relieve Candy, what do we do about a backup aircraft?" Donovan asked. "It would mean bringing somebody else in, and who would that be?"

"I could go, of course," Baker said.

"No, you know too much about uranitite," Donovan said. "I'm even uncomfortable with Grunier's knowledge of our interest."

"But if the backup aircraft were required," Baker argued, "we would have to presume that secrecy would be compromised anyway. For that reason I'd take my chances on only one plane."

"But we have to have the uranitite," C. Holdsworth Martin, Jr., said. "Even at the price of letting the Germans know we're working on an atomic bomb. For the long term, getting that ore is of greater importance than Torch."

Donovan snorted his agreement. Then, realizing that nothing more was going to come from Baker but repetition of the arguments he'd already made, Donovan cut him off.

"I want to talk to Ann Chambers," Donovan said. "Would you send her in, please, Eldon?"

As soon as he was out the door, C. Holdsworth Martin, Jr., said, "Bill, for God's sake, you're not actually thinking of locking the Chambers girl up, are you?"

"Baker thinks that may be necessary," Donovan said.

"Brandon Chambers," C. Holdsworth Martin, Jr., said, "has so far been willing and eager to cooperate with us. You lock his daughter up, and that will change. You can't tell a Brandon Chambers that his daughter is a security risk. I'm sure you're aware, further, that Richard Hoche is a very good constitutional lawyer. You lock those girls up, and you can count on Roosevelt's questionable interpretation of habeas corpus being brought before the Supreme Court. And Chambers would keep the story on page one of all his newspapers until they heard it."

"We have a mess, don't we, Holdsworth?" Donovan said.

"I repeat that I think much ado is being made about nothing," Martin said.

"And I repeat, we have a mess, don't we, Holdsworth?"

There was a knock at the door, and a female voice called, "Colonel Donovan?"

"Come in, Ann," Donovan said.

She was wearing a thin pale yellow blouse and a light blue pleated skirt. She looked as sweet and innocent as a college girl—until you looked at her eyes. She was considerably tougher than she looked at first glance, and she was clearly wary but not afraid.

"How's your family, Ann?" Donovan asked.

"Cousin Edwin's a little green around the gills, Colonel," Ann said. "But the rest of us are just fine."

Donovan smiled. "Commander Bitter may be a little green around the gills, as you put it, Ann," he said, "because he may have a greater understanding of what's going on right now than you do."

"That could well be," Ann said.

"What do *you* think is going on around here?"

"I'll take the Fifth on that one, Colonel Donovan," she said.

"Certainly you're curious?"

"Sure," she said.

"You sense you might have a hell of a story, in other words?" Donovan said.

"Is that what you're worried about?" she asked.

"A good deal of damage would be done if there is whispering about what might be going on around here," Donovan said. "If studied guesses were to appear in print . . . We just can't afford that, Ann."

"Well, you don't have to worry about that, so far as I'm concerned," she said. "I have no intention of writing a word about it."

"Well, I'm certainly relieved to hear that," Donovan said. "But I've got to pursue that a little further. I hope you won't take offense."

"Try me," she said.

"How can I be sure that your patriotism won't wear thin after you've had a chance to think it over?"

"This has nothing to do with my patriotism," she said.

"Then what?" he asked, surprised.

"Dick Canidy is obviously in deep trouble over us in the first place," Ann said. "I wouldn't do anything to add to his troubles, and I think this is the time to tell you that he had nothing at all to do with our coming. I was the one who figured out where he was and talked the others into driving up."

"Your loyalty to your friend is commendable," C. Holdsworth Martin, Jr., said.

"This has nothing to do with loyalty to a friend," Ann said. "I'm in love with Dick Canidy. I can't tell you how badly I feel about getting him in trouble."

"I didn't know," Donovan said, "that you were that close to Canidy."

"Neither does he, Colonel," Ann said. "But I hope, sooner or later, to change that."

"*Mon Dieu!*" C. Holdsworth Martin, Jr., said.

"It wasn't easy for me to tell you that," Ann said. "But under the circumstances, I thought it was necessary."

"I'm glad you told us, Ann," Donovan said. "And it won't go any further."

"Thank you," she said. "What happens now?"

"That's what Mr. Martin and I are going to decide just about as soon as you leave," Donovan said.

"If you sock it to Dick anyway," Ann said, "I'll help

him in any way I can. I've heard whispers about people being locked up for psychiatric examination. If you do something like that to Canidy, you can count on it getting in the papers. Maybe my father's papers wouldn't print it, but somebody will."

She walked out of the room. Donovan had a thought from left field: *What the hell is wrong with Canidy? That young woman is really bright. She's put together like the proverbial brick outhouse, and she's really special to boot.*

"Was that an example of the female hell hath no fury like?" C. Holdsworth Martin, Jr., asked.

"Well, she asked *the* question, didn't she?" Donovan replied. "What happens now?"

"I think we should talk to Canidy," Martin said, "before we decide."

"Yeah," Donovan said. He walked over and opened the door then raised his voice and called, "Will somebody send Canidy in here, please?"

Canidy came in wearing khaki trousers and a T-shirt.

"We seem to have a problem on our hands, don't we, Dick?" Donovan began.

"Not as much as Baker seems to think we have," Canidy said. "But a problem."

"You don't seem overly concerned about it," Donovan said sharply.

"What damage has been done has been done," Canidy said. "And I don't think you called me in here to ask for my remedy for it."

"Canidy," Donovan said, "at this moment, you're on a greased skid at the bottom of which is a long stay in St. Elizabeths."

"I thought that was probably what was going to happen," Canidy said. "I thank you, Colonel, for telling me yourself. Denying Baker that satisfaction, I mean."

He started to get up. "That's it, isn't it?" he asked.

"Sit down, Canidy," Donovan said.

Canidy shrugged and lowered himself back in the chair.

"Have you wondered why Baker is so upset?"

"Baker is a professional," Canidy said. "He holds me in the contempt he holds all amateurs. I'm not serious enough."

"I'm surprised you haven't considered that he might know something you don't."

"Oh, I've considered that, Colonel."

"Since the odds are about ninety to ten that you're going to St. Elizabeths," Donovan said, "I'm going to tell you a little more than you know. I'll be interested in your reaction."

"And if my reaction is not what you want, it's St. Elizabeths for sure?"

"Yes," Donovan said.

Canidy saw in Martin's eyes that the direction this encounter was taking had come as a surprise to him.

"The Germans have begun test-flying a jet-powered fighter aircraft, the Messerschmitt ME-262," Donovan said. "If the tests are successful, and if they can get the airplane into production in sufficient numbers, the ME-262 will be capable of inflicting tremendous losses on the bombers of the Eighth Air Force. This means that the current strategy calling for the destruction of German industry by aerial bombardment will have to be called off. At the moment, there is no satisfactory substitute available."

"Jesus!" Canidy said.

"The only way out of this problem that seems to make any sense," Donovan went on, "is to interrupt production of the engines. But that, in turn, depends on our getting our hands on either an engine or else its specifications. That will allow our technical people to determine how production can be delayed. Special metals, special smelting techniques, special machining, special machines to make those machines . . . are you following me?"

"Yes, sir," Canidy said.

"The Fokker Company has sublet the development and production contracts for the engine to FEG, that is, to Fulmar Elektrische Gesellschaft."

"And you think Eric can help?"

"We hope so."

"Then how?"

"He can help us recruit a man who we hope can do something useful in this regard. Our man in Morocco, Murphy . . . you met him, I think?"

"On my way out," Canidy confirmed.

"He has established a rather interesting contact with a man named Helmut von Heurten-Mitnitz."

"He heads the Franco-German Armistice Commission," Canidy said. "He was doing his damnedest, he and an SS officer named Müller, to get Fulmar back to Germany."

"Well, for several reasons, Murphy believes he can be very valuable to us. Fulmar is the key to his cooperation. That's why we brought Fulmar out of Morocco. It has little or nothing to do with Operation Torch."

"How is this tied in with the African flight?"

"It's not," Donovan said, after a moment's hesitation.

It was obvious that Canidy did not believe him.

"And this breach of security has fucked this up?"

"If it gets out, it will," Donovan said.

"Then, and for the first time, I am truly sorry," Canidy said. "Shit! Why didn't somebody tell me this?"

"You weren't sorry before?"

"You want a straight answer to that?" Canidy asked.

"Please," C. Holdsworth Martin, Jr., said.

"It struck me as much ado about nothing," Canidy said. Donovan coughed, as if he were trying in vain to dislodge something in his throat. Canidy waited for him to stop and then went on. "All you have to do is tell Bitter and Douglass to keep their mouths shut. To consider them security risks is patently absurd. So far as Whittaker and Martin are concerned, they don't know anything, except who's here in Deal. They also can be told to keep their mouths shut. There is a problem with one of the women, Ann Chambers. She may look like she's nineteen years old, but she's a lot smarter than you'd think just to look at her. Last night she was pumping everybody."

"You think she learned anything?"

"No," Canidy said matter-of-factly. "I'm sure she didn't. But she's smart, and we can't afford to have her speculating in the newspapers."

"Are you telling me that, with her exception, you don't see any security problem?"

"I don't suppose my opinion is worth much," Canidy said, "but if you figure some way to shut her up, I don't see a security problem, period. I never did."

"That's very interesting, Canidy," Donovan said. "It is almost exactly the opposite of the opinion Baker holds. And he's a professional."

"I'm not exactly an amateur myself anymore, Colonel. I stopped being an amateur when the sub went off without me."

"Not exactly an amateur, but not a professional either," Donovan said. "OK, Canidy, that'll be it. Thank you."

"What's my status, may I ask?"

"Mr. Martin and I are going to discuss that now. Until a decision has been reached, I think it would be best if you waited in your room."

"Yes, sir," Canidy said.

When he had gone, Martin said, "You're not going to like this, Bill, but my vote goes to Canidy."

"Oh, mine, too," Donovan said. "What you and I are going to have to do is come up with some way to stroke Baker's ruffled feathers. He's good, and we can't afford to have him feeling that we're pissing on him."

"Piss on him a little, Bill," Martin said. "It'll be good for him. He seems to think that he's the spymaster, and that's your role."

Donovan thought that over a moment.

"I'll tell you what," he said. "I'll send him in and you piss on him. Tell him you question his judgment about yelling 'Fire!' so loudly."

"Why me?"

"It was your idea, Holdsworth," Donovan said reasonably, and stood up. "I'm going to go see Canidy and read the riot act again, and then I'm going to find out if he really has laid on a clambake. I haven't been to one in years."

Eight

1

COLONEL WILLIAM J. DONOVAN was not surprised at Dick Canidy's reaction when he went to Canidy's room (actually a small apartment over the boathouse) and told him that he had decided it would be a mistake to put everybody on ice.

From the tone of Canidy's "Yes, sir," Donovan understood that Canidy had already put himself in Donovan's shoes, considered the possible options, and reached the decision that Donovan would most likely come to.

"That's all you've got to say? No questions?"

"All sorts of questions," Canidy said. "How are you going to handle Baker? How are you going to handle the Chambers girl? And that birdbrained friend of hers?"

Canidy is either more artfully deceitful than I believe or he really has no idea how Ann Chambers feels about him.

"I've spoken to the Chambers girl," Donovan said. "She's very much like her father. Once she understands how important it is to protect the secrecy of what we're doing, it wouldn't enter her mind to endanger that by writing about it.''

"The Chambers newspapers ran Drew Pearson's 'Donovan's Dilettantes' column," Canidy said.

"Brandon Chambers reserves the right to read Pearson's columns before they run in his newspapers. He has killed dozens of them over the years. I can only assume that Chambers decided that whatever I'm doing, I'm not providing a haven for well-bred draft dodgers, and thus there was no question of national security involved."

"Hmmm," Canidy grunted thoughtfully.

"Or he believed Pearson," Donovan said, chuckling, "and decided to publish that piece as his patriotic duty. It's even possible that he understood I would actually be pleased by such a story, because it would divert attention from what we're really doing."

Canidy laughed at that. He knew Brandon Chambers enough to see that Donovan might be right about that.

"In any event, I'm going to arrange to have a meal with him to express my appreciation for his discretion. I don't think we have anything to worry about with the Chamberses, *père* or *fille.*"

Canidy nodded. "And the birdbrain?"

"We're going to offer Miss Hoche," Donovan said, "whose father, incidentally, is also a friend of mine, summer employment."

"Summer employment? Doing what?" Canidy asked, surprised.

"Working at the house on Q Street, where she can relieve many of Cynthia's housekeeping chores. Cynthia can meanwhile keep an eye on her."

"I don't know how to say this tactfully, Colonel," Canidy said, "but do you understand how outraged Baker is?"

"I understand that he holds you in contempt, Dick," Donovan said. "Perhaps even more than he holds me in at this moment. But I have a plan which will, I hope, make him come to see me as profoundly wise and sound of judgment."

"How are you going to do that?"

"I'm going to promote him," Donovan said.

Canidy laughed. "To what?"

"Director of recruitment and training for the OSS," Donovan said.

"I don't know what that means," Canidy said.

"Just what it sounds like," Donovan said. "Since Baker devoutly believes that we have been recruiting the wrong kind of people for the OSS, I'm going to let him handle the recruiting. It's been taking too much of Pete Douglass's time anyway."

"I mean, what the hell is this 'OSS'? What's it got to do with us?"

"You mean you don't know?"

"I've seen it on paperwork," Canidy said. "They're now going to pay for our purchase orders, but I don't know who, or what, it is."

"Well, I can't imagine why no one has told you just who and what the OSS is," Donovan said, smiling. "Maybe Baker decided you didn't have the need to know. It happened three weeks ago."

He opened his briefcase and searched through it. "I'm sure I had it in here," he said. "It's for my personal file." He searched a moment more, and then said, "Here it is."

He handed Canidy a single sheet of crisp white paper:

MILITARY ORDER   Copy 2 of 3

Office of Strategic Services

By virtue of the authority vested in me as President of the United States and as Commander in Chief of the Army and Navy of the United States, it is ordered as follows:

      1. The Office of the Coordinator of Information,

established by Order of July 11, 1941, exclusive of the foreign information activities transferred to the Office of War Information by Executive Order of June 13, 1942, shall hereafter be known as the Office of Strategic Services, and is hereby transferred to the jurisdiction of the United States Joint Chiefs of Staff.

2. The Office of Strategic Services shall perform the following duties:

a. Collect and analyze such strategic information as may be required by the United States Joint Chiefs of Staff.

b. Plan and operate such special services as may be directed by the United States Joint Chiefs of Staff.

3. At the head of the Office of Strategic Services shall be a Director of Strategic Services who shall be appointed by the President and who shall perform his duties under the direction and supervision of the United States Joint Chiefs of Staff.

4. William J. Donovan is hereby appointed as Director of Strategic Services.

5. The order of July 11, 1941, is hereby revoked.

Franklin D. Roosevelt
Commander in Chief

"So you're now under the Joint Chiefs," Canidy said.

"Read that very carefully," Donovan said. "And start thinking 'we,' Dick."

After a moment, Canidy said, "I always wondered how you managed to get away with being a free agent. Military and Naval Intelligence must think you're an interloper on their sacred preserve."

"I'm afraid they do," Donovan said. "But ONI and G-2 are under the Chief of Naval Operations and the Army Chief of Staff."

"Who are under the Joint Chiefs," Canidy said.

"Who are under the *Chairman* of the Joint Chiefs," Donovan said. "So if there is any complaint about us, it has to pass through two levels of the military hierarchy."

"And you're not worried about the Chairman? Isn't he going to naturally side with the brass hats?"

231

"No," Donovan said. "Despite what you might have heard, he and I agree far more often than we disagree. And besides, I'm sure he has drawn the correct inference from the fact that not only was he not given the right to pick the director of the OSS, he wasn't even asked for a suggestion."

Canidy chuckled. "I get the point."

"That's about as much of a blanket authority as I think anyone could get under the existing bureaucracy," Donovan said. "It's more, frankly, than I thought I was going to get."

"Does it come with money, too?"

"Whenever possible, we're going to draw our funds from the nonaccountable funds allocated to the Joint Chiefs. If it's not there, we can get what we need from the President's discretionary funds. That airplane of yours, for example, will be charged against the Joint Chiefs. The money we're spending on the African flight operation is coming from the President."

"Interesting."

"Getting back to Baker," Donovan said. "We're about to start recruiting people on a large scale. Baker is the man to handle that, I think, and also to run the school. Have you heard about that?"

"Back when he was still talking to me, Baker threatened to send me to it," Canidy said. "But all I *know* is that there *is* a school."

"One now, more later. We're going to take over the Congressional Country Club in Washington, and we're taking over a country place, the estate of a duke, in England. The place we have right now is an estate made available to us in Virginia, not far from Washington," Donovan said. "I think we can give you and Whittaker—especially Whittaker—credit for on-the-job training and excuse you from going through it; but from now on, just about everybody we recruit will go through formal training."

"Espionage One-oh-one?" Canidy said.

"Just about," Donovan said. "Some of the people we're going to recruit will come from the military, but many others will come directly from civilian life. They'll need to acquire some basic skills, firearms for example, and a little belly flattening and muscle toning. Sort of our version of basic training."

"I understand," Canidy said.

"Baker wants Jimmy Whittaker as an instructor, and I think for once he will be a round peg in a round hole. And young Martin, too."

"You mean to go through the school, don't you? Not as an instructor?"

"Martin was commissioned when he finished basic training," Donovan said. "From then on, he's been at either Fort Bragg or Fort Benning working with the people developing parachute operations. He's actually something of an expert. He's made sixty or seventy jumps, many at night, and he's spent a lot of time learning how to drop cargo by parachute."

"I thought he was involved with us because he knew Fulmar—and because of his father," Canidy said.

"That, too," Donovan said. "If you need him to deal with Fulmar, he'll be available. Or just go get him. There's an airfield on the estate."

He dipped into his briefcase again and came up with an Esso road map. On it was marked a surprisingly large area about thirty miles from the District of Columbia.

"The field was a private strip," Donovan said. "And is not, I understand, on FAA aerial charts. Can you find it from that?"

"I can find it, but will it take the Beech?"

"I'm sure it will," Donovan said. "I was once flown there for a weekend in a DC-3."

"I can find it," Canidy said, making a careful mental note of where the estate was in relation to Washington.

"Can you get everybody in the Beech?"

"Who's everybody?"

"Baker, Cynthia, the two Douglasses, your friend Bitter, Jimmy Whittaker, and young Martin."

"Yeah," Canidy said, after thinking it over. "To this place in the country, you mean?"

"No. To Anacostia. Douglass can arrange to get them to the estate in the morning."

"You're talking about right now?"

"I heard something about a clambake," Donovan said.

"I'm responsible for that," Canidy said. "Guarding this place is really lousy duty for the white hats. I feel sorry for them. I thought they would probably like a clambake, and I showed them what had to be done."

"A pit on the beach?" Donovan asked. "Lobsters? Clams? Corn on the cob? Beer?"

"The works," Canidy said.

"Who's paying for the beer and lobster?"

"I am."

"Well, turn in a voucher for it."

Canidy was surprised. "Thank you," he said.

"You won't get to drink any of the beer, since you'll be flying, but I can't see any point in letting all that food go to waste by sending everybody to Washington right now. And Mrs. Donovan and I love clambakes."

"Considering what I feared was going to happen to me, I can cheerfully do without the beer," Canidy said.

Donovan nodded.

"How close was I to St. Elizabeths, Colonel?" Canidy asked.

"It was a close call, Dick," Donovan said. "As close as I've made lately. I hope it was a good call."

"Yeah," Canidy said, after a moment, thoughtfully, but as if he were thinking of someone else. "So do I."

As Donovan began to move toward the door Canidy asked, "What about Bitter's wife and the birdbrain?"

"I'll have Ann Chambers drive their car back in the morning," Donovan said. "If she thinks that's too much to ask of her, you can see about getting someone to drive the car."

"Oh, she can drive it," Canidy said. "She's got a commercial ticket, an instrument rating, and five hundred-odd hours. She's really a very capable young woman."

"Not bad-looking, either," Donovan said.

"Yeah," Canidy said noncommittally.

Maybe it's chemical, Donovan thought. *Maybe as there is a chemical attraction between young people of opposite sexes, there is also a chemical repulsion. Obviously, Ann Chambers does not ring bells in Dick Canidy.*

2

Summer Place
Deal, New Jersey
0015 Hours 5 July 1942

Ann Chambers had not been asleep, although she had pretended to be when Charity had finally, about eleven, returned to their room. Charity had been spending considerable time with Doug Douglass in Canidy's room above the boathouse during the clambake. And Ann—in her current state of mind—did not want to listen to Charity's impassioned rhapsodies about it.

The problem was that, unlike Charity's dashing hero, hers, rather than leaping enthusiastically into her bed, seemed oblivious to her very existence. How could she look soulfully into his eyes when she couldn't get him to look at her?

When the luminous hands on the traveling alarm clock lined up at midnight, Ann was really faced with doing what she had decided to do that afternoon. It was different now. It was not an intellectual exercise.

235

She thought some more, and when the hands of the clock reached fifteen minutes after midnight, she finally made up her mind. She would forget she was a nice girl, a virgin, an Episcopalian, and that good Episcopalian virgins who find themselves awake at midnight roll over and go to sleep.

Opportunity knocks but once, she told herself quietly as she swung her legs out and searched for her shoes under the bed with her toes. *If not now, then probably never. There is absolutely no chance I'll ever get invited back here, and where else would there ever be the opportunity again?*

There was enough light in the room for her to see Charity clearly. She was on her stomach, with her nightgown up to her waist. She was in a deep sleep.

Ann pulled a high-collared cotton robe over her baby-doll pajamas, buttoned it, and then, her lips tight in determination, reached under it and pulled the cutesy-poo balloon-leg pajama pants off. Cutesy-poo *college girl.*

Though it was a little wicked to leave her bedroom half naked under a thin robe, it gave her determination. There was no turning back now.

She went down the stairs to the foyer. A civilian security guard was sitting in an upholstered chair by the door to what had been a closet but now held a switchboard. Presuming everyone had gone to bed, he had pulled down his tie, removed his seersucker jacket, and hung his shoulder holster over the back of his chair. He looked up from his copy of *The Saturday Evening Post,* his face expressionless.

"Can't sleep," Ann said. "I think it's probably the corn. I ate two dozen ears."

He smiled. It was a friendly smile.

"That was nice, wasn't it?" he said. "I had four lobsters. I think there's some baking soda in the kitchen."

"I think I'll try a walk," Ann said. "Then the baking soda."

He leaned down then and came up with a flashlight. There were half a dozen of them, the funny-looking kind with the lens and bulb at right angles to the battery case, lined neatly against the baseboard.

"Here," he said.

"I won't need that," she said.

"The sailors may be a little nervous," he said practically. "Better they see you coming than think somebody—like the officer of the guard—is sneaking around to check up on them."

"Thank you," she said, and took the light and walked out toward the boathouse.

If he's not there already, it won't be long.

They had left Summer Place at half past seven. It was fifteen minutes to Lakehurst, and maybe another fifteen minutes to put everybody in the airplane, file a flight plan, and take off. It was about a hundred seventy-five air miles to Washington. At, say, a hundred fifteen knots, that was an hour and a half to Anacostia, call it two hours before they were on the ground. Then another two hours back to Lakehurst. He should be back about half past midnight.

Halfway to the boathouse, startling her, one of the sailors appeared suddenly out of the darkness, his rifle held diagonally across his chest.

"Can I help you, miss?"

"No, thank you," she said. "I'm just going to the boathouse."

"Yes, miss," he said, and when she started walking again, he marched behind her.

These guys had all had the riot act read to them after Douglass had glibly talked their way past the sentry on the road when they arrived. This nice-looking man had gotten the message. If she told him she was going to the boathouse, he intended to see that she did.

As Ann climbed the outside stairway to Canidy's rooms, she expected the door to be locked. But the door was open, and she let herself in. Did that mean he was home already?

There was nothing to do but turn on the lights, she realized. Otherwise, the young sailor with the rifle would climb the stairs and see if anything was wrong.

She snapped the switch. It was one big room, and he was not there. The bed was mussed, and the ashtray on the table beside it full of cigarette butts. Half had lipstick on them.

That damned Charity didn't even have the decency to clean up after herself, Ann thought angrily.

She dumped the cigarette butts into a wastebasket under the washbasin, then searched in drawers and closets for clean sheets and pillowcases.

She had just finished making the bed when she heard footsteps on the wooden stairs. Suddenly absolutely unable to face Dick Canidy, she retreated first against the wall, then into a closet.

I'll have to come out, she thought as she peered through a crack in the slatted door, *but not this instant!*

"Richard? You there?" a male voice called.

In a moment, she saw who it was. It was Eric Fulmar, someone everybody seemed to know but no one was willing to talk about.

"Shit," Fulmar said, "nobody's home."

Now he'll go. Please, God, make him go!

Eric Fulmar looked around the room, found what he was looking for—Canidy's liquor—made himself a drink, and settled himself comfortably to wait for Canidy in the room's one upholstered chair.

He didn't have long to wait. An automobile was on the drive. A car door opened and closed, then Canidy's voice: "Thanks. Sorry you had to wait up for me."

And then the sound of his footsteps coming up the stairs.

"What the hell?" Canidy said when he saw Fulmar.
"Find everything you wanted?" he asked unpleasantly.
He was wearing his Air Corps uniform. When he took
off the tunic, Ann was sure that he would want to hang
it up, pull open the closet door, and find her hiding
there. But there were two closets, and Canidy kept his
uniforms in the other one.

"I found the booze," Fulmar said.

"More important, how did you get in here? You're
supposed to be kept in the house."

"If I wanted to leave here," Eric said, "I could. I
hate to tell you this, but your security is a joke."

"What do you want, Eric?" Canidy asked.

"I want to talk to you," Fulmar said.

There was a moment's hesitation, and for a moment
Ann thought he was going to send Eric Fulmar away.
But he didn't.

"OK, we'll talk," he said. "Fix me a stiff one of
those, will you?"

He disappeared. In a moment, there was the sound
of splashing water. For a moment, Ann was confused.
Then she understood what was going on.

*My God, when he does that, it sounds like Niagara
Falls. Or a firehose!*

Canidy flushed the toilet and came back into sight.
He took the drink Fulmar had made and swallowed it
straight down.

"Jesus!" Fulmar said. "That was a little quick, wasn't
it?"

"I drank about a quart of coffee so that I wouldn't
fall asleep on the way home," Canidy said. "I hope that
two or three like that, plus a warm shower, will
overwhelm the caffeine. Make me another one, will
you?"

Then he started to get undressed. He very neatly
hung his trousers on a hanger, then tossed his shirt, his
T-shirt, and his shorts on top of the soiled sheets.

It's funny-looking, Ann decided. *He's beautiful, gorgeous, handsome, but that thing between his legs is ugly*.

"I won't be long," Dick Canidy said to Fulmar. He disappeared again, and there was the sound of a shower running. Much more quickly than Ann expected, he reappeared, still naked, toweling his head. He made a quick swipe at the rest of his body, and then wrapped the towel around his waist.

My God, I'm disappointed!

Canidy picked up his drink and went to his bed. He propped pillows against the headboard and arranged himself against it.

"OK, Eric," he said, "ask away. But make it brief, will you? This has been a bad day."

"Where did you take Jimmy and Martin?" Fulmar asked.

"To Washington," Canidy said.

"I know that," Fulmar said.

"OK," Canidy said after a minute. "Why not? The OSS is starting a school in Virginia. Jimmy and Martin are going to be instructors."

"What's the OSS?"

"It stands for the Office of Strategic Services," Canidy said. "We're all in it. Colonel Donovan is the boss."

"What are they going to teach?"

"Martin is a parachute expert. Jimmy is going to teach people to cut throats and blow things up."

"I could teach that," Fulmar said. "I could teach a lot of interesting Errol Flynn-type things. You'd be surprised how good the Berbers are at cutting throats."

"I suppose you could," Canidy said, "but as I'm sure you have already figured out for yourself, there is some question whose side you are on in this war."

"You don't believe that, do you?" Fulmar said.

"It doesn't matter what I believe," Canidy said.

"Well, do you or don't you, goddamn it?"

"No, I don't," Canidy said. "But right now, my opinion doesn't count for a whole hell of a lot around here."

"Well, what do they want with me? Since they don't trust me?"

Canidy wanted to avoid answering that. "You can't blame them, Eric," he said, "for wondering."

"Wondering what?"

"For Christ's sake, figure it out yourself. You didn't want to come to this country."

"Bullshit!" Fulmar flared. "You were with me in that goddamned boat. I didn't ask to get left behind over there. I was prepared to kill to get on that goddamned submarine, and you know it."

"I mean the second chance you were offered," Canidy said.

"What second chance?"

"You know damned well what I mean," Canidy said. "You had to be tied up and smuggled to Gibraltar because you wouldn't come voluntarily."

"Who told you that?"

"Baker," Canidy said.

"Shit!" Fulmar said. "It hasn't occurred to you that he's a lying bastard?"

Canidy was on a spot, and quickly moved to get off it. "And people have wondered why, since you've been here, you have made no attempt to get in touch with your mother."

" 'Hi, Mom, I'm in the loony bin at Fort Knox'?" Fulmar said mockingly.

"Is that the reason?"

"You know the reason," Eric said. "You and Jimmy. My mother doesn't give a shit for me and never has. If that question came up, one of you should have said something."

"You never tried to get in touch with my father, either," Canidy said.

" 'Hi, Dr. Canidy! Guess where I am, Dr. Canidy?' "

"OK," Canidy said.

"But you can't tell me what's going on, right? Or you won't."

"I can't," Canidy said.

"You know, for years I always talked myself into thinking, so what that my mother doesn't even want people to know I exist, and so what that my father made it pretty clear the big mistake of his life was not using a rubber when he screwed my mother. I've got *another* kind of family. I've got Sidi el Ferruch, and back in the States are my asshole buddies, Dick and Jimmy, and your good father. So what happens? The first chance el Ferruch gets, he sells me to that fucking Baker. And when I finally get together with you two, Jimmy acts like I have a swastika tattooed on the head of my pecker, and you're not one fucking bit better; and I can't even call Father Canidy because if I do, I'd have to tell him I can't come to see him, because you've got me locked up. He's the only person in the world who's ever given a shit about me, and I'm not going to have him worrying about me, or let him know what a prick his son is."

"Jesus Christ!" Canidy said.

"Fuck you, Canidy!" Fulmar said, and Ann saw tears running down his face as he glowered angrily at Canidy.

"You know a man named Helmut von Heurten-Mitnitz, I understand," Canidy said.

"Yeah, I know him. He's just like you, Canidy. Two peas out of a pod. If Baker hadn't beat him to it, he would have had me tied up and sent to Germany. They would trust me there about as far as I'm trusted here."

"Now, get your fucking emotions under control and think it over carefully before you answer me. From what you know of this guy, would he be useful to us?"

"No," Fulmar said, after a long pause. "What you're

asking is whether he would be a traitor. The answer is not any more than you would. Is that what this is all about? You think I can get to von Heurten-Mitnitz? You're dreaming. No way."

"One more question," Canidy said. "If we asked you to, would you stick your neck out?"

"You're asking would I go back to Morocco?"

"I didn't ask that. But answer it anyway."

"Yeah," Fulmar said. "I'm not too bright, Dick. I trust people I shouldn't. But if you tell me that it's important that I go back to Morocco, OK, I'll go. Just one condition."

"You're in no position to ask for conditions," Canidy said.

"I want a commission," Fulmar said. "A real one, like Jimmy's and Douglass's and Bitter's, not a phony one like yours."

"Douglass is a major, Bitter's the Navy equivalent, and Jimmy is a captain. They're not going to give you that."

"They made Martin a second lieutenant just because he had a college degree, he told me. I went to college. Second lieutenant would be OK."

"Why is that important?"

"Because if I get killed going back to Morocco, I want to be brought home in a casket with a flag on it and buried as a soldier, not left over there in a ditch because I was just a dumb sonofabitch who was used by people he thought were his friends."

"I'm your friend, you dumb sonofabitch. I always have been."

"Right, sure. Two choruses of 'For Auld Lang Syne.' But for the time being, try to think of some way to turn good ol' Helmut von Heurten-Mitnitz into a traitor, right?"

"Yeah, and don't tell anybody I told you to. I've already told you a hell of a lot more than I should."

"Because you're a nice guy, right?"

"No," Canidy said, "because we need you, and because I decided that was the way to get you to help."

"That sounds honest enough," Fulmar said.

"I'll raise the question of a commission as soon as I can," Canidy said. "No promises."

"Good enough," Fulmar said.

"My father knows you're safe in this country," Canidy said.

"How does he know?"

"I told him. He was worried about you."

"That's all you told him?"

"That's enough to get me locked up for the duration if anybody hears about it, so keep it under your hat."

"I had diarrhea of the mouth awhile back," Fulmar said. "Keep that under *your* hat."

Canidy got out of bed. "I'm going to call the sentry," he said. "And he will escort you back to the house."

"If you do that, the sailor sitting outside my door to keep me in the house will have his ass in a crack."

"What did you do, make a rope from your blankets and climb out the window?"

"I didn't need a rope," Fulmar said.

"You could get back without one?"

"Watch me," Fulmar said.

"No," Canidy said. "You're too valuable to have your balls blown off by a nervous sentry."

"I don't want that kid to get in trouble because of me," Fulmar said.

"I'm going to let him worry a little for the rest of the night about your getting away from him," Canidy said. "But I'm not going to squeal on him."

Then he did something which surprised Ann, and brought tears to her eyes. He put his arms around Eric Fulmar and hugged him. "Besides, asshole, if the sentry blew you away, I would miss you. You're the only thing close to a little brother I have."

They went out of sight, and Canidy called for the

sentry and asked him to "escort Mr. Fulmar back to the house."

When Canidy walked into the bedroom end of the room, she was leaning on the wall beside the closet.

"Oh, Jesus H. Christ!" he groaned.

"Hi!"

"What the fuck are you doing here?" he asked.

"That's my intention," Ann heard herself say, "but I'm not sure I like the tone of voice."

"How much did you hear?" he asked.

"I got here a couple of minutes before Eric did," Ann said. "I hid in there. I heard everything."

"Wonderful!" he said.

"I'm not going to tell anybody," she said.

"I'll have to tell Donovan," he said. "You understand what that means? You'll be hauled away for psychiatric examination. It will take years."

"Not necessarily," she said.

He turned away from her and headed for the whiskey on the sink. She took a couple of steps after him. Now he spun around and angrily demanded: "What do you mean, *not necessarily?*"

"Bill Donovan called me in this morning and asked how he could be sure I wouldn't write anything I shouldn't. I gave him an answer that satisfied him. And it covers this situation, too."

"I'd love to hear what you told him," Canidy said.

He's looking at my middle, she realized, and let her eyes drop. He had startled her when he had spun around, and she had backed up. Her leg had opened the flap of her robe. But much more than her leg was showing.

"I told him that I love you," Ann said, "and that I was consequently incapable of doing anything that would hurt you."

"What's the matter with you?" he flared. "Are you crazy? Saying something like that? And what you said before . . ."

"That's a distinct possibility," she said. "Because the facts seem to be that I do love you, and I came here to—"

"Shut up!" Canidy interrupted furiously. "Just shut up!"

"—see if I could get you to—" she went on relentlessly.

"Shut up!" he screamed again. "Goddamn you, shut your mouth! You don't know what you're saying!"

She met his eyes and saw determination in them, and knew that she had failed. Her own eyes teared, and she felt a sob rising.

There were the sounds of footsteps on the stairs.

"Major Canidy? Everything all right in there, Major?"

It was the sentry.

He pushed her against the wall. "Ssh!" he cautioned.

"Major Canidy?" the sentry asked.

"Everything's just fine," Canidy said.

"You're sure, sir? I thought I heard shouting."

"*I* didn't hear any shouting," Canidy said innocently.

Ann started to giggle.

Canidy quickly clapped his hand over her mouth.

"Well, someone was shouting," the sentry said firmly.

"Not me," Canidy said. "Everything's perfectly normal in here."

Something was pressed painfully against Ann's abdomen. She put her hand down to push it away, but when she realized what it was, she put her hand around it and held it tightly. She felt her heart pound.

"Well, good night, sir," the sentry said. "Sorry to disturb you, Major."

"Perfectly all right," Canidy said. "Keep up the good work."

When the sentry had gone down the stairs, he took his hand from her mouth.

She did not remove her hand from where she was holding him.

She heard him exhale deeply, almost as if it hurt him, and then he picked her up and carried her to the bed. She was glad that she had taken off the cutesy-poo pants, because all he had to do was push the cotton robe out of the way.

It didn't take long to become a woman, Ann thought, and she had never believed those horror stories about the pain anyway.

And when it was over, when he said, "You goddamn fool!" she heard tenderness in his voice, and was sure she had done the right thing even before he reached for her, and pulled her to him, and held her tightly against him, and said all the things she was so afraid she would never hear him say.

The second time was longer, and better, and so was the third.

3

Summer Place
Deal, New Jersey
0830 Hours 5 July 1942

When Barbara Whittaker left the table to go to the kitchen to ask for another pot of coffee, Charity Hoche smiled sweetly at Ann and said, "The tabletop is glass, so I think I should tell you that everybody can see you playing kneesie with Major Canidy."

"Charity!" Sarah Child Bitter snapped.

Captain Stanley S. Fine had trouble swallowing his coffee, while Ann Chambers and Richard Canidy flushed and separated at the knees.

Then Ann looked at Canidy.

"I don't mind if you don't," she said, and Canidy moved his knee against hers again. Ann thumbed her nose at Charity, and Fine and Sarah laughed.

This was the scene that greeted a security man and two Air Corps officers when they walked into the breakfast room: A very good-looking young woman was thumbing her nose at two other equally attractive young women and two men, one wearing an insignialess tropical worsted uniform and the other, younger, wearing swim trunks and a battered, washed-out gray sweatshirt with cutoff sleeves. On the front of the sweatshirt was still faintly visible the legend MASSACHUSETTS INSTITUTE OF TECHNOLOGY. They were all giggling and more than a little red in the face.

It was not what two officers who had volunteered for a hazardous secret mission expected to find when they reported for duty on orders conspicuously stamped TOP SECRET.

"These gentlemen have orders to report to you, Major," the security man said. "I've verified their identity."

Canidy took his knee away from Ann's. She sensed it would be a long time before she felt that delightful pressure again.

"Thank you," Canidy said, and reached out for a manila envelope the older of the two captains held in his hand.

"I'm Canidy," he said. "That's Captain Fine."

He did not introduce the women. He opened the envelope, removed another envelope from inside, and broke its seal. He then read the orders, put them back in the envelope, and passed it down the table to Fine.

"Is the car ready? You put gas in it?" Canidy asked the security man.

"Yes, sir. It's out in front."

"The weekend is over, I guess," Canidy said to Ann.

"Come see us off," Ann said as she got up.

He nodded.

When the women had left the room, Canidy waved the two officers into chairs at the table.

"Have you had breakfast?" Canidy asked.

"No, sir," the older of the two Air Corps officers said.

The "sir" came hard, Canidy thought. *If I were as old as they are, I would find it hard saying "sir" to a guy in trunks and an MIT sweatshirt.*

Barbara Whittaker came back into the room with a silver coffeepot.

"Gentlemen," Canidy said, "this is our hostess, Mrs. Barbara Whittaker."

Uncomfortably, the two officers gave Barbara Whittaker their hands and mumbled their names.

"Would you please see about getting them some breakfast?" Canidy said. "And then detour anyone else who wants to eat?"

"I'll have a table set on the porch," Barbara said.

"I'll see the girls off," Canidy said. "Stan, hold the fort, will you?"

When they were alone, the older of the two captains said to Fine with mingled annoyance and curiosity, "He's a little young to be a major, isn't he?"

"He's also a little young to be the man in charge," Fine said. "But he's an unusual young man. He was the first ace in the AVG."

"This isn't what I expected to find," the Air Corps officer said.

"Me either," Fine said. "A week ago I had a B-17 squadron at Chanute."

"What the hell is this all about?"

"I think," Fine said, "that I had better wait and let Major Canidy tell you that."

Canidy returned to the breakfast room five minutes later. He was still wearing the battered, washed-out MIT sweatshirt and swim trunks, but he no longer looked or sounded like a young man who had just found his Juliet, Fine thought.

"I'll begin with a statement of fact," Canidy said as he poured another cup of coffee. "If either of you in any way breaches the security requirements I am about to outline for you, you will spend the duration of the war in a psychiatric hospital. It is not a threat. Simply a fact. Is that perfectly clear to both of you?"

"Yes, sir," the two Air Corps officers said, almost in unison.

There was no hesitation this time, Fine thought. Was it because he had told them Canidy had been the AVG's first ace, or did they now sense a ruthlessness in him that had not been there when they had first walked into the breakfast room?

Nine

1

Le Relais de Pointe-Noire
Near Casablanca, Morocco
July 29, 1942

HELMUT VON HEURTEN-MITNITZ had reserved a *chambre séparée* for himself and Madame Jeanine Lemoine for dinner at the restaurant. Le Relais de Pointe-Noire sat on a huge granite crag thrusting into the Atlantic Ocean. The granite appeared black when surf crashed against it, hence *Pointe-Noire*.

The *chambres séparées*—there were ten—were on the floor above the main restaurant. Five of them, including the one assigned to von Heurten-Mitnitz and his companion, had large windows looking out upon the surf. The others faced inward toward the narrow road which led from the shore to the granite crag.

There was no hiding from anyone that the senior member of the Franco-German Armistice Commission for Morocco was a guest of the restaurant. For one thing, his Mercedes-Benz automobile was well known. And so, he suspected, was the Peugeot sedan with the Rabat license tag he used when he wished to be more discreet. For another, he was usually accompanied by a second Mercedes, a smaller one, carrying three members of the SS-SD[1] and one member of the Sûreté[2] who were charged with his protection.

His best protection at this moment, von Heurten-Mitnitz had concluded, was to trust that people would imagine he had brought Jeanine Lemoine here tonight for carnal purposes. He would have been pleased if it came to that, for Jeanine was an attractive, pert-breasted female with surprisingly long legs for a Frenchwoman. Despite the official policy of Franco-German friendship, she was held in contempt by the French in Morocco. The wife of an officer being held in a German POW camp, especially one who did not need the money, should not have become "the little friend" of von Heurten-Mitnitz, who, more than any other man, represented in Morocco the Germany which had so humiliated France.

The entire rear wall of the *chambre séparée* was a black mirror. Von Heurten-Mitnitz had wondered idly whether it had simply been designed that way because it made the room appear to be larger, or whether it was intended to reflect whatever might transpire on the wide, softly upholstered couch pushed against it, to cater to some French sexual hunger.

We make an attractive couple, von Heurten-Mitnitz thought as he saw their reflection in the mirror. *It's really a shame she's not what people believe, and that we're not here for an illicit liaison. Or at least not an illicit sexual liaison.*

Helmut von Heurten-Mitnitz was a tall, sharp-featured, very erect Pomeranian, thirty-five years old and blond-haired. He was an aristocrat, who like half a dozen younger sons of the Grafs von Heurten-Mitnitz

---

[1]*Shutzstaffel-Sicherheidtsdienst*: the secret police branch of the SS.
[2]The French Security Service, roughly analogous to the FBI or Secret Service.

before him had entered the diplomatic service of his sovereign. Karl-Heinz von Heurten-Mitnitz, his paternal uncle, had witnessed the German humiliation at Compiègne in 1918. And the current Graf von Heurten-Mitnitz, his elder brother, resplendent in his black honorary Standartenführer-SS's[3] uniform, had been part of Hitler's entourage at Compiègne in 1940, when humiliation had been turned into revenge.

An odd combination, von Heurten-Mitnitz thought, *a whore who is not a whore, and a patriot about to turn traitor.*

Two minutes after von Heurten-Mitnitz and Jeanine Lemoine entered the *chambre séparée,* a third man joined them. The presence of Robert Murphy, consul general of the United States to the French Republic's Protectorate of Morocco at the Relais de Pointe-Noire, could not be concealed any more than von Heurten-Mitnitz's. His official Buick was trailed everywhere by a Sûreté Peugeot or Citroën whose ostensible purpose was to provide him with the protection his rank was entitled to but whose real purpose was to keep an eye on him.

He had to hope that whoever noticed that the head American and the head German in Morocco were simultaneously at the Relais de Pointe-Noire would call it simply coincidence. That was in fact plausible. If they wanted to meet secretly, it was unlikely they would do so in a place where their presence would be so conspicuous.

The two men shook hands but did not speak.

Murphy nodded his head, perhaps made a small bow toward Jeanine Lemoine, and said, "Madame."

"Monsieur," she replied.

Helmut von Heurten-Mitnitz opened a bottle of

---

[3] An SS rank equivalent to colonel.

wine, poured three glasses, and passed one each to Murphy and Madame Lemoine.

"A toast would be a little awkward," von Heurten-Mitnitz said, "don't you think?"

"Better times," Murphy said.

Madame Lemoine and von Heurten-Mitnitz smiled and raised their glasses.

Then Murphy reached into the pocket of his suit jacket and took from it an envelope, which he handed to von Heurten-Mitnitz. The German took it, sat down at the table, opened it, and took from it half a dozen sheets of crisp white stationery.

"The White House," von Heurten-Mitnitz said. "I didn't know Roosevelt was fluent in German."

"He's not," Murphy said. "That's from Putzi von Hanfstaengel."

"Really?" von Heurten-Mitnitz said, surprised.

THE WHITE HOUSE
Washington

20 July 1942

My dear Helmut—

By the very reading of this you will, according to the laws of the Third Reich, be committing treason. I mention this because when Franklin Roosevelt asked me to write to you, I was forced to consider what that word really meant. Before, I was able to rationalize my own status: Heinrich Himmler had tried to kill me, and it was only by the grace of God that I was able to leave Germany, so therefore I could be anything I chose to be, and I chose to think of myself as an escapee, or a refugee, anything but a traitor.

I now realize that is dishonest. I am *legally* a traitor. I am consorting with my country's enemies, and doing whatever I can to help them cause my country to lose the war, including writing this letter.

But when I ask myself what I am being a traitor to, I am able to believe that I am really acting in Germany's best interests.

Roosevelt has unquestioned proof, some of it from the Vatican, of what unspeakable barbarities the Bavarian corporal and his cohorts are inflicting, not only upon Jews, but Gypsies, ordinary Polish and Russian peasants, and on *Germans*. I will not dwell on this, other than to give you my word that I *have* proof of what the bearer of this will tell you in detail. No matter what horrors he relates, I suspect that his memory will prove unable to store and recall the full obscenity of it.

That alone would be sufficient cause to overthrow Hitler and his associates.

But I will give you, if you need one, another argument why that must be done, and why you must help:

Germany will inevitably lose this war!

The genius of Germany's generals and the courage of her soldiers will never prevail against the industrial might of America. You have lived here, you know what I'm talking about.

Roosevelt tells me that he believes "as much as forty percent" of the American gross national product may be necessary to support this war. "Total war," as Goebbels and Speer envision it for Germany, is not even being *considered* by the Americans.

I will not dwell upon this.

Germany will lose the war. The degree of destruction of our cities, the number of millions of our countrymen who will be killed, is directly related to how quickly Germany loses it. There will be no armistice this time. Powerful people at Roosevelt's side are already demanding unconditional surrender.

Few know the Bavarian corporal better than I do. (God forgive me, when he knew he was going to Landshut prison after Munich, and tried to kill himself, *I stopped him!*) You must believe me, my dear Helmut, when I tell you *Unser Führer* will see Germany in rubble, her fields sown with salt, and her people extinguished from the face of the earth before he surrenders his mad dream.

It is therefore, Helmut, perfectly evident to me that it is the duty of people like you and me, whose families have guided Germany for centuries, to do our duty, at whatever cost, to see this temporary insane leadership of our country destroyed. If, after the war is lost, this will see us put in leadership positions by the victorious allies, that would probably be a good thing, but that isn't the point.

The point is that we must do our duty as we see it. Our beloved Germany cries out to you to do this.

May God give you courage and be with you, until better times.

Putzi vHan

P.S. I am guarded by an American Army sergeant in my hotel. He is equipped with a rifle and a steel helmet, and wears a baggy denim work uniform on duty. But I am as proud of Sergeant von Hanfstaengel in his baggy U.S. Army uniform as my father was of me when I went to the front in the first war, and as convinced that truly, *Gott Mit Uns*.

vHan

Helmut von Heurten-Mitnitz read the letter carefully twice, and then took a gold Dunhill lighter from his jacket pocket and burned the letter—one sheet at a time—over the ashtray. Only when he finished did he speak.

"You are aware, of course, what was in that," he said to Murphy.

"How do you know?"

"The 'better times' toast," von Heurten-Mitnitz said.

"It was sent to me unsealed," Murphy admitted. "There are no copies. I read it and then sealed it."

"That wasn't a very gentlemanly thing to do," von Heurten-Mitnitz said.

"No," Murphy admitted. "I don't suppose it was."

"He writes a very stirring letter," von Heurten-Mitnitz said. "If you see him, please don't hurt his feelings by letting him know I had already reached very much the same conclusions he has."

"I'm pleased to hear that," Murphy said. "But I still suppose it is expected of me to relate what we have learned about the extermination camps and the special SS squads."

"I probably know more about that than you do," von Heurten-Mitnitz said. "It was a factor in my decision."

"We have been led to believe that, outside of the circle of those actually involved, it is pretty much of a secret in Germany."

"Müller has a friend, wounded in Russia, who came here on recuperative leave. He got drunk and told Müller . . . and he knew about everything, not just the extermination detachments at the front. Müller had me to dinner, got him drunk again, and had him tell me all over again. I had heard whispers, and now there was proof. Müller's friend is a Leica—what's the word?— snapshot photographer."

"Why do you think Müller did that?"

"Because I tell him things I think he should know, and he does the same."

"Was he morally outraged?"

"He's a policeman," von Heurten-Mitnitz said. "Nothing shocks him."

"Motivate, then," Murphy said. "What would it take to motivate him?"

"Money," von Heurten-Mitnitz said. "A good deal of money."

"That's been thought of," Murphy said. He took two envelopes from his jacket pocket.

"There's mixed currency in each of these," he said. "Mostly Swiss francs, some Reichsmarks, some dollars, some pounds, altogether about twenty-five thousand dollars' worth."

Von Heurten-Mitnitz looked at them as if they were dog droppings.

"We wanted to make sure that you had cash available in case the need arose," Murphy said quickly. "Hence the envelope for you."

Von Heurten-Mitnitz looked closely at Murphy.

"But you wouldn't have blinked an eye, would you, Mr. Murphy, if I had said that wasn't nearly enough to buy me."

"I never believed you were for sale, Herr von Heurten-Mitnitz," Murphy said.

"I have no choice but to take your word for that, do I?"

"You have my word," Murphy said.

"I will give Müller one envelope," von Heurten-Mitnitz said. "And retain the other, should I need it. Afterward I will give you a precise accounting."

"That's not necessary," Murphy said.

"Yes, it is, Mr. Murphy," von Heurten-Mitnitz said. "To me, it is necessary."

"I was about to say I understand how you feel. But that wouldn't be true."

"Pray you never find yourself in my situation, Mr. Murphy," von Heurten-Mitnitz said.

Their eyes met for a moment, and then von Heurten-Mitnitz looked away.

"There was something symbolic about your twenty-five thousand pieces of assorted silver," von Heurten-Mitnitz said. "I presume that now you will tell me just what you want from me."

"I didn't look at the money that way," Murphy said.

"Perhaps because it is written in Scripture that it is more blessed to give than receive," the German aristocrat said dryly. "I wonder how Putzi is being paid."

"He's not," Murphy said. "Roosevelt, by executive order, exempted his art gallery from seizure under the Enemy Property Act."

"I'm surprised Putzi permitted him to do that."

Murphy didn't reply.

"I really am curious what specifically you want from me," von Heurten-Mitnitz said. "Presumably it has to do with the invasion of North Africa."

"What makes you think we're going to invade North Africa?" Murphy asked.

"Roosevelt made that clear when he abandoned the Philippine Islands. The major thrust of the American effort will first be against Germany. That leaves the question where," von Heurten-Mitnitz said. "I doubt, despite the enormous effort being made by Roosevelt to turn Joseph Stalin into Friendly Uncle Joe, that the

American people would stand for sending American troops to fight in Russia. Not the Balkans, certainly, after Churchill's Gallipoli debacle[4] in the First War. Not the Continent itself, not yet. Where, then, else?"

"Have you heard anything?" Murphy asked, poker-faced.

"Conjecture," von Heurten-Mitnitz said. "Nothing specific. The French doubt that you are capable of attacking sovereign French soil with the forces you presently have in England even if you would dare try it. They also do not believe you are capable of launching an invasion force across the Atlantic directly from the United States. I do."

"Well," Murphy said, seeing his opportunity, "since we are not, so far as I know, about to invade North Africa, where we think you could help is not connected with any such invasion."

"Then what?" von Heurten-Mitnitz asked.

"FEG is developing a jet engine for aircraft," Murphy said. "We have to have a set of authentic specifications and, if we can get it, an actual engine."

"Frankly, that's not what I expected," von Heurten-Mitnitz replied, and then added wryly, "Fulmar Elektrische Gesellschaft, the ubiquitous young Mr. Fulmar."

"From what he says, I don't think he'll be much help in this. I gather he is not the apple of his father's eye."

"Hardly," von Heurten-Mitnitz agreed. "I should think that getting the plans would be virtually impossi-

---

[4]In April 1915, in a plan devised by Winston Churchill, then First Lord of the Admiralty, fifteen British Commonwealth divisions were landed at Gallipoli with the intention of capturing Constantinople and forcing the Dardanelles Channel. After suffering 213,980 casualties, the force was soundly defeated by the Turks and withdrawn. Churchill was forced to resign as First Lord, and went to France to command a battalion of infantry in the trenches.

ble. I can't imagine they'd be left anywhere where anyone could get to them, and I daresay the plans for an aircraft engine would not fit in a valise."

"We need the metallurgical and machining specifications," Murphy said.

"I don't see how I could get them," von Heurten-Mitnitz said. "What about an engine itself?"

"Could you arrange for that?"

"From somewhere in the back of my mind I recall that on the Fulmar family estate near Augsburg FEG has an experimental electric smelter. I don't know why I remember this, but I do. I was told that it simply melts everything in, say, an auto engine. They then extract the copper and other alloying material. Wouldn't it seem likely they would send experimental aircraft engines there? Failed ones, worn-out ones?"

"Can you find out?"

"I will make inquiries," von Heurten-Mitnitz said. "It may take a little time—perhaps months. I will have to wait until I can find someone who knows. My telephone calls are monitored, and I suspect my mail is being opened."

"I'm surprised to hear about the mail," Murphy said.

"The Bavarian corporal doesn't trust people like me," von Heurten-Mitnitz said dryly. "I can't imagine why."

2

The House on Q Street, NW
1715 Hours 3 August 1942

When he heard the sliding door to the library open, Lieutenant Colonel Edmund T. Stevens, a tall, thin, silver-haired man in his late forties, looked up from a first-edition copy of *Lee in Northern Virginia* he had found on the shelves.

A young man walked in, raised his eyebrows when he saw Stevens, and said, "Good afternoon, Colonel," then walked directly to a cabinet which contained (*hid*, Stevens thought; he had had no idea it was there) not only an array of liquor bottles but a small refrigerator and a stock of glasses.

The young man selected a bottle of Scotch. "Can I fix you something, Colonel?" he asked.

Colonel Stevens, who was usually self-assured, was now surprisingly hesitant. He was on alien ground. He didn't know how to behave. There was to be a "working dinner," he had been told, with Captain Peter Douglass, and he wondered if he should appear at that with liquor on his breath.

He decided that whoever this young man was, he was probably part of the establishment (he certainly showed no uneasiness about helping himself to the hidden liquor), and that suggested that alcohol was not proscribed in a place where everything else seemed to be.

"Yes, if you'll be so kind," Stevens said. "Some of that Scotch and a splash of water will be fine."

The young man did not offer his name, and Stevens did not offer his.

Cynthia Chenowith came into the room.

"They told me you were here," she said.

"In your voice there is an implication I should have marched into your office, stood to attention, saluted, and announced my arrival formally," the young man said.

"Colonel Stevens," Cynthia Chenowith said, in control of herself but tight-lipped, "this is Major Canidy."

They shook hands. Colonel Stevens had heard a good deal about Major Canidy in the past few days. He knew he was scheduled to meet him, but was surprised by the civilian clothing.

"Dinner will be at seven," Cynthia said. "The others will be here shortly."

"Is it a command performance?" Canidy asked. "If so, what others?"

"If by that you're asking if you are expected to be there, Dick, the answer is yes, you are."

"Yes, ma'am," Canidy said. "I'll look forward to it, ma'am."

She walked toward the door and had just about reached it when Canidy said, softly but loud enough for her to hear, "Nice tail, wouldn't you say, Colonel?"

Cynthia spun around.

Canidy was stroking the tail feathers of a cast-bronze pheasant sitting on a bookcase shelf. He smiled at her benignly.

"Something else, Cynthia?" he asked innocently.

She turned around again and marched out of the room.

Canidy looked at Colonel Stevens, his eyes mischievous.

"Sometimes, if I'm lucky," he said, "I can get her to swear. You'd be surprised at the words that refined young woman has in her vocabulary."

Although he wasn't sure why, Stevens heard himself laugh. He wondered what was behind the exchange.

"She implied that you'll be at dinner," Canidy said.

"Yes, I will be," Stevens said.

"Does that mean you're one of us?"

"Yes, I suppose I am," Stevens said. "A very new one, however."

"I would ask what they have you doing," Canidy said, "and what the dinner is all about, but if I do that, tight-lipped little men will suddenly leap out of the woodwork, crying, 'Shame on you, you broke the rules,' and confiscate the booze."

Stevens laughed again. When he'd seen Bill Donovan, Donovan had told him not to be put off by Canidy's irreverent attitude, and that he was where it counted a very good man. Stevens had also been told both about Canidy's exploits in the air and that he'd completed a secret mission in Morocco.

This irreverent young man, Stevens thought, *is a veteran.*

When the Second World War started, Stevens himself was a civilian. And his somewhat sad judgment at the time was that he would not serve at all. Even if they scraped him from the bottom of the barrel and put him back in uniform, they'd make him a troop morale officer, or some such, at a remote training camp in Arkansas or South Dakota. He had made inquiries in 1940, and it had been made quite clear to him that he was persona non grata at the War Department.

In 1937, after sixteen years of commissioned service following his graduation from the Military Academy at West Point with the class of 1921, Edmund T. Stevens resigned from the Army. He had risen only, in a decade and a half, to captain in the Coast Artillery Corps.

From the beginning, his wife never liked the service, and there had been constant pressure from her, from her family, and from his own family for him to give it up. Clearly he was not destined for high rank or important command. The pay was very low, and the environment not right for the children. Subtly and bluntly they put it to him that he was no longer a child; and, as it says in the Bible, it was time for him "to put away childish things."

Bitterly disappointed when he did not find his name on the major's list in the spring of 1937, he submitted his resignation. He took his family from Fort Bliss, Texas, to New York, where a place was quickly found for him in his wife's father's business, the importing of European canned goods and wines.

By the fall of 1938, by dint of hard work (and not solely, he joked, because his wife had inherited controlling interest in the firm), he had been elected vice president for European operations and sent to London. The Stevenses had a splendid year before the war started. The boys loved their school despite the absurd hats and customs, which left Debbie and him alone together in London on what was almost a second honeymoon. On their first, there hadn't been much they could afford on his second lieutenant's pay.

When war came to England, they sadly boarded the *Queen Mary* for New York.

Shortly before Pearl Harbor, Edmund T. Stevens ran into William J. Donovan in the bar at the Baltusrol Country Club in New Jersey. Donovan asked him how he planned to spend the war, and Stevens, somewhat stiffly, told Donovan that he thought he could qualify for a commission in the Quartermaster Corps.

"You're going back in the Army?" Donovan asked, surprised.

"If they'll have me," Stevens confessed. "It's been made rather clear to me that I have let the side down. I don't think I could get a commission in artillery again, but perhaps, if there's a war, maybe in the Quartermaster Corps. I now know a good deal about how to store canned goods."

"Don't be surprised if I get in touch," Donovan said,

and then something happened to interrupt the conversation.

By the time war came, Stevens managed to get a reserve commission as a captain, QMC. This was based more on his canned-goods experience than on his West Point diploma and previous service, but there had been no telegram ordering Captain Stevens of the Quartermaster Corps to arrange his affairs so that he could enter upon extended active service. Disappointed but not really surprised, he put military service from his mind, forgot the Baltusrol Golf Club conversation he had had with Colonel Wild Bill Donovan, and went back to the family business.

And then one day, wearing a look of utter confusion on her face, his secretary put her head in the door and said there was an Army officer on the telephone, asking for *Colonel* Stevens.

"This is Edmund Stevens," he said when he had picked up the telephone.

"Hold one, please, Colonel, for Colonel Donovan," a woman on the line said.

"Ed," Donovan asked without preliminaries, "how soon can you get down here? I need you right now."

Despite a surprisingly emotional reaction—*a Pavlovian drooling at the sound of a military trumpet,* he told himself—Stevens could not, as Donovan wanted, catch the next Congressional Limited for Washington. Stevens wasn't able to get to Washington until eleven-thirty the next morning.

His wife was furious: He was simply too old to go running off the moment Bill Donovan blew his bugle. He considered his wife's arguments on the ride to Washington. They were reinforced by his uncomfortable awareness that he was wearing a uniform that no longer fit.

It was worse in Washington. As he walked across the waiting room at Union Station, a military policeman stopped him and informed him that the leather Sam

Browne belt he was wearing had been proscribed for more than a year. He was sorry, he said, but he had his orders, and would have to issue Stevens a citation for being out of uniform. He then asked for Stevens's ID card, and of course Stevens didn't have one.

Stevens had resigned himself to arrest for impersonating an officer when a man walked up, asked if he were Edmund T. Stevens, and then flashed some sort of identity card. The MP backed off immediately.

"I'm Chief Ellis, Colonel," the man said. "Captain Douglass sent me to fetch you. I must have missed you on the platform."

"It's *Captain* Stevens," Stevens insisted.

"Yes, sir, whatever you say, sir," Ellis said.

He then took Stevens to the dining room in the Wardman Park Hotel, where Colonel Donovan and Captain Peter Douglass were about to take luncheon.

That afternoon was the first Stevens heard of the Office of Strategic Services. Over broiled scrod Donovan told him that he wanted Stevens to go to London for that organization and serve as sort of secretary-treasurer of the office he had established there. What was needed over there right away, Donovan said, was someone with enough military experience to deal with the military from whom OSS was drawing ninety percent of its logistical support, as well as someone familiar with the idiosyncrasies of the "natives." Since Stevens obviously met both criteria, Donovan felt certain he would accept the job. Stevens of course agreed.

"Buy yourself some silver leaves, Colonel," Donovan said, handing him a War Department general order, four consecutive paragraphs of which promoted Captain Stevens, Quartermaster Corps, U.S. Army Reserve, to lieutenant colonel; ordered Lieutenant Colonel Stevens to extended active duty for the duration of the war plus six months; detailed him to the General Staff Corps for duty with the Joint Chiefs of

Staff; and further reassigned him to the Office of Strategic Services.

Stevens spent the next several days in briefing, most of which he didn't understand, and, honor-bound, told Captain Peter Douglass about it.

"Once you get over there, it will all fall in place," Douglass had said. "And tomorrow night there will be a working dinner, and things should be a lot clearer after that. If you'd like, you could take the day off and go home. Just be back here by, say, half past five tomorrow afternoon."

"I will have some sort of leave before I actually go to London, won't I?"

"I don't think that will be possible right now," Douglass said. "But you'll be coming back and forth, I'm sure, and we'll work something out then."

His wife was furious and heartsick when he announced he was leaving for overseas practically immediately. But his private reaction (though he was careful not to show it) was exultation, as if he had been pardoned from prison.

As Canidy made himself (Stevens politely declined) a second drink, a muscular young first lieutenant in class A uniform—pink trousers and green blouse and glossy jump boots—arrived, soon after followed by a somewhat better-looking young man also wearing pinks and greens, but with no insignia except for parachutist's wings on the breast.

"What's he dressed for, Martin?" Canidy asked.

"His commission came through, sir," Martin said.

"But no insignia?"

"He hasn't been sworn in yet, sir," Martin said. "I thought it best to wait for that before pinning on his insignia."

"If I didn't know better, Martin," Canidy said, "I would mistake you for a West Pointer."

Martin, Colonel Stevens thought, *isn't sure if he has*

been complimented or insulted. And Major Canidy, come to think of it, certainly wouldn't have made that crack if he suspected that this middle-aged retread warrior marched in the Long Gray Line.

"Do those little silver wings mean what I think they do?" Canidy asked. "That you have willingly been jumping out of airplanes?"

"Why don't you lay off me, Dick?" the handsome young man snapped.

"Eric, if you are going to be an officer and a gentleman, you will have to learn to treat your superior officers with *much* greater respect."

Fulmar glared at him but said nothing.

"Is Captain Whittaker with you?" Canidy asked.

"Yes, sir," Martin said. "He went to say hello to Miss Chenowith."

"I don't think saying hello is exactly what he had in mind," Canidy said. "Oh, excuse me, Colonel. These gentlemen are Lieutenant Martin and about-to-be Lieutenant Fulmar. They jump out of airplanes."

The announcement was not entirely necessary. As part of his briefing, Stevens had read both officers' dossiers. But now, he thought, he could put faces with names.

"My name is Stevens," he said. "I'm very pleased to meet you."

Captain Douglass, Captain Whittaker, and Miss Cynthia Chenowith came into the library together a few minutes later, trailed almost immediately by Charity Hoche pushing a butler's tray loaded with hors d'oeuvres.

They also serve, Canidy thought, *who pass the canapés.*

"I thought a small celebration was in order," Douglass said, "to mark this momentous occasion."

"What momentous occasion?" Canidy asked.

"The swearing in of Eric Fulmar as a commissioned officer," Douglass said. "I thought that I would ask

Colonel Stevens, as the senior Army officer present, to do the honors."

"I'd be honored," Colonel Stevens said.

And Fulmar put his hand on the Bible, took the oath, and stood silently as Stevens and Douglass pinned the gold bars of a second lieutenant to the epaulets of Fulmar's tunic.

Then everyone solemnly shook Eric's hand and congratulated him, during which time Canidy had a premonition that Fulmar was somehow once again getting the shaft—even if he couldn't figure out how.

Charity Hoche, meanwhile, gave Fulmar an unusually intimate kiss, and Canidy supposed that if she were half as casual with her favors as Ann claimed she was, the kiss was only a sample of what Eric would get in the way of a present later tonight. That didn't surprise him. What did was that when they went in to dinner, a place at the table had been set for her.

Douglass began the business part of the dinner by offering a flattering résumé of Lieutenant Colonel Stevens's military and civilian experience. He followed that with an announcement: on their arrival in London Stevens would assume the duty of deputy chief of station.

"On whose arrival in London?" Canidy asked.

"Yours," Douglass said. He inclined his head slightly toward Charity Hoche. Now she really surprised Canidy.

"The aircraft arrived at Anacostia at 1530," she said. "The crew was sent over to ONI. They will be here in about an hour."

"What aircraft?" Canidy asked. "I guess I'm not too bright, but I don't understand what she's talking about."

"We have borrowed a C-46—which they call the R5C—from the Navy," Charity Hoche went on, completely in charge of the situation. "They were about to put it in service as sort of a VIP transport, flying Navy brass hats between the West Coast and Hawaii, but we had a higher priority, of course. They're more than a little miffed, Dick. It may be necessary for you to smooth their feathers a little."

"*Why* have we borrowed an R5C?" Canidy asked.

"To take Admiral de Verbey and his staff to England," Captain Douglass said, "in a manner fitting a very senior French naval officer. And for other purposes, which you and I will get into a little later."

Canidy knew what the "other purposes" were. It was obvious that the Navy R5C/C-46 was the backup aircraft for the African flight. But he did not understand the business of moving Admiral de Verbey to England.

"Barring objections from you, Dick," Charity went on, "you're scheduled to depart Anacostia at 0845 hours tomorrow. The admiral and his staff will be waiting for you at Lakehurst from 0915. That should put you into Newark by 1030, with departure for England sometime tomorrow afternoon. That means you will have to leave here no later than 0800 tomorrow. It will take two cars to carry all of you and your luggage. I'll drive the station wagon and Chief Ellis the Buick. I checked just a few minutes ago, and there will be no problem with the weather, either here or in New Jersey."

"Got all that so far, Dick?" Captain Douglass asked. "Any questions so far?"

When Canidy looked at him, Douglass's eyes were smiling. He was enjoying Charity Hoche's briefing—*and* Canidy's reaction to it.

"No questions so far," Canidy said.

"London has been alerted to your arrival, and I'll reconfirm, of course," Charity went on, "once we have your departure time from Newark. You'll be met at Croydon and taken to the Dorchester, where you'll be put up for at least two days before going on to Whitbey House."

"Whitbey House?" Canidy asked.

"The Dorchester?" Stevens asked simultaneously, obviously surprised.

Canidy made a gesture, deferring to Colonel Stevens.

"Colonel Donovan thought you would like that, Colonel," Captain Douglass said.

"What's the Dorchester?" Canidy asked.

"It's arguably the best hotel in London," Stevens said.

"What's behind this touching interest in our physical comfort?" Canidy asked.

"We want to make sure that Admiral de Verbey is comfortable," Douglass said, "and that his arrival in England is not missed by certain people."

"And what's Whitbey House?" Canidy asked.

"It's been considered necessary," Douglass said, "for us to set up a close working relationship with what the British call the Special Operations Executive, SOI being much like the OSS—except, as Colonel Donovan points out, they know what they're doing.

"They operate what they call SOE Research and Development Station IX on a requisitioned estate near London. It's sort of a combination of Summer Place and the estate; it houses their agent-training facilities and serves as a hotel or billet. It is our intention to set up a similar facility as soon as possible. Another estate—they call them country houses—has been made available to us. It's called Whitbey House. It is the ancestral home of the dukes of Stanfield."

"And you're going to move the admiral there?" Canidy asked.

"*You're* going to move him there, Dick," Douglass said. "He remains your responsibility. You will report to Colonel Stevens. You know what is needed in the way of security and communications, and Colonel Stevens will arrange for you to get what you need. While you and Captain Whittaker are doing that, Lieutenants Martin and Fulmar will go through the

SOE agent school at Station IX. SOE has also agreed to make available some of their staff to help us set up and operate our own training course—at least for the time being."

"Charity," Douglass said after dinner was over, "do you think you could amuse Captain Whittaker and Lieutenants Fulmar and Martin while Cynthia and I go over some details with Colonel Stevens and Major Canidy?"

When they had gone, Douglass said, "There are some things the others don't have the need to know."

"No kidding?" Canidy asked, in sarcastic innocence.

Cynthia gave him a dirty look. Douglass shook his head in resignation, but Stevens smiled. Canidy saw it and smiled conspiratorially at him.

"Are we going to let the admiral try to steal the *Jean Bart?*" Canidy asked.

"There has been no decision about that," Douglass said, taking Canidy's question at face value. "What we're up to is a little political blackmail. General de Gaulle is giving General Eisenhower fits. More than fits. Eisenhower believes that de Gaulle can cause enormous mischief during Operation Torch. If he gets away with that, Ike is certain he'll raise even more trouble when we are ready to invade the European landmass. And if we decide to make the landing in France—Jesus! Eisenhower, therefore, wants, very badly, to get de Gaulle off his back. He has recommended that we withdraw our support from him entirely. The British rather strongly object."

"May I ask why? What do they recommend? Do they side with de Gaulle?" Colonel Stevens asked. "If that came up in the briefings, I'm afraid I missed it."

"The British completely agree that de Gaulle spells more trouble than he is worth," Douglass said evenly. "They suggested that it would be most convenient if de Gaulle were to have a fatal accident."

"My, my!" Canidy said. "Would they do it?"

"Certainly," Douglass said. "But neither Eisenhower nor the President is willing to go that far. At least not yet. Eisenhower has suggested—and Roosevelt has approved—another tack. If General de Gaulle learns that we have 'secretly' brought the admiral to England, perhaps he will find it in himself to be a bit more cooperative. He just might realize that he is only self-anointed head of the French government in exile."

"Why bring in the admiral secretly?" Canidy asked.

"If we *officially* imported the admiral, that would be a confrontation," Douglass explained. "Eisenhower doesn't want that confrontation if it can be avoided. If we secretly import him, while taking pains to make sure de Gaulle knows, that's something else. And, of course, the threat to replace de Gaulle with Admiral de Verbey will not be entirely a bluff. If Roosevelt decides that de Gaulle has to go, we'll have de Verbey in place."

"So we continue to let the admiral believe we're going along with his steal-the-battleship idea in order to make him behave in England?"

"It really is still under consideration," Douglass said. "It has gone from 'impossible' to 'possible, but probably not worth the effort.'"

"What about the plane? Is that just to make sure de Gaulle doesn't miss the admiral? Or is there anything else?"

"I'm impressed, Dick," Douglass said. "You're learning that simply asking questions often gives things away. In this case, your concern is not necessary. Colonel Stevens knows all about the African flight. To answer your question, yes, the Navy plane is the backup aircraft for the African mission. As soon as you land in England, it will be taken to a guarded hangar and stripped of its seats, the way the Pan American plane has been. We hope that de Gaulle will believe the airplane has been reserved for the admiral's exclusive use and put in a hangar to await his pleasure. De Gaulle's been after Eisenhower to get him a personal C-47, and Eisenhower hasn't elected to give him one. We think de Gaulle's monstrous ego will be bruised."

"You are a devious man, Captain Douglass," Canidy said, chuckling.

"Somehow, that sounds like a compliment," Douglass said. "I guess around here it really is."

"Right up with there with chicanery, fraud, and false pretense," Canidy said.

"There's one thing," Douglass said, "that I don't want you to think of as simply another stage prop in this scenario."

"What's that?"

"We have arranged for a battalion of infantry to guard Whitbey House," Douglass said.

"There are twelve hundred men in a battalion!"

"I thought a battalion was a bit excessive," Douglass said. "But Eisenhower overrode me. He seems to feel that de Gaulle couldn't help but be impressed with the admiral's importance if we chose to guard him with that large a force."

"I could use maybe a company," Canidy thought aloud. "The others could just be there and do what they normally do."

"Rather than make an issue of it, I decided just about the same thing," Douglass said. "But I'd like to make the point that you're *really* going to have to guard him, Dick."

Canidy looked at him curiously. "You're suggesting something," he said.

"The admiral didn't pose a real and present danger to de Gaulle so long as he was in New Jersey," Douglass said. "He will at Whitbey House. You'll have to keep that in mind. More important, you will have to impress it upon the commanding officer of the infantry battalion."

"This Brigadier de Gaulle seems to be a charming fellow," Canidy said.

"I think he really believes God appointed him to save France," Douglass said. "People who take their orders directly from God are often difficult and dangerous."

"How much of this can I tell Whittaker, Martin, and Fulmar?" Canidy asked.

"When you think Whittaker should know, you are authorized to tell him there is a bona fide threat to Admiral de Verbey's life."

"And the others?"

"I'll leave it up to you, but I can think of no reason they have to know."

"Then why are you sending them along in the first place?"

Douglass and Stevens exchanged glances.

"Tomorrow morning," Douglass said, "Chief Ellis will deliver to Colonel Stevens a small suitcase. It will contain a little over one million dollars in American, English, French, and Swiss currency. Most of it will be used for other purposes by the London station, but possibly two hundred fifty thousand dollars of it—Murphy is still negotiating with Sidi el Ferruch—will be sent to Morocco. Fulmar and Martin will take it in."

Canidy looked at Douglass for a long moment considering that. The money didn't surprise him. Fine was carrying a hundred thousand dollars in cash. Something else bothered him.

"And you're not going to tell me, are you," he asked, "why you just don't send it in the diplomatic pouch?"

"Not in specifics," Douglass said.

"How about philosophically?" Canidy asked.

"Before you ask someone to do something important, it's often necessary to ask him to do something somewhat less important, to see how he handles it."

"You mean to see if he can be trusted," Canidy said, and then he understood. "You're not talking about

275

Fulmar," he said. "You're talking about von Heurten-Mitnitz. You're going to put Fulmar on his plate like a bone in front of a dog, and see if he can resist it."

"That's *your* scenario," Douglass said.

"Oh, Christ!" Canidy said. But that was all he said.

Donovan was right, Stevens decided. *Canidy was, where it counted, a very good man.*

3

The House on Q Street, NW
Washington, D.C.
1730 Hours 5 August 1942

Charity Hoche came to the door when the security man rang the bell. Taking one look at Ann, she announced: "You're not supposed to be here, Ann, and you know it."

"She's got a press card, and she said she had an appointment with Miss Chenowith," the security man said.

"Do you?" Charity challenged.

"Yes," Ann said. "Ask Cynthia."

Charity knew Ann was lying, but she still said, "Just a moment, I'll check," and closed the door.

Cynthia Chenowith opened it two minutes later.

"I'll handle this," she said to the guard. "Come in, Ann."

She led her no farther into the house than the vestibule.

"Now, what's all this?" Cynthia said.

"I thought it was understood I was sort of an honorary Dilettante," Ann said.

"What was understood was that you would write nothing and ask no questions. You should know better than to come here."

"Where's Dick?" Ann said.

"You thought he was here?" Cynthia asked. "What gave you that idea?"

Ann didn't reply. To do so would have been an admission that Dick had called her from Deal and told her that he had been ordered to come to Washington with enough clothes for two weeks. He'd said he couldn't promise he would be in Washington, but if she could get away and wanted to take the chance . . .

Cynthia took the meaning of the silence.

"He's not here, Ann," she said. "And he won't be."

"Where is he?" Ann asked.

"I really don't know," Cynthia said.

"You mean you won't tell me," Ann said.

"I mean he's not here," Cynthia repeated, and then she took just a little pity on Ann. "He won't be here, Ann, for some time."

"You mean he went overseas," Ann challenged.

The reporter in her saw she had hit home.

"I said nothing of the kind," Cynthia said.

"Well, thanks for nothing," Ann said, and turned around and started to leave.

"Wait a minute," Cynthia said. "I'll have Charity take you back downtown."

"Don't bother," Ann said.

"Don't be any more of a fool than you already are," Cynthia said, then called Charity.

Despite her best efforts—including what she hoped were credible sobs—Ann got nothing out of Charity in the station wagon on the way downtown.

But then she thought that Dick's whereabouts weren't completely the mystery they at first seemed to be. He was almost certainly overseas. And he was involved in Europe and Africa, not the Far East. That French admiral was somehow connected, and so was that Fulmar character.

The American headquarters for Europe was in London. It was going to be difficult finding him in London, but there was absolutely no way she was going to find him if she were in Memphis, Tennessee.

"Charity," she commanded, "drop me at Woodward and Lathrop's."

The landmark Washington department store was several blocks from the Washington bureau of the Chambers Publishing Company. Two could play at the Big Secret, she thought. She did not want Charity to report to that damned Cynthia Chenowith that she had gone directly from the Secret Mansion to a news bureau.

"I'm really sorry," Charity said when she dropped her off.

"I know," Ann said.

There was a good omen at Chambers Publishing. When she went into the newsroom and called her father's office on the tie line to Atlanta, his secretary told her he was in Washington.

He was right there in the office—and torn between pleasure and annoyance when he saw her.

"You're a little off your beat, aren't you, honey?" he asked.

"Well, since you got me the job, Daddy," Ann said, "I thought it only fair that I hand my resignation to you."

"May I ask why?"

"Since you won't send me overseas, I'm going to get a job that will."

"We've been over this before," he said.

"I remember."

"This has something to do with Dick Canidy?"

"Yes, it does."

"He went overseas and you want to follow him, is that it?"

"I didn't say that," she said.

"You didn't have to," he said. "But the point is, I simply cannot send you overseas. The War Department allocates the spaces. Every war correspondent has to be housed and fed. I've got good men I'd love to have over there, and I cannot justify sending you in place of one of them."

"I thought that's what you would say," she said. "Which is why I'm resigning."

"And you think you can get someone else to send you?" he asked. His clear implication was that she was dreaming.

"I'll send you a postcard from London," she said.

"Who's going to send you to Europe?"

"Lots of people," Ann said.

"Hey, for every guy you might charm into giving you a job," he said, "I know two senior editors who will be happy to do me a favor by *not* giving you a job. Don't get too big for your britches, missy."

"How about Cowles?" she said immediately. "You think he'd do you that kind of favor?"

She saw from his look that the lie could not possibly have been a better choice. The Cowles Publishing Company published, among others, a *Life*-like photo magazine called *Look*. Since her father and Gardiner Cowles had been warring for years, he apparently immediately concluded that Gardiner Cowles had offered her a job just to make him angry.

Now that I think about it, the sonofabitch is perfectly capable of doing just that!

"Doing what?" Brandon Chambers asked, making a valiant effort to sound only mildly curious.

"Women's-interest things, the WACS, the WAVES, and whatever it is they call the lady Marines," Ann said.

"And you would really work for Gardiner Cowles?" he asked.

"I would work for the *Daily Worker* if they agreed to send me to Europe," Ann said.

"You don't mean that," he said.

"I'll try to get home before I go," Ann said.

They locked eyes for a moment, and then Brandon

Chambers said: "Greg Lohmer, who runs our radio stations, is sending a news announcer, a man named Meachum Hope, over to London from WRKL in New Orleans. He'll make a nightly broadcast via shortwave which all the stations will carry. Greg Lohmer says the fellow has a splendid voice but some difficulty with basic journalism. He'll need somebody to write his scripts. If I could somehow arrange to send you over there to write his scripts—call you a technician or something, maybe administrative assistant—would you be interested?"

"Gardiner Cowles," Ann said, "is arranging for my correspondent's accreditation right now. How can he do that if you can't?"

"Why don't I call him and ask?" he said.

"Why don't you?" Ann said.

"It would have to be clearly understood between us, Ann," her father said, in conditional surrender, "that you would be going over there to write Meachum Hope's scripts."

"Until other arrangements can be made," Ann said. "Thank you, Daddy."

"I don't know how I'm going to explain this to your mother," he said.

"You're a very clever man, Daddy. You'll think of something."

Ten

1

Croydon Air Field
London, England
August 7, 1942

IT WAS RAINING softly but steadily when the R5D with NAVAL AIR TRANSPORT COMMAND letters along its fuselage landed. When they stopped on a taxiway and just sat there, Canidy went forward to the cockpit to see what was going on.

Making it plain he resented being questioned, the pilot told Canidy he had been ordered by the tower, without explanation, to hold where he was. This wasn't the first trouble the pilot had given them. He was a regular navy full commander who Canidy suspected had put in a lot of time flying long slow Catalina patrols before the war had promoted him to pilot in command of transoceanic NATC aircraft.

The pep talk ONI had given the man in Washington hadn't taken very well. Even before they left Washington he had made it plain that so far as he was concerned, this flight to carry some foreign admiral, his tiny staff, and a handful of relatively Junior American officers to London was a typical Washington boondoggle diverting an important aviator like himself and his important aircraft from making an important contribution to the important war being fought in the Pacific.

Between Gander, Newfoundland, and Prestwick, Scotland, their European landfall, Canidy had gone forward to offer to relieve one of the pilots at the controls.

"Do you have any R5D time, Major?" the pilot had asked.

"About twenty hours," Canidy said. "I'm rated in it."

"Not with twenty hours you're not, not by Navy standards," the commander had told him abruptly.

Between Prestwick, where they had refueled, and London, Colonel Stevens had politely asked the commander to come into the cabin. He told him then that in London the aircraft would be taken to a hangar, where the seats would be removed and auxiliary fuel tanks installed. During this time quarters for him and his crew would be provided at Croydon, where they were to hold themselves in readiness for departure on twelve hours' notice.

"I'm afraid I will require authority from a competent naval authority before I could permit any modifications to the aircraft," the commander said.

Canidy was amused and pleased at Colonel Stevens's reaction to that. Icily Stevens snapped, "So far as you're concerned, Commander, until I relieve you, I'm the Chief of Naval Operations."

Canidy felt sure that as soon as the commander had the chance, he would get in contact with the highest-ranked admiral he could find to relate his tale of woe. Eventually he would be told that so far as he was concerned, Stevens was in truth speaking with the authority of the Chief of Naval Operations, and his ass would be thoroughly chewed for talking about a mission he had been specifically ordered not to talk about.

On the other hand, if the R5D was needed to fly to Africa, the commander probably was just the guy they needed, someone with a lot of experience in flying great distances where there would be no navigational aids worth speaking about. He had probably, Canidy thought, been selected for just that reason. Douglass had requested from the Navy (which really meant Eddie Bitter's Vice Admiral Hawley) the best R5D they had and the best crew to fly it. Hawley had provided a nearly new R5D and the commander.

The major risk that Canidy saw was that the commander would run off at the mouth. He thought that over a little, and then mentioned it to Stevens.

"Our minds run in similar paths," Stevens said, with a smile. "I was just thinking that I should talk with the commander and give him the 'loose lips sink ships' speech suitably revised for the circumstances."

They sat on the taxiway for fifteen minutes before the tower directed them to a hangar some distance from the terminal building. There a small caravan of vehicles was waiting for them, an English limousine with its fenders outlined in white reflective paint; an Army three-quarter-ton truck; and four American Ford staff cars.

The moment the plane door opened, Canidy realized he was back in the war. There was a familiar, pervasive odor of burning and open sewage. The smell of burning he remembered from Burma and China. It was the aftermath of bombing. The sewers had already been open in Burma and China. Here the smell came from sewers ruptured by bombs.

Two colonels wearing the SHAEF[1] patch spoke briefly with Colonel Stevens, who then came back on the airplane and said that he was going to take Admiral de Verbey with them, and Canidy should come along to the Dorchester with the others when the plane had been unloaded.

---

[1]*Supreme Headquarters Allied Expeditionary Force*

The limousine, preceded and trailed by two of the Ford staff cars, each occupied by three men wearing U.S. Army uniforms with civilian technician insignia[2] drove off into the rain.

When the truck had been loaded, the remaining Fords drove them into London. Almost immediately they saw signs of the bombing, fire-scarred holes, like missing teeth, where German bombs had landed on row houses. They passed a bomb crater from which the rear of a bus still protruded, and when they got to the Dorchester Hotel, the entrance was piled high with sand bags.

There was still a doorman in a top hat, and small uniformed boys who came out to unload the truck. But the luxury of the hotel was war-tarnished, and the lobby was crowded with headquarters types.

One of the civilian technicians from Croydon was waiting for them inside, and led them to an elevator. There was another civilian technician sitting at a small desk in the corridor of the sixth floor, barring access to the wing where Colonel Stevens, alone, was waiting for them. The civilian technician who had met them in the lobby was introduced as Mr. Zigler, of the Counterintelligence Corps.

Zigler told him that he would be responsible for Admiral de Verbey until Canidy felt that the security of Whitbey House was such that he could take over. Zigler explained that after a survey of the estate, he'd made certain recommendations for its security. The first elements of the infantry battalion had begun arriving that morning.

"If you feel up to it, Dick," Stevens said, "I thought you might go out there first thing in the morning. You

---

[2] An embroidered blue triangle with the letters US, worn sewn to the lapels.

could drop Martin and Fulmar off at Station IX on your way. There will be a car for you here at eight o'clock."

"Fine," Canidy agreed, although he would have preferred to sleep for twenty-four hours.

Stevens, Canidy, and Whittaker had a room service dinner with Admiral de Verbey in the three room suite provided for him. The service was shabbily elegant, Canidy thought, and the portions very small. He had ordered roast beef, envisioning a juicy slice of rib. He got a two inch square, tough, chunk of overdone meat.

During the dinner, Colonel Stevens told the admiral politely but firmly it would be best if he didn't leave his suite or contact anyone while he was in London.

The admiral seemed resigned to whatever indignities the OSS had planned for him. Canidy felt a little sorry for him.

Breakfast in the hotel dining room was much like dinner. The coffee, and they were allowed only one cup, was watery, the jam for the single piece of cold toast was artificial, and the scrambled eggs were powdered. But precisely at eight o'clock a bellboy wearing a round hat cocked over his eye like Johnny in the Phillip Morris advertisements came into the dining room paging Canidy by holding up a slate on a pole with *Major Canidy* written on it.

"Your car and driver are here, sir," he announced when Canidy waved him over.

The car was a Plymouth sedan driven by a GI. Even with some of their luggage on the front seat, the trunk would not close over the rest of it, and it had to be tied closed with twine. They made it that way, however, to Station IX.

Canidy found the British Special Operations Executive training school officers to be an insufferably smug collection of bastards who made no effort to conceal their "superiority" over their American cousins.

The lieutenant colonel in charge told Canidy and Whittaker in great detail what was planned for "your young chaps." What was planned that didn't sound childish sounded sadistic, and Canidy toyed for a few minutes with the notion of somehow rescuing Fulmar and Martin from the Englishman before he realized that was out of the question. And so was telling the Englishman that Fulmar had lived among the Berber tribesmen of Morocco—some of the most vicious fighters in the world—long enough to be accepted as one of them. He was also tempted to tell the English officer (a parachutist who made it plain that parachuting was an exclusively English specialty) a story that Fulmar had told him: At the OSS school in Virginia, Martin had given his own high-altitude jump trainees a long moment's horror by "falling out" of his harness and, with a bloodcurdling scream, dropping out of sight. It turned out that he did not become hamburger. He had hidden a second reserve chute under his field jacket, and was waiting, smiling broadly, immensely pleased with himself, when they themselves had landed.

Martin had made sixty-odd jumps, which Canidy suspected was far more than any of the Englishmen who were going to teach him how it should be done had made.

The temptation to tell the colonel that story was great, but he resisted it, and he went even further in the interest of hands across the sea: he had told both Fulmar and Martin, as sternly as he could, that they were to keep their eyes open and their mouths shut and absolutely no fucking around with their English hosts.

When he and Whittaker went outside to get in the Plymouth to be taken to Whitbey House, the Plymouth was gone, the driver having apparently decided on his own that he had done his duty for that day.

The British found this frightfully amusing, of course, but ultimately produced an automobile for them. It was a worn-out Anglia, an English automobile which obviously had not been designed to accommodate two large American males, their luggage, and a driver at the same time.

But it was better than walking, Canidy told himself, as the Anglia roared along (it sounded, Whittaker solemnly pronounced, like an overworked lawn mower) at what must have been all of thirty miles an hour, bouncing and lurching in the rain down what seemed like an endless country road.

There was an American GI in a steel helmet and a raincoat guarding access to Whitbey House with a rifle hung muzzle down over his shoulder, but their pleasure at seeing him ("Thank God, a GI! Where there are GIs there is a mess hall," Whittaker had cried. "Dying for my country is one thing; starving painfully to death on English food is something else!") was quickly replaced by annoyance.

The guard had been ordered to pass no one, and so far as he was concerned, that included two Army Air Corps officers. It was ten minutes before the officer of the guard responded to the sentry's summons, and another five minutes before he received permission from the "colonel" to pass the Anglia through the gate.

Whitbey House was enormous and, like everything else he'd seen so far in England, it looked run-down. But even run-down, Canidy reflected, it looked comfortable—sort of like the rectories he'd known as a boy, except that genuine suits of armor were hung up on the walls, as if they'd been put up to dry.

The officer from the London station, a nice-looking young lieutenant named Jamison, waited for them with a bulletin from Colonel Stevens. And the English officer who was going to make himself helpful to the new tenants of Whitbey House announced that the duchess of Stanfield herself was going to make an appearance.

"Colonel Stevens said to tell you he has absolute faith in your ability to handle the duchess," Lieutenant Jamison said.

"Captain Whittaker, Lieutenant," Canidy said, "is herewith appointed officer in charge of dealing with duchesses."

"And Colonel Innes is waiting to see you, Major," Jamison said. "And I think I should warn you, Major, he's more than a little pissed."

"Why?"

"I told him he couldn't move his officers into the house, Major," the man from the London station said. "And he said he would have to hear that from you."

"Why can't he move his officers in?" Canidy asked. "Christ, from what I've seen of this place, he could move his whole battalion in here."

"The final decision's yours, Major, but this is what they recommend."

"They being Mr. Zigler of the CIC?" Canidy asked.

"Yes, sir," Jamison said. "He left a map for you."

The map showed that the house was to be surrounded by a double barbed-wire fence. The guard battalion was to be placed between the inner and the outer barrier. There was a note on the map: "For self-evident reasons of security, it is not anticipated that the guard force will have any reason to enter the interior perimeter."

"Did you show Colonel Innes this?" Canidy asked.

"It's classified secret, sir," the lieutenant said. "I didn't think I should."

"Where is he?"

"There's a . . . I don't know what to call it, sir . . . a great big room, down the corridor."

"Let's go deal with him. They told you, I suppose, that you would be here awhile?"

"For as long as you need me, sir," Lieutenant Jamison said.

Canidy offered his hand.

"You and I may grow old in this place, Lieutenant Jamison," Canidy said. "With that in mind, you better stop calling me 'sir' so often. It's liable to go to my head. This, on the other hand, is Captain Whittaker. He would prefer if you bowed to him a lot."

"Jim Whittaker, Jamison," Whittaker said, offering his hand.

They followed Jamison down a corridor, and then through tall double doors into what looked, Canidy thought, like a furnished roller-skating rink—a huge, high-ceilinged room with parquet floors and what looked like battle flags from the Wars of the Roses hanging from the walls.

A plump, bald infantry lieutenant colonel, wearing an open-collared shirt, stood up when he saw Canidy.

That is not in respect, Canidy thought dryly, *it is so he will look military when he returns my salute.*

"Good afternoon, Colonel," he said. "My name is Canidy, I'm in charge here. May I see some identification, please?"

It was not what the colonel expected. He produced an AGO card, and as Canidy was examining it he took from his shirt pocket a piece of paper, and unfolded it. When Canidy handed him the AGO card back, the colonel gave him the sheet of paper.

"Those are my orders," he said.

"Why didn't you give them to Lieutenant Jamison?" Canidy asked.

"I was told to present myself to the commanding officer," the colonel said.

"For the future, Colonel, Lieutenant Jamison is my adjutant," Canidy said. "Captain Whittaker is my executive officer."

"I understand," the colonel said.

"Jamison, give Colonel Innes the map," Canidy said.

"Yes, sir," Jamison said crisply.

"I authorize you herewith, Colonel," Canidy said, "to make the contents of this map known to such officers, in the grade of captain or above, as you deem necessary. I would like your thoughts about the fences, together with an estimate of materials and construction time, by, say, zero eight hundred hours tomorrow. Can you do that?"

"Yes, sir," the colonel said.

That's what I was waiting for. Now I don't think you'll give me any trouble.

"When things get under control, Colonel," Canidy said, "perhaps you would join me for dinner. But right now there's a good bit to do, and precious little time to do it in, so I'll have to ask you to excuse me."

"I understand, sir," Colonel Innes said.

Canidy marched purposefully down the long hall and passed through a door, with Jamison on his heels.

"Where are you going?" Jamison asked when he stopped.

"Damned if I know," Canidy confessed. "I just thought a purposeful march seemed called for."

2

Headquarters
Free French Forces
London, England
1305 Hours 12 August 1942

The deputy chief of the Deuxième Bureau of Free French Forces was responsible for the most delicate intelligence function: gathering information from allies. Because the consequences of discovery while conducting such operations were not pleasant to consider, these consequences had to be constantly kept in mind. Spying on one's friends, especially when one is drawing one's entire financial and logistical support from them, has a considerably different flavor from spying on the Boche.

One can accept the loss of compromised agents to a German firing squad. It is quite another thing—*quite impossible*—to accept the penalties which would likely result from the compromise of a mission against one's allies.

As he made his way to *le Général*'s office, the deputy chief of the Deuxième Bureau of Free French Forces went over these considerations in his mind. Under the circumstances, it would be appropriate to remind *le Général* of the operational limits his agents were forced to work under: In a "friendly" country they *must* not get caught. That imperative preceded any seeking of intelligence.

The deputy chief could tell from the look of *le Général*'s personal adjutant that *le Général* was already annoyed.

He marched into *le Général*'s office and saluted.

"*Mon Général—*" he began.

"Let's have the information I requested," *le Général* snapped.

The deputy chief of the Deuxième Bureau handed *le Général* the report. *Le Général* went into his desk drawer, took his spectacles from it, and put them on. Normally, because *le Général* believed that eyeglasses detracted from correct military appearance, he wore them only in private. Normally, the deputy chief of the Deuxième Bureau would have been dismissed and made to wait outside while *le Général* read the report in private.

Le Général, his round eyeglasses perched uneasily on his prominent nose, began to read:

> At 1605 hours 7 August 1942, a U.S. Navy R5D long-range transport of the Naval Air Transport Command landed at Croydon Air Field, the usual terminus of flights originating in the United States.
>
> Rather than taxiing to the terminal, the aircraft stopped some distance from the terminal buildings. Two senior

officers, the London chief of station of the American OSS and Oscar Zigler of SHAEF counterintelligence, met the aircraft. Two passengers debarked, a naval officer and an American lieutenant colonel, presumably Colonel Edmund T. Stevens, the new number two man for the OSS in London. They entered an Austin Princess limousine assigned to the OSS and were driven to the Dorchester Hotel, accompanied by two unmarked American CIC cars.

The driver of a U.S. Army three-quarter-ton truck, plus a man in the uniform of a French Navy seaman, began unloading luggage and several wooden crates from the Navy aircraft. Four American officers then debarked from the aircraft, entered two more Ford CIC cars, and were driven, with the truck following, to the Dorchester Hotel.

Almost immediately, the aircraft was moved to a guarded hangar.

It has been impossible to penetrate the rooms the OSS maintains in the Dorchester Hotel, because that entire wing of the eighth floor is being guarded by both the British (who have a man riding the elevators and another stationed in the fire escape stairs) and by the American Army's CIC.

It had been learned, however, that the largest of the three OSS suites had been reserved for an unidentified "senior personage."

The next morning it was determined that the American Air Corps major is a man named Canidy, who was in charge of the safe house where Vice-Amiral de Verbey was interned in the United States.

Based on information previously received from our operative in the safe house in Deal, New Jersey, it is probable that the other three officers are Captain James M. B. Whittaker, an intimate of President Roosevelt; Lieutenant C. Holdsworth Martin III, formerly a French resident and a 1939 graduate of the École Polytechnique in Paris; and Eric Fulmar, a German-American last known to be in Morocco. (There is a rather extensive dossier on Fulmar. In Morocco, he was intimately associated with Sidi Hassan el Ferruch, the pasha of Ksar es Souk. Although there is no intelligence previously connecting him with Vice-Amiral de Verbey, it seems logical to conclude that he is a longtime American agent.)

The dossier of C. Holdsworth Martin, Jr., reveals that he is married to a French national, and was general manager of LeFreque, S.A., the engineering firm, before the war. He and his wife have a long-standing personal relationship with Vice-Amiral de Verbey. Now residing in New York City, he is known to be associated with Colonel William Donovan of the OSS.

At 0810 8 August 1942, Canidy, Whittaker, Martin, and Fulmar left the Dorchester Hotel in an OSS automobile and were driven to the British SOE Station IX. At 1420, Canidy and Whittaker, in a vehicle assigned to SOE, were driven to Whitbey House, Kent, which is the seat of the duchy of Stanfield, where they remained until 1915 hours 11 August 1942, when they returned to the Dorchester Hotel.

The estate has been turned into an OSS installation. A double barbed-wire fence has been erected by American troops, a battalion of which (Infantry, Lieutenant Colonel Innes) has been encamped on the estate since 3 August.

At 0615 hours 12 August, the naval personage and his immediate staff departed the Dorchester Hotel in the Austin Princess limousine of the OSS and were driven to Whitbey House. An attempt is presently under way to penetrate Whitbey House, or in some other manner confirm the identity of the naval personage.

"Merde!" said the commander in chief of Free French Forces and head of the French State. "*'Confirm the identity?'* Who *else* do you think it could possibly be?"

"The possibility exists, *mon Général,* that they wish us to believe that it is Amiral de Verbey. That, perhaps, the man is a double."

"Of course it's de Verbey, you idiot!" *le Général* fumed.

"In that case, it would seem, *mon Général,*" the

deputy chief of the Deuxième Bureau said, "that Bedell Smith has lied to you."

De Gaulle fixed him with an icy glare.

"Find out for me," he said finally, "why that Navy airplane is being held in reserve. Find out where it's going."

3

Newark Airport
1130 Hours 13 August 1942

Three of the four men in the 1941 Ford wooden-bodied station wagon were wearing the uniforms of Pan American World Airways' air crews. The two middle-aged Air Transport Command captains had in fact been Pan American Airways pilots before volunteering for the Air Corps. They had taken Pan American uniforms—including one for Stanley S. Fine—out of mothballs for the African flight.

The C-46 now had painted on the fuselage the insignia of CAT, the Chinese Airline, and Chinese registration numbers. Pan American's experienced pilots were routinely hired by aircraft manufacturers to deliver aircraft to foreign airlines. All departing transatlantic flights, military and civilian, were controlled by the Air Corps. The great majority of these flights left from Newark. The C-46 had consequently been flown from Lakehurst to Newark three days ago; the more routine their flight appeared, the better. From all outward appearances, theirs was just one more routine ferry flight.

As the station wagon approached the airfield, with the skyscrapers of New York City visible beyond the ironwork of the Pulaski Skyway, a B-17E passed over them, flaps and wheels lowered, and touched down.

"Pretty, isn't it?" Fine said dryly. *"Four* engines, too."

"Oh ye of little faith!" Homer Wilson, the older of the two ex–PAA pilots, chuckled.

Once they had shown their papers to the guard and been passed inside the fence, they drove past long rows of B-17Es sitting on parking ramps. As many as a hundred B-17s left Newark every day for England. The details of these ferry flights had been explained during one of their briefings—an operation Fine thought remarkably casual. They simply formed up flights of twenty or twenty-five aircraft. Two of the planes in each flight had pilots and navigators familiar with the route—qualified people who did nothing but fly back and forth across the Atlantic. The rest of the flight just followed the leaders. The trip was in two legs, first to Gander Field, in Newfoundland, and then across the Atlantic to Prestwick Field, Scotland.

They drove to a Quonset hut with a sign nailed above its door: TRANSIENT FLIGHT CREWS REPORT HERE.

The hut was jammed with Air Corps fliers, officers and enlisted men, almost all of them carrying Val-Paks and duffel bags. Some of them, Fine thought, were behaving like a high-school football team en route to a game. A few others, the brighter ones—or perhaps those who weren't so new to this sort of thing—sat quietly and thoughtfully, as if they knew what they were getting into and were considering their chances of living through it.

There were a harassed-looking captain and several sergeants behind a small counter. The officer spotted the civilians.

"You're the CAT guys?" he asked.

"Right," Fine said.

The captain flipped through sheets of paper on a clipboard and pulled one loose and handed it to Fine.

"They took it out of the hangar," he said. "It's on the parking ramp, way down at the end. You got wheels?"

Fine nodded.

"When you've checked it over, come back here," the captain said, "and we'll see about getting you off."

The C-46, surprisingly, looked larger than the B-17E parked next to it. It was in fact a larger airplane, even though it had only two engines to the B-17E's four.

As they were walking around it, starting the preflight check, a B-17E on its landing approach came over them at fifty feet, the noise of its throttled-back engines deafening.

They found a work stand, manhandled it into place, and removed the inspection plates on the engine while the B-17E taxied up the ramp, turned, and parked beside them.

"I am losing my mind," Homer Wilson said. "If the kid in the left seat of that thing is a day older than sixteen, I'm Eddie Rickenbacker."

Fine looked up but couldn't see anything.

By the time they finished inspecting the engine and were pushing the platform around the nose to the other engine, the B-17E crew had shut the airplane down, done the paperwork, and climbed out. They were standing by the nose, waiting for a ride down the parking ramp.

"You're right," Fine said incredulously, "that's a boy."

"No, I'm not," one of the B-17E pilots said to him, shaking her head. Her hair, which she had had pinned up, came loose and fell across her shoulders. "We're WASPs."

"I'm afraid to ask what that is," Homer Wilson said.

"Women Auxiliary Service Pilots," she said. "We ferry these from the factory." She nodded at the C-46. "I thought they were flying these over from the West Coast."

"Not this one," Wilson said.

"If somebody with fifteen hundred hours plus of

multiengine time wanted a job with CAT," she said, "who could she ask?"

"There's an office in Rockefeller Center," Wilson said. "But I don't think you'd want to go to China."

"Yeah, I would," she said. "Three trips a week here from Seattle get a little dull."

They gave the WASP crew, two pilots and a flight engineer, all women, a ride back up the ramp. Both the Pan American pilots seemed stunned, Fine saw.

They were sent to base operations for a pilots' briefing. A major, an older pilot, told them, using a map and a pointer, that a flight of twenty-three B-17Es would soon begin taking off. They would form up at cruise altitude, nine thousand feet, over Morristown, New Jersey. Then, in four- and five-plane Vs, they would fly north over Connecticut, Massachusetts, and Maine, toward Newfoundland.

"If you can get off the ground now," he said, "within the next thirty minutes or so, the flight will catch up with you somewhere over Maine. By the time the tail of the flight has gone past you, you should be pretty close to Gander. In other words, you'll have some company on the scary part of the first leg."

"Let's go wind it up," Homer Wilson said, and they went directly back to the plane, loaded their luggage aboard, and climbed up the ladder into the cabin. There were several fire extinguishers on wheels scattered along the parking ramp, and Fine drafted the security agent to help him wheel one into place.

Once he had his engines running, Homer Wilson paid no attention to Fine at all. Fine heard the hydraulic hiss as the brakes were released; then the C-46 moved onto the taxiway and headed for the far end of the field.

4

Whitbey House
Kent, England
14 August 1942

Lieutenant Jamison went looking for Dick Canidy late in the afternoon, carrying with him a six-inch-thick stack of printed forms. He found him in Colonel Innes's command post, formerly the gamekeeper's cottage, listening with something less than enraptured fascination to the colonel's most recent inspiration (Jamison had learned that Colonel Innes had fresh ideas on the subject at least twice a day) about what he called "perimeter security."

Jamison decided that Canidy would probably like to be rescued.

"Sorry to interrupt, sir," he said, crisply military. "But there are some matters that require the major's immediate attention."

"I'm afraid I'll have to get back with you later, Colonel," Canidy said.

"I understand, of course," Colonel Innes said.

As they walked back to the house, Canidy asked, "What's up?"

Jamison hoisted the stack of requisitions.

"Well, I appreciate being rescued, Jamey," Canidy said. "If I had spent another five minutes in there, I would have fallen asleep and really hurt his feelings. . . ."

"He does try hard, doesn't he?" Jamison said.

"Still—as a manifestation of my boundless faith in your ability, and also because I don't know what I'm signing anyway—you should know that I want you to go

298

right ahead and forge my name to requisitions whenever you think you have to."

"That sort of puts me on a spot," Jamison said after Candy had flipped through the stack of requisitions.

"How?"

"One of those requisitions you requisitioned is for a car," Jamison said. "A real car, not a jeep. I am prepared to defend it, but I'd rather you knew about it. You won't if you haven't even seen it."

Candy looked at him curiously.

"A car?" he asked. "You mean an American car?"

"Three jeeps and a couple of three-quarter-ton trucks are supposed to arrive tomorrow with the service troops," Jamison said. "I thought a car would be nice to have. You just signed what I consider to be a splendid justification for a sedan."

"OK," Candy said, smiling. "If you think you can 'persuade' them to give us one, fine."

"They just got half a dozen Fords," Jamison said, and added: "I have a spy planted in the enemy headquarters. I can't promise, but there's a chance I can steal one from the motor pool, and we can worry about returning it later."

"Lieutenant," Candy said, "are you actually standing there and proposing theft of an automobile from the *OSS* motor pool? You don't really think you could get away with that, do you? Christ, it's the OSS. They probably chain each vehicle to the pavement. And have you considered the trouble *I* would be in if you got caught?"

"I guess," Jamison said uncomfortably, "it's not such a hot idea."

"Now," Candy went on, "Captain Whittaker could probably get away with it. And he could probably figure out how we could keep it after we stole it. Where is he?"

Jamison smiled. "Playing billiards," he said.

"How do you plan to get to London?"

"With the message-center car," Jamison said.

"I am going to hold you responsible if Captain Whittaker returns from London with a social disease," Canidy said. "With that caveat, you have my permission to have at it. But you should keep in mind that I will follow sacred OSS tradition in this. If you get caught, I never saw you before in my life."

He handed the requisitions back to Jamison, and they went looking for Whittaker.

Canidy had dinner with Admiral de Verbey, and they played chess for an hour afterward; then Canidy went to his room. The ducal chambers, which Canidy had claimed for himself, were large, beautifully furnished, and had an alcove with a desk and telephone he used as an office. Both for reasons of protocol and because he liked the old man, Canidy had originally planned to put the admiral in the ducal chambers, but Lieutenant Jamison talked him out of it. The apartment had so many entrances that guarding the admiral there would be more difficult than in a smaller apartment with only one door.

Whittaker was in the connecting apartment, where the duchess of Stanfield had slept. Despite the warning Canidy had received from Colonel Stevens, Her Grace had not appeared at Whitbey House, and neither had the British Army officer who was supposed to "liaise" with him. Canidy wasn't sure exactly what that meant; and so far as he was concerned, he hoped neither ever showed up.

He wrote Ann Chambers a letter—exactly the same letter he had written her every day since his first night in Whitbey House: "Having a smashing time, wish you were here. Love, Dick."

The letters (all with the return address Box 142, Washington, D.C.) went to London, where they were put in a pouch and flown to the States. They would be stamped with a Washington postmark and mailed. Presumably, eventually there would be letters from Ann.

He was smugly pleased with the idea of sending her what amounted to a daily postcard the censors and letter readers could find no fault with. Ann's incoming mail was not supposed to be censored, of course (actually, he was not entirely sure about that), and she would, he told himself, understand why he was not writing more than he was. He was sure she'd get the message that he was indeed thinking about her at least daily.

The truth of the matter was that he was thinking of her all the time, like a lovesick high-school kid. And the simple act of sitting down and writing those very few words to Ann had become enormously important to him.

Having finished this day's letter to Ann, he decided to take a drink from one of the bottles of Chesty Whittaker's twenty-four-year-old Scotch he had "borrowed" from the library in the house on Q Street just before they'd come to England.

He was sitting in a brocade upholstered armchair with the almost untouched drink in his hand, his mind full of the myriad physical charms of Ann Chambers, when there came a knock at his door.

"Come!"

It was the officer of the guard, a Southern second lieutenant with a double chin.

"Theah's an officer heah wants to see Loo-tenant Jamison," the officer of the guard said. "An English officer. I mean an English *lady* officer."

"Lieutenant Jamison isn't here. What does she want?" Canidy said. As he spoke he realized what was up: The missing British officer with whom he was supposed to "liaise" had finally shown up.

"Ah don't know, suh. But she's got the right pass to get inside the innuh perimetuh, Majuh."

"Would you ask her to come in, please?" Canidy said.

The captain marched in, came to attention, and saluted crisply.

"Sir!" the captain barked, with an accompanying stamp of boot heel.

The captain was about five feet four, Canidy judged, maybe 125 pounds, maybe thirty-two, maybe a little older, and her Women's Royal Army Corps cotton uniform did not do much to conceal what was obviously a fine set of knockers.

"I'm Major Canidy," he said.

"I'm sorry to bother you, Major. I had hoped to report to Lieutenant Jamison."

"The lieutenant's off stealing a car in London, I'm afraid," Canidy said.

Not willing to believe what she heard, the captain said: "I am reporting for duty, sir. I am to liaise with you."

It sounded vaguely obscene, Canidy thought, and became aware he was smiling. He was greatly tempted to pursue that line of thought.

"You were expected a couple of days ago, Captain," Canidy said, and then gave in to the temptation. "I might as well tell you right now, Captain, that when people liaise with me, I expect them to be on time. There's nothing I dislike more than working myself up to liaise and having no one to liaise with."

The captain did not find that at all amusing.

"I'm sure the major will find my orders are all correct," she said. She handed them to him, and he tossed them on the desk.

She has remarkable eyes. Very light blue. They disturb me, as if she read my mind and knew I was thinking about her knockers. Which, come to think of it, I am not supposed to be doing anymore.

And what the hell, that was a lousy joke, and she's

probably scared half to death of the American barbarians.

"As it has been explained to me, Captain," Canidy said, "you have a dual mission here. You will handle the English for us, and for the English you will do your best to preserve this ancestral mansion from the ravages to be expected from the barbarians from across the sea."

"Oh, I don't think you're all barbarians," she said with a little laugh, "but that's about the size of it, yes."

"Your first responsibility, Captain," Canidy said, "deals with duty A."

"I don't quite understand," she said.

"We were supposed to be graced with a visit from the duchess a couple of days ago, when we expected you. I don't suppose you have any idea where the old bat is, do you?"

"I do know exactly where she is, Major," the captain said.

"Great!" Canidy said. "At my best, I would not be very good dealing with an elderly English noblewoman. I'm a simple American boy from Cedar Rapids, Iowa, and we have very few noblewomen out there. And this one is apparently a holy terror."

"Why do you say that?"

"My colonel warned me to handle her with kid gloves," Canidy said. "I am herewith delegating that responsibility to you. You handle the old lady when she shows up. Tell her that we shall guard her furnishings as if they were our own, thank her for the use of this monstrosity, and then get rid of her as politely as possible."

"I understand completely, sir," she said.

"Jamison handles room assignments," Canidy said. "There's a couple of rooms set up on the first floor, more or less for transients. I suggest you put up overnight in one of them, and then Jamison can place you where he wants in the morning."

"I believe I saw them as I came in," the captain said.

"The lieutenant who brought you up here can show you," Canidy said. "If you need anything, ask him."

"Thank you very much, sir," she said. "Have I your permission to withdraw?"

"Good night, Captain," Canidy said.

The captain stamped her foot, did an about-face, and marched militarily out of the room.

The captain had worn a wedding ring. Canidy wondered where her husband was—and whether the wedding ring would have an effect on Whittaker. All things considered, he'd rather the captain were a man.

He finished his drink, undressed, and went to bed.

5

Shannon Air Field
Republic of Ireland
14 August 1942

One of the B-17Es in their flight had lost an engine over New Brunswick, left the formation, and turned around and landed safely at Presque Isle, Maine. A second experienced engine trouble over Cape Breton Island, but because of weather conditions at alternative airports, they decided to make the first scheduled stop at Gander Field, Newfoundland. Homer Wilson, who was convinced the B-17 pilot was probably going to get lost flying by himself, got on the radio and told the other pilot he was above and behind him.

"Suggest you go on oxygen, climb to one-five-thousand, and get on my tail," he said. "I'll throttle back so you can."

The B-17E pilot's voice, even clipped by the radio, was emotional with gratitude.

Slowing down caused them to reach Gander two

hours after the other B-17Es. And they were on the ground there only long enough to refuel, even though many of the B-17Es "required attention." One of the lead pilots told them this was standard practice. The mechanics would in fact find very little wrong with engines or anything else, once they investigated the reported red X's.[3] But faced with flying a thirty-four-hundred-mile leg across the North Atlantic, pilots with only a couple of hundred hours could reasonably be expected to be a little nervous.

"I can't say I blame them. When I had as much time as most of these kids, I thought New York–Boston was a dangerously long hop."

They took off and headed east on the course the B-17Es would fly en route to their destination in Scotland. Wilson made the takeoff, but before they had even reached cruising altitude, he got out of his seat and turned it over to Fine. He needed rest, and there was no sense sitting there watching the fuel gauge needles move.

Twelve hours into the flight, after his second two-hour stint at the controls, Fine went aft, sat on the round, backless radio operator's stool, and began cranking the radio direction finder antenna, a circle of aluminum tubing mounted on top of the fuselage.

A half hour later, the needles of the direction finder jumped into life. Although he could not yet make out the Morse code through the static, Fine went forward and suggested to Wilson that he change course and try to pick it up on his own separate RDF system. When he did, the needle jumped, but the little X flag on the dial, indicating a signal too weak to be reliable, remained in view.

Fine returned to the radio operator's station and

---

[3]On the postflight examination form, mechanical problems which would make further flight hazardous are marked with a red X.

rotated the RDF antenna again. Before long the needle jumped, and he could hear the Shannon identifier. The plane immediately began to bank in that direction.

Fine stood on the navigator's stand and watched through the plastic navigator's hemisphere on the top of the C-46 until the last of the B-17Es, on a course for Prestwick, had faded from sight.

The Irish coastline appeared twenty minutes later, a black blur on the horizon which gradually came into focus. An hour later, they made contact with the Shannon tower on the communication radio. They touched down at Shannon with forty-five minutes' fuel remaining.

"I have just had a profound thought," Fine said as he stood behind the pilots' seats while Wilson taxied the C-46 down a taxiway toward the terminal buildings. "Mrs. Fine's little boy, Stanley, has just flown the ocean."

Wilson laughed.

"It may be routine to you," Fine said. "But it's extremely exhilarating. If I weren't a happily married man, I would get drunk and chase immoral women."

The Irish customs officials who met the plane were not the smiling, genial Irishmen of lore. There were four of them, pinch-faced and scowling, and they examined the C-46's papers and their passports suspiciously. Then they conducted a thorough search of the airplane itself, as if they had been tipped it was carrying contraband.

Fortunately, they did not go so far as to strip-search the crew, for if they had, they would have learned that Fine was wearing a money belt that held one hundred thousand dollars' worth of assorted currency and a dozen Hamilton aviator's chronometers. Possession of either the money or the wristwatches was not illegal, but it was unusual, and he would have been asked questions.

Two of the customs officers stayed with them when

they went through the paperwork at the terminal, and stayed with them when they went to the shabby, unpleasant restaurant for dry rolls, artificial strawberry preserves, and tea, but no coffee. The custom officials even followed them into the men's room, leaning impatiently against cracked and dirty washbasins until they had come out of the stalls.

They took off again after an hour and fifteen minutes on the ground. First they flew west but then turned on a southeasterly course which would carry them over the southern tip of Ireland, and then over the Atlantic on a straight course toward Lisbon.

Eleven

1

Whitbey House
Kent, England
0400 Hours 15 August 1942

Captain the Duchess Stanfield, WRAC, was not at all surprised when wakened by the sound of a whistle, and then a cheerful voice bellowing, "Awright, awright, drop your cocks and pick up your socks, it's that time, haul your ass out of the sack!"

There had been an essentially identical announcement last night at 10:00 P.M., shortly after she had gone to sleep on an American Army folding canvas cot in a nine-by-twenty-foot room that had been, she recalled, her downstairs housekeeper's broom closet.

Similar whistle blowing and picaresque admonitions to the guard came at midnight and at 2:00 A.M. The racket lasted about five minutes. The whistle blowing and obscenities (some clever, some simply vulgar) roused the thirty-odd men of the guard relief from cots in tents erected close behind her window. After they were up, the guards were formed in ranks and loaded aboard two large trucks. The trucks were then driven off with loud clashes of gears and roaring whines of transmissions. Ten minutes or so later—just long enough for her to begin to fall asleep—the trucks returned with the just-relieved guard, who, following another picaresque announcement from the sergeant, entered the tents, exchanged colorful obscenities as they removed their boots, then slept.

The difference between the British Army and the American Army, she concluded afterward, is that the British Tommy suffers the obscene exhortations of his sergeant in silence, while the American GI, to the delight of his peers, is quick to exchange obscenity for obscenity, and he apparently does it with impunity. She could scarcely imagine a British sergeant accepting a suggestion shouted from the ranks that he "knock off the fucking bullshit!"

Captain the Duchess Stanfield, WRAC, whose Christian names were Elizabeth Alexandra Mary, knew by now she would probably not get back to sleep. She usually was a sound sleeper. But once woken it was hard for her to get back to sleep. This was the third time she had been awakened.

She was naked between the American Army sheets. It had either been that or her underwear. She did not like to sleep in a brassiere, and her slip was standard issue, which meant it was skimpy and abrasive. One of the supplemental benefits of her new assignment would be access to her own linen, presuming she could find it.

When Whitbey House had been requisitioned, the staff had of course carefully packed away all her personal things. But the staff was now gone, and she had not a notion where in the house her trunks had been stored. Because she had not been able to go looking for them last night, she thought she had slept naked in the broom closet while a young and distinctly unpleasant American major slept in her husband's bed.

But then she came to realize that there was no reason why she could not turn her wakefulness to her own advantage. She would start looking for her things right now. In seconds she was standing on the balls of her feet on the cold, gritty stone floor and reaching for her discarded underwear.

Then she decided to ignore the soiled underthings. In five or ten minutes she would have fresh, clean, soft underthings. In the meantime, all she had to do was pass the officer of the guard in the adjacent room and head down the corridor to the rear stairs. It was entirely likely that he would not even come out of his little office.

She slipped her bare feet into her oxfords and tucked her shirt into the waistband of her khaki shirt. There was a bloody sexual injustice in women officers' uniforms. Despite the shortages, prewar-quality material was somehow made available to gentlemen's tailors. Male officers had at least several uniforms of prewar quality, while officers' uniforms of the Women's Royal Army Corps came from the same manufacturer who made uniforms for enlisted men, and were thus of the to-be-expected quality and fit. It had been possible for a seamstress to tighten her uniform skirts where they bagged over her rear end, but there had not been enough material to let out her shirts and tunics to make room for her bosom. Unless she wore a tight brassiere, she strained buttons.

She looked down at her shirt now. The buttons looked about ready to pop.

That was something else she would now do, now that she was assigned at Whitbey House. She would go into the village and find some seamstress who could take care of uniforms for her. Somewhere in the house with her personal things were a dozen or more of Edward's uniforms. They could be cut down for her, even if every stitch had to be taken out of them and the uniform started from scratch.

With her nakedness now more or less covered, she carefully opened the door, found no one in the foyer, and slipped out, walking quickly down the corridor toward the kitchen. From there stairs lead upstairs.

With no one in it, the kitchen seemed enormous. The six huge black stoves—now cold—were larger than she remembered them. The Americans apparently were not going to trouble themselves with coal stoves, as there were now two stainless-steel field ranges where the butcher blocks had been. And still in a crate addressed to Quartermaster ETO[1] was a huge, restaurant-size refrigerator. Beside it, the Whitbey House refrigerator looked incongruously small.

She gave in to the temptation to see if there was something to eat in the old refrigerator. She had missed supper the night before, and she would be damned if she would ask Major Canidy for a meal.

Inside she found an almost unbelievable cornucopia of foodstuffs. There were, for starters, at least six dozen fresh eggs. The British ration was one fresh egg per week—when available. There were two-gallon containers of milk marked CONTAINER PROPERTY QUARTERMASTER CORPS US ARMY. Only children under four, pregnant women, and nursing women were given a milk ration. There were steaks, chickens, two enormous tinned hams, pound blocks of fresh butter [BUTTER, I LB Block, Grade AAA, Schmalz's Dairy, Oshkosh, Wisc. USA], and the most incredible thing of all, three or four dozen SUNKIST FLORIDA ORANGES.

Captain the Duchess Stanfield could not remember the last time she had had an orange. They were rationed out to British children even more strictly than eggs and milk.

No wonder, she thought as she slammed the door angrily, *our refrigerator is inadequate for their needs.*

When she was in the stairwell she began to consider the most likely place the staff would have put her clothing. The answer was immediately obvious. There

---

[1] European Theater of Operations.

were two small rooms just above what had been her
own apartment where her personal maid (now a lead-
ing aircraftswoman in the Royal Air Force) had lived.

Just as she hoped, a neatly lettered sign was thumbtacked to her personal maid's door:

These rooms contain the personal effects of Their
Graces, the Duke and Duchess of Stanfield. We ask
that they not be disturbed.

And the door was not locked.

The small room was crowded with steamer trunks,
ordinary luggage, and even some paper cartons, all
neatly labeled.

She was lifting a cardbox labeled HG Personal
Summer Linen when an automobile horn blared. It was
cheerfully tooting *Shave and a haircut, two bits*. She
wondered what peculiarity of American culture that
represented. When the horn sounded again, she grew
more curious. When it sounded a third time, she went
to the window and looked down.

An American army car, a Ford, had pulled up to the
house. As she watched, a young American Air Corps
captain stepped out. He had his cap, with its crown
crushed, on the back of his head. For some reason,
American pilots felt that was chic. His jacket was open,
his tie pulled down, and he wore the self-pleased look
of someone in his cups. He went to the trunk and
opened it, then returned to the driver's door and blew
the horn again, this time a long, steady, almost angry
blast.

At the same moment the duchess was noticing that
the Ford's left front fender was crumpled, a window
below her, *Edward's window*, opened and Major Canidy looked out.

"I thought you were in the stockade," he called
down.

The duchess remembered Canidy had said something

about Lieutenant Jamison being off "stealing a car in London."

"We ran off the road and hit a stone post," the captain called up, "and we couldn't get it out of the ditch in the dark. Aside from that, it was worthy of John Dillinger."

"Does anyone know you stole it?" Canidy asked. "Are you a half mile ahead of the MPs?"

"I told you, Dick, it went like clockwork."

"Until you ran it off the road." Canidy chuckled. "Where's Jamison?"

"We also stole some whiskey," the captain reported. "He drank some of it."

At that moment, a lieutenant stumbled out the other side of the car. Since he was deeper in his cups than the captain, the duchess concluded that this one was Lieutenant Jamison.

"You can't leave the car there," Canidy said. "Not out in the open."

My God, they did steal it!

"I stole a tarpaulin for it," the captain announced, then went back to the trunk and hauled out a huge canvas tarpaulin. Lieutenant Jamison went into the backseat of the car and began to unload cases of whiskey and beer.

"Did you steal that from the OSS, too?"

"No," the captain said. "We found it in the middle of the road."

"Jimmy, behave yourself and come in," Canidy called. "That English captain we've been waiting for showed up. It's a female, a real tight-assed bitch. I'm sure she's been sent to spy on us, anyway, so keep your hands off her and your mouth shut. That applies to you too, Jamison."

Deeply offended, the duchess of Stanfield stepped back from the open window and very carefully closed it. She rummaged through her summer linen for suitable underclothing, and then went through the steamer trunks until she found nightgowns. She wrapped one of the nightgowns around everything else, and descended the stairs to the kitchen.

When she pushed open the door, she startled Major Canidy, the captain, and Lieutenant Jamison, who were sharing various breakfast preparation tasks. One of the unused stoves was littered with what they obviously planned to eat; this amounted to a week's ration for a British family of six, not counting the oranges.

"Up early, aren't you, Captain?" Canidy asked sarcastically.

"Tight, all right," the captain observed, "but not *too* tight."

"I told you to watch your mouth," Canidy snapped.

"I was gathering some personal possessions," the duchess blurted, and exhibited her nightgown bundle.

"You've been here before, then?" Canidy accused.

"Yes," she said, "I have."

Obviously, he never even looked at my orders. If he had, he would know who I am.

"The captain has been sent by the War Office to 'liaise' with us," Canidy said. "Apparently, 'to liaise' means to roam through the place before anybody is up."

"I'm Jim Whittaker," Whittaker said, advancing on her with his hand extended. "I think I should warn you that I am a pervert and find females in uniform terribly exciting."

He was looking with great fascination and obvious approval at her breasts. She flushed when she realized that her nipples were clearly evident beneath the cloth.

"I'm not going to tell you about your mouth again, Jimmy," Major Canidy flared.

"I didn't catch the name, Captain," Whittaker said. He had her hand now and seemed reluctant to let it go.

"My name is Stanfield," the duchess said.

"Like the duke?" Canidy asked.

"I am the duchess," she said.

It did not produce the reaction she expected: Canidy was annoyed, and not awed.

"You should have told me that last night," Canidy said.

"You didn't give me the chance," she said.

Jim Whittaker bowed deeply, with an accompanying sweep of his arm.

"How's that, Duchess?" he asked. "Is that the way to do it?"

She had to restrain herself from smiling at him. He was a happy drunk, and a *rather* good-looking young man. And a happy young man who is drunk cannot really be faulted for staring at her nipples. Major Canidy was the unpleasant one.

A question of protocol occurred to Lieutenant Jamison.

"If you're the duchess," he asked somewhat thickly, "what are we supposed to call you? Captain or Duchess?"

"I had a dog named Duchess one time," Captain Whittaker announced. "You remember her, Dick? Great big Laborador bitch?"

"You're supposed to call me Your Grace," she said. "But I think that would be a bit awkward, wouldn't it? My Christian name is Elizabeth."

"Isn't that the other extreme?" Canidy asked.

"Please," she said softly. "You and I seem to have gotten off on the wrong foot."

He's thinking that over, the insufferable bastard!

"OK," he said. "We'll start all over. Put your package down and have some breakfast. The cooks don't show until half past six, so I'm afraid it'll have to be an omelet."

A sudden rage swept through her, unstoppable. "My God, you Americans are something! 'Since there's nothing decent to be had, we'll have to make do with an omelet'!"

He looked at her curiously.

"Is there something wrong with an omelet?" he asked.

"Do you know what the British egg ration is?"

"No, and I don't really give a damn," Canidy said.

They locked eyes for a minute, and then she gave in.

"Sorry," she said.

"No," Canidy said. "Sorry won't wash. Let's have it out in the open."

"I beg your pardon?"

"I don't like your attitude, Duchess," Canidy said. "I may have to put up with those arrogant bastards at SOE, but I'll be damned if I'm going to put up with you. I don't like the way you came in here last night, playing captain without letting me know this is your house. And I have no intention of putting up with a litany of 'what's wrong with you Americans is' from you, duchess or no duchess. Whittaker here ate cavalry horses in the Philippines until the horses ran out . . ."

"Hey, Dick . . ." Whittaker tried to interrupt, but Canidy was not to be stopped.

". . . and neither of us needs any lectures on short rations from the likes of you. If you feel uncomfortable eating our fresh egg omelets, *Your Grace,* I think you should ask to be reassigned. As long as I'm running this place, I'm going to get my hands on and pass out to the people here all the goddamned luxuries—from fresh eggs to high-class whores—that I can. And I don't want you standing around with a corncob up your ass looking down your aristocratic nose at us."

"Jesus *Christ!* Dick!" Whittaker said.

The duchess of Stanfield took a moment to find her voice. Then she said, "Perhaps it would be best if someone else were assigned to liaise with you, Major Canidy. And now, if you'll please excuse me?"

She marched out of the kitchen and down the corridor to what had been the downstairs housekeeper's broom closet, closed the door, threw herself on the folding cot, and with a great deal of effort managed to keep from crying.

She was going to look like a bloody fool when she had to report back to the War Office that she had immediately gotten into it with the man she was supposed to liaise with over something as bloody silly as how many eggs the Americans had. She *could* report, of course, that they apparently spent much of their time drunk, and that they considered it great fun to steal automobiles from one another. The problem was that the War Office didn't give a damn about such things. They would simply see that *she* had failed.

What she was going to have to do was go to the bastard and apologize and sound as if she meant it.

She pushed herself off the bed.

And be properly dressed when I do it.

She picked the bundle off the floor and unrolled it on the bed. She picked out underwear, then started to take off her shirt.

There was a knock at the door.

"Yes? Who is it?"

"Room service," a voice she recognized as Captain Whittaker's called cheerfully.

She went to the door and pulled it open.

He had found a butler's cart somewhere. It was covered with food: ham, eggs, toast, and what certainly —since it was American—was genuine strawberry marmalade.

"No matter what," he said, "you have to eat."

"I made a fool of myself in there, didn't I?" she asked.

He rolled the cart to a chair at the far end of the bed and stood behind it like a waiter.

"I don't know what happened between you two last night," he said. "But I know what's generally wrong with him."

"*Generally* wrong with him?"

"For the first time in his life, he's in love," Whittaker

317

said, "and almost immediately upon getting jabbed with Cupid's arrow, they shipped him over here."

"Being in love produced that tirade?" she asked.

"That, and knowing that a mission he set up is under way," Whittaker said. "Despite what he says, he really thinks he should be doing it."

"You seem to know a great deal about the major," she said.

"We've been pals since we were kids," Whittaker said.

"What did he mean about you eating cavalry horses in the Philippines?"

"Eat your ham and eggs, Duchess," Whittaker said. "After which, Friendly Jim Whittaker will take you to Nasty Dick Canidy so that you can kiss and make up."

"But you were in the Philippines?" she pursued.

"Yeah," he said. "I was in the Philippines."

She looked down at the huge slice of ham and the four fried eggs on her plate. And saw that her shirt was unbuttoned halfway to her navel. She felt her face color.

He was still behind her, which meant that he was almost certainly looking down her dress. She was not furious with him. He was, she reminded herself, in his cups.

2

Lisbon, Portugal
16 August 1942

There were German fighter bases at Brest and Saint-Nazaire, whose pilots would have been happy to shoot them down, but they had come no closer to Brest than two hundred miles. And they'd been four hundred from Saint-Nazaire. En route to Lisbon, they picked up some air-to-air conversation in German, which gave Fine time to vicariously experience what bomber pilots went through, but four and a half hours after taking off from Shannon, the Lisbon tower operator, in a strangely accented English, cleared China Air Transport Two-naught-six to land on runway twelve.

The Portuguese customs officials, who were accompanied by an Air Force officer, were considerably more pleasant than the Irish had been. The Air Force officer's request to be shown around the airplane was pure flier's curiosity. The C-46 was the first he had ever seen.

When they asked him if there was someplace they could get something to eat and a few hours' sleep, he summoned a taxi, bargained with the driver for them, and sent them to "a place I think you will like" in Lisbon. It turned out to be an elegant turn-of-the-century hotel. They were met by a desk clerk in a morning coat who told them he had had a telephone call about them from the Air Force officer.

He then took them to a finely furnished two-bedroom suite on an upper floor overlooking Rossi Square and the Dona Maria II National Theater. The bathroom contained an enormous bathtub and thick towels. After Fine came out of his bath, he found the others sitting before a large assortment of hors d'oeuvres.

"No Scotch," Homer Wilson said dryly. "The war, you know. But they did manage to scrape this up." He raised a quart bottle of I. W. Harper.

The dining room offered a full menu at incredibly low prices, and they ate ravenously. Wilson arranged with the maître d'hôtel for box lunches to be prepared for the morning, chicken and ham sandwiches.

At half past six the next morning, China Air Transport Two-zero-six requested taxi and takeoff for Porto Santo, in the Madeira islands.

Almost exactly four hours later, they were telling another smiling, friendly Portuguese Air Force officer that all they were going to do was top off the tanks and get back in the air.

The next leg was a long one, twenty-six hundred miles, ten hours plus, to Bissau in Portuguese Guinea on the lower tip of the Horn of Africa. They climbed slowly to twenty thousand feet and set up a course which would place them no closer than a hundred miles off the African coast. They also planned to fly just to the west and out of sight of the Spanish Canary Islands. If they were spotted by Spanish aircraft, it was likely that the Spanish would make their presence known to the Germans.

Twenty minutes after Wilson had turned the pilot's seat over to Will Nembly, the other ex–PAA pilot, and gone back into the cabin to sleep, a buzzer sounded and the oil pressure warning light for the starboard engine lit. Almost immediately, there was another warning buzzer, louder than the first, and the fire light for the starboard engine lit.

"You better go get Wilson," Nembly ordered calmly as he quickly shut off fuel to the starboard engine and pulled the lever that engaged the carbon dioxide fire extinguisher. Fine looked out the window as he entered the cabin. Thick black smoke was pouring from the engine nacelle. It turned gray and white as carbon dioxide mixed with the smoke, and then the gray smoke vanished.

Wilson, instantly awake, went to the cockpit and sat down, hastily fastening his seat and shoulder harness. Fine stood between the two pilots' seats. He could see that the starboard propeller, feathered, had stopped spinning, and that the airspeed was already down well under two hundred miles per hour and dropping.

Wilson did not take over the controls from Nembly. He didn't even seem especially upset.

"We have an oil leak," he announced conversation-ally.

"No shit?" Nembly asked sarcastically.

"What the hell do we do now?" Homer Wilson asked rhetorically. "Go back? How long can we rely on the other engine? And where the hell are we?" He reached beside him for the chart.

"We're a hundred fifty miles, roughly, from Santa Cruz in the Canary Islands," Nembly said. "The *Spanish* Canary Islands."

"Christ, if we sit down there, we'll be interned for six months," Wilson said. "And when they finally let us go, there will be a flight of German fighters waiting for us."

Nembly began to adjust the engine controls. Fine saw that he was unable to maintain altitude without moving the RPM needle into the red.

"We're just going to have to dump some fuel," Nembly said finally. "And try to make it back."

"Set a course for Lanzarote," Fine said. It was an order.

"That sounds like an order," Wilson said with a hint of annoyance.

"I suppose that's what it amounts to," Fine said.

Wilson considered that a moment, then looked at the chart.

"Lanzarote, you said?" he asked. "There's only a fighter strip on Lanzarote, according to the chart."

"There is a contingency plan," Fine said, "for an emergency like this."

"Why is this the first I've heard of it?" Wilson said, but then, without waiting for a reply, told Nembly to "Steer zero-eight-five." Nembly began a slow, wide turn to the east.

"I'm going to start dumping fuel," Nembly said.

"No," Fine said.

Wilson looked at him questioningly.

"Our only hope to continue the mission is that when

we have a look at the engine, we'll be able to fix it. A loose—not broken—oil feed line. If we have fuel aboard, we can take off again."

"What makes you think they'll let us take off? Or that there won't be a squadron of Messerschmitts waiting for us? Lanzarote is close to the Moroccan coast, well within the range of German fighters."

"If the Spaniards at Lanzarote don't tell them we've landed, they won't come looking for us," Fine said.

"Why wouldn't they?" Nembly asked.

"I've got a name to use," Fine said. "And a bunch of money."

"Then the only small little problem we have," Wilson said, "is trying to set this big sonofabitch down on a fighter strip with nearly full tanks."

"I think we have to try," Fine said.

"That's presuming, of course," Wilson said, "that Nembly can keep us in the air until we get there, and that the Spanish don't shoot us down for violating their airspace. I don't suppose this contingency plan of yours says we can call the name you have before we get there?"

"We'll just have to try to set it down at Lanzarote," Fine said. "I don't see where we have any other choice."

The island appeared to their right forty minutes later. When they got closer to the island, they could see the single strip, running diagonally across the only level part of it, a sort of plateau on the northern shore.

"Should we try to call their tower? You have the frequency?" Wilson asked.

"No," Fine said. "Let's just go in. Straight in."

"If I screw this up with all this fuel aboard, I won't be able to go around," Nembly said.

"Then don't screw it up," Wilson said reasonably.

Fine wondered why Wilson, as the senior pilot, didn't take over the controls himself, but this was not the time to ask.

Homer Wilson turned and looked at Fine. "You better go strap yourself in," he said.

"I will," Fine said. "There's time."

He continued to look out the windshield until he saw they were lined up on the runway. Then he dropped to the floor, braced his feet against the bulkhead of the radio panel, put his arms over his knees, then rested his head on his arms.

Nembly, unused to the sink rate of the aircraft on one engine, misjudged, and came in too low. He reached up and shoved the throttle to full emergency power. The airplane turned to the dead engine. He made a violent crab maneuver, then chopped the throttle, and crabbed nearly as violently in the other direction.

They landed heavily, bounced, and then touched down again. Nembly reversed pitch on the propeller, which sent the plane off the center line of the runway. The right tire screamed as he applied the brake. Fine felt himself being thrown into the aisle and for a moment sensed the aircraft was on the edge of turning over. But then it settled, and there was a lower-pitched scream as both brakes locked. The plane skidded for a moment, stopped when the brakes were released, and then screamed again as they were reapplied. Finally the plane lurched to the left and shuddered still.

Fine got to his feet and went forward. Out of Wilson's side window, he saw that they were perhaps a hundred feet from the end of the runway threshold. Beyond that, fifty feet below, was a pile of rocks, onto which the waters of the Atlantic splashed in slow rolling waves.

"Here comes somebody," Homer Wilson said, nodding his head toward his side window.

A procession of vehicles was racing down the runway toward them. It was led by an automobile of a make none of them could identify. Next came a small fire truck on a Ford chassis. And finally two Mercedes trucks.

"I think we should shut the engine down," Wilson said, "and then practice smiling. You're going to do the talking, right, Stan?"

Fine went back through the fuselage and, with great difficulty, because a strong wind was blowing from the sea, pushed the large door open.

The Spaniards were waiting for them.

The trucks each carried a dozen soldiers. They now formed a ring around the door. The muzzles of their rifles were toward the ground. They were wearing German helmets, and the rifles were Mausers. Fine did not need to be reminded that the sympathies of Generalissimo Francisco Franco were with the German-Italian-Japanese Axis.

Behind the line of soldiers were three officers. To judge both by his more luxurious uniform and by his air of arrogance, one was a senior officer. He was standing there, Fine thought, with all the insolence of a Marine Corps second lieutenant. He was tall, stocky, mustachioed, and good-looking.

"It is forbidden to land here," the Spanish officer said, in British-accented English. "You will consider yourselves under arrest."

"It was an emergency, Colonel," Fine said. If the officer were not a colonel, flattery would not make things worse. "We lost an engine."

The officer snapped his fingers, and two of the soldiers laid a wooden ladder against the fuselage. The officer climbed up it.

"I don't think you're Chinese," he said. "English?"

"American," Fine said. "Is Colonel di Fortini available?"

"I am not familiar with that aircraft," the officer said, ignoring the question.

"It is a Boeing," Fine said. "A Stratocruiser transport. We're ferrying it from the factory to China."

"May I see your documents, please?" the officer asked.

"I'll get them for you," Fine said, and turned toward the cockpit. When he returned he held a stack of one-hundred-dollar bills. These were bound together with a paper band marked $10,000 in $100.

"It really means a great deal to me to be able to get in touch with Colonel di Fortini," he said.

"Colonel di Fortini is not here," he said. "He may be on Las Palmas. I will make inquiries."

He took the stack of money and put it in an inner pocket of his tunic.

Or maybe you'll just put the money in your pocket and not make inquiries, Fine thought.

"And now if I may have your documents, please?" the officer said.

3

The Dorchester Hotel
London, England
1720 Hours 17 August 1942

Two American field artillery officers, a colonel and a lieutenant colonel, were standing under the marquee when the Austin Princess limousine rolled up to it. Except for a narrow slit, the headlights of the limousine had been painted black, and the front fenders were outlined with white paint, in the standard if not very successful attempt to prevent fender benders on streets that were no longer illuminated. These small irregularities, however, did little to mask the elegance of the limousine.

It stopped under the marquee, and the driver, a young Englishwoman in the uniform of a sergeant of the Royal Women's Army Service Corps, stepped quickly out from behind the wheel, trotted around the front of the limousine, and opened the rear door.

The American officers had their luggage at their feet. They had come to London on seventy-two-hour passes and had just been politely but firmly denied accommodations in the hotel. They both looked at the car out of the corners of their eyes, partly in simple curiosity, and partly because the limousine more than likely carried a general officer entitled to a salute.

The officer who got out of the limousine was American. He wore a leather-brimmed fur felt cap and a finely tailored Class A uniform. (It was, in fact, brand-new.) But he was not a general officer, just a lowly lieutenant colonel. Nevertheless, the full colonel and the lieutenant colonel knew him.

"I'll be damned," the full colonel said. "Stevens!"

Stevens looked at him, and then saluted. "Good evening, sir," he said.

After the colonel returned the salute and shook hands, Stevens then offered his hand to the lieutenant colonel.

"Hello, Bill," he said, "how are you?"

"Awed by your car," the lieutenant colonel said. "And surprised to see you."

They had been classmates at West Point, and they had served together at Forts Bliss and Riley. The last time the lieutenant colonel had seen Edmund T. Stevens, they had both been captains, and Stevens had been in the limbo of an officer who has submitted his resignation but has not yet been released from duty.

Stevens ignored the implied questions. "Just checking in?" he asked.

"Just turned away," the full colonel said. "This place is apparently reserved for VIPs." His question was direct: "What are you doing here?"

"Dealing with a VIP," Stevens said. "There's a hotel reserved for field-grade officers, the Cavendish by St. James's Square, if you need a place to stay."

"So we have been informed," the full colonel said. "We were just wondering how we were going to get there."

"No problem," Stevens said. He turned and made a gesture with his hand to the driver of the Princess, who had just backed the limousine into one of the half-dozen reserved spots between the marquee and Park Lane. She started the engine, drove up to them, got out of the car, and waited for orders.

"Sergeant," Stevens said, "would you run these officers over to the Cavendish and then come back?"

"I'm curious, Ed," the lieutenant colonel said. "What have they got you doing?"

Stevens pointed to the SHAEF insignia on his shoulder and the General Staff Corps (GSC) insignia on his lapels. "I am now a member of the palace guard," he said.

"Nice work, if you can get it," the full colonel said.

"It has its compensations," Stevens admitted.

"So we see," the full colonel said. "Well, I appreciate the ride, Stevens."

"My pleasure, sir," Stevens said.

The lieutenant colonel shook his hand. Then he followed the colonel into the backseat of the Princess.

As soon as they hit Park Lane, Stevens thought, *they will begin to commiserate among themselves about the goddamned injustice: A man who had resigned his captain's commission was now winding up a light bird on the SHAEF staff with a chauffeur-driven limousine. The story would quickly move along the West Point grapevine. He now knew the word for that: "disinformation." It was far better having his former peers think of him as a chair-warming sonofabitch at SHAEF than to suspect that he was deputy chief of station for the OSS in London.*

Lieutenant Colonel Edmund T. Stevens had already come to the not-unpleasing conclusion that not only did he seem to perform well as a concierge to Bill Donovan's spies, saboteurs, assassins, safecrackers, and other "specialists," but that by doing so he could make a greater contribution to the war than he would in command of an artillery battalion.

He and the chief of station had hit it off right away. The day he arrived, the chief of station told him that the less he heard of administrative problems the better he would like it. He went on to say that since Stevens had come to him with Donovan's personal recommendation, he was granting Stevens full authority to act in his name in all matters.

The next day, the chief of station had sent him over to Grosvenor Square, where Ike had his SHAEF headquarters. There General Walter Bedell Smith neatly solved virtually all of Stevens's potential problems by giving him a letter stating that in the event SHAEF units were unable to comply with any request of the OSS, the reasons therefor were to be reported to him immediately.

Stevens's role, as he saw it, was to be as helpful as possible. He had no notion that he would ever become operationally involved. He would simply assume the administrative burdens for the people who were carrying out the OSS mission. He would be the billeting officer, the finance officer, the transportation officer, the communications officer, and quite probably, he thought after meeting some of the operational people, the VD-control officer too. He had, for instance, just spent two hours with a detective inspector from Scotland Yard, going over with him in boring detail the results of their investigation into the theft of a staff car from the motor pool and two and a half cases of mixed liquor from a storeroom. That wasn't important. What was important was that his spending the two hours with Scotland Yard spared the station chief from having to do so. The station chief had more important things to do than help to bring a couple of car thieves to justice.

Stevens passed through the revolving door to the

Dorchester lobby and walked to the bar. It was very crowded, mostly with officers of the Allied armies, among whom he was sure was at least one officer sent by the intelligence service of Free French Forces to see what he could learn to substantiate their suspicions regarding Vice Admiral d'Escadre Jean-Philippe de Verbey.

Major Richard Canidy was sitting at one of the tiny tables against the wall. When Stevens had made his way through the crowd to their table, Canidy stood up.

"Good evening, sir," he said.

There was no empty chair in sight, so Stevens squeezed in beside Canidy on the padded bench.

A waiter appeared immediately, which was a surprise.

Stevens looked at Canidy, who nodded.

"Just ice and a glass, please," Stevens said.

Sometimes the Dorchester had whiskey and sometimes it didn't. It never had much. Stevens had unlimited access to the Class VI stocks at SHAEF, and had sent several cases of this to Whitbey House. Canidy's nod told him that Canidy had a bottle with him. The Dorchester would charge them corkage for the privilege of drinking their own whiskey, but Stevens preferred to do that than use up what was available to others who did not have access to SHAEF Class VI.

"I have just spent two hours," Stevens said, "discussing whiskey with Scotland Yard."

"Oh?"

"We have been burgled. After two days of extensive investigation, Scotland Yard has come to the tentative conclusion that it's an inside job. Party or parties unknown, in the dead of night, made off with three cases of whiskey, *plus* a staff car."

"You don't say?"

"Scotland Yard is taking it very seriously," Stevens said. "They consider it most unpatriotic for their thieves to prey on their American cousins. I have been told that there 'have been developments' and that we 'may expect to hear something shortly.' I doubt if we'll get the liquor back, but maybe the staff car. If we get the car back, I'll send it over to you."

"Big flap, is it?" Canidy asked.

"If Scotland Yard catches the thieves, I think they plan to behead them at the Tower of London to set an example," Stevens said. "A chief inspector is devoting all of his time to the case."

"What would happen, do you think, if the Ford were found on a country lane somewhere? Would they be satisfied with that?"

"Interesting question, Major Canidy," Colonel Stevens said. "Particularly since I don't recall mentioning that it was a Ford staff car."

"Didn't you?" Canidy asked innocently.

"Whittaker?" Stevens asked. "Goddamn! I want to change this subject before I am faced with a moral dilemma."

"Apropos of nothing whatever," Canidy said, "I have taken to heart what Mr. Baker said about our training. I have tried, consequently, to make it as realistic as possible."

"Such as 'practicing' stealing objects and vehicles from an allegedly well-guarded intelligence establishment?" Stevens asked.

"Something like that."

"As I said, I think we should change the subject," Stevens said. "How, for instance, are your relations with Her Grace?"

"Sort of an armed truce," Canidy said. "I think Her Grace was not amused when I told her she had a corncob up her ass. It may take her some time to get over that."

Stevens had not, in the balance, been disturbed when Canidy had reported his battle with the duchess. Canidy had felt duty-bound to mention it, even though it made him look foolish. But he was pleased that Canidy had apparently worked it out with her.

"I would rather have her there than some of the other liaison officers I've met," Stevens said. "I hope you can maintain the armistice."

Canidy nodded, and then said, "Christ, what games we play."

"And, unfortunately, for such high stakes," Stevens replied.

The waiter appeared with a glass and ice. Canidy took a flask from his pocket and splashed Scotch into Stevens's glass.

"Found a source of liquor, have you?" he asked, but when Canidy chuckled uncomfortably, he raised his glass. "To realistic training and hands across the seas."

They sipped at their drinks.

"When we finish this one, and perhaps another," Stevens said, "I think we should go upstairs and have a room-service dinner."

"You've heard something?" Canidy asked.

"I want to tell you some things I know," Stevens said.

When they got upstairs, a Signal Corps lieutenant was in the suite Admiral de Verbey had occupied. He told Colonel Stevens that the suite had just been swept and that nothing had been found. He also reported that a phone tap on the lines to Whitbey House had been discovered. It had been put there, as Colonel Stevens had thought it might be, by the Free French. As Colonel Stevens directed, it had been left in place. They were still working on the installation of a secure line. It was difficult, he said, because of the old-fashioned British telephone equipment.

After he had gone, and their dinner was laid out for them, the reason for having the room swept became apparent. Stevens gave Canidy a report on the African flight first because he knew Canidy was concerned about it. The report was encouraging: The CAT C-46 was by now off the west coast of Africa, past danger of interception by German fighters. There should be word shortly that they had landed at Bissau, in Portuguese Guinea. Having got that over with, Stevens got down to what was more pressing for him.

"I wanted to talk to you about future operations, Dick," he said.

"Torch?"

"Beyond Torch," Stevens said matter-of-factly.

"We intend," he went on, "to establish an OSS detachment in Switzerland. When Fine returns from Africa he will be sent there. He has contacts in Europe, both in the motion-picture business and with the Zionist organization. There are people in Germany and Eastern Europe that we're going to have to try to get out. There are already a couple of pipelines, but Colonel Donovan wants us to establish more. I'm sorry, but I can't tell you anything more about that except that it has the highest priority."

"I'm surprised you're telling me this much," Canidy said.

Stevens did not respond to that.

"Another high priority is getting our hands on a German jet engine. Depending on how things work out when we send him back into North Africa for Torch, Eric Fulmar will probably be involved with that. It may be necessary to send him into Germany. But in any event, when Torch is over, it is planned to send him to Switzerland. There is even an idea—which I consider pretty farfetched—to steal a jet aircraft."

"Have we got anybody who knows how to fly one?"

"No," Stevens said. "And from the information we have, the jets don't have sufficient range to make it out of Germany. But since Colonel Donovan hasn't rejected the idea out of hand, you can see the priority he places on getting concrete information on the jet fighters."

"Are you thinking of using me to steal one of these airplanes?" Canidy asked. An unlikely occurrence, he knew, but still . . .

"As you don't know how to fly one," Stevens said, "I think that's probably not in the works. But on the other hand, we're in an unlikely business. There is one aviation operation in which you will be involved, however. You and Whittaker. The Germans have built submarine pens at Saint-Nazaire that are apparently bombproof. The Navy has come up with an idea. I'm told the idea actually came from a young lieutenant named Kennedy. . . ."

Thinking he was being asked if he knew him, Canidy shook his head. "I don't know him, I don't think," he said.

"No reason that you should," Stevens said. "I do. He's the son of Ambassador Kennedy. And what he wants to do is turn worn-out B-17s into radio-controlled flying bombs. The aircraft would be loaded with explosives, and then flown directly into the submarine pens."

"Can that be done?" Canidy asked incredulously.

"Taking out the submarine pens is of such importance . . . we simply can't accept the damage the submarines are doing to the Atlantic supply line . . . that the Joint Chiefs have given them authority to have at least a shot at it. We have been directed to support them as far as we can. You're an aeronautical engineer . . ."

"Who has never even been in a B-17," Canidy said.

"And Jim Whittaker is an explosives expert," Stevens went on. "I've arranged for the British to demonstrate an explosive of theirs, something called Torpex, to our experts. One of those experts should be Jim Whittaker. I think you should be the other one. Go talk to Kennedy, at least."

"A lieutenant is running this?" Canidy asked.

"Not only is Lieutenant Kennedy a very bright young man," Stevens said, "but his father owns the Merchandise Mart in Chicago, just about controls the import of Scotch whiskey into the United States, and was the ambassador to the Court of Saint James's."

"Almost as well connected as Jimmy, in other words," Canidy said dryly.

"I think that ran through Colonel Donovan's mind when he suggested we involve Captain Whittaker in the flying-bomb project," Stevens said dryly.

Then he looked at his watch. "Hadn't you better start heading back to Whitbey House?"

"I sort of hoped I could stick around here until we hear something more about Fine," Canidy said.

"Sure," Stevens said. "Stay right here, if you like. As soon as I hear anything, I'll let you know."

4

Whitbey House
Kent, England
2100 Hours 17 August 1942

As he pulled the heavy tarpaulin from the trunk of the Ford and dragged it in place over the car, Captain James M. B. Whittaker wondered if he was being subtly punished by Major Richard Canidy. There was no reason Canidy couldn't have driven the Ford himself into London, but he had insisted that Whittaker drive him. And there was no reason Whittaker could not have stayed in London, but Canidy had insisted the risk of leaving the stolen car (despite new numbers painted on the hood and a valid trip ticket) in London overnight was too great to take.

So he wound up, in the car he had stolen for his *own* convenience, playing chauffeur to Canidy and being sent back to Whitbey House like any other chauffeur.

Canidy could be subtle at times, and this was probably one of those times.

When he walked into Whitbey House, the officer of the guard told him that Lieutenant Jamison had gone to the movie they were showing. The movie started at 2000 hours, so there was no point in walking down there just to see the end of it. If Jamison had gone to the movies, the duchess had probably gone with him.

With Canidy gone, he could have at least tried to have a shot at the duchess even though he knew Canidy was dead serious when he told him the duchess was off limits. As Whittaker made his way up the wide staircase to his apartment—the one that was once the duchess's —he was forced to conclude that the world was often cruel to kind, gentle, and all-around worthy people like himself.

When he got to the apartment, he felt he was entitled, by way of solace, to a drink or two of the Scotch Canidy had had the foresight to steal from the cabinet in the library of the house on Q Street. If he didn't drink it now, he thought, it would be all gone. And technically, it was his anyway.

He went into the ducal chambers, found the Scotch, poured a glassful, and carried the glass back into the apartment. There he carefully poured two inches of it into a second glass, added water, and sat down in a high-backed chair. He was sipping it when there was a loud and almost vulgar gurgling sound. He looked around the suite in surprise and for the first time saw there was a crack of light under the door to the bathroom.

The duchess is shamelessly taking advantage of the American hot water, he thought. *Naughty. And she is not at the movies with Jamison.*

Elizabeth, Duchess Stanfield, came into the room several minutes later. She was wearing a thick terry-cloth robe, and her hair was wrapped in a towel.

"I'd hoped to be done before you returned," she said.

"No apologies required," he said. "My bathtub is your bathtub, as they say in ol' Meh-hi-co."

She smiled at him. "That was a quick trip," she said.

"Our leader elected to stay in London," Whittaker said.

"And you didn't?" she teased.

"Oh, he was on business," Whittaker said. "And I guess he . . ."

"What?"

"There's a mission on. I think he wanted to stick close to London to get word on it. A couple of pals of ours are involved."

"I see," she said. "Waiting is difficult, isn't it?"

"Can I offer you a little belt of this?" he asked. "Guaranteed to cure what ails you and to take the hair off your chest."

Now that was a goddamned dumb thing to say.

"What is it?" she asked.

"Genuine Scotch whiskey," he said.

"Yes, I think I would," she said. "I feel a bit down, myself."

She has forgiven you. Watch the mouth from here on in.

He made her a drink. She surprised him by saying she would take it neat.

"This is very nice," she said.

"Imported from the United States by our leader," he said.

"Will he be angry when he finds it gone?"

"Probably," Whittaker said. "Why do you ask? Has he been jumping on you again?"

"Oh no," she said, and then laughed.

"What's so funny?"

"Two people speaking the same language differently again," she said. "The vernacular is different. I would not use that slang, if you don't mind the suggestion, in mixed English company."

"Jumping is screwing in English English?" he asked.

"Why did I bring this subject up?"

Why indeed?

"In Australia it's 'rooting,'" Whittaker offered.

"Did you have a nice ride to and from London?" she asked, diverting the conversation to what she obviously hoped was a sexless subject.

"Lovely," he said. "Why are you down? Is there anything I can do?"

"You've done it," she said, raising the whiskey glass.

"That's not an answer," he said.

"I took advantage of everyone's absence to wander through the house," she said. "I'm afraid it was a mistake. It made me miss my husband."

Well, there goes the ball game.

"Where's he stationed?"

"My husband is down," she said. "He was flying a Wellington. It went down over Hanover. There were some parachutes, but there's been no word."

"Jesus," Whittaker said. "I'm sorry. I didn't know about that."

Her eyes met his for a moment, and then she looked away.

"Could you possibly spare some more of that?" she asked. She could not let things stand like that, she decided. It would be unfair.

"Of course," he said, and emptied what was left of the Scotch in the glass into hers. "When that's gone, we'll go steal some more."

"Have you ever wondered why there are two apartments?" she asked. "Why I lived here, and my husband there?"

The question confused him; it showed on his face.

"I suppose that goes back a long time," he said.

"The purpose of marriage between the nobility is to

ensure the line, to buttress alliances," she said. "That sort of thing."

"I'm about to misinterpret this whole conversation," he said.

"No," she said. "You already have misinterpreted this conversation, with that sweet, hopeless look on your face when I told you Edward is listed as missing."

"You said you missed him," Whittaker said.

"As indeed I do," she said. "He's a fine, amusing, decent human being, and I pray he's all right."

"But?"

"We were married because it was expected of us," she said. "One does what one is expected to do. And avoids what one is expected to avoid, which includes doing anything that would cause talk. In other words, I had to be Caesar's wife while I was assigned to the War Office."

He looked at her in surprise. He saw in her eyes that he had not misunderstood her meaning.

"This isn't the War Office," Whittaker said.

"And we are alone in the house," she said.

"Jesus H. Christ!" Whittaker said.

She licked her lips nervously. "I shock you, don't I?" she asked. "Would you rather I leave?"

"No," he said. "I wish you would stay."

He stood up and went to her and pulled the cord of her robe loose.

"I probably shouldn't tell you," she said. "But I have thought about this from the moment I saw you looking at my breasts."

She shrugged out of the robe and let it fall to the floor. Then she pulled the towel off her head and shook her hair. After that she ran to the canopied bed and slipped under the cover.

"If Canidy finds out about this," he said, "both our asses will be in a crack."

"Then," the duchess of Stanfield said, "we shall have to be careful that he doesn't find out, shan't we?"

He went to the three doors to the apartment and carefully locked them. Then he walked toward the bed, shaking out of his clothes.

He was later glad that he had locked them, for at ten minutes after four, several minutes after the duchess had woken up feeling frisky, and had wakened him in what he thought was a delightfully wicked way, Lieutenant Jamison attemped entry without knocking.

"Whittaker!" Jamison called impatiently. "Open the damned door!"

Whittaker tried to open the door just wide enough to see what the sonofabitch wanted, but Jamison pushed his way inside, looked in genuine surprise at the duchess, and thereafter pretended she was invisible.

"Colonel Stevens was just on the horn," he said. "You're to come to the hangar at Croydon as soon as you can get there."

"He say why?"

"No," he said. "But he said bring a change of clothes, and either come by jeep or bring somebody along to drive the Ford back here."

"Go take the tarpaulin off," the duchess of Stanfield said. "I can drive the Ford."

Then she got out of bed and trotted regally, stark naked, across the room.

Twelve

1

THEY HAD A bit of trouble, as it turned out, gaining entrance to the field itself; The red-hatted soldiers of His Majesty's Military Police, who guarded it, had been ordered to be on the lookout for a stolen American Ford staff car meeting the description of the one they were driving.

The MP officer of the guard, however, backed down before the icy indignation of Captain the Duchess Stanfield, WRAC, a passenger in the car. Her Grace was incensed that anyone could imagine for a moment that she could possibly be found in the company of a car thief. And they were passed onto the field.

The R5D was out of the hangar, and a snub-nosed English fuel truck was parked beside it. Its hose led to the auxiliary fuel tanks inside the fuselage. Canidy was standing in the aircraft door watching the proceedings. When he saw the Ford drive up, he came down the ladder.

"What's going on?" Whittaker asked.

"I hate to say this, but the duchess doesn't have the need to know," Canidy said.

"The War Office and the OSS agreed that any actions taken with regard to Admiral de Verbey would be a joint decision," the duchess said.

"So file an official complaint," Canidy said, and took Whittaker by the arm and led him inside the hangar.

"The captain," he said to the guards loud enough for the duchess to hear him, "is not authorized to enter the hangar."

Inside, Whittaker saw Colonel Stevens standing expectantly beside a telephone. Next to him, a cigarette dangling from his lips, was the London chief of station.

"Are they down?"

"They're overdue at Bissau," Canidy said. "They will run out of fuel in about fifteen minutes."

"So the backup flight is on?"

"Well, that's being decided," Canidy said dryly, nodding toward Colonel Stevens and the chief of station, "at the highest levels. Things are just fucked up, Jimmy."

"Well, then, tell me what's going on," Whittaker said reasonably.

"I'll start from the beginning," Canidy said. "At seventeen hundred hours yesterday, purely as a precautionary measure, Colonel Stevens called over here and asked to speak to Commander Whatsisname. He wanted to put him on a six—as opposed to a twelve—hour alert. The flight engineer told him that Commander Whatsisname was with Captain Somebody at the moment. So Stevens, being a nice guy, said that's all right, when he comes back, tell him you're on a six-hour alert, and ask him to call me for details. That's fuckup number one."

"How?" Whittaker asked.

"Bear with me," Canidy said. "Then he went over to meet me at the Dorchester, where he told me that

Scotland Yard is on the case of the stolen Ford, and that they expect to have the criminal behind bars in the immediate future."

"Are you serious?"

"Dead serious," Canidy said.

"Christ, and Elizabeth's going to drive it back to Whitbey House."

"I'm fascinated to hear you refer to her as Elizabeth," Canidy said. "But I thought you wanted to hear about this."

"Go on."

"We had a drink, and then he took me upstairs to a just-swept room, where I was, as they say, brought into the big picture. That was fuckup number two."

"I don't understand that."

"I am now possessed, the London station chief feels, of such hot secrets that my capture cannot be risked, and therefore I can't go on the backup flight."

"So I'm to go," Whittaker said.

"I'm not finished," Canidy said. "After I was admitted to all the secret crap, and Stevens went back to the OSS, the duty officer told him that Commander Whatsisname . . ."

"Logan," Whittaker impatiently furnished the name of the NATC aircraft pilot.

". . . Logan had yet to report in. So Stevens called back out here, and the flight engineer said he had heard from him. They were in Liverpool, and Liverpool is socked in. The captain Commander Logan had gone to see was in Liverpool. That was the first time Stevens had heard that."

"What time is Logan due here?"

"The train will get them here sometime around noon, I understand," Canidy said. "The weather has been updated . . . would you like a report? I've been running over to the weather office every fifteen minutes or so since about one this morning, when the chief of station arrived out here. . . . Liverpool is thick ground fog, visibility about two and a half feet, and expected to worsen. Oh yeah, and I seem to have left out that at midnight Colonel Stevens woke me up and told me it might be a good idea if I came out here."

"What about another crew?" Whittaker said. "There ought to be lot of people who can fly C-46s around here."

"Not as many as everybody thought," Canidy said. "And none we can find with a top secret security clearance, which the station chief has thrown into the equation. The Air Force is working on that. If they find somebody, then we have the problem of getting them here."

"You and I could fly it," Whittaker said. "You said the engineer is here."

"You weren't listening," Canidy said. "I can't go. I know too much."

"So what happens now?"

Canidy nodded again toward the station chief and Colonel Stevens, who were hovering around the telephone.

"We wait for the phone to ring," Canidy said.

"Jesus Christ," Whittaker said.

The phone never rang. But ten minutes later, after Canidy had looked at his wristwatch yet again, a motorcycle messenger arrived outside the hangar.

"I don't like that," Canidy said.

"How do you know what it is?" Whittaker asked.

"If it were good news," Canidy said, "they would have called and said something mysterious that would have let him know. Shit, they're down. They've probably been down for hours."

The chief of station took the message, read it, and handed it to Colonel Stevens. They exchanged no more than six words, and then Stevens waved Canidy and Whittaker over to them. As they approached, the station chief took the message back from Stevens.

"We can't wait any longer," Stevens said. "We have

just been authorized to take any risk considered necessary."

"Such as sending two fighter pilots to Africa in a C-46?" Canidy said.

"The risk, Major Canidy," the station chief said coldly, "is that you would find yourself being interrogated by the Germans. It has been decided that the mission is worth running that risk."

"So we go?" Canidy asked.

"Yes, Dick, as soon as you can get in the air," Stevens said.

"I want to see you alone a moment, Whittaker," the station chief said.

"I'll go wake up the engineer and tell him to wind the rubber bands," Canidy said. "Colonel, where's the flight plan?"

"The engineer has it," Stevens said.

Ten minutes later, Canidy called the Croydon tower and reported that NATS Four-oh-two was at the threshold of the active and requested takeoff clearance.

"NATS Four-oh-two, hold your position. I have a C-54 trying to land at this time."

"Roger, Croydon," Canidy said. "Four-oh-two holding on the threshold."

Whittaker got out of his seat. "Don't go anywhere without me," he said.

Canidy wondered where the hell he was going, then realized that Whittaker needed to take a leak.

Whittaker came back as an Air Transport Command C-54 roared past and touched down.

"I hope the rubber bands don't break and we have to come back," Canidy said. "I'd hate to try to land here in this shit."

He looked at Whittaker as he spoke.

Whittaker was extending a small snub-nosed revolver, Smith & Wesson toward him.

"Put this where you won't shoot yourself," he said.

"Where'd you get that?"

"The station chief gave me one, and he gave the engineer one. I just took that one away from the engineer."

"Why?"

"Because when the station chief gave me mine, he said I was to use it on you in case it looked as if you were going to fall into enemy hands, and I figured he probably told the engineer the same thing."

Canidy looked at him incredulously.

Whittaker nodded.

"Jesus Christ," Canidy said.

"Yeah," Whittaker said.

"NATS Four-oh-two, you are cleared for takeoff. Maintain a heading of two-seven-zero magnetic until you reach seven thousand feet."

Canidy looked over his shoulder at the engineer.

"Stand by to give me takeoff power," he said into his microphone. Then he released the brakes, tapped the throttles enough to get him onto the runway, and lined up with the white line down the center.

"Give me full takeoff power," he said to the microphone, and then switched to transmit. "Understand two-seven-zero, seven thousand. NATS Four-oh-two rolling."

The C-46 began to gather speed very quickly, and he felt the controls come to life. Just as he lifted off, he saw the C-54 that had just landed taxiing toward the terminal area.

The C-54 stopped three minutes later in front of the terminal. Ground crewmen pushed steps to the door. An officer in a trenchcoat ran through the rain from the terminal and up the stairs. It took the flight attendant longer than he expected to open the door, and he was drenched when he finally stepped inside the aircraft.

"Gentlemen," he said, "welcome to the European

Theater of Operations. We are delighted to have so many distinguished members of the press with us. We have buses waiting for you, which will take you to the press center, where we will serve breakfast. By the time breakfast is over, we'll have your luggage sorted out and in your rooms. I must remind you that from this moment you are subject both to censorship and military authority. Now, if there are no questions that won't wait, gentlemen, I suggest you begin to debark the aircraft."

The last distinguished gentleman of the press off the aircraft wore a pink skirt beneath her brand-new green tunic with the shiny WAR CORRESPONDENT brass pins. There was an official hat that went with the ensemble, but she thought it made her look ridiculous, and she had already "lost" it.

She carried a canvas suitcase, a typewriter, and a Leica camera that had cost her an arm and a leg in Washington just before she left.

Well, here I am, Ann Chambers thought. *Now the question is, where's Dick Canidy?*

2

Over Exeter, England
0715 Hours 19 August 1942

The P-38, with flaps down to dirty it up enough to slow it to the speed of the C-46, appeared so suddenly that Canidy was a little shaken.

They were over the soup, and the early-morning sun made the thick layer of clouds beneath them look like an endless layer of cotton batting.

Canidy reached forward, took the cans from the throttle quadrant, and held one to his ear.

"Good morning, big fat Navy lady," the cheerful voice of the fighter pilot said.

"Good morning," Canidy replied.

"There seems to be some doubt that big fat Navy lady could find the ocean by its loncsome," the fighter pilot said. "We have been sent up to lead you to it."

Whittaker grabbed his microphone.

"This is Admiral Wellington," he said. "Not only are you fifteen minutes late to the rendezvous point, but you have an intolerable notion of proper radio procedure. I recommend that you take up a position five hundred yards above and in front of this aircraft, and maintain radio silence until directed otherwise."

The flaps went up, the P-38 moved ahead, and the fighter pilot came back on the air.

"Tangerine, this is Tangerine Leader. Form on me in a V formation," he said, considerably less cheerful.

There were six P-38s in Tangerine, and they quickly formed a V five hundred yards above and ahead of the C-46.

Whittaker went back on the radio.

"Tangerine Leader, drop back to the rear of the formation," he ordered.

Very slowly, the other aircraft in the flight passed the P-38 which had been the point of the V. When the leader was trailing the formation, Whittaker went back on the radio again.

"Tangerine Six," he ordered, "wiggle your wings."

The wings of the last P-38 on the right of the V dutifully dipped to the left and then to the right.

"Tangerine Leader," Whittaker went on, "exercising due caution, move up behind Tangerine Six, until such time as you have your nose up his ass."

Tangerine Leader's P-38, which had begun obediently to ease up behind Tangerine Six, now moved to the center of the V, and then back to the point.

"Let that be a lesson to you, Tangerine Leader,"

Whittaker said. "Never try to fuck with a couple of old fighter pilots," Whittaker said.

"Score one for the Navy," Tangerine Leader said, chuckling. "We have enough benzine to stick with you for maybe two hours. We were already up here when they sent us looking for you. Hope that helps."

"We're glad to have you," Canidy said, meaning it. German fighter aircraft from fields in Normandy and Brittany patrolled the Atlantic off the western coast of England.

"What are a couple of old fighter pilots doing flying that thing?"

"One of us stole a car," Canidy said, "and we are being punished."

The P-38s left them over the Atlantic when they were about halfway between Brest and Cape Finister on the western coast of Spain. Two and a half hours later, without incident, Canidy put the C-46 down at Lisbon.

3

Arrecife Field
Lanzarote, Canary Islands
1800 Hours 19 August 1942

Fine, Wilson, and Nembly had been taken in the back of one of the trucks to an ancient stone barracks on Lanzarote, and held in a sparsely furnished basement room long enough for Wilson and Nembly to conclude that whatever Fine was up to, it wasn't going to work. They were going to be interned for God alone knew how long.

There was no breeze in the room and the air was hot and humid. They were fed, three times, on speckled blue porcelain-over-tin plates. The first meal was sausage and peppers, a chunk of bread, and coffee. The second meal was ground meat and peppers, a chunk of bread, and coffee. The third meal was identical to the first.

When the door to their basement room opened again, Wilson cracked, "Gee, I hope they serve peppers for a change."

But this wasn't another meal. It was a tall, aristocratic-looking officer in a well-cut uniform, who announced that he was Colonel di Fortini. Di Fortini went to each of them in turn, formally and expansively shook their hands, and told them, in vaguely British-accented English, that he was very happy indeed to have the pleasure of meeting them.

Then he politely asked if he could have a word in private with Stanley S. Fine, took him to a corner of the room, and, whispering confidentially, said that he was sure Fine was aware of the arrangement made between certain mutual friends of theirs.

Fine gave him forty thousand dollars. Colonel di Fortini very politely said he understood the figure agreed upon was fifty thousand dollars. Fine told him he had given the other ten thousand dollars to the officer who had met them on landing. Colonel di Fortini said that whatever Fine had given anyone else was between *them*, the figure that *he* had agreed to was fifty thousand dollars.

There was something unreal, almost comical, about the conversation.

All he has to do, Fine thought as he took another ten-thousand-dollar stack of bills from his money belt and handed it to di Fortini, *is help himself.*

As Fine stuffed his shirt over the remaining forty thousand dollars in his money belt, di Fortini carefully distributed his five ten-thousand-dollar stacks of currency in his tunic pockets, and then shook Fine's hand again.

Then he gestured dramatically toward the door. Fine told him that it would be necessary to work on the engine, and that he would be most grateful if the colonel could arrange for a ladder to do so.

"Your mechanical irregularity has been detected and corrected," di Fortini said, "by our very best workmen. It was a loose oil line."

Fine said that he would like to have a look at the engine anyway, just to be sure there was nothing else wrong.

"That will be unnecessary," di Fortini said. "You have my personal assurance that there is no longer any sort of mechanical irregularity."

Fine decided not to press the point. If the leak had not been repaired, that would be evident when they started the engine. To insist on checking would have been an insult to Spanish pride, and they were in no position to insult anything Spanish.

There was a little smoke when Wilson cranked the engine, but that was residual lost oil, and it disappeared before they had taxied back down the runway and turned around to take off.

Wilson was flying. He didn't say so, but it was clear that he thought the runway much too short. He ran the engines to full takeoff power before releasing the brakes, and they were within a hundred yards of the end of the runway before he could get it in the air.

There was nothing to worry about now, Fine thought, but two small problems. First, there was the very real possibility that the charming Colonel di Fortini had contacted his German friends in Morocco.

Second, they were now going to arrive at Bissau before daylight. Arrangements had been made for them to land there, but they were long behind schedule. Bissau would naturally have assumed that they had gone down in the drink, and there would be no one available to turn on the landing-field lights.

Thankfully, there were no Germans, but there was another problem. As they reached ten-thousand feet, Nembly began to complain of cramps. By the time they had climbed to twenty-thousand feet, his cramps had turned to diarrhea. With a portable oxygen mask clamped to his face, he had gone into the cabin to fend as best he could with the situation on the makeshift toilet.

4

Aeroport de Bissau
Portuguese Guinea
0225 Hours 20 August 1942

There was a radio direction transmitter at Bissau, a weak one. And when the CAT aircraft reached the area, they spotted a rotating beacon. But aside from a few faint lights—which could have been streetlights or anything—the beacon was the only aviation light. There were no runway lights. And there was no answer when Fine tried to reach the tower on the air-to-ground radio.

There was an hour-thirty fuel aboard. Sunrise was at 0455, twenty-five minutes after they would run out of fuel. There was no alternative airport.

They were flying two-minute circles around the flashing beacon, when all of a sudden approach lights and runway lights flickered, blinked, and then stayed on, and a voice came over the air.

"Aircraft in vicinity Bissau aerodrome, this is Bissau tower."

The runway was rough, narrow, short, and—when they finally slowed enough—they saw that it was paved with some sort of shell.

When they went into the cabin, Nembly was sitting on the makeshift toilet, hunched under a blanket. He was obviously quite ill.

"Fucking Spaniards and their fucking peppers," Nembly said.

One man was both tower operator and airport manager. He was plump and olive-skinned and he wore a loosely woven shirt with square tails outside his trousers.

In broken English, he told them that when they hadn't shown up on schedule, he had assumed they weren't coming.

Fine managed to explain that they would need a ladder to inspect the engines.

A heavy wooden ladder was produced, which proved too short to reach the C-46's engine nacelles. The airport manager sent for a truck. With the ladder on the truck bed, it was high enough. Wilson climbed very carefully up, worked the Dzus fasteners, and opened the nacelle cover.

"Looks all right to me," Wilson called, after three minutes of close inspection. "Maybe that Spaniard knew what he was doing."

And then the ladder rung he was standing on made a cracking noise and gave way. Wilson fell outward, arms flailing. His forehead struck one of the propeller blades a glancing blow, but enough to open the skin. Then he fell onto the roof of the truck. The steel roof made a dull thump, and then Wilson slid off the roof onto the hood and then the ground.

He was unconscious when Fine reached him, and blood from the cut on his forehead covered his eyes and lower face. It was immediately evident that his left arm was broken.

Fine went quickly up the ladder and snatched the first-aid kit from its mounting just forward of the door. When he saw Nembly on the toilet, he realized for the first time that the C-46 was without a competent pilot.

He went back down the ladder and rolled Wilson onto his back. First he applied a pressure dressing—a pad of bandage attached to cloth—to Wilson's head to stop the bleeding. Then he found an ammonia ampoule, snapped the top, and put it under Wilson's nostrils.

Wilson groaned, shook his head, tried to sit up, and then cried out in agony as the broken ends of the bones of his left arm ground against each other.

"Oh shit!" Wilson said. "It hurts."

Fine found morphine syringes in the first-aid kit and injected Wilson in the buttock.

There was a hospital, the airport manager told Fine, run by Catholic nuns. They put Wilson in the cab of the truck and took him there, a fifteen-minute drive over a very bumpy road. Twice Wilson asked to stop so that he could throw up.

With infinite gentleness, but no local anesthetic, two very obliging nuns, wearing thin cotton robes and headpieces, cleaned and sutured the deep cut in Wilson's forehead, and then, making him scream despite the morphine, set his broken arm and wrapped it in a heavy plaster of paris cast.

Wilson sat up, his face gray and covered with beads of sweat.

"It's a hell of a place to be marooned," he said. "But it looks like this cockamamy operation is suspended again, at least until we can cure Nembly of his terminal shits."

"There's a schedule," Fine said.

"Is the schedule that important?" Wilson asked, after a moment.

"I think so," Fine said.

"Well, I can sit there and work the flaps, I suppose," Wilson said.

Four hours after they landed at Bissau, they took off again.

When he had it at cruising altitude and trimmed up,

Fine went back in the cabin to check on Nembly. He was off the portable toilet, but not far from it, curled up under blankets. As he went back to the cabin, Fine consoled himself that the worst case of diarrhea probably wouldn't last more than twelve hours. By the time they reached Luanda, Nembly would be well enough to take the controls.

When he had strapped himself in the pilot's seat, Wilson asked him if there was any Benzedrine. "I'm getting pretty damned groggy," he said.

"Why don't you get some sleep?" Fine said. "And take the Benzedrine when you wake up? I can handle it for a while."

"I've just got to take a couple of winks," Wilson said, making it an apology.

He fell asleep almost immediately.

Fine found the Benzedrine. It was guaranteed to keep you awake, he had been told, the price being that you slept like you were dead when they wore off. He decided against taking any yet. He would wait until he really needed one.

There was very little to do in the cockpit. The C-46 was on autopilot on a southeasterly course that took them over the South Atlantic. It was twenty-four hundred miles, say ten hours, from Bissau to Luanda. He knew he could not expect to hit it using only dead reckoning. It was like flying from Pensacola to Boston and back with no reference to anything on the ground and with no assist from navigational aids.

They were also now out of oxygen, which meant that he could fly no higher than twelve thousand feet, which in turn meant the fuel consumption was considerably higher than it would have been at twenty or thirty thousand.

He drank all but what he guessed were two cups of the now-cold coffee in the thermos. He had to leave some for Nembly, he knew, presuming he recovered, or for Wilson if he didn't.

He dozed off, caught himself, shifted in the seat, and flexed his legs and arms. He thought that perhaps if he took the plane off the autopilot and flew it, that might keep him awake. He really didn't want to start taking the Benzedrine just yet.

He woke up, he didn't know how much later, looked at the altimeter, and felt bile in his throat. The altimeter indicated seven-thousand feet.

He knew what had happened. When he had dozed off, he had apparently been in a very slight nose-down position. If the nose had been elevated as much as it had been depressed, they would have just as gently climbed five-thousand feet, which would have taken them to seventeen-thousand. From thirteen-thousand up there would have been increasing oxygen starvation. He would have been unconscious at around fourteen-thousand; and at seventeen-thousand, they would have all been dead.

He reached for the trim wheel and set up a slight nose-up altitude. Then he popped three of the Benzedrine capsules into his mouth and washed them down with a swallow of cold coffee. Benzedrine was no longer an option for later use; he needed it now.

He took the C-46 to ten-thousand feet, and then went aft again to check on Nembly. If anything, he was worse. Whatever was wrong with him, Fine decided, it had nothing to do with Spanish peppers.

But when he got back to the cockpit, Wilson was awake.

"Is there any coffee left?" Wilson asked. "I can watch the gauges awhile."

"I just took some Benzedrine," Fine said as he poured a cupful of coffee for Wilson.

"You should have woken me up," Wilson said.

What I should have done, Fine thought, suddenly furious, *when Canidy waved the flag at me, was tell him to stick it up his ass. Then I wouldn't be in this fucking mess.*

The depth of his anger surprised him. After a moment, he decided it was a symptom of fatigue. And fear.

The next thing he knew, he was coming awake. His bladder ached to be relieved of all the coffee.

The damned Benzedrine doesn't work, he thought angrily.

The forty-eight-hour clock on the instrument panel had stopped. He looked at his watch. He had been asleep for two hours. The clock had stopped long before that. They had forgotten to wind it.

What else, in our fatigue, have we forgotten to do?

He wound the clock and set it, and then went aft to relieve himself. Nembly was shivering beneath his blankets, and the square aluminum box they were using as a toilet smelled so foul when Fine lifted the lid he thought he was going to be sick.

5

Luanda, Portuguese Angola
1000 Hours 20 August 1942

For some reason (perhaps, Whittaker thought, because the London station chief had given him a gun so he could shoot Canidy, or perhaps because Whittaker had shoved his own gun into the man's face and taken the gun away), the flight engineer was growing more and more nervous and irritable as the flight progressed. And ten hours and fifteen minutes after they had taken off, he had come forward and angrily but wordlessly switched on the radio direction finder (because its hiss annoyed Canidy, he had turned it off hours before) with a vehemence that seemed no less a challenge than an upraised middle finger.

Whittaker looked over at Canidy, who was sound asleep with his head resting at an angle that was going to give him a stiff neck when he woke. Very tenderly, Whittaker leaned over and pushed Dick gently, so that his head hung down over his chest. He would not wake him, he decided, until they were twenty minutes or so out of Luanda.

When they shut down the engines in front of the corrugated tin building that was the Luanda terminal, they saw waiting for them—in addition to the khaki-uniformed Portuguese customs officials—a civilian, obviously American, wearing a seersucker suit, a necktie, and a natty straw hat.

Canidy climbed down the ladder and approached him.

"I'm Canidy," Canidy said. "I presume you're from the consulate?"

The man gave him his hand. The handshake was perfunctory.

"My name is Spiers," the man said, "Ronald I. Spiers, and I'm the United States consul general for Angola."

"Have you any word on what happened to the other plane?" Canidy asked.

Ronald I. Spiers ignored the question. "Excuse me, but you'll understand the necessity of this," he said. "Do you have any identification?"

"Who the hell else do you think would be flying that airplane?" Jim Whittaker asked.

He looks and talks like Baker, Canidy thought. *They must have a mold somewhere where they turn them out like Hershey Bars, each one just like every other one. And how did you fuck up, Mr. United States Consul General, to get stuck in an asshole of the world like this?*

"One never knows, does one?" Spiers said.

Canidy handed over his AGO card. Spiers examined it and passed it back.

"There has been no word on the other aircraft," he said.

"Shit!" Canidy said.

"Goddamn it!" Whittaker said.

Spiers looked at them with distaste. Then he opened his briefcase and took from it an envelope stamped TOP SECRET. He opened it and took out a single sheet of paper and handed it to Canidy.

```
URGENT
DEPTSTATE WASHINGTON
VIA MACKAY
FOR USEMBASSY JOHANNESBURG SOUTH AFRICA
EYESONLY AMBASSADOR
DIRECTION SECSTATE RELAY FOLLOWING US CONSUL
GENERAL LUANDA BEST POSSIBLE MEANS INCLUDING
COURIER STOP REPORT DELIVERY RADIO STOP QUOTE
DIRECTION SECSTATE RELAY TO STANLEY S FINE ABOARD
CHINA AIR TRANSPORT C-46 AIRCRAFT SCHEDULED REFUEL
LUANDA 19 AUGUST STOP IF UNABLE ARRIVE CARGO
LOADING POINT FOUR HOURS PRIOR DAYBREAK 21 JULY
ABORT MISSION PROCEED CAPETOWN SOUTH AFRICA STOP
CANNOT OVEREMPHASIZE IMPORTANCE OF CARGO PICKUP
STOP SIGNATURE CHENOWITH STOP END MESSAGE
```

"Inasmuch as we must presume the other aircraft has been lost," Spiers said, emotionless, "I thought I should make the contents of the cable known to you."

Canidy handed the cable to Whittaker.

"You should have no problem," Spiers said. "I have arranged for your aircraft to be refueled. That should take no more than an hour. You can arrive in Kolwezi in plenty of time to load your cargo and depart within that time frame."

"We'll take off about half past seven tonight," Canidy said. "That should put us over the border at half past eight. By then it should be dark."

"I'd really rather you continue on with this mission just as soon as you could," Spiers said.

"You would?" Canidy asked dryly.

"I was led to believe that the aircraft would bear civilian markings," Spiers said. "There is liable to be trouble with the Portuguese authorities over a military aircraft"

"Well, you'll just have to handle the Portuguese," Canidy said.

"I'm afraid I must insist," Spiers said.

"I have no intention of flying an aircraft with US NAVY in large letters on the wings over the Belgian Congo in the daylight," Canidy said.

"I hadn't considered that," Spiers said. "It will make things difficult for me, but I suppose you're right."

"I'm glad you feel that way," Canidy said. If Spiers detected the sarcasm, he gave no sign.

"Is there someplace we can get something to eat, and maybe some sleep?" Canidy asked.

"Do you think that's wise?" Spiers asked.

"The eating or the sleeping?" Whittaker asked innocently.

Spiers could not ignore the sarcasm.

"There is a hotel in town," he said. "I'll take you there."

The hotel rooms were dirty, and none of them could read the menu in the dining room. Whittaker solved the problem by flapping his arms and making sounds like a rooster. Soon they were served a large platter of eggs and a large loaf of freshly baked, very good bread.

The mosquito netting over the beds had holes through which a variety of winged insects flew with ease. Although he remembered being bitten only once or twice, when Canidy splashed water on his face and looked in the mirror, he saw at least a dozen round, angry insect bites.

He found that Whittaker had suffered equally when

he met him in the lobby. But when he went to wake the flight engineer, the room was empty. Spiers had already joined Whittaker by the time Canidy returned to the lobby.

"Where do you think he is?" he asked.

"He's around town somewhere," Canidy said. "He's going to wait until we take off and then reappear, all apologies for having missed the flight."

"Why would he do that?"

"He probably came to the slow realization while we flew that this flight was hazardous duty," Whittaker said.

"What am I supposed to do with him?" Spiers asked. "That could pose a very embarrassing situation."

"When he does show up," Canidy said angrily, "you can brighten his day by telling him that when he does get back, I will press charges."

Even as he said it, he knew it was an empty threat. To charge a man with avoiding hazardous duty, you would have to specify *what* hazardous duty. Officially, this flight—whether or not they made it—didn't exist.

They didn't absolutely have to have a flight engineer. It was a really chickenshit thing for the engineer to do, of course, but he knew that they could do without him. He wondered if that had entered into the man's thinking.

Spiers drove them back to the airport, where, obviously relieved to be rid of them, he gave them another perfunctory handshake and watched them climb into the aircraft and start the engines.

Before they taxied to the end of the runway, they saw his car driving off.

Once they left Luanda, navigation was surprisingly simple. Twenty minutes out of Luanda—still in a slow climb passing nine-thousand feet—Canidy saw a light to their right and pointed it out to Whittaker.

"Probably Salazar," Whittaker said, but then corrected himself. "It has to be Salazar. According to the chart, there's absolutely nothing down there but jungle and that town."

Canidy leveled off at ten-thousand feet, flew to the left (and out of the hearing) of Salazar, and pointed the nose toward Malange, one hundred ten miles farther along. Five minutes later, faint but unmistakable against the absolute blackness, they could see another glow of lights. He flew the lights to Cacolo, then to Nova Chaves. And ten minutes after passing Nova Chaves, they spotted a yellow glow that had to be Kasaji, in the Belgian Congo, for there was nothing else for three hundred miles.

They were now over the border—which made them now absolutely illegal. They had entered the airspace of a neutral, German-occupied country without permission. The least offense they could be accused of now would be violating airspace. Later, after they loaded the ore, they would be smuggling.

Then the glow that had to be Kolwezi appeared dead ahead, a soft yellow spot that seemed even from a distance larger than the other towns. As they got closer, the lights came into focus and took on a strange pattern—like a lopsided bull's-eye—lines of lights forming concentric circles.

"What the hell is that?" Whittaker asked.

"The copper mines," Canidy said, "the largest man-made hole in the world."

"Kolwezi," Whittaker said to the microphone, "this is Belgian African Airways Two-zero-six, five miles west. Request you light the runway."

The lights came on a moment later, not at all bright, but two parallel lines of them, with three Vs, forming an arrow at one end. Canidy had never seen lights like that before.

Though there was no communication from the tower, when he had touched down and begun to slow, he saw the headlights of a car racing down what had to be an unlighted taxiway parallel to the runway.

He taxied all the way to the far end of the runway, and concluded that getting out of here with a full load was not going to be as difficult as he had feared. The runway was wide and very, very long. It was paved with some sort of crushed stone that was almost certainly mine tailings.

Canidy shut down the engines as Whittaker went aft to open the door. When they climbed down the ladder, a man cradling a shotgun in his arm like a hunter was standing there next to another European.

"*Bonsoir, Monsieur Grunier,*" Canidy said.

"We were beginning to give you up," Grunier said.

He did not seem surprised to see Canidy, although the last time they had seen each other was in a small boat off Safi, Morocco. Grunier had been bound and gagged because his pathetic pleading to remain in Morocco had been more than Canidy could stand.

Awkwardly, because of his shotgun, Grunier climbed into the C-46 and looked around. Then he climbed down again. While he was in the airplane, the runway lights went off.

Grunier looked at Whittaker and, matter-of-factly, said, "I will kill you if you attempt to leave without me."

"What the hell is he talking about?" Whittaker asked.

"The last time he was offered government transportation, they left me behind. I guess he doesn't want that to happen to him." He turned to Grunier. "My orders are to take you," he said. "Where's the cargo?"

The European took a small flashlight, pointed it, and blinked it on and off three times.

Several hundred yards off in the darkness, there was the sound of an engine starting, and then the sound of a vehicle approaching. When headlights came on, Canidy saw two trucks, a 1938 or 1939 Chevrolet panel truck and a large, canvas-roofed French Renault. Both had the legend UNION MINIÈRE painted on their doors.

The larger truck approached the C-46 and then made a turn so that the headlights shone on an area of spillings. The Chevrolet stopped so that its headlights lit the C-46 door.

An astonishing number of Africans, tall, muscular, good-looking men wearing white cotton shirts and what looked like American dungarees, poured out the back of the Renault.

There must be thirty of them, Canidy thought.

The last couple of men off the truck reached back inside and began to pass out shovels. Several others went to the Chevrolet and came out with bundles of cloth bags.

"It isn't bagged?" Canidy asked incredulously.

"I could move it here without suspicion," the European said. "But I could not bag it without attracting the attention of the wrong people."

"Jesus!" Canidy said.

There was the sound of another truck engine, and Canidy looked with alarm in that direction.

"The fuel truck," the European said. "Nothing to worry about."

"How long is this going to take?" Canidy said.

"As long as it takes thirty *noires* to fill one hundred twenty bags," the European said, "and load them on the airplane."

The Africans, the *noires,* seemed to know exactly what they were doing. One man held open the mouth of one of the bags while two men shoveled the material into it. As Canidy watched, a bag was filled. The man who had been holding the mouth picked it up, shook it to settle it, held it for another couple of shovelfuls, shook it again, and then took several steps back. As he tied the bag, another African with a bag moved into position so the shovelers could fill it.

At the rate they're going, Canidy thought, *they'll be finished long before we're refueled.*

6

Luanda, Portuguese Angola
2030 Hours 20 August 1942

When the Luanda radio direction finder signal had finally grown strong enough to be trusted, Fine knew they were a hundred fifty miles or so almost dead south of where they were supposed to be. A little farther south and they would not have picked up the Luanda transmitter at all. But they flew the needle, and ten hours and fifty minutes after taking off from Bissau, they received permission from Luanda to land.

The landing, Fine thought, was a real greaser, the best one he had ever made in the C-46. That had to be just pure dumb luck—and he almost immediately had good cause to suspect that was all the good luck they were going to have.

Three Portuguese customs officials walked out from the small terminal to the C-46 and, as soon as Fine put the ladder out, climbed aboard.

They saluted, bowed, and shook hands—and then saw Nembly, asleep or unconscious, and Wilson with his bandaged head and his arm in a splint.

"You have befell a misfortune?" the senior of the customs officials asked.

"He fell," Fine said. "And he's sick. Is there a doctor?"

They seemed to be genuinely sorry to report there was no doctor.

"There is supposed to be a gentleman from the U.S. consulate waiting for us," Fine said.

They seemed to be just as genuinely sorry to have to tell him that the gentleman from the U.S. consulate had only recently departed, a matter of only hours before.

Fine went down the ladder and on unsteady legs walked to the terminal building, where he tried and failed to get through on the telephone to the U.S. consulate.

Wilson came up to him as he was putting the telephone down.

"No guy from the consulate?" he asked.

"No," Fine said.

"So what do we do now?" Wilson asked.

"Kolwezi is nine hundred miles from here. None of us is any shape to fly that thing around the pattern, much less nine hundred miles."

"You're not suggesting we give up?" Wilson asked.

"Have you got a better idea?" Fine said. "We have done all that could possibly be expected of us. We have flown without any real rest nine thousand miles in thirty-six hours."

"We've come this far," Wilson continued. "I'd hate to quit now."

As if to make a joke of it, he spilled a handful of Benzedrine pills into his hand and mimed swallowing them all at once.

"They wouldn't do any good," Fine said. "We need to lie down in a bed and sleep."

"And then?" Wilson asked.

"Then we go," Fine decided.

When he saw Nembly, huddling under his blankets, he was not at all sure he had made the right decision.

Getting the lie-down-in-a-bed type of sleep he had told Wilson they needed proved to be impossible. By the time they had refueled the airplane, the customs officials were gone; the driver of the fuel truck (who had ridden to work on his bicycle) said that he was forbidden to take the truck from the airfield, and was immune—never having seen any before—to the large amount of American currency with which Fine tried to bribe him.

Fine and Wilson lay down on the floor of the fuselage making what beds they could from a few blankets. Immediately, hordes of insects found them. They gave up, went into the cockpit, and started the engines.

7

Kolwezi
Katanga Province, Belgian Congo
0630 Hours 21 August 1942

When Canidy climbed off the wing, walked under the plane, and looked up at the door, Grunier was standing in it, still carrying the shotgun and wearing a look of mingled fear and determination.

"If you have anything to put aboard," Canidy said to him, "do it now. We're going."

He had decided last night that there was no sense taking chances now that they were so close. Two things (in addition to his own and Whittaker's fatigue) bothered him. Since there were no cabin lights, the lashing down of the bags of ore could not be inspected. And he wanted to be very careful when he made the preflight inspection, which meant doing it when there was light stronger than a flashlight or the headlights of a truck.

"I am ready," Grunier said, without emotion.

Whittaker came up from the tail.

"OK back there," he said. "You about ready?"

Canidy waved him up the ladder.

The European touched his arm.

"Bon voyage, bonne fortune," he said.

"Thank you," Canidy said, and climbed up the ladder.

Grunier backed into the cabin, as if afraid at the last moment Canidy would somehow keep him from going along.

Canidy pulled the ladder into the airplane and tried to put it in its rack. It was blocked by ore bags.

That didn't matter; he laid it on top of some ore bags. Whittaker had had the Africans arrange these on the fuselage floor in stacks of three: two on the cabin floor, one on top of the two. Whittaker had then lashed the stacks down and had done a good job even by lantern light.

By the time Canidy went into the cockpit Whittaker had started the engines. Canidy strapped himself in, released the brakes, turned the C-46 back onto the runway, and taxied slowly down to the other end. It steered heavily.

"It's heavy," Canidy said, hoping he sounded less concerned than he felt. "You can feel it."

"A hundred twenty bags at a hundred pounds," Whittaker said. "Twelve thousand pounds. Six tons. That's heavy."

"Even heavier if those bags weigh, say, a hundred twenty pounds," Canidy said.

Whittaker's smile faded.

"Jesus Christ, you're serious!"

"I don't think anybody weighed them," Canidy said. "But this won't be the first plane ever to take off a little over max gross weight."

"The runway's pretty long," Whittaker said. "We'll be all right."

"I thought about weighing a couple of bags," Canidy said; "then I wondered where we could get a scale this time of morning."

"It'll be all right," Whittaker said.

There was no point contacting the tower, and he didn't. He ran the engines up, checked the gauges, took off the brakes, and advanced the throttles.

The rumble of the takeoff roll was heavier and more muted than it usually was, and acceleration was noticeably slower.

"Goddamned thing doesn't want to go," he said.

"I wonder," Whittaker said thoughtfully, "just how much weight we do have aboard."

The C-46 finally came off the tail wheel.

Canidy was watching the airspeed indicator move with maddening slowness to takeoff velocity when there was a sound like an enormous shotgun being fired.

A terrible vibration followed. Instinctively, he applied right rudder and pulled a little harder on the wheel, and the vibration stopped. But the rumble of the takeoff roll seemed undiminished.

"We've blown the left tire," Whittaker said, and then very calmly, "and we're running out of runway."

There seemed, perversely, to be all the time in the world to make a decision.

"What should we do?" Canidy asked. There was bile in his mouth again.

"Cut the switches and pull the wheels," Whittaker said. "If you get this big sonofabitch in the air and then come down, it'll blow up for sure. And it's not going to fly."

Canidy dropped his eyes to the control panel. The airspeed needle was very far from indicating even a marginal takeoff velocity.

"Wheels up," he ordered calmly as he reached forward to cut the main switch.

There was a split second when he thought he felt life in the controls, and there was a terrible temptation to take a chance, to ease back on the stick and see if he could get it in the air. He resisted it. Their only chance was to stay on the ground and pray that sparks generated by metal against the runway would not ignite the fuel that would almost certainly leak from ruptured tanks.

Then there was a loud, very frightening scream of tortured metal as the wheels folded inward, and the prop tips and then the fuselage dropped down to encounter the runway.

Canidy felt himself being thrown violently against his harness and for a moment heard an absolutely terrifying screech of metal being violently torn apart. Then his head struck the bulkhead by his side window, and everything went red, and then black.

Whittaker had the wind knocked out of him but did not lose consciousness as the plane skidded for what seemed like a very long time to the end of the runway and then off. With a final crash of crumpling metal, the C-46 came to a stop against a mound of dirt.

The windlessness frightened Whittaker. He was convinced that it was a symptom of grave injury, most probably paralysis. But then, in short, painful intakes, he began to breathe. The terror of being paralyzed was then replaced by the terror of being burned alive.

He tore off his harness, leaned over Canidy, unfastened his harness, and picked him up from his seat by brute force. He dragged him to the crew door. It was wedged shut. He laid Canidy to one side and kicked it open with both feet. Then, dragging Canidy after him, he left the aircraft, threw Canidy over his shoulders, and ran for a hundred yards, expecting to hear the dull grump of igniting avgas any second. He found an undulation in the dirt, and dropped Canidy down in it.

There was no explosion. The plane just sat there.

He thought of Grunier.

Fuck him, I don't owe him a thing!

He ran to the airplane, went back through the crew door and into the fuselage. Grunier was crumpled against the bulkhead, his face bloody, his neck broken, quite dead.

He stayed in the fuselage long enough to confirm the

incredible. The auxiliary tanks had not ruptured. They were warped, but the seams had held.

He walked back to where he had left Canidy. Canidy was awake and sitting up, holding a handkerchief to a cut on his forehead.

"I wondered where the hell you were," Canidy said.

"Who did you think carried you here? The good fairy?"

He knelt over Canidy and examined the cut.

"You'll live," Whittaker said. "Only the good die young."

There was the sound of aircraft engines.

Whittaker stood up, and then reached down and hauled Canidy to his feet so that he too could see the Curtiss C-46 with CHINA AIR TRANSPORT painted on the fuselage making its final approach to the Kolwezi runway.

8

The House on Q Street, NW
Washington, D.C.
1340 Hours 23 August 1942

Colonel William J. Donovan and Captain Peter Douglass were having a private business lunch to which Miss Cynthia Chenowith, to her very carefully concealed displeasure, had not been invited. She suspected, correctly, that the luncheon had very little to do with the national security generally, but a very great deal to do with one particular activity of the OSS.

Fine and the CAT transport were missing and presumably lost. As the result of a series of fuckups (Cynthia was fully aware that the *f* in the acronym *snafu* did not represent *fouled*) it had been necessary to send Canidy and Whittaker rather than the qualified Navy crew on the backup flight. And they had not been heard from.

It was one thing to order a faceless agent on a mission. It was something else entirely when you knew the participants, were *fond* of the participants.

Colonel Donovan and Captain Douglass wished to be alone. That was their real reason for the "private" working luncheon.

It was *her* mission too! She had been involved in it from the beginning. She was, for God's sake, the damned case officer!

And it was worse than that, worse than being banished to sit over a cup of cold tea in the kitchen while the colonel and the captain waited in splendid masculine isolation in the dining room. She had been considering over the past thirty-six hours the very real possibility that Canidy, that sonofabitch, and Jimmy Whittaker would not be coming back. As time passed, she was no longer able to convince herself that her concern was primarily because poor Mrs. Whittaker would be devastated if poor Jimmy were lost. The truth was that she was going to be devastated herself, and not even because Jimmy was a dear old friend. She realized that Ann Chambers had done at Summer Place with Dick Canidy what she should have done with Jimmy. It would have been very unprofessional, of course, and unladylike, but she should have given him that—and not only because he was going in harm's way, but for her own selfish purposes.

When an unsmiling Chief Ellis came into the kitchen of the house on Q Street, she knew that he had word, and that it was not good news.

"They said they didn't want to be disturbed unless it was important," Cynthia said. Her voice, she noted with bitter pride, had not broken.

"This is addressed to you," Ellis said, and handed her the sheet of light green paper on which decrypted TOP SECRET messages were typed.

"Thank you, Chief," she said, and unfolded it and read it.

URGENT TOP SECRET
FROM STEVENS LONDON
1600 GREENWICH 22 AUGUST 1942
FOR OFFICE OF DIRECTOR WASHINGTON
EYES ONLY CHENOWITH
FOLLOWING FROM BLUEBELL PRETORIA
LIFEBOAT CRASHED ON TAKEOFF LEADCITY STOP REMAINS
NAPOLEON BURNED WITH WRECK STOP SANDBAGS AND
HARDY BOYS EVACUATED KEYWEST BY CHOPSUEY WHOSE
ARRIVAL DELAYED BY INTERNMENT BIRDLAND STOP
SANDBAGS TRANSFERRED TOMATO SAILED BROADWAY
0515 GREENWICH 22 AUG STOP CHOPSUEY DEPARTED
KEYWEST WITH ALL HANDS 0910 GREENWICH 22 AUG
STOP JULIET VERY NOSY STOP ADVISE STOP STEVENS

It was a coded message within an encrypted message, but Cynthia did not need her little black code book to read it. *Lifeboat* was the relief R5D aircraft borrowed from the U.S. Navy. *Leadcity* was Kolwezi. *Napoleon* was the French mining engineer, Grunier. *Sandbags* was the uranitite ore. *The Hardy Boys* was Donovan's droll contribution to the list of code names for Canidy and Whittaker. *Chopsuey* was the C-46 with China Air Transport markings. *Birdland* was the emergency landing field in the Spanish Canary Islands. *Keywest* was Capetown, South Africa. *Tomato* was the destroyer ("tin can") U.S.S. *Dwain Kenyon*, DD-301, a brandnew, very fast vessel which had been waiting in Capetown to transfer the uranitite to *Broadway,* which was the Brooklyn Navy Yard.

And *Juliet* was, of course, Miss Ann Chambers, who was in London, and was determined to find Canidy. Colonel Stevens was fully aware of the trouble she could cause if she were aroused. The standard solution —"psychiatric evaluation"—could not be applied to the daughter of the owner of the Chambers Publishing Company.

Cynthia finished reading the message, and looked up at Chief Ellis. He was fuzzy. Cynthia realized her eyes were wet.

"If I didn't know better," Chief Ellis said, "I'd think you were really worried about them."

She didn't trust herself to speak. If she opened her mouth, she realized, and could find her voice, she would have said "Fuck you!" or something else she shouldn't.

She went to the dining room, slid open the door, and handed the decrypted message to Colonel Donovan. He read it, and wordlessly handed it to Captain Douglass.

Everybody was smiling.

Douglass finally broke the silence.

"I think under the circumstances it would be all right if you sent Colonel Stevens a cable authorizing him to inform Miss Chambers that Major Canidy will shortly be in London, and there will probably be an opportunity for her to meet with him."

"We can do better than that, Pete," the director of the Office of Strategic Services said. "Chief Ellis, send a separate Urgent to Colonel Stevens over my signature. The message is, 'HAVE JULIET MEET ROMEO AT THE AIRPORT.'"

The refining of sufficient quantities of uranium ore to manufacture nuclear weapons, should this theoretical possibility prove actually feasible, began in early September 1942 at a secret facility at Oak Ridge, Tennessee, using a stock of uranium ore secretly imported from the Belgian Congo at the direct order of the President of the United States.

On December 2, 1942, in a laboratory under the seats of the University of Chicago's football stadium, the first chain nuclear reactor, composed of graphite and urani-

um, operated as predicted, resulting in the sustained, controlled production of atomic energy.

An atomic bomb was now possible. It would be irresistible against any enemy.

The problem now became to produce a functioning weapon before the Germans, who were known to be working on the idea, could build one.